DO242426

THE DOMESDAY SERIES
The Wolves of Savernake • The Ravens of Blackwater
The Dragons of Archenfield • The Lions of the North
The Serpents of Harbledown • The Stallions of Woodstock
The Hawks of Delamere • The Wildcats of Exeter
The Foxes of Warwick • The Owls of Gloucester
The Elephants of Norwich

THE RESTORATION SERIES
The King's Evil • The Amorous Nightingale • The Repentant Rake
The Frost Fair • The Parliament House • The Painted Lady

THE BRACEWELL MYSTERIES
The Queen's Head • The Merry Devils
The Trip to Jerusalem • The Nine Giants
The Mad Courtesan • The Silent Woman
The Roaring Boy • The Laughing Hangman
The Fair Maid of Bohemia • The Wanton Angel
The Devil's Apprentice • The Bawdy Basket
The Vagabond Clown • The Counterfeit Crank
The Malevolent Comedy • The Princess of Denmark

THE CAPTAIN RAWSON SERIES
Soldier of Fortune • Drums of War • Fire and Sword
Under Siege • A Very Murdering Battle

THE ELEPHANTS OF NORWICH

EDWARD MARSTON

Allison & Busby Limited
11 Wardour Mews
London W1F 8AN
allisonandbusby.com

First published in Great Britain in 2000.
This edition first published by Allison & Busby in 2021.

A CIP catalogue record for this book is available from
the British Library.

10 9 8 7 6 5 4 3 2 1

ISBN 978-0-7490-2690-5

Typeset in 11/16 pt Adobe Garamond Pro by
Allison & Busby Ltd.

The paper used for this Allison & Busby publication
has been produced from trees that have been legally sourced
from well-managed and credibly certified forests.

Printed and bound by
CPI Group (UK) Ltd, Croydon, CR0 4YY

To Conrad and Gaynor
beloved son and daughter-in-law
as a belated wedding present

King William caused all England to be surveyed: how much each of his barons possessed; and how many enfeoffed knights; and how many ploughs, villeins, animals, and livestock, each one possessed in all his kingdom from the greatest to the least; and what dues each estate was able to render. And as a consequence the land was vexed with much violence.

Florence of Worcester

Prologue

'Elephants?' she said in astonishment. 'You brought elephants back to England?'

'Yes, my lady. Two of them.'

'Where did you find them?'

'That's a secret,' said the other with a quiet smile.

'But I thought that you were visiting your estates in Normandy.'

'My search took me further afield.'

'Search?'

'For the two elephants,' he explained. 'When I set my heart on something, I'll move heaven and earth until I possess it. That's why I hunted them down with such patience. You'll not see two such beasts in the entire kingdom. Those elephants will make a perfect wedding gift to my bride.'

Richard de Fontenel gave a confident grin. He was a big man

in his forties with the build and rugged features of a soldier. Time had thickened his waist, thinned his hair and lent him a florid complexion but he could still be accounted a moderately handsome man. Ten years younger, the lady Adelaide had retained the beauty and poise that made her such a desirable prospect as a wife. The great wealth she had inherited from her late husband only served to intensify desire.

'Nothing has been agreed, my lord,' she reminded him.

'Until today.'

'I'm in no rush to make a decision.'

'Wait until you see the elephants.'

'Why should they make any difference?'

'Because I got them for *you*, Adelaide.'

'It's a curious way to court a lady,' she teased. 'Tracking down two monsters in the hope that they may further your suit. To be honest, my lord, I had grave doubts that such things as elephants even existed. I've heard the tales, naturally, but I never met anyone who had actually laid eyes on the creatures. Since you have brought two of them to Norfolk, I shall be interested to see them, but I cannot promise that they'll win me over.'

'Why not?'

'Elephants are, by report, large and dangerous. I'm more likely to be frightened by them than enamoured.'

His grin widened. 'There's no chance of that.'

'How can you be so sure?'

'Because I would never dream of doing anything to upset you,' he said with rough courtesy. 'I seek only to delight your senses. That's why I went to such trouble to secure the elephants for you.' He moved to the door. 'I'll have them brought in at once.'

'Here?' she gasped, suddenly afraid. 'Are they not tethered and penned?'

'No, my lady. They are tame enough to handle.'

Richard de Fontenel opened the door of the parlour and barked an order. When he turned round, he saw that his guest had withdrawn for safety to a corner of the room. Torn between curiosity and apprehension, the lady Adelaide waited in silence. Her host ran covetous eyes over the shapely body beneath the long blue gown. She looked even more entrancing than when he had taken ship for Normandy. Absence had increased his fondness for her and, he suspected, melted away some of her reservations about him. She was finally within his reach. The wedding gift would remove any lingering doubts she might have.

There was a tap on the door, then Hermer, the steward, came in with a wooden platter in his hands. Silken cloth covered some objects on the dish. A short, stout individual in his thirties, Hermer had the cautious look of a man who walked in fear of his master. He stood beside de Fontenel.

The guest was mystified. 'Where are the elephants?' she asked.

'Waiting for you,' said her host, indicating the platter.

'Is this some kind of jest, my lord?'

'Far from it. Lift the cloth and see for yourself.'

'I expected two vast animals.'

'These are not *live* elephants, my lady.'

'But you led me to believe that they were.'

'I did nothing of the kind,' he said, beckoning her over with a crooked finger. 'I would never offer a fragrant lady like you such foul-smelling pets as a pair of elephants. These creatures are designed to excite and allure.'

The lady Adelaide crossed slowly towards him and looked down at the platter. Taking the edge of the cloth between thumb and forefinger, she pulled it tentatively away to reveal two objects that made her gape in wonderment. They were miniature elephants, made from solid gold and standing four inches in height. Affixed to the top of each head was a small crucifix. Richard de Fontenel picked one of the gleaming animals up and handed it to her. She was entranced. Its sheer weight gave her some idea of its value but it was the craftsmanship that really appealed to her and she ran her fingers gently over the smooth contours. Never having seen an elephant in the flesh, she could not tell how accurate a representation the miniature was, but the large head, long trunk and curved tusks held a thrilling novelty for her. And she was not just being offered a piece of treasure. The crucifix gave each object a religious significance.

It was impossible not to be touched. She looked up at de Fontenel.

'You brought these back for *me*, my lord?' she said with gratitude.

He gave a nod, took the elephant from her and put it back on the platter. When the two animals were covered once more with the cloth, Hermer went out of the room, but not before he shot a sly glance of admiration at the lady Adelaide. She was sad to see the miniature animals go. The tips of her fingers were still tingling from the touch of the gold. The very sight of the objects had stirred something akin to lust in her, but possession came at a price.

'Well?' said de Fontenel, searching her eyes.

'They're exquisite, my lord.'

'An exquisite gift for an exquisite lady.'

'That remains to be seen.'

'Did you not like them?'

'I adored them,' she confessed, 'but then you knew that I would.'

'I'm well aware of your tastes,' he said softly. 'I've studied them long enough. I seek to please you in every way, Adelaide. Precious as they are, those elephants are only a means to an end that is far more precious to me. I've offered you my hand already but I do so again now,' he continued, extending a palm towards her. 'I think that I'm entitled to an answer from you.'

'You'll get one, my lord,' she said, politely ignoring his hand.

'When?'

'In due course.'

'You've been saying that for months.'

'Marriage is not something into which I'll enter lightly.'

'You were swift enough to wed Geoffrey Molyneux.'

'That was different,' she said with a note of reprimand in her voice. 'I was young and inexperienced in the ways of the world. I was also very much in love with my husband. I still grieve over Geoffrey's untimely death.'

'So do I, Adelaide,' he assured her. 'So do I.'

'Were he still alive, you could not buy me with a hundred gold elephants.'

He feigned indignation. 'There is no sense of purchase here, I swear it. No amount of money could attract such a wife. I offer you love and devotion, not riches and finery. You already have those in abundance. What you don't have – and what you need – is a husband who will cherish you.'

'The lord Mauger said the selfsame words.'

'Mauger is a fool!' he retorted.

'He offers me everything that you do, my lord.'

'Including two gold elephants?'

'No,' she conceded. 'He lacks the imagination to find such a gift.'

'That's not all that he lacks,' said the other, still bristling. 'Let's put Mauger aside for the moment. He has no place in this discussion. Unless, that is,' he added, arching an inquisitive eyebrow, 'some promise was given during my absence?'

'Not by me, my lord.'

'Mauger has been rejected?'

'Neither rejected nor accepted. I've still to make up my mind.'

'Does my wedding gift carry no weight at all?'

'Considerable weight.'

'Then why do you hesitate?'

'Because it's my privilege to do so.'

Bestowing a warm smile on him, she turned away and moved across to gaze out of the window. She pondered. Richard de Fontenel had much to recommend him as a husband. He had wealth, position and power. His manor house was one of the largest in the county, his estates scattered across Norfolk, Suffolk, Lincoln and Essex. In Normandy, too, he had substantial holdings. The lady Adelaide was tempted by his proposal but two things held her back. The first was the fact that her beloved husband, Geoffrey, had been killed in a hunting accident while riding out with de Fontenel and that memory still festered. The second obstacle concerned her host's relationship with his two previous wives. One had died in childbirth and the other had been carried off by a fever, but it was rumoured that he treated both with a harshness unbecoming in a devoted husband.

Richard de Fontenel was a hard man in a world that punished softness. He was ruthless, ambitious and acquisitive. The lady Adelaide's fear was that she would be one more prize to be added to his collection. Though he was wooing her gently now, his manner might change sharply once she had succumbed. There was the additional problem of providing an heir for a childless husband. That phase of her life, she hoped, was over. Having already brought two children into the world, she did not wish to go through the ordeal again. Her hesitation shaded into reluctance.

Watching her carefully, he moved across to stand behind her shoulder. 'What are you thinking?'

'How fine your garden is,' she said, pointing at the avenue of trees.'

'Fine enough to make you yearn to share it with me?'

'Perhaps, my lord.'

'And perhaps not?'

She turned to face him. 'It's not an easy decision.'

'What's making it so difficult?'

'Memories,' she whispered. 'And the presence of a rival.'

'Mauger is no rival,' he snarled. 'He's a grasping rogue. While I was away on my travels, he had the temerity to claim land that is rightfully mine. Fortunately, when they compiled their returns for this county, the commissioners did not believe him. Even as we speak, a second team of commissioners is on its way to Norfolk to settle the dispute between us.' He became earnest. 'Settle the more important dispute between us, Adelaide. Mauger is no fit husband for you. Discard him and choose me.'

'Why must I accept either of you?'

'Because it's my destiny!' There was anger as well as exasperation in his voice. The lady Adelaide was too composed to let her feelings show but he sensed her disapproval. Making an effort to control his temper, he showered her with apologies, then conducted her to a chair.

'You must do as you wish, Adelaide,' he said.

'I intend to, my lord.'

'All I ask is that you hear me out.'

'That's the least you deserve.'

Her smile encouraged him to show his hand more clearly. Richard de Fontenel had admired her from afar for years. He spoke of his continuing affection and of the deep sympathy he felt for her at the tragic death of her husband. Honest about his faults, he was profuse in his vows. The lady Adelaide listened attentively, enjoying the flattery without being taken in by it and making an occasional mention of her other suitor in order to prick him into a response. Courtship was preferable to marriage. While she had two suitors paying their attentions to her, she could play them off against each other in order to secure advantages for herself. Eventually, however, the game would have to end.

Richard do Fontenel was persuasive. As the time slipped past, he slowly began to gain ground. He talked so fondly about his previous wives that she disregarded all the rumours she had heard. She even forgot some of the dire warnings her husband had given her about the man who was now bidding to replace him. The lady Adelaide was tempted afresh. When he pleaded with her to marry him, she gave the matter serious thought.

'Let me see them again,' she said at length.

'See what?'

'The two elephants, of course.'

His hopes rose. 'Then you accept my proposal?'

'Allow me a little more time.'

Concealing his disappointment, he gave a nod, then escorted her out of the room. They went down a passageway until they reached a door at the far end. He unhooked the keys from his belt and inserted one into the lock.

'This door is solid oak,' he boasted. 'I like to protect my property.'

She was almost flirtatious. 'Is this where you would lock me up as well?'

'No, Adelaide. I'd never let you out of my sight.'

He opened the door and they stepped into a small room that smelled of damp. Light came in through the cracks in the shutters but the iron bar that held them in place made it impossible to open them from outside. Three large wooden chests took up most of the floor space. Her companion went to a smaller chest that stood on the table. Made of elm, the chest was reinforced with iron bands. He chose a key and offered it to her.

'You open it,' he suggested.

'Shall I?'

'The elephants are yours.'

She took the key and pushed it into the lock before giving it a sharp twist. Lifting back the lid, she expected to feast her eyes on the two gold miniatures, but a rude shock awaited her. The chest was completely empty.

'Where are they, my lord?' she asked.

'My steward should have put them back.'

'Who else has a key?'

'Nobody apart from Hermer and myself.' He stepped back into the passageway and roared at the top of his voice. 'Hermer! Hermer, where are you, man!'

When repeated yells failed to elicit a response, he went charging off in a fury. The lady Adelaide could hear him calling for his steward and howling at his servants. It was minutes before he appeared. Richard de Fontenel's face was puce with rage.

'He's not here,' he said, biting his lip. 'Hermer has gone.'

His guest heaved a sigh and looked down at the empty box.

'So have the elephants,' she said.

Chapter One

Love had finally won the battle against caution. Protracted absences from home made Gervase Bret miss his young wife so much that he eventually decided to take her with him when he next ventured out of Winchester on royal business. Hitherto, he had always persuaded himself that Alys was too delicate to undertake a long journey and that it was wrong to expose her to the potential dangers of travelling through open country. Gervase was also concerned that his wife's presence would be a distraction, taking his attention away from the important judicial work that he and the other commissioners had to complete in each designated county. Long nights in a lonely bed made such arguments less convincing. Setting aside his reservations, therefore, he invited Alys to join him on the trip to Norfolk and was delighted at the alacrity of her response.

Early fears were soon confounded. Though small and slight,

she had an innate strength that kept fatigue at bay. No additional periods of rest were necessary on her account. Alys proved herself a competent horsewoman and revelled in the opportunity of leaving her native Hampshire and seeing something of the rest of the country. What was an onerous assignment for her husband was a wonderful adventure to her. After only one day, Gervase realised that he did not, after all, have to watch over her so anxiously. Alys was well ableto take care of herself and she was an ideal companion for Ralph Delchard's wife, Golde, a seasoned traveller with the commissioners. They might come from different backgrounds but the beautiful young Norman lady and the Saxon thegn's daughter showed a sisterly affection for each other. Gervase was able to relax. The decision to bring his wife was already yielding up more than one bonus.

Her value to the expedition had not gone unnoticed by Brother Daniel.

'You are a fortunate man to possess such a wife,' he observed, fondly.

'I know,' said Gervase.

'Anyone can see that you bring each other great joy. Your good lady also helps to cleanse the minds and mouths of the company.'

'In what way, Brother Daniel?'

'Soldiers can be very coarse when they're alone together. Yet I've not heard an offensive word from them since we left Winchester almost a week ago. They've been becalmed by our two charming female companions.'

'I'm glad of that.'

'So am I. Obscenity offends me.'

'I'd hate it if Alys were forced to listen to warm words from our escort.'

'She's subdued them, Master Bret,' said the other with a grin. 'And given them something far more interesting than my tonsure to stare at as we move along.'

Gervase was riding beside the Benedictine monk and directly behind Alys and Golde. He was finding Brother Daniel a talkative companion. Brother Simon, their usual scribe, had many virtues but his undisguised fear of the female sex and his hatred of soldierly banter ensured that every journey with the commissioners was an extended ordeal for him. Brother Daniel, by contrast, was a much more worldly man with a twinkle in his eye that suggested he was not unacquainted with physical pleasure before he took the cowl. Devout and learned he might be, but the lean, wiry, sharp-featured monk with the greying circle of hair was a red-blooded human being as well. His gaze was fixed admiringly on the two women in front of him.

'I hope that I'll not let you down,' he said.

'There's no question of that, Brother Daniel,' replied Gervase. 'You come with the highest recommendation. I'm sorry that Brother Simon is indisposed but you'll be an able deputy, I'm sure.'

'Simon instructed me with meticulous care.'

'Did he tell you what to expect?'

'Yes,' said Daniel, turning to him with amusement. 'But I've so far encountered none of the things I was warned about. 'Simon spoke well of you, Master Bret, though he was less complimentary about the lord Ralph.'

'Only because Ralph enjoyed poking fun at him.'

'I take such teasing in my stride. It's always good-humoured.'

'What else did Brother Simon say?'

Daniel was discreet. 'Enough to show that he didn't appreciate the privilege he was being given. I do appreciate it, Master Bret. Very much.'

'Let's see if you still feel that way at the end of our visit.'

'I've no doubts at all on that score.'

He returned to his contemplation of the two graceful figures in front of him.

They were eighteen in number, wending their way at a steady trot through the Norfolk countryside. Six knights from Ralph Delchard's own retinue provided half of the escort, the remainder belonging to the new commissioner, Eustace Coureton. Like their men, Ralph and Coureton wore helm and hauberk and carried weapons. Gervase, too, though wearing the attire of a Chancery clerk, had a sword in his scabbard and a dagger at his belt. Such a show of force was necessary on a journey that took them through six separate counties. Outlaws would think twice about trying to ambush such a well-defended group of travellers. Alert and disciplined, the soldiers rode in pairs. Sumpter horses followed on lead reins at the rear of the column.

Leading the cavalcade were Ralph Delchard and Eustace Coureton. Ralph had been pleased when his habitual colleague, Canon Hubert, was replaced by a veteran soldier, but Coureton was not turning out to be the hardy warrior he had anticipated. A solid man of medium height, the newcomer had a vigour that was surprising in someone who was approaching his sixtieth year. He also had a scholarly turn of mind. Instead of wanting to discuss the finer points of military strategy or past battles in which he had fought, Coureton preferred to enthuse about Greek and Roman authors whose work he was reading in their original language. Ralph liked him immensely but was quite unable to follow his colleague through the thickets of Classical literature.

'My favourite author is Horace,' Coureton observed.

'Who?'

'Quintus Horatius Flaccus.'

'Another noble Roman?' said Ralph without enthusiasm.

'A poet and a satirist.'

'The only Romans I know are soldiers.'

'Oh, Horace did his share of fighting,' explained the other. 'When Julius Caesar was assassinated, Brutus fled to Greece. Horace joined his army and fought at the battle of Philippi. Unfortunately, he chose the losing side. Horace had to obtain a pardon before he was allowed to return to Rome.'

'I've never been on the losing side,' said Ralph, proudly.

'Then you're too young to have borne arms when King William was merely the Duke of Normandy. They were desperate days, my lord. Feuds broke out from time to time in every part of the duchy. Unlicensed castles were built all over the place. Fighting never ceased. None of us won all the skirmishes in which we were forced to take part.' He gave a shrug. 'Perhaps it's just as well.'

'What do you mean?'

'Too much success can lead an overweening arrogance. Failure in battle tempers a man's character. It did so in my case. I learnt the value of humility.'

Ralph laughed. 'Humility is only fit for monks.'

'Monks and beaten armies.'

'Victory sharpens the edge of ambition.'

'That's why I came to distrust it.'

'Would you rather we had lost at Hastings?'

'Of course not.'

'Then why not enjoy the spoils of war?'

'Because war is not always something that we should enjoy.'

They argued happily for a couple of miles. Ralph then lifted an arm to call a halt so that they could have a rest, water the horses and see to the wants of nature. The place he had chosen met all three needs. A fallen tree offered seating to the women while verdant grass welcomed the rest of them. Water rippled invitingly in a twisting stream and the nearby copse supplied enough privacy for those wishing to relieve themselves. Everyone was grateful for the break in the journey. It was a warm day and the sun kept peeping through a veil of wispy white cloud to test its strength on them. Soldiers in heavy mailshirts were eager to dismount and find some shade. Horses whinnied in approval.

Ralph helped his wife down from her palfrey and escorted her across to the fallen tree. Gervase was equally attentive to Alys, taking her by the waist to swing her gently to the ground. She gave him a dazzling smile of thanks.

'I'm enjoying this so much, Gervase,' she said.

'You're not bored, my love?'

'How can I be when there is so much to see and so many things to talk about with Golde? She really is the perfect travelling companion.'

He pretended to be hurt. 'What about me?'

'You're perfect in other ways.'

'I'm relieved to hear it.'

'Where are we?' she asked, moving across to sit beside Golde.

'I'm not sure,' he replied. 'But it can't be more than ten miles to Norwich.'

'That's my reckoning as well,' agreed Ralph.

'What sort of a town is it?'

'Who knows, Gervase? I've never been there. And if it were left to me, I'd not be going anywhere near the place now. Norwich holds no appeal for me.'

'It will, my lord,' promised Coureton.

'You've visited the place?'

'Once or twice. I was impressed and saddened at the same time.'

'Saddened?'

'War has been unkind to it.'

Ralph was wary. 'Are you going to lecture me again about the defects of victory?'

'Only if you're prepared to listen,' said Coureton with a chuckle.

Removing his helm, he settled down on the grass and explained his remark about Norwich. Though it was ten years since he last visited the city, it remained a vivid memory. He talked with affection and regret, holding their interest and sparking off a flurry of questions. The two women wanted to know about the castle where they would be staying, Brother Daniel enquired about the spiritual life of the community and Gervase asked about the trade in the area. Ralph's attention soon wandered. It was not from lack of curiosity. He was as eager as any of them to learn something of the city, but another development took priority. Out of the comer of his eye, he saw movement in the bushes and let a hand drift at once to his sword. Having drunk their fill in the stream, the horses had been tethered nearby. To give the animals a rest, packs and leather satchels had been removed from the backs of the sumpters who now grazed contentedly.

What alerted Ralph was the sight of a hand reaching out slowly from behind a bush to grab one of the satchels and drag it away. Hauling himself up, Ralph drew his sword and gave a signal to his men. Three of them immediately leapt to their feet to support him as he strode quickly towards the bushes. The rest of the escort also got up and drew their weapons. Coureton broke off his narrative and Gervase, fearing an attack, got up to stand protectively in front of the two women. There was, however, no danger. When Ralph and his men plunged into the undergrowth, they met with no opposition. All they saw was a bedraggled figure limping off into the copse with the satchel under his arm. Even in their hauberks, the soldiers had no difficulty in overhauling the man. He was old, grizzled and close to exhaustion. Tripping over the exposed roots of a tree, he fell full length and let out a cry of pain.

Ralph turned him over with a foot and held a swordpoint at his throat.

'Where do you think you're going?' he demanded.

'Spare me, my lord!' pleaded the other.

'Why should I spare a thief?'

'I was only after food.'

'You and who else?' said Ralph, eyes combing the trees

around them.

'Nobody else, my lord.'

'Are you sure?'

'I swear it.'

Ralph nodded to his men and they fanned out to search the copse. Eustace Coureton joined Ralph to see what quarry he had run down. The man at their feet was a pitiful sight, cadaverous, hollow-eyed and caked in filth. His tunic was badly torn, his gartered trousers ripped in several places to expose skeletal legs. He was trembling violently, fearing for his life and wondering how a Norman lord could speak his language so fluently. Coureton looked down with sympathy at the bearded captive.

'Is this all you found?' he said.

'He stole one of our satchels,' explained Ralph, reclaiming it from the ground. 'The rogue claims that he was only searching for food.'

'Then I'd say he was telling the truth, my lord. I'd also suggest that you take your weapon from his neck or hell die of fright. Let him be. He's hardly likely to outrun mounted pursuit, and he's not armed.'

Ralph relented and sheathed his sword. The remainder of the escort was now picking its way through the copse, searching in vain for any confederates. The old man was patently alone.

Golde had instructed her husband well. His mastery of the Saxon tongue enabled him to speak to the captive on his own terms.

'What's your name?' he said.

'Alstan, my lord.'

'Where are you from?'

'Taverham hundred.'

29

'What are you doing here?'

'I was driven out,' whimpered the other. 'When King Edward sat on the throne, I was a villein and happy to work the land for my master. Times have changed. Under the new king, I became a mere bordar, then my master treated me as a slave. When I tried to protest, he had me whipped and driven out.'

'Whipped?'

'Yes, my lord. I still bear the scars.'

Alstan struggled up into a kneeling position so that he could peel off his tunic. When he turned his bare back to them, they saw the livid wounds across the pale torso. It was surprising that the old man had survived the punishment. Coureton was shocked and Ralph felt a surge of sympathy.

'We'll give you food, then you can tell us the full story.'

'Thank you, my lord,' said Alstan, weeping with gratitude.

'That doesn't mean I condone theft,' warned Ralph. 'On the other hand, I don't condone savage punishment such as you've endured. Taverham hundred, you say?'

'Yes, my lord.'

'Who is this cruel master of yours?'

'The lord Richard.'

'Richard de Fontenel?'

'He drove me out to starve in the wilderness.'

'For what offence?'

'Old age.'

'Do something!' insisted Richard de Fontenel. 'Summon your men and do something!'

'My deputy is already looking into the matter.'

'I don't want a mere deputy. I want the sheriff himself in charge of the case.'

'I have more important things to do than to go searching for missing trinkets.'

'Trinkets!'

'And you'll not endear yourself to my deputy by insulting him. Why not calm down, Richard? Nothing will be gained by trying to browbeat me.'

De Fontenel held back a tart rejoinder. Roger Bigot, sheriff of Norfolk, was not a man to be intimidated by a loud voice and a threatening manner. While his visitor ranted at him, he remained icily calm. Bigot was a power in the land, a man who had the King's trust and a place at his Council table. Constable of the castle, he had recently been elevated to the shrievalty of Norfolk and of its southern neighbour, Suffolk, two large counties with a healthy respect for the name and reputation of Roger Bigot. He was a tall, slim man of middle years with a sagacity and imperturbability rare in a soldier. When de Fontenel came riding angrily into the castle to harangue him, he was given short shrift.

'Return home,' advised Bigot. 'Let justice take its course.'

'How can it when you stand idle here, my lord sheriff?'

'I'm never idle, Richard. In addition to affairs of state that require my attention, I have to welcome the commissioners who'll soon arrive in Norwich.'

'Not before time!' grumbled the other. 'They can oust Mauger from my land.'

Bigot was amused. 'Mauger is hoping that they'll shift you from what he claims is his property. Don't expect too much from the commissioners. They'll be quite impartial.'

'In that case, I'm bound to win.'

'Mauger feels the same.'

'I don't care what he feels. Mauger is a sly rogue. An unscrupulous cheat.'

They were standing in the bailey of the castle, a timber fortress that had been erected soon after the Conquest to attest Norman supremacy and to act as a bulwark against any Danish incursions along the eastern seaboard. The conversation between the two men could be clearly heard by the guards on the battlements. Richard de Fontenel was not a man to lower his voice in a public arena.

'I'd not put it past him to be involved here,' he declared.

'Mauger?'

'The crime has his mark upon it.'

'You told me that the gold elephants were stolen by your steward.'

'They were. Hermer made off with them.'

'Then how does Mauger come into it?'

'Hermer was acting at his behest,' decided the other. 'He must have been. My steward gave me very loyal service for years. Only someone like Mauger could corrupt him and turn him against me.'

'Are you quite sure that your steward was the thief?'

'Completely, my lord sheriff.'

'How can you be so certain?'

'Apart from myself, he was the only person with a key to the chest in which they were locked. Nobody else could even have got into the room where my valuables are stored. Or, indeed, into my house. Besides, the man has vanished into thin air. The facts are irrefutable. It has to be Hermer.'

'I doubt very much that he was in league with the lord Mauger.'

'Why?'

'What motive could he have to instigate the theft of those elephants?'

'Spite, my lord sheriff.'

'Concerning this property dispute?'

'And property of a different nature.'

'Ah,' said Bigot with a knowing smile. 'I begin to understand.'

'The gold elephants were to be a wedding gift.'

'The lady Adelaide has accepted you, then?'

'Unhappily, no. But she will,' added de Fontenel, defensively. 'The lady Adelaide was enchanted by my gift. Once those elephants are back in my possession, shell not be able to refuse me. That's why they must be found immediately.'

'My deputy will do his best, Richard.'

'Order him to arrest Mauger.'

'On what evidence?'

'Search his house. I'll wager that you find the stolen property there.'

'A foolish wager,' argued Bigot. 'Even if those gold elephants were taken on Mauger's instructions – and I refuse to countenance that notion – he would never be stupid enough to conceal them in his own home where they might be found by a search. As you know better than anyone, Mauger is as cunning as a fox. My advice is to forget him altogether, Richard. He has no place at all in this investigation.'

'But he has. He's trying to lure the lady Adelaide away from me.'

'That's a personal matter between the two of you. What concerns me is the crime that's been committed. If your steward is responsible for the theft, you should be looking at yourself rather than at the lord Mauger.'

'At myself?'

'Yes.'

'Why?'

'You said a moment ago that Hermer was very loyal to you.'

'He was, my lord sheriff. Unswervingly so.'

'Then what happened to undermine that loyalty?'

'Nothing at all.'

'Nothing?' said Bigot levelly. 'Be honest with yourself, Richard. You're a hard man with a rough edge to your tongue. You like your own way and you make sure that you get it, no matter how many toes you may have to trample on in the process. What did you do or say to upset your steward?' He looked his visitor in the eye. 'Has it never occurred to you that you may actually have provoked this crime?'

The last few miles began to tell on the travellers. Weary from so much time in the saddle, they were finding the heat more oppressive and the terrain less diverting. When their destination finally came within sight, they heaved a collective sigh of relief.

Gervase Bret was riding beside his wife, who was bearing up bravely.

'Take heart, Alys,' he said. 'We're almost there.'

'Good.'

'I'm sorry that the journey has been so tiring.'

'I was enjoying the ride until we met that poor man. He was all skin and bone.'

'At least we were able to give him one good meal today.'

'It was distressing to see someone in that terrible state,' she said. 'Did I hear Ralph tell you that he'd been turned out to fend for himself?'

'Yes, my love.'

'What kind of master could be so cruel?'

Gervase did not answer. The name of Richard de Fontenel was already known to him because the man was involved in one of the property disputes they had come to settle. Alys was upset enough already. Her husband did not wish to alarm her by telling her that he would soon be locking horns with the very Norman lord who had treated the old man so callously. Gervase had promised himself to keep his work and his domestic life rigidly apart. His wife would hear nothing of his deliberations with his colleagues.

He glanced across at her and was disturbed by what he saw. 'Are you unwell?' he said with concern.

'No, Gervase.'

'But you look pale.'

'This heat is bothering me.'

'Do you wish to stop for another rest?'

'I can hold out until we reach the castle.'

'It's not very far to go.'

'I long for a cool drink and a place in the shade.'

Gervase reached out a consoling hand. 'You'll have both very soon.'

'Thank you.'

'I hope that you don't regret coming with us.'

'No,' she said, rallying slightly. 'For the most part, it's been very exciting. I am simply in need of a long rest now. I shall sleep very soundly tonight.'

'So will we all.'

The closer they got to Norwich, the more able they were to appreciate its size and character. It was the principal town in one of the most populous counties in the entire kingdom. The soil was rich, the harvest plentiful and the rivers stocked with fish. Larger boats ventured out to sea in search of even bigger catches. Extensive deposits of salt supported a flourishing trade and there were dozens of other occupations in what was the fourth largest county in England. Much of the country was plagued with drought that summer, but Norfolk seemed to have suffered less from its effects than some of the other areas through which they had travelled. Sheep and cows grazed in the fields. Pigs could be heard in patches of woodland. There was an abiding sense of contentment.

It disappeared the moment they rode into Norwich. Eustace Coureton's description of the place was accurate. It bore the scars of war as blatantly as Alstan bore the mementoes of his whipping. Almost ninety buildings had been destroyed to make way for the castle, creating a huge hole in the fabric of the city. Of those that remained, the best part of two hundred houses were unoccupied, abandoned by owners who had fled for a variety of reasons. The streets were full and the market was busy, but there was no zest about Norwich. Its indigenous population had yet fully to accept that it was now under Norman control. When Ralph Delchard led his party towards the castle, they gathered the usual mixture of hostile stares and muttered resentment.

Riding beside her husband, Golde was grateful for their safe arrival.

'The journey didn't take as long as I'd feared,' she said.

Ralph grimaced. 'The best road in Norfolk is the one that

takes us out of it.'

'Aren't you looking forward to our stay here?'

'No, Golde. I'd rather be at home with my lovely wife.'

'Travel adds body to a marriage.'

'You sound like the brewer you once were,' he remarked with a grin. 'What did you add to your ale to give it some sparkle?'

'That's a closely guarded secret.'

'Even from your loving husband?'

'Especially from you, Ralph,' she pointed out. 'When you were in Hereford, you refused to touch my ale. You're a true Norman. Wine is all that you'll drink.'

'I'm glad you mention Hereford, my love.'

'Why is that?'

'Do you recall your ill-fated earl?'

'Of course.'

'Well, this is where he sacrificed his earldom,' said Ralph, pointing to the castle ahead of them. 'My namesake, Ralph Guader, was earl of Norfolk, a man of mixed parentage and uncertain temper. He decided to marry Emma, sister of Roger, earl of Hereford.'

'You don't need to remind me of that. It was the talk of the town. We could not understand why the wedding was not held in Hereford cathedral. Had the ceremony occurred there, I might have been engaged to provide ale for the table. Not all the guests were as fond of wine as you are.'

'It was not only drink that flowed at the wedding, Golde. Blood was up and passions ran high. The noble earl of Hereford conspired with Ralph Guader and with Waltheof, earl of Northumberland, to overthrow the King with the help of Danish invaders. A doomed enterprise from the start,' he said with contempt. 'It robbed Waltheof of his life and both Norfolk and Herefordshire of an earldom. This is where the plot was first hatched. Norwich has much to answer for.'

'That was well over ten years ago, Ralph.'

'You still see the effects, my love. Look around you. Much of the destruction here came as a result of Earl Ralph's forfeitures. His supporters quit the city in fear. Houses that were not burnt to the ground still stand empty.'

Golde gazed around her. 'I'd certainly prefer to live in Hereford.'

'Are you not happy in our home?'

'On the few occasions when we actually spend time there,' she said with a teasing smile. 'But at this moment, after a long day in the saddle, I have to confess that I am delighted to be here in Norwich.'

'So am I.'

'What kind of welcome may we expect?'

'A cordial one, I hope.'

No sooner had he spoken than a man came riding out of the castle at a reckless speed, heedless of what lay ahead and jabbing his spurs hard into his horse's flanks. Richard de Fontenel was in no mood to bid the commissioners welcome. Face dark and teeth gritted, he rode straight at the cavalcade, scattering it uncaringly as he headed for the city gate. Ralph had grabbed the reins of Golde's palfrey to pull it out of the way of the galloping stranger who missed others in the party by a matter of inches and went hurtling on to send the townspeople scurrying for safety. There was great commotion in his wake. Everyone turned to look in bewilderment after the furious rider.

It was left to Ralph Delchard to put their thoughts into words.

'Who the devil was *that!*' he exclaimed.

Chapter Two

Mauger Livarot arrived at her manor house with an escort of six knights. When he was admitted to the parlour, the lady Adelaide could not resist teasing him.

'Have you come to arrest me, my lord?' she said, feigning apprehension.

'In a manner of speaking.'

'Does it take seven men to overpower one woman?'

'We've been hunting,' he explained, indicating the mounted riders who could be seen through the open shutters. 'Since our way home led directly past your house, I felt it only courteous to call on you.'

'You are always welcome here.'

'More welcome than Richard de Fontenel?'

Her smile was calculated. 'Both of you are equally welcome.'

'How long will you keep us on the same footing?'

'Only time will tell.'

'You're as evasive as ever, my lady.'

'Would you be interested in a woman who submitted without any delay?'

Livarot grinned. 'There's only one woman who excites my interest.'

She waved him to a seat, then lowered herself on to an oak bench with her back straight and her hands folded in her lap. His gaze never left her. A tall, thin, angular man with a long face that tapered down to a pointed chin, he was now in his late forties, the once attractive features ravaged by a life of excess. The lady Adelaide would never have chosen him as a husband on the strength of his appearance. It was his other assets that appealed to her. Livarot was a wealthy man with estates in England and Normandy. He was also a skilful politician, employed by the King on occasional diplomatic missions abroad and, it was rumoured, destined for high office in the fullness of time. His bride might find that she had wed a future sheriff.

'I hear that the lord Richard is having domestic problems,' he said, complacently.

'You have keen ears, my lord.'

'Little that happens in Norwich escapes me.'

'Then you'll know the circumstances in which the robbery took place.'

'I can guess at them.'

'Go on.'

'Richard de Fontenel acquired some costly gifts in the hope that they might make you look more favourably upon his ugly visage. Exactly what they were I don't know, but they seem to have disappeared.' Another grin surfaced. 'I must confess that I regard the theft as an act of God.'

'Can crime ever be providential?'

'This one is.'

'Evil can surely never come out of good.'

'To steal from such a confirmed thief as the lord Richard is not exactly an evil act. He's spent the last twenty years grabbing land at will from those too weak to defend themselves. The loss of a little gold is small retribution for his misappropriations.'

'They were elephants, my lord.'

'Elephants?'

'Fashioned out of gold. Objects of great beauty.'

'He'll need more than two elephants to plead his case.'

'They were powerful advocates,' she admitted. 'I coveted them.'

'Then I'll have something similar made for you.'

'Why bother when the originals may soon be recovered?'

'Whatever he offers you,' said Livarot, jealousy flickering, 'I'll match. Remember that, my lady. There's no gift that the lord Richard can dangle in front of you that I'll not give you as well. Simply name it and it's yours.'

'There's nothing I want.'

'You wanted those gold elephants.'

'I was tempted by them,' she corrected, 'but the animals did not, alas, come alone. They bore the lord Richard on their backs. His gift was conditional upon my accepting his hand in marriage.'

'That would be a disaster for you.'

'Not necessarily.'

'Look at his reputation,' he urged, leaning forward to

41

gesticulate. 'The man is a household tyrant. He's already buried two wives and their deaths were a blessed release from a bullying husband. Do you wish to be his third victim?'

'You've been married yourself,' she noted, bluntly, 'and that union was scarcely an example of wedded bliss.'

Livarot was stung. 'My wife and I were reasonably happy together.'

'Reasonably?'

'We had no more unhappiness than most marriages.'

'Then why did she try to flee back to Normandy?'

'She didn't, my lady,' he retorted, smarting at the accusation. 'That was a wicked lie put about by the lord Richard. Judith was a good wife to me and bore two fine sons. But she could never settle in England. Judith missed her parents sorely. That was why she longed to return to Normandy.' He sat back with a sigh. 'Her death came as a great shock to me. I mourn her still.'

'I didn't mean to offend you,' she said, adopting a more conciliatory tone. 'Only those involved in a marriage know its true nature. But I must warn you that you'll not win my hand by speaking ill of the lord Richard. He is just as harsh in his judgement of you and it does him no good. If you must woo me, do so by telling me about your own virtues and not about the supposed vices of others.'

'The lord Richard's vices are established fact.'

'I'm already aware of them.'

Mauger Livarot pursed his lips to hold in any further comment. Taking a deep breath, he spread his hands in a gesture of apology. The lady Adelaide was right. He would make more headway by emphasising the positive aspects of his own character than by listing the negative attributes of his rival. Long before his wife died, the marriage had crumbled, not least because of his repeated infidelity and his long absences abroad. Though there were mercenary instincts involved as well, he saw a union with the lady Adelaide as a means of atoning for the mistakes of his first marriage. She would be altogether more outspoken and self-possessed than her predecessor. As he now reminded himself once again, she was also considerably more beautiful and gracious. Infidelity would no longer be a factor.

'I offer everything that I have, my lady,' he said. 'And everything that I am.'

She was direct. 'I'd look for more honesty than you've so far shown.'

'Honesty?'

'Yes, my lord,' she continued, pointing towards the window. 'You claim that you're on your way home from a day's hunting yet none of your men have any carcasses with them. You travel empty-handed. Was it such a poor day in the forest or am I the only prey you seek?'

'You're no prey,' he assured her.

'Then why invent this tale about hunting?'

'It was no invention. The truth is that we hunted this morning. I thought it a pretty excuse to gain admission to your home. Forgive me, Adelaide. It was a small deception.'

'Small deceptions hold the seeds of larger ones.'

'You'll have no cause to doubt my honesty.'

'None at all?'

'You have my word on it,' he said, rising to his feet. 'Put me to the test.'

'I will,' she replied, watching him closely. 'When you first arrived, you said that you'd heard about the theft from the lord Richard's house but you didn't know exactly what was taken. A little later, you mentioned that gold had been stolen and, when I told you about the elephants, you knew that they were two in number. How?'

Mauger Livarot weighed his words carefully before replying. 'If you want a straight answer, my lady, you shall have one.'

'I'd appreciate that.'

'My steward's name is Drogo,' he said airily. 'He's a resourceful man who acts as my eyes and ears. Drogo has a friend who's employed in the household of Richard de Fontenel. By that means, I get to know almost everything that occurs under his roof. In short,' he added with a smirk, 'I follow the rules of combat.'

'Combat?'

'I keep a spy in the enemy camp,'

'Oh,' she said with astonishment. 'I see.'

'You did ask for honesty.'

Ralph Delchard was impressed with the way that they were received. Everything was in readiness. As soon as they entered the castle, the sheriff himself greeted them. Servants were on hand to conduct the guests to their respective apartments while their escort was taken to lodgings in the bailey by one of the guards. When his wife was safely bestowed in their chamber, Ralph went off to speak at more length to their host. Gervase Bret joined the two men in the hall.

'A fine castle,' observed Ralph. 'Well-sited and heavily fortified.'

'Yes,' replied Bigot. 'Of necessity we keep our defences in good repair. Raiding parties have a habit of sailing up the River Yare. Intime, of course, we'll replace the timber with stone and make Norwich Castle into an even more impregnable fortress.'

'There's safety enough *inside* your walls, my lord sheriff,' said Gervase. 'The danger we encountered was on your threshold.'

'Danger?'

'Some madman tried to run us down with his horse.'

'Yes,' Ralph affirmed. 'Had we not moved out of the way, we'd have been knocked from our saddles. He came riding hell-for-leather out of the castle as if the hounds of Hades were on his tail. I'll tell you this, my lord sheriff. But for the fact that I had ladies to protect, I'd have been on his tail as well. And I wouldn't have stopped until I'd caught up with the rogue and taught him some manners.'

'That lesson would have been long overdue,' said Bigot, ruefully.

'Who was the fellow?'

'Richard de Fontenel.'

'No wonder he didn't wait to be introduced.'

'What do you mean?'

'We had already heard about his lack of courtesy,' said Ralph, hands on hips. 'On our way here, we met an old man who'd been a bordar on one of the lord Richard's estates in Taverham hundred. When he was reduced to the status of a slave, the old man made the mistake of complaining to his master. The lord Richard not only turned him out of house and home, he had the poor devil whipped until he was half dead.'

Bigot rolled his eyes. 'That sounds like Richard de Fontenel.'

'We offered to bring the man to Norwich,' explained Gervase, 'so that we could intercede on his behalf. But he was too terrified to come anywhere near the lord Richard. So we gave him food and directed him to a church we'd passed earlier. The priest will take him in and show him a kindness he never got from his master.'

'Kindness is not one of the lord Richard's virtues.'

'Does he have any virtues?' wondered Ralph.

'You might well ask.'

'I will, my lord sheriff. He's due to come before us in a property dispute. I'll tax him with his rudeness and beat an apology out of him. He had no cause to scatter us all over the street like that.'

'The lord Richard will claim that he did,' said Bigot, wearily. 'What's more, he'll point an accusing finger at me.'

'At you?'

'Yes, my lord. A robbery occurred at his home. Something of great value was taken. When the crime was reported, I ordered my deputy to investigate but that only served to enrage the lord Richard. He accosted me here and demanded that I abandon all my other commitments to take charge of the enquiry myself. When I refused, my angry visitor leapt on his horse and galloped out of here. I'm sorry that you met him at such a bad time.'

'I'm sorry that we met him at all,' said Ralph.

'What was stolen from his house?' asked Gervase.

'Two elephants.'

'Elephants? Here in Norwich?'

'They were not live animals, Master Bret, but gold miniatures.'

He gave them a full account of the crime and explained its significance. Ralph had no sympathy for the victim, hoping that the theft would at least rescue the lady Adelaide from the fate of marrying him. Gervase's ears pricked up at the mention of another person.

'The lord Mauger is a suspect?'

'Not in my estimation,' said the sheriff. 'But he and the lord Richard are arch-enemies so he takes the blame for everything that upsets his rival. The truth of the matter is that each man is as bad as the other.'

'Which one will the lady Adelaide choose as a husband?' said Ralph.

'Neither, if she has any sense.'

'And does she?'

'Oh, yes. She's a redoubtable woman.'

'Then why does she let them court her?'

'You'll have to ask her that, my lord,' said Bigot with a note of sadness. 'Geoffrey Molyneux was her first husband, as decent and upright a man as you could wish to meet. Compared with him, her two suitors are arrant rogues.'

'Rich ones, however,' commented Gervase. 'I went through the returns for this county with great interest. The names of Richard deFontenel and Mauger Livarot crop up time and again. They have substantial holdings.'

Talk turned to the work that had brought the commissioners to Norwich. Roger Bigot could not have been more helpful. He gave them friendly advice and told them of arrangements he had already made on their behalf. Ralph and Gervase were grateful. Other sheriffs had been more grudging in their hospitality, trying to hurry their guests on their way and resenting what they saw as interference. Bigot seemed genuinely interested in the disputes that had come to light during the visit of the earlier commissioners. Unlike most people, he did not view the Great Survey as an odious imposition.

'It helps to clarify the situation,' he decided.

Ralph chuckled. 'That's a polite way to describe it, my lord sheriff,' he said. 'Most people call it the Domesday Book, for it represents a Day of Judgement. Our job is to lift stones so that the truth can crawl out into the sunlight. I'm afraid that there'll be a lot of stones to lift in the county of Norfolk. And I'm not only referring to men like Richard de Fontenel and Mauger Livarot.'

'No,' said Gervase, taking a signal from Ralph. 'The Church's hands are not entirely clean in this county. Bishop Alymer set a bad example. When he succeeded his brother, Stigand, he seized manors such as Thornage, Hindringham, Hindolveston, North Elmham and Helmington in addition to outliers like Colkirk and Egmere. Other prelates followed suit with a vengeance.'

Gervase rattled off a score of misappropriations and left the sheriff gaping in admiration at his mastery of detail. He had already been struck by Ralph's air of authority. It was the lawyer's turn to impress him now. Bigot could see that the two men would make a formidable team when they sat in judgement.

'What manner of man is your colleague?' he asked.

'Eustace Coureton will make a fine commissioner,' said Ralph. 'He's a shrewd man who'll show neither fear nor favour. All we have to do is to ensure that he's not allowed to quote Greek and Latin authors at us.'

'Is he a scholar, then?'

'His only fault.'

'I see it more as a strength,' argued Gervase.

'You would.'

'A Classical education is a source of joy.'

'Not for the person on the receiving end of it, Gervase. For several miles, I had Eustace riding beside me. It was purgatory. How would you like to have someone called Horace poured relentlessly into your ears?'

'I'd love it, Ralph.'

'Well, it gave me a headache.'

'*Vos exemplaria Graeca, nocturna versate manu, versate diurna.*'

'Now you're doing it!' wailed Ralph.

'Horace gives sage counsel.'

'What's the translation?' asked Bigot. 'My Latin is a trifle rusty.'

'Our colleague, Eustace Coureton, has been doing what Horace urges. "For your own good, turn to the pages of your Greek exemplars by night and by day." Do you hear that, Ralph?'

'I hear it and I ignore it,' said the other. 'Keep your Greeks and your Romans. I'll do my duty by day and turn to my wife at night.'

'We must agree to differ. *Concordia discors.*'

Ralph waved an arm in protest. 'He's at it again!'

'Even I can translate that,' said Bigot. 'It means "harmony in discord". Correct?'

Gervase nodded. 'Yes, my lord sheriff.'

'You provide the harmony and the lord Ralph supplies the discord.'

All three of them shared a laugh. The commissioners warmed to their host. He treated them as welcome guests rather than interlopers. It boded well for their stay.

Roger Bigot became serious. 'Will you hear the cases in strict order?'

'Yes,' said Ralph. 'Gervase has devised the plan. Minor cases will be dealt with first before we move on to more complicated disputes like the one involving that surly horseman, Richard de Fontenel.'

'Couldn't you deal with him and the lord Mauger first?'

'For what reason?'

'It would get him off our back while we investigate this robbery. My deputy will be able to work more effectively if the lord Richard is entombed in the shire hall with you for a few days.'

Ralph pondered. 'We'll consider that possibility,' he said at length.

'Thank you. Meanwhile, you might consider something else.'

'What's that?'

'An invitation to the banquet we're giving in your honour this evening.'

'That's very kind of you, my lord sheriff,' said Gervase.

Ralph was circumspect. 'I take it that the lord Richard will not be there?'

'No, my lord.'

'Then we accept with gratitude.'

When Golde called to see her in her chamber, Alys was just waking up from a short sleep. She rubbed her eyes with a white knuckle. Her visitor was contrite.

'Did I wake you, Alys? I'm so sorry.'

'I didn't mean to doze off.'

'The long ride tired us all. To be honest, I had a nap myself.'

'Gervase left me alone in here so that I could rest,' said Alys. 'The bed was too tempting to resist. I only intended to lie on it for a while.'

'It looks to me as if you needed the sleep,' said Golde, studying her friend's puckered features. 'You're pale and drawn, Alys. Do you feel unwell?'

'No, no. I'm in good health.'

'Perhaps you'd like a longer sleep?'

'Not at all,' said the other, detaining Golde with an outstretched hand when the latter moved to the door. 'Don't leave me. I'd value some company.'

'You'll have plenty of that this evening.'

'Will I?'

'Gervase hasn't told you, obviously.'

'Told me what?'

'We're bidden to a feast. The lord sheriff and his wife have prepared a banquet for us and invited a number of guests they wish us to meet. Ralph is delighted. We've not always had such warm hospitality on our travels.'

'That's what Gervase told me.'

'You chose the right part of the country to visit.'

Alys forced a smile. 'So it seems.'

'Put the rigours of the journey behind you,' advised Golde. 'We'll not have to take refreshment in open country any more. You I'll be going to a banquet on your husband's arm this evening.'

'I look forward to it.'

'You don't sound very excited at the prospect.'

51

'Oh, I am, Golde,' said the other, trying to inject more interest into her voice. 'When I've woken up properly, I'll be as excited as you clearly are. It's a wonderful surprise. I've never feasted in such august company before.'

'Nor had I until I met and married Ralph. The life I lead now is a far cry from working as a brewer in Hereford.'

'Do you have any regrets?'

'None at all, Alys.'

'I'm sure that Ralph would say the same.'

'What about you?'

'I couldn't be happier.'

'Gervase is thrilled to have you at his side. He's a changed man.'

'I just hope that I don't let him down.'

'What a strange thought!'

'This is all so new to me, Golde.'

'You'll have nothing to worry about, I promise you. Gervase will be even more proud of his lovely wife than he already is. Be yourself, Alys. That's all you must do.'

'I'll try.' Alys crossed to the window. The room was at the top of the keep, a timber structure that was perched on a huge mound of earth to make it easier to defend. Down below in the bailey, there was considerable activity. Soldiers were exercising, the guard was being changed and the armourer was busy in his forge, hammering on the blade of a new sword and producing a rhythmical noise that could be heard throughout the entire castle. Horses were being groomed. Servants ran to and fro. An elderly priest ambled towards the chapel. An unseen dog barked a slow lament. Alys was fascinated.

'I've never stayed in a castle before,' she confessed. 'What is it like?'

'Very draughty in the winter,' said Golde, crossing to stand beside her. 'These places are built for safety rather than comfort. We're lucky to be here in the summer, Alys. We'll be able to spend less time around a fire.'

'What will we *do* all day?'

'See something of Norwich, for a start.'

'I'd like that.'

'We may even do some shopping in the market.'

'What will we buy?'

'Things that we're unlikely to see in Winchester,' said Golde. 'Norwich does a thriving trade with other countries. Goods are brought upriver from Yarmouth. We may well find silks and cloths that catch our eye, not to mention small items of jewellery.'

'Gervase doesn't like me to wear anything too gaudy.'

Golde gave a subversive smile. 'Please yourself, not your husband.'

'I'm not sure that I'd dare. Doesn't Ralph tell you what to buy?'

'Of course, but I usually ignore him.'

Alys laughed. 'You're so bold.'

'I lived alone for some time after my first husband died. That taught me to stand on my own feet. And to follow my own instincts when I went to the market.'

'Then I'll do the same,' said the other, conspiratorially.

'There's one way to ensure that Gervase doesn't criticise what you buy.'

'Is there?'

'Yes, Alys. Get something for him as well.'

The younger woman laughed again and turned to face her companion. It was Golde's presence on the expedition that had convinced her to join it. Eager as she was to be with her husband, Alys would never have left Winchester if she had been the only woman in the party, yet that hitherto had been Golde's position. She marvelled afresh at her friend's courage and independence. To be with her husband, Golde had ridden to places as far apart as Chester, York, Canterbury and Exeter. Bad weather and uncomfortable accommodation n had been endured without complaint. It made Alys resolve to make light of any problems she encountered. The slight queasiness had passed off now. She would soon be able to respond to the notion of a banquet with real enthusiasm.

Golde sensed that something was troubling her and stepped in closer.

'What ails you?' she asked.

'Nothing.'

'The life seems to have drained out of you.'

'It will come back.'

'Are you not in a mood for celebration this evening?'

'Yes, yes,' Alys lied.

'Something's on your mind, Alys. What is it?'

Alys gave a shrug and moved back to the middle of the room to give herself a moment to collect her thoughts. She looked at Golde again. 'It was that old man,' she said. 'The one we met on our way here.'

'Poor wretch. I felt so sorry for him.'

'How could anyone treat a human being like that? Ralph wouldn't beat a dog the way that that old man was beaten. It was painful to look at him.'

'I know. But his is not an isolated case, I fear.'

'What do you mean?'

'Perhaps we should break off this conversation,' suggested Golde tactfully. 'I don't want to say anything out of place.'

'How could you possibly do that?'

'I'm from Saxon stock and you're not, Alys. You were born in Winchester, I know, but your father came from Normandy and fought at Hastings. That sets the two of us apart. I belong to the conquered and you to the conquerors.'

'What does that have to do with the old man we met?'

'I've seen him before a hundred times,' explained Golde. 'Sometimes he's old, something young, sometimes neither. But he's always badly treated by his master. He's always a reminder that a Saxon peasant lives at the mercy of his Norman overlord. Not that all members of your nation are harsh,' she added, quickly, 'because they're most certainty not. Some are much kinder than the thegns they replaced. But I can't change what I am, Alys. Though I married a Norman soldier and love him to distraction, I never forget where my roots lie. That old man we saw today was a symbol to me.'

'Of what?'

'You'll understand in time,' Golde brightened. 'But enough of such thoughts! A banquet is being prepared for us. That should raise our spirits.'

'Are we all invited?'

'Oh, yes. Including Brother Daniel.'

'Is a monk allowed to eat rich food?' asked Alys, innocently.

'You wouldn't pose that question if you'd ever seen Canon Hubert at table. He has the appetite of half a dozen men. My guess is that Brother Daniel will not restrict himself to bread and water either,' said Golde cheerfully. 'He's not just a scribe to the commissioners. He's a Benedictine who's been released for a while from his abbey.'

'So?'

'He's here to enjoy himself, Alys.'

Brother Daniel was brimming with energy and filled with curiosity about his new abode. After he had been shown to the tiny room where he was to sleep, he found his way to the chapel and knelt down to offer up a prayer of thanks for their safe arrival. He then befriended the ancient chaplain, pumped him for information about the castle, and went out into the town to take stock of his surroundings. A paradox confronted him. Though there were plenty of people about, Norwich seemed curiously empty. In a city of almost five thousand souls, the monk felt oddly alone, as if the crowds that were drifting away from the market were mere assemblies of ghosts. Daniel was puzzled. It was not so much a question of what he could see as what he felt. He sensed bitterness, neglect and a resignation that bordered on despair. The castle was casting a long shadow.

As he walked down one of the side streets close to the fortress, he saw evidence of a destructive past. During the ill-fated revolt of the earl and his confederates, the castle had been besieged for three months. Many of the nearby dwellings were razed to the ground or simply abandoned by their panic-stricken owners. Those that remained were grim reminders of those troubled times. Daniel glanced into a few of them. The first was barely standing and the second boarded up with pieces of rough timber. Through the cracks in the shutters, he saw a small room with a sunken floor that was littered with rubbish. Something was crawling about in the gloom. Flies buzzed noisily. The stench made him hold his breath and move away.

The third house was in a more dilapidated state. Its wooden walls were pitted, its thatch all but done and its shutters hanging off like torn limbs. Brother Daniel went up to the entrance, then stepped back in surprise as a cat suddenly darted out between his bare legs. He gave an indulgent smile. The front door was simply propped against the opening. When he took hold of it, he was able to lift it aside. The room into which he now gazed was long, low and covered in the charred remains of furniture. The stink was even more powerful but it did not dispatch him on his way. Something had captured his attention. Revealed by the light that came in through the open door and the broken shutters was a piece of sacking in the far corner. It was heavily stained and seemed to be covering a large uneven object. Picking his way through the ashes, the monk took hold of the corner of the rough material and drew it slowly away.

Daniel was shocked. His stomach heaved and his temples pulsed. His legs went limp. Sweat broke out all over his body. He wanted to replace the sacking and hurry away to raise the alarm but he had no strength even to move. He was forced to stand there and gaze down in silent horror at the mutilated corpse.

Staring back at him were the sightless eyes of Hermer the Steward.

Chapter Three

The discovery of the dead body threw the castle into a turmoil. When the trembling Brother Daniel broke the news, the sheriff immediately surrounded the derelict house with an armed guard. Ralph Delchard and Gervase Bret went into the building with him to investigate. The murder victim was in a sorry condition. The blood that stained the sacking came from a series of stab wounds in the chest. Hermer's throat had also been cut and both hands had been hacked off. Congealed blood from a head wound formed a gruesome mask across the upper half of his face. All the ritual humiliations of death had set in. The foul smell made Ralph turn away in disgust.

'What a way to end a life!' he said. 'Who is the poor devil?'

'Hermer the Steward,' said Bigot.

'You *recognise* him?'

'More by his apparel than his face, my lord. But that's the

lord Richard's man, I'm sure. I've met the fellow often enough to pick him out even in that hideous state.'

'When did he go missing, my lord sheriff?' asked Gervase.

'A couple of days ago.'

'That accounts for the stink.'

'It's not the only cause,' said Ralph, looking around at the accumulated excrement on the floor. 'This place is a latrine. No wonder there are so many flies in here.'

'One thing is certain,' observed Bigot.

'What's that?'

'Whoever stole those elephants, it wasn't Hermer. The lord Richard was wrong about that. His steward is a victim, not a villain.'

Gervase knelt down to peer more closely at the corpse. Evidence of a violent death was horribly clear but the killer had left no clues as to his identity. Gervase peeled the sacking away to reveal the lower half of the body. The feet were tied together with a stout rope. To the surprise of his companions, Gervase then rolled the man briefly on his side so that he could look at his back before lowering him gently into his former position. Shaking his head in bafflement, he stood up again.

'Where are his hands?' he said.

'Heaven knows,' said Ralph.

'That's not the question that his master will ask,' said Bigot, leading he two of them out of the room. 'He'll want to know where his priceless gold elephants are. The lord Richard will insist that the killer be brought to justice, but not out of consideration for Hermer. A steward can be replaced; those two gold elephants cannot.'

All three men took a deep breath when they came out into the fresh air again. The sheriff was decisive. He ordered his men to disperse the small crowd that had gathered, then sent two of them to fetch a litter so that the body could be carried to a more dignified resting place in the morgue at the rear of the chapel. Reflecting on what they had seen, Roger Bigot and the two commissioners walked back towards the castle.

'I feel that I owe you both an apology,' said the sheriff.

'Why?' asked Ralph.

'This is a poor welcome for such important guests. Examining a corpse like that is hardly the best way to whet your appetite for a banquet.'

'True, my lord sheriff, but no blame attaches to you. Any apology is unnecessary. It's not as if you deliberately arranged to have a murder victim laid at your very door.'

'Someone did,' remarked Gervase.

'What do you mean?'

'The steward was meant to be found, Ralph. Why leave him so close to the castle when he could have been buried where nobody would ever have found him? There's calculation here. That house was empty but I dare say that children play in it occasionally and,' he added, wrinkling his nose, 'it's certainly used by people for another purpose. It was only a matter of time before the body was discovered.'

'Unfortunately,' said Bigot, 'it just happened to be on the day of your arrival.'

Gervase was unconvinced. 'I wonder.'

'Why?' demanded Ralph.

'Because it might not be such a coincidence.'

'What else can it be?'

'A warning.'

'To whom?'

'To the lord Roger and to us.'

Ralph frowned. 'How do you reach that conclusion, Gervase?'

'It's not a conclusion,' replied the other. 'It's just a possibility that we have to consider. On the very day that we ride into Norwich, a dead body is found in the shadow of the castle. It's no anonymous corpse left there at random. The murder victim is Hermer the Steward.'

'So?'

'You've not read the returns for the Taverham hundred as closely as I have, Ralph. Hermer was not only going to support Richard deFontenel when he appeared before us in the shire hall. He was actually claiming land in his own right, one of the outliers at the heart of the dispute. It was a gift from his master for services rendered.'

'And the lord Mauger contests that?'

'Not against the steward any longer,' said Gervase, sadly. 'The only place where Hermer will be able to state his claim is before his Maker. I trust that God will be more merciful than the murderer.'

'And more merciful than *I'll* be when I run that killer to ground,' vowed Bigot. 'This was a brutal murder and it must be answered. But go on with what you're saying, Master Bret,' he continued as they strolled in through the castle gate. 'You spy a link between this crime and your presence in the city?'

'A potential link, my lord sheriff.'

'I have my doubts,' said Ralph.

'Suspend them until we learn the truth,' advised Gervase. 'It may be that my guess is wide of the mark. What does seem clear is that the murder of the steward and the theft of the gold elephants are somehow connected.'

'I'd already decided that,' said Bigot.

Ralph nodded solemnly. 'So had I. Hermer was probably killed by someone who wanted the keys to the room where the gold elephants were kept. What puzzles me is this. The lord Richard's manor is several miles away. Why bring his steward all the way here in order to stab him to death?'

'That's not what happened, Ralph,' said Gervase.

'No?'

'Hermer was killed elsewhere then brought here. Under cover of darkness, most likely. You didn't see the man's back. His tunic was badly torn as if he'd been dragged along the ground and there were wounds in his scalp and neck. I think that his feet were tied together so that he could be pulled along behind a horse.'

'Who could do such a thing to another human being?'

'We've both seen worse on a battlefield, my lord,' said Bigot.

'That's different,' said Ralph. 'We're not on a battlefield now.'

'Yes, we are,' said Gervase as they came to a halt in the bailey. 'We're royal commissioners who're caught in the middle of a battle over land. Instead of fighting with deeds and other legal documents, someone is resorting to more effective methods.'

'That can only mean the lord Mauger,' reasoned Bigot.

'Is he capable of such an act?' said Ralph.

'Capable of ordering it, if not committing it.'

'Then he's the villain you must arrest.'

'Not so fast, my lord,' said the sheriff. 'I prefer to gather evidence before I make an arrest. Mauger is the first person I'll question but I'll do so cautiously. He's as slippery as an eel. Be warned. You'll have to deal with him yourself.' He ran a meditative hand across his jaw. 'The crimes may seem to have Mauger's signature on them but that could be an illusion. He and the Lord Richard are at each other's throats. Mauger will rejoice in anything that upsets his rival but that isn't evidence enough to convict him.'

'You think that he may be innocent?'

'It's not inconceivable.'

'But he's the person who stands most to gain.'

'Perhaps,' said Gervase, thoughtfully, 'but the lord Mauger is also the person who stands least to gain. Here we are, only a short time after we've examined a murder victim and we're already naming him as the chief suspect. He's too obvious. What if someone is setting out to incriminate the lord Mauger?'

'Who?'

'Someone who wants to stir up bad blood between him and the lord Richard.'

'That's easily done,' said Bigot.

'What advantage would they gain, Gervase?' asked Ralph,

'I don't know,' confessed the other.

'Then they'd have no motive. The lord Mauger does.'

'Motive and means,' agreed the sheriff, 'but I was struck by the words that Master Bret just used. He said it was "too obvious". That's my feeling. Mauger is cunning and devious. He works in the shadows. Why should he leave a dead body on my doorstep when he knows that it'll bring me down on his neck?'

They continued to review the situation and speculate on the possible identity of the murderer. Roger Bigot did not try to exclude them from the investigation in any way. Sensing their ability to give practical help, he took pains to invite their comments. Ralph and Gervase were duly touched. It was not the first time that their arrival in a town had been greeted by a violent death, but they usually had to track down the killer against the express wishes of the sheriff. Bigot was less possessive. He would cooperate with anyone who could end valuable assistance to him in a murder inquiry.

It was only when the body was carried past them that they broke off. Placed on a litter and covered with some rough cloth, Hermer the Steward was taken off towards the chapel. The sheriff was reminded of a priority.

'The lord Richard must be informed at once,' he said.

'Will you go in person?' asked Ralph.

'No, this is a task for Olivier.'

'Olivier?'

'Yes, my lord. Olivier Romain is my deputy. He won't relish this particular duty but it has to be discharged. The lord Richard has the right to know of his steward's fate.'

'How will he react?'

'Violently.'

Richard de Fontenel was at first stupefied by the news. He took an involuntary step backwards as he absorbed the shock and took in the implications. When he spoke, his voice was hoarse with anger.

'Dead?' he cried. 'You're telling me that Hermer is dead?'

'I fear so, my lord.'

'Where was he found?'

'In a deserted house close to the castle.'

'What on earth was he doing there?'

'We've no idea.'

'Who found the body?'

'Brother Daniel, a scribe who travels with the commissioners.'

'Why should a monk go poking around in an empty house?'

'I don't know, my lord,' said Olivier Romain, 'but we should be grateful that he did. The corpse might have lain there unseen for even longer. We believe that your steward's been dead for a couple of days.'

'What state was he in?'

'That's immaterial.'

'Tell me, Olivier!' demanded the other, lurching towards him. 'God's tits, man! My steward has been murdered. I want to know what condition he was in when he was found. Tell me the truth.'

'I wasn't there when the lord sheriff went to investigate.'

'But he must have told you what he saw.'

Romain nodded sadly. 'The killer left nothing to chance.'

'In other words, Hermer was butchered.'

'That's what I heard.'

They were standing in the hall of the manor house, a long room with an oaken floor. A table stood at the far end. Swinging on his heel, de Fontenel marched the full length of the room as he tried to subdue the rage that was building inside him. His efforts were in vain. With a loud bellow, he used an arm to dislodge everything that stood on the table, sending goblets and platters clattering to the floor. He turned to face his visitor.

'Were my gold elephants found on him?' he asked.

'No, my lord.'

'Are you sure?'

'There was nothing of value on his person. Or so I'm told.'

'Then where are those miniatures?'

'The lord sheriff is more interested in finding the murderer first,' said Romain. 'In solving that crime, he believes, we will also solve the other.'

'Then you must seize Mauger Livarot at once,' insisted de Fontenel, striding back down the hall. 'He's behind all this. He bribed Hermer to steal the two elephants from me then had him hacked to death by way of reward. Mauger is the culprit. I've said that all along. If you'd had the sense to listen to me at the start, my steward might still be alive and those elephants would be back under lock and key.'

'That's pure supposition, my lord.'

'Don't argue with me, man!' yelled the other. He raised an arm as if about to strike, but Olivier Romain held his ground. The sheriff's deputy was a stocky man of medium height, a conscientious officer who took his work with intense seriousness. Still only thirty, he had a composure and fearlessness that made de Fontenel hesitate. The older man lowered his arm and glowered at him. Romain did not flinch. His voice was calm.

'You're blaming the messenger for bringing bad tidings, my lord.'

'I blame the lord sheriff,' snarled the other.

'He's not culpable here.'

'Yes; he is. A robbery takes place yet he refuses to take charge of the case and fobs me off instead with his deputy. A murder occurs and he sends you to report the matter to me. Why isn't Roger Bigot here himself? What does it take to get him off his backside at the castle?'

'The lord sheriff is already making enquiries,' said Romain, defensively.

'His place is here, breaking the news to me. I want to know exactly when and how my steward was discovered. I also expect to be told that Mauger has been arrested and thrown into a dungeon for his heinous crimes.'

'If the lord Mauger is guilty, he'll be taken in due course.'

'Why the delay?'

'Evidence has to be gathered, my lord.'

'The man hates me,' said de Fontenel, jabbing a finger at him. 'He's stolen my land, he's trespassed on my estate, he's done everything he can to annoy or obstruct me. Now he's trying to wreck a marriage that is very dear to my heart. How much more evidence do you need, Olivier?' He gesticulated wildly. 'Mauger is a thief and murderer. Take him.'

'The lord sheriff means to interview him first thing tomorrow.'

'Why wait until then?'

'You'll have to ask him that.'

'Save valuable time and put him in chains this very evening.'

'I don't make the decisions,' said the other, reasonably. 'I simply carry out orders. You needed to be told about the fate of your steward and that's why I rode out here post haste. It's bleak news, my lord, and I offer you my sincere condolences.'

'What use are they!' Richard de Fontenel stormed around the hall, feet clacking noisily on the oaken floor. One hand was on the dagger at his belt, the other clutched at his hair. It was as if he were feeling the full impact of the news for the first time. He came to an abrupt halt.

'The commissioners have arrived, you say?' he snapped.

'This afternoon, my lord.'

'How many in number?'

'Three with one scribe.'

'Take a message to the leader of the embassy.'

'If you wish.'

'I do wish, Olivier,' said the other, approaching him again. 'My message is this. Until these crimes are solved, I refuse to be called to the shire hall to be examined by them. Theft and murder take precedence over their deliberations. Besides,' he went on with a harsh laugh, 'I'll spare them time and trouble. When Mauger is arrested, he'll have to forfeit his claim to my property. The commissioners will not have to adjudicate between us. I'll only have to dispute lesser matters before them.'

'Your message will be delivered.'

'Take a second with you.'

'For the commissioners?'

'No, Olivier. For your revered Roger Bigot, sheriff of Norfolk and Suffolk.'

'What am I to say to him?' asked Romain, warily.

'That he must do his duty and call Mauger to account.'

'Or?'

The other man drew his dagger and brandished it menacingly. 'I'll take the law into my own hands.'

Impervious to the discomfort, Brother Daniel knelt at the altar rail in the chapel for a long time and offered up prayers for the soul of the dead man. Since he had discovered the corpse he felt a personal responsibility towards Hermer the Steward even though he had never met him. When he finally got up, genuflected and turned, he was astonished to see Eustace Coureton waiting patiently for him at the rear of the nave.

'How long have you been there, my lord?' he asked.

'Long enough to appreciate how devout you are, Brother Daniel.'

'I wasn't only prompted by devotion. To be honest, I went down on my knees in abject fear. I asked God to send me the courage to face this horror. For that is what it was, my lord,' he admitted. 'When I looked into the eyes of the dead man, I felt the cold hand of mortality gripping me by the throat.'

'A natural reaction,' said Coureton easily. 'We all feel like that when we look upon violent death for the first time. As a soldier, I, alas, grew hardened to such sights. There's nothing as sickening as a walk across a battlefield that's strewn with corpses. Man's inhumanity to man is writ largest there. Yet I did it without a tremor eventually. I knew that life must go on.'

'That's why I feel so guilty.'

'Guilty?'

'He lay dead at my feet, I was still alive.'

'Thank the Almighty for your good fortune.'

'I did, my lord. Several times.'

'Then you've no cause to be troubled by guilt.'

'So why does my conscience plague me?'

'I don't know, Brother Daniel.'

'My head is still pounding.'

'Rest awhile,' said the other, lowering him on to a bench and sitting beside him. 'You need time to come to terms with what you saw.'

In the short time they had known each other, Eustace Coureton had grown fond of the monk. Brother Daniel was a congenial member of the party, intelligent, willing and quick to learn, but on the long road from Winchester, when the two men had enjoyed several conversations together, Coureton had detected a more sensitive side to his friend. Behind the amiability and the spiritual exuberance was a decided vulnerability. Hearing of Daniel's unwitting discovery of the murder victim, Coureton had guessed that the monk would be duly appalled by the experience and might welcome a friendly face, and it was for this reason that he sought him out in the chapel.

Daniel spoke in a whisper. 'When one of the holy brothers passed away at the abbey it was always a peaceful event. Sadness was tinged with relief that the departed would be going to a far happier station than they had enjoyed on earth. But not in this case, my lord.'

'I know. Gervase Bret gave me the details.'

'It was a ghastly sight. I'll never forget it.'

'Yes, you will,' said Coureton soothingly. 'Time is considerate towards us. It suppresses darker memories. I knew that you'd be shaken by the ordeal and repair to the chapel. That's why I came to find you.'

'I'm grateful for your kindness, my lord.'

'You shouldn't be left alone. Come and join us, Brother Daniel.'

'Where?'

'In the hall.'

The monk was amazed. 'The banquet is still being held?'

'It begins very soon.'

'How can anyone enjoy a feast when a foul murder hangs over us?'

'In the circumstances, I don't think there'll be much enjoyment, but the banquet had to go forth. It was too late to abandon it. Besides,' he said, philosophically, 'we have to keep body and soul together. Even a monk must eat and drink.'

'I lack any appetite.'

'Then at least sit with us in the hall. Company will distract you.'

'It's more likely to sadden me, my lord,' said Daniel. 'Don't worry about me. You go to the banquet with the other guests. I'm only a humble scribe. I don't really belong there. The chaplain has invited me to share more homely fare with him, so I'll have someone to comfort me.'

'What will you do after that?'

'Come back here to pray once more.'

Coureton gave a tired smile. 'Who knows? I may even join you.'

'You'll be too busy sleeping off the effects of too much wine,' said Daniel with a flash of his old spirit. 'I don't begrudge you that. Drink a cup for me – but raise another for Hermer the Steward.'

'We'll all do that, Brother Daniel.'

'Do the ladies know of the murder?'

'It would be impossible to keep it from them.'

'I hope that they're not too distressed. The lady Golde is robust enough to cope with such grim tidings but Master Bret's wife is a more delicate creature.'

'I fancy that she may be tougher than she appears.'

'You probably thought the same about me, my lord,' said the monk with a self-deprecating shrug. 'Yet look at me now. Cowering in the chapel because I stumbled upon a corpse.'

'There's rather more to it than that.'

'Is there?'

'Yes, Brother Daniel,' explained the other. 'To begin with, what you found was a mutilated body that turned your stomach. You were bound to turn to God for support. Then again, you may have made a critical discovery that will simplify our work here.'

'In what way, my lord?'

'Hermer the Steward was set to be a crucial witness in the major dispute we've come to witness. Alive, he would have been vital to his master's chances of success.'

'And dead?'

'He becomes a key that may unlock the door to the truth. A grotesque truth at that. It's small consolation to you, I know,' Coureton said with a hand on the monk's shoulder, 'but your walk outside the castle may have been providential. In finding that dead body, you did us a kind of favour.'

The banquet was a muted affair. Fine wine and delicious food were served but they were consumed without any relish. News of the murder hung over the occasion like a pall and, though few people discussed the details, all of them had the crime very firmly in their minds. The long table in the hall was presided over by Roger Bigot and his wife, Matilda, a handsome woman in rich apparel who did everything with a natural grace, but not even her smiling affability could put the guests at their ease. Apart from the three commissioners and the two attendant wives, over a dozen others had been invited to dine at the sheriffs table and they had been chosen with care. Both Richard de Fontenel and Mauger Livarot had been passed over because they were implicated in one of the disputes that Ralph Delchard and his colleagues had come to settle and they would, in any case, be fractious guests if forced to take part in a feast together. Others who might try to curry favour with the commissioners because they, too, would appear before them at the shire hall in due course were also excluded from the guest list.

Those who remained were Norman barons of some standing in the county, outwardly eager to hear of affairs in Winchester, the nation's capital, yet inwardly suspicious of royal agents whose remit included the imposition of taxes. The men were cautious, their wives largely subdued. Nobody dared to offend the commissioners. Sporadic laughter echoed along the hall but it often had a hollow ring to it. Eustace Coureton took more pleasure from the evening than most, talking volubly to those around him and seizing the opportunity to learn as much as he could about the county to which they had been sent. The discovery of a murder victim did not diminish his appetite in the least. He set about his food with a gusto worthy of Canon Hubert and visibly lifted the jaded spirits of his neighbours with his military anecdotes.

Gervase Bret looked at his colleague with envy, wishing

that he had Coureton's ability to put an horrific event aside in the interests of social decorum. Memories of his visit to the empty house inhibited Gervase. He ate little, drank sparingly and spent most of the timekeeping a worried eye on his wife who, dismayed at the tidings, had lost what appetite she possessed and merely picked at her food out of politeness. Gervase regretted having told her about the crime but it was not something he could easily keep from her and he preferred to give his own carefully doctored version of events before she heard the details from anyone else. Though unable to savour the banquet, Alys nevertheless slowly came to take some enjoyment from it, feeling increasingly relaxed in the company of strangers and shooting her husband affectionate glances whenever she felt a surge of pride. The banquet was, after all, being held partly in his honour and that gave her an associated status. Alys warmed to the new sensation of importance.

She was not able to match Golde's aplomb. Seated beside the sheriff, Golde held her own as if born to the situation, speaking to him in his native tongue with a fluency schooled by her husband. She was lively, attentive and well informed. Roger Bigot and his wife were entertained by her comments and struck by her strong opinions on all manner of subjects. Ralph Delchard did not need to support her in any way. Golde's ability to sustain an intelligent conversation liberated him to pay attention to the guest on his immediate right. Apart from being one of the most attractive women in the room, the lady Adelaide was a central figure in the feud between the two most prominent Norman lords in the vicinity. Ralph attempted some gentle probing.

'You were married to Geoffrey Molyneux, I believe,' he said.

'Yes, my lord,' she replied softly. 'Happily married for several years'

'His family lived not far from Lisieux.'

'You knew them?'

'Only as distant neighbours. I grew up on the other side of Lisieux and inherited my father's estates when he died. Had I gone back to Normandy, I might well have met your husband, but there was a huge obstacle to overcome.'

'Obstacle?'

'Yes, my lady,' said Ralph, grimacing. 'The English Channel.'

She gave a brittle laugh. 'You're no sailor, I take it.'

'The sea terrifies me. I'm a soldier. I like dry land beneath my feet. That's why I rarely return to Normandy. I've promised to take my wife, Golde, there one day but I'm not sure if that promise will ever be honoured.'

'Shame on you, my lord!' she teased.

'Why?'

'A husband should never let his wife down.'

'Even when it would spare him great distress?'

'Especially then,' she argued, good-naturedly. 'It's a sign of true love to endure distress for someone else's sake. Your wife would be duly grateful.'

'I doubt that she could summon up much gratitude if she saw her loving husband leaning over the side of the boat throughout the voyage. But you raise an interesting point about marital promises, my lady,' he said, artlessly. 'Should they be fulfilled only if they're freely given by the husband, or if they're extracted deliberately by the wife?'

'In both cases.'

'Did you keep your own husband to that rule?'

'There was no need, my lord. He spoilt me wonderfully.'

'Is that what you look for in a husband? Someone who'll spoil you?'

'I'd need to be loved and cherished first.'

'Few men could resist doing either for you,' he said, gallantly. 'The wonder is that you've remained a widow for so long. You must fight off suitors in droves.'

'One or two, perhaps.'

'You're being too modest, my lady.'

'Am I?'

'Every man in the room has been staring at you.'

'But they're all married. They stare without consequence.'

'Only because it gives them so much harmless pleasure. But there must be enough single men in Norfolk to make up a posse. If I were not wed, I'd be among them.'

'No woman wishes to be hunted by a pack.'

'Then you must pick out a favourite. Who will it be?'

'Why not ask the lord sheriff?' she said meaningfully. 'I can see that you've already discussed my marital prospects with him. It's one of the penalties of becoming a widow. No sooner is one husband consigned to his grave than everyone wonders who will follow him. I'm surprised that a royal commissioner should take an interest in such pointless tittle-tattle.'

Ralph backed off. 'Accept my apologies,' he said, penitently.

'I'm not offended, my lord.'

'You've every right to be. I should mind my own business.'

'I'd agree with that,' she said with a cold smile.

'You see? I did upset you.'

'It will take a lot more than that to upset me.'

A servant came between them to refill her cup with wine. When the man stood back, Ralph saw that the lady Adelaide was talking deliberately to the man on her other side and he chided himself for being too inquisitive. He had learnt something about her character but nothing at all about the competing claims of her two suitors. Ralph was still wondering which of the men would finally lure her into marriage when one of the contenders made a dramatic appearance.

Throwing open the door, a furious Richard de Fontenel came marching down the hall to stand accusingly in front of the sheriff. Servants froze in their positions and the buzz of conversation died instantly. Everyone turned to look at the enraged intruder. He gazed at the banquet with utter disgust before pointing directly at the host.

'So this is where you are, my lord sheriff!' he shouted. 'My steward is savagely murdered and all you can do is fill your belly. Perform the office that's required of you,' he said, banging the table with a fist for emphasis. 'Arrest the lord Mauger – *now!*'

The festivities were at an end.

Chapter Four

Covered with a shroud, the body lay on a stone slab in the morgue. Although it was a warm evening outside, there was an abiding chill in the air and Ralph Delchard gave a slight shiver as he followed the sheriff and his turbulent guest into the chamber. Richard de Fontenel was more restrained, cowed by a rebuke from Bigot and showing a respect for the dead now that he was on hallowed ground. Darkness was closing in on the castle and what little natural light penetrated the morgue was now spent. The dancing flame of a single large candle illumined the scene. Hermer somehow looked much smaller than when alive, a shapeless lump beneath the shroud. Herbs had been used to sweeten the smell of decay but it still invaded their nostrils. At the sheriff's invitation, de Fontenel stepped forward to tug back the shroud. A gasp escaped his lips. The body had been washed and most of the wounds had been bound up, but the corpse was still repulsive to behold. After taking a quick inventory, de Fontenel covered his steward up again.

'What happened to his hands?' he asked.

'They were not found with the body,' said Bigot.

'Hacked off?'

'Presumably, my lord.'

'But why?'

'I was hoping that you might suggest an answer.'

'It's needless butchery.'

'Can you think why someone would wish to commit it?'

'You know what I think, my lord sheriff,' growled the other.

He lifted the shroud again to take another look at Hermer's face. Ralph studied his reaction. He and Gervase had visited the morgue earlier to scrutinise the body in the hope of finding that telltale evidence had been revealed by its tending. Neither of them had ever met the steward yet they treated his corpse with a reverence they felt appropriate. There was nothing reverent about de Fontenel's perusal. As he gazed down at the bruised face for the second time, he might have been appraising some rotten food served up to him by mistake. Ralph saw no hint of grief, still less of affection. He was grateful that the sheriff had asked him to accompany them. It meant that he was able to lend support to his host and take the measure of a man whose extraordinary behaviour had interrupted the banquet in the hall. Richard de Fontenel did not endear himself to the commissioner.

'Let's get out of here,' the visitor said, flicking the shroud back into place. 'I've seen all that I need to of Hermer.'

'What will you do with the body?' said Bigot.

'Take it back with us. My men have brought a cart for the purpose. Hermer will be buried in the local church. And soon,' he added. 'Before that stink grows worse.'

'Death is never fragrant, my lord,' observed Ralph.

Ignoring the remark, de Fontenel led the way out. When all three of them stepped back into the fresh air, they saw torches burning in the bailey. The last of the guests were leaving the castle. Roger Bigot now gave vent to his own anger.

'I've indulged you far enough,' he said, sharply. 'It's time for recompense.'

'I owe you nothing, my lord sheriff.'

'An apology is the least that you could offer,' prompted Ralph.

The visitor rounded on him. 'Who asked you for your opinion?'

'Nobody. I offer it of my own free will.'

'Then I treat your advice with the contempt it merits.'

'Don't insult my guest,' warned Bigot. 'I'll have no more of that.'

'Then tell the lord Ralph to hold his tongue.'

'Tell me yourself,' said Ralph, squaring up to him. 'If you dare.'

'I'd dare more than that,' asserted de Fontenel, truculently.

'Would you?'

Their eyes locked in a silent tussle. Richard de Fontenel was smouldering but caution slowly got the better of anger. Ralph's stare was calm but steadfast, conveying a challenge that was too daunting for his adversary to take up. The fact that he was a royal commissioner also had to be weighed in the balance. If rough hands were laid upon his agent, the King himself would come in search of the malefactor. It was Richard de Fontenel who eventually gave way and averted his gaze. The sheriff issued a stinging reproach to his uninvited guest.

'Take care, my lord,' he said, confronting him. 'Offend anyone else beneath my roof and you'll pay dearly. The banquet you so rudely interrupted this evening was held in honour of important visitors. It was arranged days ago and could not be cancelled at the last moment because of a sad turn of events. No disrespect was being offered to your steward. As you saw, his body was treated with care and respect. Its very presence in the morgue ensured that little merriment took place in my hall this evening.'

'I can vouch for that,' Ralph confirmed.

'There was no excuse at all for your boorish behaviour,' continued Bigot, glaring at de Fontenel. 'It disgusted me, upset my wife and outraged my guests. While I'm sheriff here, I'll obey nobody's wild demands. Mark that well, my lord. The next time you ride unbidden into my castle with a troop of men at your back, I'll have each one of you clapped in irons. Is that understood?'

'Yes,' murmured the other.

'Speak up, man!'

'Yes, my lord sheriff. I was perhaps a little intemperate.'

'Is that all you have to say?'

Richard de Fontenel shifted his feet and threw a hostile glance at Ralph, annoyed that he was being reprimanded in front of the commissioner and reluctant to yield up the apology that was being asked of him. Cold facts had to be accepted, however. In the county of Norfolk, the power of the sheriff was paramount. It was backed by the King's own writ and it was fatal to violate that.

'I crave your forgiveness, my lord sheriff,' he said at length.

Bigot was brusque. 'Some things are unpardonable.'

'I was crazed by the news about my steward.'

'That's not how my deputy viewed your response. Olivier tells me that you seemed more concerned about the loss of your gold elephants than you did about the murder of your steward. Have you no loyalty to the men you employ?'

'I'm their master,' retorted the other. 'It's they who owe loyalty to me.'

'What sort of man was Hermer?' asked Ralph.

'A good one until he was corrupted by Mauger.'

'You've firm proof of that, my lord?'

'I will have,' vowed de Fontenel. 'When I shake the truth out of him.'

'You'll do nothing of the kind,' said Bigot, peremptorily. 'The lord Mauger is under my protection. I'll conduct any interrogation that is called for and I'll do so at my own discretion. I'll not be stampeded into action by you.'

'Besides,' said Ralph, mischievously, 'If memory serves me aright, the lord Mauger has more knights at his beck and call than you. If you try to threaten him, he'll beat you all the way back to your manor house.'

'There'll be no violence between the two of them,' continued the sheriff. 'This county is subject to the rule of law and I'm charged with the duty of enforcing that law.' He gave de Fontenel a meaningful look. 'Do you still intend to go your own way?'

'Not if you apprehend Mauger.'

'That's not the answer I look for, my lord. You warmed the ears of my deputy with a blunt message for me. You swore to take the law into your own hands. Are you still of the same mind? If you are,' Bigot said, unequivocally, 'I'll give you time to reflect on your stupidity in one of the dungeons. Is that what you want?'

'No, my lord sheriff.'

'Then repudiate your boast.'

There was a long pause. 'Perhaps I spoke in haste,' conceded the other at length.

'Spoke in haste and acted in fury.'

'I'm sorry about that.'

'Rein in your temper,' ordered Bigot, 'and say no more about the lord Mauger. 'He'll not escape close questioning. Other lines of enquiry must also be explored.'

'That's why I asked about your steward,' said Ralph, seriously. 'Did the fellow have many enemies?'

'None at all, as far as I know,' grunted de Fontenel.

'Was he married, my lord?'

'Hermer lived alone.'

'He must have had family or friends of some sort.'

'His parents came from Falaise but they died years ago. As for friends,' he said with a slight smirk, 'Hermer took his pleasures where he could find them. He liked the girls to be young and pretty.'

'Why do you think he was murdered?' asked Ralph.

'Because he knew too much. Hermer was bribed to steal the elephants from me. When he handed them over to his paymaster – and I know who *that* was – his tongue was silenced in the most brutal way.'

'It's the brutality that worries me, my lord.'

'For what reason?'

'Put yourself in the position of this alleged paymaster,' suggested Ralph. 'For the sake of argument, imagine that you bribe someone to steal precious items from a rival. When that's done, you decide to have your hireling killed.'

'Go on.'

'Wouldn't you take care to hide your tracks? Wouldn't you bury the body some distance away instead of leaving it under the nose of the lord sheriff?'

'Probably.'

'I certainly would,' opined Bigot.

'There's another point,' continued Ralph. 'Your steward looks to have been sturdy enough, but he was no soldier. It wouldn't have been difficult for someone to take him unawares with a sly dagger.'

'So?'

'Why stab him a dozen times or more when one well-placed thrust would've done the task? Your steward was defenceless, he wore no armour. Why was his body so cruelly abused? If you had seen his ankles, you'd have noticed the ugly weals left by a piece of rope. Your steward was dragged on his back over rough ground, my lord. Who'd wish to do that?'

'Mauger.'

'Keep his name out of it,' ordered the sheriff.

'I agree,' said Ralph. 'The man who murdered your steward had a personal score to settle. It was a vengeful death. That rules out the lord Mauger. From what I hear, he's no saint but neither is he a cold-blooded killer. Remember those missing hands, my lord. Why were they cut off? There has to be a meaning in that brutality.'

'The lord Ralph is right,' concluded Bigot. 'The man we seek didn't bribe your steward into stealing those elephants. He slaughtered Hermer for a purpose.'

'To strike at me,' said de Fontenel.

'No,' argued Ralph. 'To get revenge. I come back to my original question, my lord. This is an intensely personal crime. Who were Hermer's enemies?'

'I told you. He had none.'

'Think hard.'

'There's no need. Hermer was a conscientious steward who carried out my orders to the letter. Nobody could have any cause to dislike him, let alone hate him enough to carry out such a barbaric attack.'

'What about Alstan?'

'Who?'

'An old man we met along the way,' said Ralph.

'One of your bordars.'

'There are dozens of such men on my estates,' said the other, dismissively. 'I can't be expected to remember the name of every churl.'

'You should remember Alstan. Old age didn't deprive him of his spirit. You reduced him to slavery. When he had the gall to complain, you had the fellow whipped and chased off your land.'

'It was no more than the wretch deserved.'

'That's a matter of opinion, my lord. I saw Alstan's scars. They'll remain till his dying day. I was reminded of them when I went into the morgue earlier and looked at the wounds on your steward's back. As a matter of interest,' Ralph went on, 'Who actually administered that beating?'

'I don't know. I left the matter to Hermer.'

'Could he have wielded the whip himself?'

'Possibly.'

'Then it seems he did have an enemy, after all. Who'd have a better reason to drag him at the tail of a horse than a man whose back had been lashed to shreds? I'm not saying that Alstan is the culprit here,' Ralph emphasised, 'because I'm certain that he's not. The old man can barely walk, leave alone commit murder. But others might want revenge on his behalf. Others might want to cut off the hand that used that whip on Alstan. Do you see what I'm telling you, my lord?'

'What?'

'Forget, the lord Mauger. Look nearer home for the killer.'

Gervase Bret lay on the bed and cradled his wife lovingly in his arms. Moonlight slanted in through the gaps in the shutters to create a striped pattern on the bare floor. He kissed Alys softly on the forehead.

'I'm sorry, my love,' he whispered.

'It's not your fault, Gervase.'

'I should never have brought you with us.'

'You weren't to know that a terrible murder would be committed. Besides,' she said, squeezing his hand, 'I'd rather be with you whatever may befall us.'

'The ride was too exhausting for you. I should have realised that.'

'I'd be well enough after a night's sleep.'

'You'll be able to rest all day tomorrow, Alys.'

'I wouldn't dream of it. Golde and I want to see something of Norwich.'

'Take some of Ralph's men as an escort.'

'Don't fuss over me,' she teased. 'I can manage, especially with Golde at my side. You just worry about the work that brought you here in the first place. The sooner that's done, the sooner we can head back home to Winchester again.'

'There may be some delay, I'm afraid,' he sighed.

'Why is that?'

'This murder has complicated matters, my love. It has a direct bearing on the major dispute that we came to settle. Ralph has decided that we can't even begin our deliberations until the crime has been solved.'

'Surely, that can be left to the lord sheriff.'

'We feel obliged to help him.'

'No, Gervase,' she objected with sudden alarm, 'it's far too dangerous.'

'We'll move with caution, I promise you.'

'But you're dealing with a brutal killer. I overheard some of the remarks made at the banquet. The victim was not merely killed. He was butchered to death.'

'Don't believe all the gossip,' he warned, keen to allay her fears. 'At times like this, people always exaggerate. The murderer was callous, it's true, but he'll soon be caught and punished.'

'Why must you and Ralph join in the hunt?'

'Because we need to, my love. No more questions.'

He kissed her softly on the lips to terminate the conversation. Along pause ensued. Hearing the change in her breathing, he thought that his wife had drifted off to sleep and he began to doze off himself. Alys brought him awake again.

'Gervase?' she murmured.

'Yes?'

'Who was that dreadful man?'

'Which one?'

'The one who stormed into the hall in the middle of the banquet.'

'That's Richard de Fontenel. He has extensive holdings in the county. Ralph and I will have to see rather a lot of him, unfortunately. He'll have to show better manners in the shire hall or we'll have him removed.'

'He was so rude and frightening.'

'That's typical of the man, I'm told.'

'Could she really be thinking of taking such a brute as her husband?'

'Who?'

'The lady Adelaide,' she explained. 'You must have seen her. She was that beautiful creature who sat beside Ralph.'

Gervase grinned. 'I thought that was Goile.'

'The *other* side of him. You know full well the lady I mean. Every eye in the room was on her at some point. Her name is Adelaide. She's a rich widow and someone told me that she was considering a marriage proposal from the lord Richard.'

'He's a rough wooer, if tonight is anything to judge by.'

'She didn't appear to be surprised by his behaviour.'

'Perhaps she expected him, then,' he speculated. 'It may even be that his performance in the hall was put on largely for her benefit. Perhaps he wanted to impress his future bride by showing her that he was a law unto himself.'

Alys was firm. 'That certainly wasn't the case,' she said. 'What woman in her right mind would be impressed with that crude behaviour? Besides, the lord Richard obviously didn't know that she'd even be at the table. His manner changed at once when he noticed her. He even had the grace to look apologetic.'

'You obviously watched him carefully.'

'I watched her, Gervase. The lady Adelaide was the person who interested me.'

'Why?'

'Because she held every man in thrall.'

'Not me, my love.'

'I saw you sneaking a look at her,' she said, nudging him with an elbow.

'Idle curiosity.'

'Well, my curiosity wasn't idle. I made a point of speaking to her as we left.'

'What did she say?'

'That banquets at the castle didn't always end so prematurely. She's clearly someone who's in her element on such occasions. I have to admit that she made me feel rather awkward and out of place.'

'Nonsense!'

'It's the truth, Gervase.' She snuggled into his shoulder. 'But I'm glad that I went. I was enjoying it until the lord Richard burst in. That was why her comment was so odd.'

'Odd?'

'Yes. The lady Adelaide could see that I was dismayed by the commotion. She told me to make allowances for the intruder because he was the victim of a crime. The odd thing was the way that she said it.'

'I don't follow.'

'Everyone else was shocked and angry,' recalled Alys. 'But not the lady Adelaide. Instead of being appalled at the bad behaviour of a friend, she sounded like a loyal wife apologising for an erring husband.'

Gervase propped himself up on his elbow to look down at her in the half-dark. 'What else did the lady Adelaide tell you?' he asked.

Mauger Livarot pored over the documents that were set out on the table in the parlour and smiled with satisfaction. Standing at his shoulder was his steward, Drogo, a small, stringy man in his fifties with darting eyes and a pale forehead that was visibly crisscrossed with tributaries of blue veins. Both of them looked up when they heard the approach of horses' hooves. Drogo went swiftly across to the window to peer out.

'Well?' asked Livarot.

'The lord sheriff and his men.'

'I expected them earlier than this.'

'Two strangers are riding with him.'

'Men of consequence?'

'The one most certainly is,' said Drogo as he looked at Ralph Delchard. 'The other lacks any authority but he bears himself well.'

Livarot got up from his chair and joined his steward at the window. He watched as Roger Bigot and the two strangers dismounted before walking towards the house. A servant admitted them and conducted them straight to the parlour where there was an exchange of greetings and introductions were made. When he heard that two royal commissioners had come calling, Livarot's interest quickened.

'You're most welcome,' he said with a smile that barely stopped short of ingratiation. 'I thought that I'd have to give evidence before you at the shire hall. It's heartening to see that the whole matter can be settled in the privacy of my own home.'

'We've not come here to discuss any property claims,' explained Ralph. 'The lord sheriff was kind enough to ask our help on a separate – but perhaps related – subject.'

'And what might that be?'

'The murder of Richard de Fontenel's steward.'

'Murder!' echoed the other.

His surprise appeared to be genuine but the news provoked no reaction from Drogo. The older man simply lurked watchfully in the background. The sheriff gave them a terse account of the events surrounding the discovery of the body.

'I can see why you came to me,' said Livarot, wearily. 'To interrogate me. Richard no doubt thinks that I'm the killer.'

'That was the kindest thing he called you, my lord,' said Ralph.

The other man grinned. 'He and I have never been kindred spirits.'

'This is a serious business,' Bigot reminded him. 'There are some questions we need to ask you and it will save us all time if I put them bluntly.'

'Be as blunt as you wish, my lord sheriff,' said Livarot, indicating the seats, 'but at least be comfortable while you speak.' He waited until they sat down, then lowered himself into a chair opposite them, leaving Drogo on his feet alone. 'Now,' he went on, composing his features into a token solemnity, 'ask what you must.'

'Are you involved in any way in the murder?' said Bigot crisply.

'No, my lord sheriff.'

'Where have you been for the last couple of days?'

'Here on my estates.'

'You've not left them for any reason?'

'Only for a morning's hunting,' admitted the other. 'Oh, and I did pay an important call on a friend yesterday afternoon.'

'May we know his name?'

'It was a lady, my lord sheriff. I think you'll guess who she might be. Talk to her, if you wish. I'm sure that the lady Adelaide will tell you exactly when I arrived at her house and when I departed. As for my movements on the estate,' he went on, turning to his steward, 'Drogo will confirm that I was here for the vast majority of the time and I can call a dozen other witnesses who'll say the same.'

'Tenants of yours?' asked Ralph.

'Yes, my lord, but honest men who'll not speak up for me simply because they pay their rent into my coffers. I won't pretend that I'm distressed to hear of Hermer's death. I never liked the fellow so he'll not be mourned here. But that doesn't mark me out as his executioner.' An oily smile spread. 'Given the choice, I'd far sooner kill his master but I'm too God-fearing to do anything like that.'

'What do you know of a theft from the lord Richard's house?' said Bigot.

'I know that it has nothing to do with me.'

'But you're aware of the crime?'

'The lady Adelaide mentioned it to me.'

'Did she tell you what was stolen?'

'Two gold elephants that were destined to be a wedding present to her. If she accepted the hand of Richard de Fontenel, that is. The lady Adelaide was spared that fate, fortunately for her.'

'And fortunately for you as well,' noted the sheriff, bluntly.

'Luck has always sat on my shoulder.'

'Is it only a case of luck?' asked Ralph.

'What else might it be, my lord?'

'The profit of calculation.'

Livarot stiffened. 'Are you accusing me of the theft?'

'Of course not. I merely point out the interesting coincidence that you stand to gain a great deal from it.' He ran an appraising eye over his host. 'Though I doubt if the same can be said for the lady Adelaide.'

'Don't rush to judgement on that score.'

Ralph beamed. 'I'd never do that, my lord.'

'May I ask a question?' intervened Gervase, turning to Livarot. 'You told us a moment ago that you didn't like Hermer.'

'I loathed the man,' confessed the other.

'Why?'

'Because he was working with Richard de Fontenel to dispossess me of land that's rightfully mine. Drogo and I were going through the deeds once again when you arrived, Master

Bret. My claim is incontrovertible.'

'That remains to be decided, my lord.'

'At the appropriate time,' added Ralph.

Gervase was tenacious. 'Tell us more about Hermer.'

'I scarcely knew the fellow.'

'You knew him well enough to loathe him.'

'Naturally,' replied Livarot. 'He was the lord Richard's creature. I'd hate anyone who was employed by that unprincipled rogue.'

'Did you ever meet Hermer?'

'A number of times, Master Bret.'

'Describe him to us.'

'A short, stout, ugly fellow, somewhat older than you but younger than the lord Ralph. He looked solid enough, but Hermer was a weak, frightened, cringing man when his master was near. Able, I daresay, but terrified to contradict the lord Richard.'

'And you say that you hardly knew the man,' observed Gervase with irony.

'I know *of* him and that's quite different.'

'How would he deal with his master's tenants?'

'Unmercifully.'

'You just told us that he was weak,' said Ralph.

'Only in the presence of Richard de Fontenel. When his master wasn't around, Hermer could strut and bully very effectively on his behalf.'

'Was he capable of whipping a slave on the estate?'

'Easily.'

'Even if the man were old and defenceless?'

'That would give the punishment more appeal.'

Gervase took over again. 'Hermer must have been very unpopular, then.'

'Only among the men,' said Livarot with a sly grin. 'From what I gather, it might have been another story with the women. Isn't that so, Drogo?'

'According to the rumours,' said the steward, trying to conceal a snigger.

'You seem well informed about life on another estate,' remarked Gervase.

'News travels, Master Bret.'

'So I see.'

'Is there anything else you wish to know?' asked Livarot with a benign smile. 'I'm always more than ready to indulge royal commissioners.'

'That wasn't the experience of our predecessors, my lord.'

'No,' said Ralph, pointedly. 'If you'd been more honest and less evasive with them, our journey might not have been necessary. But that's something we can resolve in the shire hall when these crimes have been solved.'

Livarot shrugged. 'I'm sorry that my steward and I were unable to help you there.'

'But you *did* help us,' Ralph countered.

'Immensely,' said Gervase. 'Without even realising it.'

Their host exchanged a baffled glance with Drogo.

'We'll probably need to speak to you again,' decided the sheriff, rising to his feet. 'Meanwhile, if anything comes to mind that's in any way relevant to our investigations, I'd be grateful if you'd let us know.'

When Ralph and Gervase got up as well, Livarot escorted his visitors to his front door, pausing to scratch his head when he got there.

'There is one thing that I should perhaps mention,' he began.

'Well?' prodded the sheriff.

'It may have nothing to do with the murder, of course, but who can tell?'

'Does it concern Hermer?'

'I think so, my lord sheriff. Some weeks ago, a man was seen trespassing on my land near nightfall. When he realised that he'd been spotted, he turned tail and ran off.'

'What's the significance of this story?'

'According to the tenant who saw him, the man was Hermer the Steward.'

'Why should Hermer be creeping around your property?'

Mauger Livarot opened the door and waved his guests through it. 'I'm afraid that it's too late to ask him,' he said. 'Goodbye.'

Slumped in a chair, Richard de Fontenel brooded on his misfortune. A few days earlier, he had been confident that he could at last overcome the resistance of the lady to whom he wished to be married. It was something for which he had worked zealously over a period of months. What gave him additional pleasure was the fact that his joy would provoke rage and frustration elsewhere. The imminent arrival of royal commissioners appeared to offer him another opportunity to secure an advantage over a despicable rival. Mauger Livarot would be completely routed. On other fronts, too, the tide seemed to be running in de Fontenel's favour. Then, suddenly, everything had changed. The gifts intended to ensnare his bride were stolen, his steward vanished and his plans began to fall apart. Discovery of Hermer's corpse served to exacerbate the situation. He was deprived of a vital ally in the property dispute that lay ahead and, while he was embroiled in a murder investigation, the field was clear for Livarot to court the lady Adelaide. It was galling.

The unannounced visit to the castle had been a grave mistake. He saw that now. Anger had clouded his judgement. Not only had he insulted Roger Bigot, the person on whom he relied for justice, he had also lowered himself in the esteem of the very woman he sought to impress. Unaware of the lady Adelaide's presence in the hall, he had blundered in and shocked her along with all the other guests. It would take more than two gold elephants to woo her once more to the verge of accepting his proposal. He meditated for a long while on how he might win back her good opinion. Recriminations were still sweeping through his mind in waves when there was a knock on the door. He did not even hear it. A louder knock made him sit up and listen.

'Come in!' he called.

The door opened and a servant entered with a wooden box in his grasp.

'Yes?' said his master.

'This was brought to the house, my lord.'

'What is it?'

'I've no idea, but it bears your name.'

'Who delivered it?'

'I can't tell you, my lord. I found it lying on the step.'

'Bring it here.'

The servant trudged across the room. He was a tall, gangly young man with a mop of dark hair and a curly beard. He gave the box to his master. Attached to the top by a nail was a scrap of paper on which the name of Richard de Fontenel had been scrawled.

'Stand off, Clamahoc,' he snapped, waving the servant away with an irritable hand. 'I don't need you to bend over me like that.'

'No, my lord,' said Clamahoc, taking a few paces backwards. 'Shall I go?'

'Not until I see what this is.'

The box was crudely made. Having no lock, its lid was secured by means of two hooks that were hammered into a tight embrace. It took de Fontenel some time before he could prise the hooks apart with his dagger. He replaced the weapon in its sheath and lifted the lid. One glance was enough to make his blood run cold. Slamming the lid shut, he jumped up from the seat and thrust the box at his servant.

Clamahoc took it, mystified. 'What am I to do with it, my lord?'

'Take it to the priest. Ask him to put it into Hermer's coffin.'

'Coffin?'

'That's where it belongs. See for yourself.'

The servant was tentative. He slowly raised the lid of the box to peep in, then gaped in horror. His master's command was explained. Lying side by side in the box were two blood-covered hands. On one of the fingers, he recognised Hermer's ring.

Chapter Five

Seen from the vantage point of the castle, Norwich was a large
city built in the loop of the river and replete with rows of timber
dwellings whose thatched roofs shone in the morning sunlight
like burnished gold. The dominating influence of religion was
attested by the presence of almost forty churches and chapels,
many of them constructed of local flint and possessing the
distinctive round towers for which the city was justly renowned.
Norwich had a sense of order and permanence to it. Closer
inspection, however, revealed it to be a more decayed and
cluttered place than at first appeared. As Golde and Alys rode
through the dusty streets escorted by two of Ralph's men, they
saw countless examples of dire poverty and the fell hand of war.
The weight of resentment was heavy. Even after twenty years
of occupation, Normans were seen as odious foreigners, an
imposition to be endured ratherthan a people with whom the

inhabitants could make common cause.

Alys had never met such open disapproval, evidenced, as it was, in cold stares, hostile comments, insulting gestures and mute insolence. She found it disturbing. As a Saxon woman in the garb of a Norman lady, Golde was in a more ambiguous position, understanding the feelings of the bystanders they passed while identifying herself with a conquering elite about whom she had many reservations. Not all the citizens were unfriendly. The latent animosity of the many was offset by the cheerful greetings of the few. Others simply ignored the quartet, coping with the sight of Norman soldiers in hauberks by pretending that they were not there. Murder added a dimension of unease. News of the homicide had spread throughout the community and it hung in the air like a noisome stench. People looked warily over their shoulders.

'Well,' said Golde, turning to her friend, 'what do you think of Norwich?'

'I like it far more than it likes us,' replied Alys.

'You get used to that sort of thing.'

'Do you?'

'I met it in York, Chester, Exeter and every other place I visited with Ralph.'

'It's never been quite so obvious in Winchester, perhaps because that's where I grew up. I don't simply sense their condemnation here; I can reach out and touch it.'

'People are slow to accept change.'

'It goes deeper than that, Golde.'

After their short tour of the city, they rode into the noisy market, itself a symbol of discord. Moved from its original site in Tombland to the east of the city, it now occupied land in the parish of St Peter Mancroft to the west of the castle, serving the many Norman families who had settled in the district and causing a stream of protest that still flowed with a strong current. During the banquet the previous evening, Golde had been told about the enforced change of venue. She raised her voice above the hubbub.

'It upset everybody,' she said.

'What did?'

'Shifting the market here from its old site. It used to be in the parish of St Michael Tombland, the richest in the city, according to Ralph. It stood there for many years. They met a lot of opposition when they took it away.'

'I can understand that, Golde.'

'A market is really the heart of a town.'

'Don't let Brother Daniel hear you say that,' warned Alys.

'Why not?'

'He'd argue that a cathedral or an abbey was the heart of a community.'

Golde took a more practical view. 'We all have to eat.'

Caught up in the mild frenzy around them, they picked their way through the milling crowds. The stallholders had been busy since dawn but the haggling was still at its height as fresh customers came in from outlying villages and hamlets to swell the numbers. Alys took note of a blaze of colour to her left.

'Can we look at that stall selling cloth?' she asked.

Golde laughed. 'We'll look at *everything*.'

'Look or buy?'

'Both.'

Helped by the two soldiers, they dismounted and made their way across to a display of silks, satins and woollen materials. Alys was soon entranced. The market was an education. It told them far more about the city than they could learn inside the confines of the castle. They heard the voices, shared in the emotions and observed the habits of the local people. Crafts of all kinds were on display. Stalls were set out in a higgledy-piggledy fashion. The two women followed a meandering route that took them past luscious fruit, fresh vegetables, slabs of meat, piles of fish, squawking poultry, baskets of eggs, jewellery, pottery, wine, beer, shoes, clothing, cutlery and all the other items that vendors promoted with loud competitive zeal. The powerful aroma of the market was compounded of many individual elements, the most enticing being that of freshly baked bread. The two women enjoyed it all immensely. Golde was pleased to see how well Alys stood up to what was a tiring expedition. They were on their feet for a long time and buffeting shoulders took their toll.

'How do you feel?' she asked.

'Very well.'

'You looked quite ill during the banquet.'

'I was tired, that's all.'

'You've certainly got your colour back today.'

'And my appetite,' said Alys with a smile. 'The sight and smell of all this food is making me hungry. Shall we go back?'

'I think we'd better or they'll wonder what's happened to us.'

Lifted back on to their horses, they made their way to the castle through the steady throng with the few items they had purchased safely packed into a satchel. Their journey took them past the deserted house where the dead body had been found, now attracting the ghoulish interest of some children and a barking dog. When they rode into the castle, an ostler was waiting to assist them to the ground before taking their mounts away to be stabled. Somebody else was waiting for them as well.

'There you are,' said Brother Daniel, beaming happily as he swooped down on them. 'I was hoping to find you.'

'We've been to market, Brother Daniel,' explained Golde.

'Yes,' said Alys. 'It was wonderful.'

His face clouded. 'I'm glad that you found something to take your mind off the dreadful crime that came to light yesterday. It still preys on me. Perhaps I should've come with you to the market, though I doubt if even that would wipe away the memory of what I saw in that house.'

'The lord Eustace told us how distressed you were,' said Golde.

'He's been very kind to me.'

'It must have been a horrid experience for you.'

'It was, my lady,' he confessed, 'but God directed my footsteps for a purpose. I was meant to find that body. It chastened me. Shocking as it was, I think the experience has left me a better and more considerate person.'

'Nobody could be more considerate than you, Brother Daniel,' says Alys.

'Thank you,' said the monk, shaking off his melancholy. He held up a letter. 'But this is why I'm so pleased to see you. I have something for you.'

'For me?' Alys said in surprise.

'It's addressed to both of you.'

'Who could be writing to us?' wondered Golde, taking the missive.

'The servant belonged to the lady Adelaide's household.'

'The lady Adelaide?'

'Open it, Golde,' urged Alys.

'No, you take it,' said the other, passing it to her. 'You spoke to the lady Adelaide last night. I didn't.' She gave a wry smile. 'Though I heard a great deal about her from my husband. Ralph sat next to her.'

Alys broke the seal. 'I'll see what she says.'

'I'm sorry that you missed the banquet, Brother Daniel,' said Golde.

'So am I,' he replied. 'But I hear you had an uninvited guest.'

'Richard de Fontenel. It was his steward whose corpse you found.' She saw the astonishment on Alys's face. 'Good news or bad?'

'Excellent news,' said Alys. 'We've been invited to visit the lady Adelaide.'

'Alone or with our husbands?'

'Oh, alone. She makes that quite clear.'

Eustace Coureton had no intention of being excluded from the investigation of the two crimes. He plied Ralph Delchard and Gervase Bret with searching questions about their visit to the manor house of Mauger Livarot.

'What sort of man is the lord Mauger?'

'The kind that no sensible person would trust,' said Ralph. 'Behind that leering smile of his was a selfish, cunning, deceitful man who'd stop at nothing to gain the upper hand over a rival.'

'Not even at murder?'

'No, my lord.'

'Then he could be the culprit?'

'I didn't say that. The lord Mauger is certainly capable of stabbing a man to death, though he'd be more likely to thrust the blade into his back than his chest. But I don't think he's guilty of this murder. He looked too surprised when he was told about it. Too surprised and too peeved.'

'Why was that?'

'He felt cheated out of the pleasure of killing Hermer himself.'

'Is that what he told you?'

'I read it in his eyes.' Ralph told Coureton in detail about the interrogation of Livarot and the old soldier took it all in, nodding sagely throughout. When the recital was over, he turned to Gervase.

'Do you have anything to add to that?'

'Only that I'm also convinced that the lord Mauger didn't commit or instigate the murder. It came as a welcome bonus to him. We could see that. As for the theft of the gold elephants, however,' reflected Gervase, 'I'm not so sure. The lord Mauger may well be implicated there. So might Drogo.'

'Drogo?'

'His steward.'

Ralph gave a snort of disgust. 'A wizened little weasel of a man.'

'He was too knowing,' said Gervase. 'Too shifty, artful, sure of himself. He and the lord Mauger are well matched. They'll be subtle advocates when they appear before us to ratify their claim to the disputed property. We'll have to watch them like hawks.'

'We will,' vowed Ralph.

'I look forward to meeting them,' said Coureton. 'But I'm glad you mentioned the theft of those elephants, Gervase. In pursuing a killer, the sheriff has rather lost sight of the earlier crime. His efforts are concentrated on solving a murder.'

'He believes that the two crimes are linked,' said Gervase.

'All the more reason to look more closely into the first because that may lead directly to the second. I thought that the sheriff's deputy was investigating the theft,' Coureton went on, 'but when I spoke to Olivier Romain earlier, he told me he was riding out to the lord Richard's estate again to look for clues relating to the murder.'

'That won't please the lord Richard,' commented Ralph. 'Nothing is more important to him than the return of his precious elephants. And we all know why. They're the bait for the lady Adelaide. What a hideous choice confronts her!' he said, pulling a face. 'Richard de Fontenel or Mauger Livarot. She wouldn't be selecting a husband. She'd be choosing between death and damnation.'

'The lady Adelaide may reject both,' said Gervase.

'That's her business,' said Coureton. 'Ours is to do what we can to solve two crimes that are holding us back from the work that brought us here in the first place. To that end, I think that we should go hunting.'

'For what, my lord?'

'Elephants.' He leant forward to explain. The three men were sitting at a table in the hall over a light meal. Ralph had a cup of wine in front of him; Gervase and Coureton had opted for ale. The latter's voice lowered to a conspiratorial whisper.

'I had a long talk with Olivier Romain,' he said. 'He admitted that he'd made little progress in solving the theft of those gold elephants. But he had stumbled on one promising fact.'

'What was that?' said Ralph.

'A year ago, the lord Richard employed a man who worked hand in hand with Hermer as his assistant. They got on well at first. Then they fell out. Hermer had the man dismissed and he went off swearing that he'd get his own back.'

'On the steward or on the lord Richard?'

'On both.'

'Who is the fellow?'

'His name is Starculf.'

'Then why hasn't he been questioned?'

'Because there's no sign of him,' said Coureton, frowning. 'Starculf left the area months ago and hasn't been seen since. The sheriff's deputy looked everywhere and the search will continue. Starculf not only had a reason to steal, he had a motive to kill.'

'Also,' said Gervase, thinking it through, 'he'd be familiar with the estate. He'd know his way around extremely well. If he was Hermer's assistant, he might even have had keys to the house.'

'Apparently, the lord Richard spoke very harshly of him. He flew into a temper at the very mention of Starculf's name.'

'It doesn't take much to enrage him.'

'*Ira furor brevis est.*'

'What does that mean?' said Ralph.

'"Anger is a short madness." I was quoting Horace.'

'Then he must have had someone like Richard de Fontenel in mind.'

'Starculf must be tracked down,' said Gervase. 'He's an obvious suspect.'

'I agree,' said Coureton, 'but I think we'll uncover some others before too long. Starculf was only one of several people with a grudge against the lord Richard.'

'Alstan, for instance.'

'I wasn't forgetting that poor old man.'

'It's a pity we didn't get him to tell us more about the way the estate was run.'

Coureton shook his head. 'He knew little that would be of value to us. No, I fancy there are far more eloquent witnesses to his master's ruthlessness. And you're the person to find them for us, Gervase.'

'Me?'

'You're our sharp-eyed lawyer.'

'Where am I supposed to look?'

'Where else,' said Coureton, 'but in that sheaf of documents you brought with you? The lord Richard is contesting the ownership of a large acreage of land with Mauger Livarot, but it must have belonged to someone else before either of them tried to take it into their possession. Who was that original owner and how was his property seized from him?' He offered a helpful grin. 'Does my suggestion make sense?'

'Considerable sense,' said Gervase, gratefully. 'I went through the returns for this whole county and saw just how often the name of Richard de Fontenel was associated with dubious claims. He acquired land by all manner of subterfuge.'

'Make a list of those he dispossessed.'

'I will, my lord.'

'Especially in the Taverham hundred.'

'Leave it to me.'

'We may turn up suspects that would not occur to the sheriff and his deputy.'

'I'll go through my satchel with care.'

Ralph was lost in thought. Emerging from his silence, he brought the flat of his hand down hard on the table and startled them. They looked quizzically at him.

'What if we're wrong?' he demanded.

'About what?' said Gervase.

'Everything. What if the two crimes are unconnected? We're all assuming that one person is responsible for both but that may not be the case at all. In any event, we're more likely to solve the first crime if we treat it in isolation.'

'Why?'

'Because then we can examine it properly,' argued Ralph. 'If we treat it as a prelude to murder, we only confuse the issue. Reduce it to the simple facts. Richard de Fontenel buys an expensive gift for the lady he wishes to marry. That gift is stolen from his home. What's his immediate conclusion?'

'That the lord Mauger took the elephants,' said Coureton.

'Exactly. A deadly rival trying to ruin his marriage plans. That's one reason for the theft but isn't there a much more obvious one?' He looked from one to the other. 'Sheer gain,' he said, grinning at them. 'Those elephants were made of solid gold. They'd be dangerous to keep because they're so distinctive. Besides, they were very valuable. So what would the thief do?'

'Have them melted down.'

'Yes, my lord.'

'That way, the evidence disappears from sight,' said Gervase.

'And he sells the gold for a handsome profit.' Ralph got up suddenly from the table. 'Let the sheriff go chasing after Mauger Livarot,' he said with a chuckle. 'I'm going to acquaint myself with the goldsmiths of Norwich. One of them may have had some unusual items presented to him recently.'

'Sound reasoning,' complimented Eustace Coureton. 'You and Gervase are engaged in the selfsame search, my lord.'

'Are we?'

'Yes. While you're hunting through some shops in the city, Gervase will be scouring his documents. I'll be interested to see which of you finds gold first.'

Roger Bigot lifted the lid of the rough-hewn wooden coffin and peered in. Wrapped in a shroud, Hermer's corpse had been reunited with his hands but they were not attached to his wrists. They had been placed either side of the body.

'Are you certain they belonged to your steward?' asked the sheriff.

'There's no doubt about that,' said de Fontenel, testily. 'The left hand bears his ring and there's a scar on his right palm that I recognise. Those are Hermer's hands, my lord sheriff. Who else's could they be?'

Bigot took one last look at them before he closed the lid of the coffin. 'When is the burial?' he said.

'This afternoon. There's no point in delaying it.'

'At least he'll be whole when he's lowered into his grave.'

'That won't be the case with his murderer,' promised the other with a glint in his eye. 'I'll cut off more than his hands. I'll gouge out his eyes for a start.'

'You'll do nothing of the kind,' warned the sheriff. 'When we arrest the villain, *I'll* decide what punishment to inflict.'

'Not if I get to him first!'

They were in the tiny church on Richard de Fontenel's estate, less than half a mile from his manor house. Since the building lacked a separate chamber, the coffin had been placed on trestles in the nave. The smell of incense filled the air. Summoned by a message from de Fontenel, the sheriff had ridden out to view the missing hands and to hear how they had reappeared. It was a puzzling development. Bigot waited until they left the church before he resumed his questioning.

'Who found the hands, my lord?'

'Clamahoc, one of my servants.'

'Where were they?'

'Left outside my front door in a box.'

'Did this Clamahoc see who put them there?'

'No,' said the other, grimly, 'and nor did anyone else. But I know who it was.'

'I hope that you're not going to say that it was the lord Mauger.'

'It's just the kind of taunt he would favour.'

'How can you be sure that it was a taunt?'

'What else could it be, my lord sheriff?'

'An act of penitence.' His companion snorted. 'It could, Richard. Suppose that the killer repented of his savagery and returned the hands to lighten the burden on his conscience.'

Richard de Fontenel scowled. I don't believe in penitent murderers. If the man was so conscience-stricken, why not confess his crime? No,' he insisted, 'this was a gibe at me. Those hands were sent back to give me a deliberate shock.'

'Well, they weren't placed at your door by the lord Mauger. That I can affirm. Not long before your servant found that box, I was talking to Mauger at his house. He would never have been able to cover the distance here in time.'

'Then he must have sent that verminous steward of his.'

'Drogo was present throughout my visit.'

The other man was adamant. 'Mauger had those hands delivered here somehow.'

'I don't agree,' said Bigot, 'and neither do Ralph Delchard and Gervase Bret. They came with me on my visit. Both are shrewd men, used to rooting out deceit and dishonesty. They came to the same conclusion that I did. Mauger is not the culprit.'

'Then he fooled all three of you.'

'My deputy is of the same mind. Olivier still believes that the most likely person is the man who was Hermer's assistant. What was his name?'

'Starculf.'

'He left here under a cloud, it seems.'

'We found him unreliable.'

'Why was that, my lord?'

'That's a private matter. Starculf had to go.'

'But he left embittered, vowing vengeance.'

'True,' admitted the other. 'He did have cause to strike at Hermer, but why leave it so long? Why attack at this particular moment? Starculf has not been seen or heard of for months, my lord sheriff. I doubt that he's even still in the county. It would be too much of a coincidence if he returned to take his revenge at the precise moment when I had those gold elephants in my possession.' He gave a dismissive shrug. 'How could he arrange to steal something he didn't know I owned?'

'We'd still like to speak with him.'

'Only one other person was aware that I'd acquired those elephants.'

'Mauger Livarot.'

'Exactly!'

'But how did he know, my lord?'

'The way that he gets to know everything,' sneered de Fontenel. 'By means of bribery. My wedding gift vanished on the very day I showed it to the lady Adelaide. That was no accident.'

'According to you, Hermer made off with it.'

'He must have done.'

'Why?'

'Because he had the elephants on a platter when he left the room. The lady Adelaide and I talked alone at some length. Above an hour, probably. During that time,' de Fontenel asserted, 'Hermer must have sneaked off to deliver the takings to the man who put him up to the crime – Mauger Livarot.'

'You really believe that your steward betrayed you?'

'What I believe is that Mauger used him then cast him aside.'

'Yet Hermer's body lies in your church. It'll be buried on your land.'

'I couldn't deny him that.'

'Even though you suspect him of being party to a conspiracy?' said Bigot. 'I would have thought you'd want to burn the body or tear it to shreds.'

'That rage has passed,' confessed the other, solemnly. 'Hermer gave me good service for many years. I owe him something for that. Besides, there's an element of doubt. Not about Mauger's involvement,' he said, wagging a finger. 'Only about Hermer. Part of me wants to believe that a loyal steward would never sink so low.'

'Olivier Romain reached the same conclusion.'

'All that your deputy can talk about is Starculf.'

'With good reason, my lord. He was disaffected when he left your estate.'

'The only way that he would have been drawn into this was as Mauger's agent.'

'Stop harping on the lord Mauger. He's innocent.'

'Not from where I stand!'

Bigot sighed wearily as they walked towards their horses. Four of the sheriff's men were already in the saddle. They waited while the two men exchanged their last words. Bigot recalled something that had been said earlier.

'You claim that nobody knew that you had those gold elephants.'

'Nobody except Mauger.'

'What about the man who sold them to you?'

'I bought them abroad. In a private transaction.'

'Where did the transaction take place?'

'That's no concern of yours, my lord sheriff,' said de Fontenel, sharply. 'Just do your office and get them back for me.'

'When are you bidden?' asked Ralph Delchard, interested to hear the news.

'Tomorrow,' said Golde.

'Did the invitation extend to me?'

'No, Ralph. Nor to Gervase.'

'A pity. I'd rather like to see where the lady Adelaide lives.'

'Be honest.' she teased. 'All you'd like to see is the lady Adelaide herself. '

'Not for the reason you think, my love. I enjoy her company, I won't deny it, but that's not why I'd seek it out. Two men are vying for her hand in marriage. One of them has been robbed of the wedding gift intended for her and his steward has been murdered. That's why I'd like to speak with the lady Adelaide again,' he said, kissing

114

her on the forehead. 'To find out more about her relationship with the lord Richard than she was prepared to divulge at the banquet.'

'Does she still have a relationship with him? I'd have thought that his behaviour last night ended all hopes he had of marrying her. He was raging.'

'*Ira furor brevis est.*'

Golde was taken aback. 'What did you say?'

'"Anger is a short madness".' he replied airily. 'It's from the Roman poet, Horace. You didn't know that your husband was a Latin scholar, did you?'

'I think you've been talking to the lord Eustace.'

'How did you guess?' He gave a ripe chuckle. 'As for the lady Adelaide, you'll be able to judge for yourself if she's cast the lord Richard aside as a suitor. He's no worse than her other swain, the lord Mauger.'

'A beautiful woman can't always choose the men who're attracted to her.'

'Tell that to the lady Adelaide.' he said, cheerily. 'But I must away, my love.'

They were in their chamber at the castle. Golde had just shown him what she had bought that morning and told him of the invitation. Ralph had no time to linger. After giving her another kiss, he moved towards the door. 'You went to market this morning.' he said, 'and now it's my turn.'

'What are you after?'

'Gold!'

He let himself out and went down the stairs. Minutes later, he was riding alone through the main gate, with directions from the captain of the guard. There were three goldsmiths in Norwich and he intended to visit them all. The first could be discounted at once. He had been sick with fever for over a week and his shop was closed. The second had been offered nothing to buy or melt down and was a man of such patent honesty that Ralph wasted no more time questioning him. It was when he called on the last of the three that he sensed he might make more progress.

Judicael the Goldsmith was a portly man with heavy jowls, rounded shoulders and flabby hands. He was older and more prosperous than either of his two rivals. His shop was larger, his apparel richer and his manner more confident. When he saw Ralph entering his premises, he rubbed his palms and gave an unctuous smile.

'Good morning, my lord.' he said.

'Are you Judicael?'

'Yes, my lord. What can I do for you?'

'I'd like your help.'

'Certainly. I keep a very large stock. Rings, brooches, necklaces, bangles.' His voice took on a confiding note. 'I take it that we're talking about a gift for a lady?'

'We are,' confirmed Ralph.

'Good. What would you like to see?'

'Two gold elephants.'

Judicael's face went blank. 'Elephants, my lord?'

'Do you know what elephants are?'

'Well, yes, of course. Not that I've ever seen one in the flesh. But I have an idea of what they look like. You want me to *make* two elephants? Is that my commission?'

'No,' said Ralph, irritated by his manner. 'Your commission is simply to give me the answers I need. I'm not here to buy anything.'

116

'Oh, I'm disappointed to hear that.'

'My errand is more important than your disappointment.'

'Is it, my lord? Why is that?'

'I'll ask the questions. Now, has anyone brought any gold elephants to you?'

'No, my lord.'

'I'm told they're so big,' explained Ralph, using his fingers to give some idea of dimensions. 'Made of solid gold, with a crucifix on each head. Has anything like that been brought to your shop?'

'Nothing at all, my lord.'

'Are you sure?'

'Absolutely sure.'

'So you weren't asked to melt them down?'

'No, my lord.'

'But you do buy the occasional gold item?'

'Only if I have proof of ownership,' said Judicael firmly. 'Otherwise, I turn it away. I'm a respectable goldsmith, my lord. I don't trade in stolen goods.'

Ralph was not persuaded by the claim. Judicael was too sleek and plausible. There was an evasive look in the man's eye. Ralph tried to press him.

'Where is your stock kept?'

'Under lock and key, my lord.'

'Here on the premises?'

'In my strong room.' The unctuous smile returned. 'You wish to buy something?'

'No, my friend. I just want to see what you have.'

Judicael was cautious. 'I'm sorry, my lord. That would be out of the question.'

'What if I were to come back here with the sheriff?' Ralph introduced himself properly and stated the nature of his business. The goldsmith became even more circumspect. Although anxious not to impede a murder investigation, he was at first unwilling to take Ralph on trust. The commissioner grew impatient.

'Will you open your strong room or do I have to break the door down myself?'

'That won't be necessary, my lord,' said the other in alarm.

'Then why dither, man? Are you hiding something?'

'No, no. Of course not.'

'Those two elephants are here. Is that it?'

'I swear I've never seen any gold elephants.'

'Then you have nothing to worry about, have you?'

Judicael gave way. After first locking the door of the shop, he took Ralph into the room at the rear and approached a stout door. Two keys were needed to open it. Inside the strong room was a series of small boxes, each locked and chained to the wall. The goldsmith fumbled with his keys.

'Which one shall I open, my lord?' he gibbered.

'All of them.'

Ralph was certain that the missing property was not there but he was determined to make the goldsmith sweat a little. He looked into each box and examined each separate item of jewellery. Nothing even remotely like an elephant came to light. Yet the visit was not fruitless. The more time he spent with Judicael, the more he sensed that the man was holding something back from him. When the last of the boxes had been locked up again, he fixed the goldsmith with a cold stare.

'Where are they, Judicael?'

'I don't know, my lord. As God's my witness.'

'Someone brought those elephants to you, didn't they?'

'No, I've never laid eyes on them.'

'But you've heard of their existence?'

The goldsmith squirmed helplessly. 'I may have,' he admitted.

'Go on.'

'If they're anything like the objects you describe, they're very unusual. Only an expert goldsmith could fashion such objects. They're far beyond my skill.' He squinted up at Ralph. 'Where did you say they came from?'

'Somewhere abroad. Brought to England only recently.'

'I doubt that, my lord.'

'Why?'

'You mentioned that the elephants each had a crucifix on its head?'

'According to what I was told.'

'That jogged my memory,' said the other. 'What I said was true. I've not seen the pieces myself but I've heard tell of them. You were misinformed, my lord.'

'Oh?'

'They weren't recently brought to England.'

'How do you know?'

'Because they've been in this country for quite some time,'

Chapter Six

Alone in his chamber at the castle, Gervase Bret went patiently through the documents he had brought with him from Winchester. It was a task he thoroughly enjoyed. Ralph Delchard was at his most effective when confronting awkward witnesses in the shire hall. Legal niceties only exasperated him. They were meat and drink to Gervase who read the abbreviated Latin on the pages in front of him with continuous pleasure, knowing that his retention of detail would be vital when the commissioners sat in judgement on the various disputes. The name he was after was proving elusive. He knew that it was somewhere in his sheaf of papers but he could not recall the exact spot. Richard de Fontenel had separate holdings in the hundreds of Forehoe, Taverham, Blofield and Humbleyard and Gervase picked his way carefully through them all. It was amid land in the Depwade hundred that he eventually located the person he was seeking.

'In Boielvnd. 1 car tre. Qua tenuit Olova.t.r.e.'

'In Boyland, 1 carucate of land which Olova held in King Edward's time.'

His satchel contained only a fraction of the returns that were brought back to the Exchequer by the first team of commissioners to be checked and collated. All that concerned Gervase and his colleagues were patent irregularities and unresolved disputes. Olova's claim was among them. She had definite cause for complaint. Not only had she lost a carucate of land in Boyland to Richard de Fontenel, he had also taken two carucates from her in Tharston. It was not clear by what mean she had acquired the property but, since it amounted in total to over three hundred and fifty acres, Gervase could understand why Olova was eager to contest ownership of it. Others had also been dispossessed by de Fontenel but she had been deprived of most land. Her losses did not end there. Gervase noted that Olova had also been relieved of two smaller holdings in the West Flegg hundred by Mauger Livarot. It was a familiar tale. She was one of many people in Norfolk who had been ground down remorselessly between the mill wheels of de Fontenel and Livarot.

Gervase was putting the documents away again when his wife opened the door.

'Am I disturbing you?' she said, pausing in the doorway.

'No, no. Come on in, Alys.'

'I promised that I wouldn't get in your way while I was here.'

'I know.' he said, giving her a welcoming kiss and closing the door. 'But I've just finished what I was doing. You could not have come at a more apposite time.'

'Good.'

'Did you enjoy your visit to the market?'

'Oh, yes!'

Alys laughed with girlish delight and recounted the details of her visit to the town. Her voice saddened when she talked about the hostility that she and Golde had met. It had been the one small blemish on an otherwise pleasant morning. Gervase was glad that his wife had found so much to divert her and was interested to hear about the invitation that had arrived at the castle from the lady Adelaide.

'You've no objection, have you?' she said, eager for his approval.

'None at all, Alys.'

'Thank you. I'm so keen to go and so is Golde.'

'Ralph will certainly not hold her back,' he observed.

'That's what Golde said.'

'He'll do everything in his power to make sure that she calls on the lady Adelaide. It could help us. The more we can glean about her, the better. Look and listen, Alys.'

'I will.'

'She occupies a unique place in our enquiries. You might say that she holds the balance between the lord Richard and the lord Mauger.'

'It must be exciting to have two men vying for your hand.'

'Not if they happen to be those reprobates. Besides,' he said, slightly nettled, 'one honest suitor is enough for any woman, surely? Wasn't I sufficient for you, Alys? Or did you want a whole pack of wooers banging on your door?'

'I was grateful to have one.'

'You had several admirers.'

'None that I cared to notice,' she said, sweetly. 'Apart from you, that is. If there'd been a hundred suitors hammering on my door, it would only have been opened to Gervase Bret.'

He smiled with relief. 'Thank you, Alys.'

'Could you ever doubt me?'

'No, my love.'

'As for the lord Richard, I wouldn't look twice at such a man. I pity the lady Adelaide if she is forced to marry him. I'd be terrified of a husband who could work himself up into such a violent rage.'

'You're not terrified of me, are you?'

'Only now and then,' she teased.

He took her by the shoulders to kiss her again, then stood back to appraise her.

'You look much better now, Alys.'

'I've got my strength back after the journey.'

'So have I,' he said, 'and it's just as well because I'm going to need it. We came here to act as judges but we're deputies of the sheriff instead. That will take all the energy we can muster.'

'Have you any idea who the murderer might be?'

'Not at this point. We have a short list of names but we've yet to put faces to them. And the lord Richard is only muddying the waters by his wild behaviour. It could be some time before we manage to solve the crimes.'

'Is there anything that I can do to assist you?'

'You're doing it by visiting the lady Adelaide.'

'What would you like me to ask her?'

'Nothing,' he said, quickly. 'Leave any questions to Golde.

'She's played this game before. You haven't. Just behave as you would on any other visit to a friend. Be polite to your hostess – and take note of every word she says.'

'Ill try, Gervase. What will you be doing, meanwhile?'

'Paying a call on another Norfolk lady.'

'And who's that?'

'Olova.'

Roger Bigot was astounded by the news. He pressed Ralph Delchard for more detail. 'The elephants were stolen?'

'So it appears, my lord sheriff.'

'From whom?'

'The abbot of Holme.'

'Who told you this?'

'Judicael the Goldsmith,' said Ralph. 'Except that he didn't exactly volunteer the information. I had to prise it out of him like a pearl from an oyster.'

'If this intelligence proves to be correct,' said Eustace Coureton, 'It will be a pearl indeed. Who is this man, Ralph?'

'Not one that I could ever bring myself to like.'

'Can his word be trusted?'

'In this instance, I believe that it can.'

The three men were in the hall at the castle. Bigot and Coureton were intrigued to hear what Ralph had learnt from his visit to the goldsmith. It cast a whole new light on the disappearance of the two gold elephants.

'No wonder that the lord Richard is so desperate to reclaim them,' said Ralph. 'It's not simply a question of using them to dazzle the eyes of the lady Adelaide. He wants them back in his possession before anyone starts asking where they came from in the first place.'

Coureton chuckled. 'And now we know. He stole them.'

'A thief is now the victim of theft,' said Bigot.

'We can't be certain of that,' suggested Ralph, 'and it would be very foolish of us to show our hands before the facts have been verified. It may be that the lord Richard bought them in good faith, ignorant of their origin.'

'Where did he say that they came from?' asked Coureton.

'Somewhere abroad,' said Bigot. 'The lord Richard went to Normandy recently to visit his estates. When he came back, he had those miniature elephants with him.'

'That doesn't mean that they actually came from Normandy.'

'I agree,' said Ralph. 'Why should anyone bother to steal them from the abbey of Holme, take them across the Channel then sell them to someone who was returning to this country? That would be perverse.'

'Had the goldsmith actually seen those elephants?' said Bigot.

'No, my lord sheriff. 'But they'd been seen and admired by someone who had dealings with Judicael. A man who'd visited the abbey. The pieces were so unusual that he described them in detail to the goldsmith. That description tallied with the one given to you by the lord Richard.'

'Then they *have* to be the same miniatures.'

'And I'll wager that the lord Richard stole them,' asserted Coureton.

'That's only a guess,' Ralph reminded him. 'We'll need proof and the best way we can get that is by moving stealthily.

Whatever we do, we mustn't alert the lord Richard to the fact that we've uncovered an earlier crime relating to those elephants. We can rest assured that they were taken illegally from the abbey of St Benet at Holme. No abbey would part willingly with anything so valuable.'

'Don't forget the spiritual aspect, my lord,' said Bigot. 'Each animal had a crucifix on its head. The monks of St Benet will regard them as holy treasures.'

'What will they think when they hear that their holy treasures have been waved in front of a beautiful woman to inveigle her into a marital bed?'

'The abbot will be mortified.'

'He must be aware of the crime. Why hasn't he howled at the outrage?'

'Perhaps he's yet to discover it,' said Bigot. 'If they keep their valuables locked away in a chest, the abbot may not have realised that those elephants have vanished. On the other hand, he may know the truth yet not wish to report the crime for some reason. Abbot Alfwold is a venerable man. He's far more likely to pray for the return of his treasures than to come running to me.'

'That fact probably weighed with the lord Richard,' said Coureton. 'When he stole those gold elephants, he counted on the fact that you would not even get to hear of the theft. And if the lord Ralph hadn't been so astute,' he added, winking at his colleague, 'you might never have known of the crime.'

'I'm very grateful to him.'

'And we're grateful to you, my lord sheriff,' resumed Ralph. 'You sought our help and we're pleased to give it. This enquiry has already thrown up some fascinating detail about one of the men we came to Norwich to investigate and I'm sure that it will yield far more. None of it, I suspect, remotely flattering to the lord Richard.'

'He's not a man to court popularity.'

'Especially not in monastic quarters!' said Coureton.

Ralph grinned. 'It's just as well that Canon Hubert is not with us. He'd want to excommunicate the lord Richard on the spot.'

'If he's found guilty of theft,' said Bigot, 'there'll be other punishment as well.'

'All in good time, my lord sheriff.'

'What should our next step be?' Bigot asked.

'To confirm that Judicael the Goldsmith was telling the truth,' Ralph replied.

'Shall I send a messenger to the abbey?'

'He stands before you. This is an errand that I claim for myself. After all,' said Ralph, cheerfully, 'I won't just be riding to Holme to see the abbot. I might well find the man who took those elephants there.'

Coureton was doubtful. 'Surely a monk wouldn't steal?'

'Some do little else,' said the other, irreverently. 'I've met too many grasping abbots and lying monks to put much faith in a Benedictine habit. In any event, it would not really be a case of theft. The abbey would simply be reclaiming something that was theirs in the first place.'

'What about the murder?' asked Bigot.

'What about it, my lord sheriff?'

'Do you expect to unearth a suspect in Holme for that as well?'

'Of course,' said Ralph. 'It's the main reason why I wish to go there.'

* * *

Expecting a visit from him, the lady Adelaide took pains with her appearance. Over a pure white chemise, she wore a light blue gown. Her hair was coiled neatly at the back and only the curls at the front peeped out of the white wimple. Around her waist was a gold belt that hung down between her thighs. She looked immaculate and dignified. When her visitor was admitted to the house, the lady Adelaide was posed on a bench that was carefully placed beneath a window so that it acted as a frame to her head. She rose to welcome Mauger Livarot.

'Good day, my lord,' she said.

'You look more charming than ever, Adelaide,' he remarked, crossing to place a kiss on her outstretched hand. 'It's wonderful to see you again.'

She resumed her seat. 'Have you been out hunting again today?'

'In a manner of speaking.'

'What do you mean?'

'I've been helping the lord sheriff in his pursuit of the murderer.' He smirked down at her. 'The first thing I had to do, of course, was to assure him that I was not responsible for Hermer's death. For some reason, he seemed to think that I might be.'

'The lord Richard is certain of it.'

'Yes, I heard about his performance at the castle last night.'

'It caused quite a commotion.'

'I hope that it also showed you the kind of man that he really is.'

Her tone was artless. 'Forceful and strong-willed?'

'Arrogant, bullying and headstrong.' he said, curling his lip. 'Those aren't qualities that a lady should look for in a husband.'

'I like a man who speaks his mind and the lord Richard certainly does that.'

'Are you drawn to someone with a vile temper?'

'No,' she conceded. 'That has little appeal.'

'Then my rival must stand aside, for he has the vilest temper in the county.'

'I think he could be taught in time to curb it.'

'Would you take on such a monstrous task?'

'If there were sufficient inducements.'

'I, too, can offer inducements, my lady.'

Mauger Livarot was wearing a green tunic with a floral pattern. His mantle was of a dark crimson hue that matched the belt at his waist, and his brimless cap was peaked in the centre. Hands on his hips, he gazed at her with an almost proprietary air. He lowered his voice to a caressing whisper.

'Come, Adelaide,' he coaxed. 'Why choose a wild animal for a husband when you might have one who is already tame?'

'Nobody would describe you as tame,' she said with polite scorn.' Least of all, your tenants. You have a reputation for harsh treatment.'

'Firmness is a virtue.'

'Until it's taken too far.'

'Oh, I always know the exact point at which to stop,' he boasted, leering at her. 'Tenants are like children. To school them properly, you have to be firm or they'll take advantage of your weakness.'

'Isn't that what you're doing now?'

'Perhaps, my lady.'

'The lord Richard has been weakened by events. A serious

129

theft from his house has been followed by a gruesome murder. He's very preoccupied at the moment. You came here to take advantage of his weakness.'

'Do you blame me?' he said with another smirk.

'Not at all,' she replied, easily. 'I knew that you'd visit me again sooner or later.'

'I always choose the best time to strike.'

'True.'

'Isn't that a recommendation?'

'Yes, my lord, but I need rather more than that.'

'You shall have it,' he asserted, becoming more earnest. 'Richard de Fontenel is mired in trouble. Spurn him, my lady, or you'll share the same fate. Accept me instead.'

'You mentioned inducements.'

'You shall have whatever you want.'

'Unfortunately, that's not possible.'

'Anything is possible when you say that you'll be mine. Put me to the test.'

'There's no point.'

'Why not?'

'Because I'd ask for the one thing you could never give me, my lord.'

'Then it doesn't exist.' he declared.

'Oh, it does.' she said with a nostalgic smile. 'To be more exact, they exist. I've seen them and marvelled at them. I all but fell in love with them. That's what I want more than anything else – those exquisite gold elephants that the lord Richard bought for me.'

'Do they really mean that much to you, Adelaide?'

'They do.'

'Nothing similar would entice you?'

'Perfection cannot be imitated. I want those particular elephants.'

He was decisive. 'Then you'll have them, my lady.'

'How?'

'That's for me to worry about.'

'But they're stolen property. They could be hundreds of miles away by now.'

'Then they'll have to be found and brought back, won't they?' he said, confidently. 'I stand a far better chance of retrieving them than the sheriff, believe me. I have intelligencers all over the county. Before I set the search in motion, of course, I need to extract a promise.'

'Of what?'

'Discretion, my lady.'

'It's second nature to me.'

'When I capture those elephants, you'll be my accomplice.'

'Nobody else will know that I have them, I promise you,' she said with quiet sincerity. 'I'll keep them entirely to myself. I'll feast my eyes on them in private. All that concerns me is the joy of possession.'

'Then we share the same impulse, Adelaide.' he said, taking her hand. 'I, too, want to revel in the joy of possession. And it will be all the more sweet because of the means by which I accomplish it.'

'In what sense?'

'I'll turn thief to give you another man's wedding gift.'

'The lord Richard would kill you if he ever found out.'

'That's a risk I'd willingly take for you.'

'I'm impressed.'

'Just think, my lady.' he said, emitting a cackle of delight. 'While the lord Richard is scouring the kingdom for his missing elephants, they'll be right here all the time. They'll be ours.'

'No, Mauger,' she said, softly. 'They'll be mine.'

Ralph Delchard was not a man for delay. Once a decision had been made, he liked to implement it at once. Shortly after his conversation with the sheriff, he was ready to go.

'Three choices confront you, my lord.' he said, putting a foot in his stirrup.

'What are they?' asked Eustace Coureton.

'You can visit an abbey with me, call on a lady with Gervase or simply stay here and take your ease. You're under no compulsion.'

'I certainly can't be idle. As for the abbey, I think that Brother Daniel would be a more useful companion for you. I'll ride with Gervase,' he said, turning to his young colleague. If you have no objection, that is?'

'None whatsoever, my lord,' replied Gervase. 'You'll be most welcome.'

'Then it's settled.'

'Where does this lady live?' said Ralph, hauling himself up into the saddle. 'It may be that we can all ride part of the way together.'

Gervase shook his head. 'No, Ralph. You ride north-eastwards while we strike due south into the Henstead hundred. That's where we'll find her.'

'Remind me of her name.'

'Olova.'

'And you really think that she's worth questioning?'

'We won't know until we get there.'

'What do you know about this Olova?'

'Very little beyond the fact that her land was annexed by the lord Richard. She spoke up well in the shire hall in front of our predecessors but the dispute could not be brought to a resolution.' Gervase mounted his own horse. 'Olova is clearly a lady who's prepared to fight for her rights.'

'To the extent of theft and murder?' said Coureton.

'I don't know. It's highly unlikely.'

'Nothing is unlikely in Norfolk,' complained Ralph. 'Gold elephants that disappear, a steward who gets himself hacked to death, an uninvited guest who ruins a banquet at the castle, human hands that arrive in a wooden box. These seem to be normal events here. It wouldn't surprise me in the least if Abbot Alfwold stole those two elephants in person, killed Hermer in the process, then threw Olova over his shoulder and carried her off to Holme to celebrate.'

'That's a blasphemous suggestion,' said Daniel, suppressing a smile.

Attended by their escort, the four men were in the bailey, making preparations for their departure. Gervase had been told about the discovery made by Ralph when he called on the goldsmith and he, in turn, had confided his suspicions about Olova. Two new lines of enquiry had suddenly opened up and both had to be explored.

'Don't forget Starculf,' Coureton reminded them. 'His name

has rather slipped out of our minds, but when all's said and done, he's the man who swore to get revenge.'

Ralph was sceptical. 'I doubt if he's still in the county.'

'Yet he has to be our chief suspect.'

'If the lord sheriff and his men can't locate Starculf, how can we hope to do so?'

'The same way that you and Gervase have discovered other things that have eluded the lord sheriff's officers,' said Coureton. 'By instinct and vigilance.'

'Ask after Starculf at the abbey,' said Gervase.

'Yes,' agreed Brother Daniel. 'It's surprising how many missing persons are tracked down that way. An abbey is not just a place of worship and self-denial.'

'Self-indulgence, more like!' said Ralph. 'I've seen the belly on Canon Hubert.'

'It's a refuge for travellers,' continued Daniel, ignoring the good-humoured interruption, 'and, as such, a gathering-place for news. It's amazing how much you get to hear if you stay in one place. That's the case in Winchester and, I dare say, in Holme. We'll make a point of mentioning Starculf's name to Abbot Alfwold.'

'We'll do the same when we meet Olova,' said Gervase. 'Meanwhile, the lord sheriff can devote his time to keeping Richard de Fontenel and Mauger Livarot apart.'

Coureton raised a finger. 'Another name we mustn't forget. The lord Mauger.'

'He's not the killer,' said Ralph, seriously. 'Gervase and I were agreed on that.'

'He could be involved in some other way.'

'I know and we're bearing that in mind, my lord. We rule nothing out.'

'This case gets more complicated by the minute.'

'That's what makes it so interesting,' said Gervase. 'But I'm sorry that you have to endure such a distraction from our work, my lord. You were appointed as our fellow-commissioner. It's unfair to entangle you in a murder inquiry.'

'Not at all!' said Coureton robustly. 'I relish the challenge.'

'Then let's take it up!' announced Ralph.

He and Brother Daniel set off with half a dozen armed men as their escort. Accompanied by their own six soldiers, Gervase and Coureton followed them out through the castle gates. The two parties soon split to go their separate ways, Gervase pleased to be riding alongside the new commissioner. Eustace Coureton was turning out to be a more than adequate replacement for Canon Hubert. He brought an experience and sagacity that only old age could bestow yet it was allied to a youthful zest.

'I never anticipated this much excitement,' said Coureton, happily.

'The real excitement will come if we manage to unmask the killer.'

'We've already unmasked a thief, Gervase. The lord Richard himself.'

'I can't say that I'm surprised,' observed the other. 'Having read between the lines of the returns for this county, I suspect that Richard de Fontenel acquired very little by legal means. Why buy something when he could get away with theft? How he got the gold elephants from the abbey I don't know, but I'm certain that he was behind the crime somehow. Ralph will tease out the truth, have no fear.'

'I've every confidence in the lord Ralph but I have to admit that I prefer to be riding with you at the moment, Gervase.'

'Why is that?'

'You're more receptive to the wisdom of ancient Rome.'

Gervase grinned. 'Do you hear another whisper from Quintus Horatius Flaccus?'

'I do, and it concerns the lord Richard.'

'Well?'

'*Vis consili expers mole ruit sua.*'

'"Force, if unassisted by judgement, collapses under its own weight."'

'A good translation, Gervase.'

'And an accurate comment on Richard de Fontenel.'

The burial service was so short that it was almost perfunctory. Like everyone else in the tiny church, the old priest was unnerved by the presence of Richard de Fontenel and gabbled the Latin at speed in a high, quavering voice. A mere handful of mourners had turned up, men from the household who came out of duty rather than out of any respect or affection for the dead man. Hermer had made few friends on the estate and none of them were there to see his remains laid in the bare earth. Conscious of the violent manner in which he died, the small congregation watched it all with a mixture of anxiety and trepidation. They shed no tears for the murdered steward. What worried them were the repercussions that might follow. In a space as confined as that of the church, they could feel the growing discontent of their master as if it were a fire slowly building up.

Richard de Fontenel saw little and heard nothing of the service. What occupied his thoughts was the sight of the corpse inside the coffin, trussed up in a shroud with a severed hand resting each side of him. Uncertainty chafed him. He could not decide if Hermer was a loyal steward who died in his lord's service or a traitor in the pay of a loathed rival. Whichever he was, the man had paid a fearsome price. When the coffin was taken out into the churchyard, the congregation formed a ragged circle around the grave. Mass was sung by the priest, then the mutilated body of Hermer the Steward was lowered into its final resting place. A fresh spasm of doubt seized de Fontenel. While he watched the earth drumming down on to the coffin, he wondered yet again if he was looking at a hapless victim or a man who had foolishly betrayed him.

As his anger swelled, he decided that there was only one way to find out the truth and that was to confront the man he believed to be responsible for the crimes. Revenge was a matter of honour. The theft of the gold elephants and the loss of his steward were bitter blows to sustain. He simply had to strike back. No help could be expected from Roger Bigot or from the royal commissioners who were assisting him. They had all been taken in by Mauger Livarot. Unaware of his true character, they had accepted his lies as a convincing alibi. That, at least, was what de Fontenel thought. He knew the passion that his rival had conceived for the lady Adelaide, a feeling surpassed in intensity only by his own. Such passion drove a man to any limits. It was, he sensed, the impulse behind Livarot's actions. It was time to respond. Brutality had to be met with brutality. A funeral that left everyone else numbed into immobility only served to provoke him into life.

His departure was abrupt. Richard de Fontenel did not even linger to spare a word of gratitude to the priest. Stalking out of the churchyard, he mounted the waiting horse and cantered off with the two men-at-arms who had come with him. It was not a long ride. As soon as he reached his house, he dropped to the ground and summoned one of his companions into the parlour.

'Huegon?'

'Yes, my lord?'

'How long would it take you to round up my knights?'

'That depends how many you want, my lord?'

'All of them!'

Huegon was astonished. 'That may take a while, my lord.'

'Then make a start now.'

'What do I tell them?' asked the other.

'That I need them immediately.'

'They are bound to ask why, my lord.'

'Say that we're going to teach someone a lesson he'll never forget.'

'Who might that be?'

'The lord Mauger.'

'You want all your men summoned to pay a visit to the lord Mauger?'

'We'll be doing much more than simply paying a visit,' said de Fontenel. 'We're going to exact revenge. Now hurry, man! There's no time to lose.'

In spite of his age, Eustace Coureton was an accomplished horseman. Long years spent moving from one battlefield to the next had given him a natural affinity with his destrier. No matter how hard they rode, he never seemed to tire even though he was wearing a hauberk beneath his tunic. It was Gervase Bret, in much lighter apparel, who showed the first signs of strain. Sweat glistened on his brow and his breathing was laboured.

'How do you manage to do it, my lord?' he asked, gulping in air.

'Do what?'

'Ride so fast yet remain so calm.'

Coureton chuckled. 'You're looking at a centaur, Gervase. I was half man and half horse for over thirty years. War leaves its mark.'

'That's what Ralph always says.'

'The lord Ralph is a soldier still at heart. So am I.'

'Yet you've renounced that world,' noted Gervase. 'You turned to scholarship.'

'Yes,' said the other with a philosophical smile. 'I wanted something to occupy my mind while I was riding a horse.'

They had slowed to a steady trot to rest the animals and to make conversation a little easier. Their journey had taken them due south of Norwich over flat countryside with an abundance of sheep grazing on it. Woodland slowed them down and put them on the alert against a possible ambush but they emerged unscathed into the sunlight again.

Gervase had got his breath back. He studied the horizon ahead. 'It shouldn't be too far now,' he said.

'And what do you expect to find when we get there?'

'A lady with good reason to hate Richard de Fontenel.'

'Hatred doesn't always drive someone to murder,' said

Coureton, 'or there'd be homicides by the hundred every day of the week. I can think of a few victims that I might have added to the list.'

'You don't strike me as a man capable of deep hatred, my lord.'

'I'm only human, Gervase. When I've been hurt, I want to return that pain. In my position, you'd feel the same, I dare say.'

'Would I?'

'You've a beautiful young wife who dotes on you. But supposing that some injury was inflicted upon her. An assault that left her badly wounded, for instance. Or a rape.' He saw Gervase tense. 'Yes, my friend. You, too, would feel hatred burning inside you then, but I doubt very much if it would drive you to kill. You're a lawyer. You'd use the might of the law to bring the miscreant to heel.'

'Prevention would be my first duty,' said Gervase, ruffled at the thought of any harm befalling his wife. 'I'd make sure that Alys was never in a position to suffer harm.'

'That's why you're such a good husband.'

'I try my best.'

Another mile brought them within sight of their destination. The woman they sought lived in a modest house on the remains of an estate that had dwindled almost to nothing over the previous twenty years. Of the seven timber huts that stood in a rough circle, only three were still occupied by the people who built them. The others were either derelict or inhabited by chickens or pigs. Brushwood fences surrounded the little encampment, which was situated beside a stream and in the shadow of a wooded hill. When the visitors rode into the middle of the dwellings, there was no sign of anyone at first. A sturdy young peasant then emerged from one of the huts and looked resentfully up at the Norman soldiers. Gervase nudged his horse forward so that he could speak to the man in his native language.

'Good day, my friend. We're looking for someone by the name of Olova.'

'Why?' grunted the other.

'That's our business.'

'Have you come to take even more land from her?'

'No,' said Gervase, taking no offence at the man's gruff hostility. 'My name is Gervase Bret and my colleague here is the lord Eustace of Marden. We're royal commissioners who've come to settle property disputes in this county and we are more likely to restore land to Olova than to take it away. Not that I can promise that,' he stressed, quickly, 'because I would never prejudge a case. But nothing here is under threat. That I can assure you.'

The other remained tense. 'Is that your business with Olova?'

'No, my friend. We come on a more urgent matter.'

'Nothing is more urgent than getting our land back.' the youth declared.

'*Our* land?' repeated Gervase. 'You're related to Olova, then?'

'Yes.' said a loud voice behind him. 'Skalp is my grandson.' Gervase turned to take his first look at Olova. Standing in the doorway of the largest hut, she surveyed the newcomers with a blend of dislike and disdain. Olova was a proud woman, declined in years but lacking none of the spirit she had possessed when she was the wife of a Saxon thegn of considerable standing in the county. The estates that she inherited on his death had been steadily whittled away by her Norman overlords and it had transformed a handsome face into a mask of bitterness. Gervase dismounted and walked across to her. Eustace Coureton followed his example. The old woman was surprised by the courtesy they were showing.

'What do you want?' she asked, eyeing them both.

'To ask you a few questions.' said Gervase. 'We've ridden from Norwich to speak to you. You know a man called Hermer, I believe.'

'More's the pity!'

'Why do you say that?'

'He's the man who helped to rob me of my estates,' she said. 'Hermer is steward to the lord Richard. Two such black-hearted men never existed before.'

'When did you last see Hermer?'

'Not for several months.'

'Is that the truth?' he pressed.

'Why should I lie?'

'Have you been into Taverham hundred recently?'

'I've no cause to do so. What land I once owned there was taken from me.'

'What about your grandson? Has he been there?'

'Skalp looks after me. He rarely stirs from here.'

'Do other members of the family live with you?'

Olova was irascible. 'Why are you pestering me?' she said, flaring up. 'Isn't it enough that you strip me of land that's rightfully mine? Have you come to gloat?'

'No,' said Gervase. 'We mean you no harm.'

'Then ride on your way. I haven't seen Hermer the Steward for months and neither has anyone here. We keep well away from that evil rogue.'

Gervase exchanged a look with Coureton. Even though he could not understand all she said, the latter got a clear impression of the woman's honesty. Olova clearly had no idea that the man she hated had been killed. Convinced that she was not involved in the crime, Gervase turned back to her. 'You'll have no more trouble from the lord Richard's steward,' he said.

'If only that were true!'

'It is true,' he announced. 'Hermer was murdered two days ago.'

Olova was stunned. The change in her manner was dramatic. All the anger seemed to drain out of her face and the cold eyes lit up with sudden hope. Tears began to stream down her cheeks as she clutched her hands to her breast.

'Thank God!' she exclaimed, looking upward. 'Our prayers have been answered.'

Chapter Seven

Progress was slower than Ralph Delchard expected. After riding at a steady pace from Norwich, he and his companions eventually came to broadland and were obliged to follow a tortuous track that snaked its way between the recurring expanses of water. Sheep held sway on the marshes, looking up with dull unconcern as the travellers passed before returning to the important task of foraging for grass. Salt pans appeared from time to time and the occasional windmill waved its sails at them in the stiff breeze. One of the lakes was so large that they wondered if they had reached the coast, but dry land stretched out on the far side of it. Men were busy in the freshwater fisheries. A lone thatcher was spotted, gathering a supply of reeds. Birds dipped, wheeled or waded in the shallows. Gilded by the sun, it was a tranquil scene but it merely served to irritate Ralph.

'I've never seen so much water,' he complained. 'It would be quicker for us to swim there than ride on horseback.'

'The site was chosen with a purpose, my lord,' said Brother Daniel.

'Yes – to annoy me.'

'The abbey was founded long before you were born. King Cnut deliberately had it built in a remote spot so that the monks would be free from interruption and isolated from the temptations of the world.'

'There aren't many temptations here,' said Ralph, looking around. 'Unless you want to chase sheep or catch one of those wading birds. Why should anyone want to live in such a place? What do the monks *do* all day, Brother Daniel?'

'Serve God, my lord.'

'In this wilderness?'

'An ideal place for contemplation.'

'All that I wish to contemplate is the abbey itself. This ride has left me hungry. I hope that the abbot's larder is well stocked. I'm in need of refreshment.'

Ralph and Brother Daniel were riding beside each other. The monk was an indifferent horseman but he clung on bravely and ignored the pounding on his buttocks. Behind them, the six knights rode in pairs, their harness jingling as they trotted briskly along, their profiles mirrored in the water that stretched out all around them.

'How many of these ponds are there?' said Ralph in exasperation. 'I'd have thought that God would have grown tired of making them in such profusion.'

'I'm not sure that they're natural, my lord.'

'What else can they be, Brother Daniel?'

'Peat was dug here for centuries,' said the monk. 'I'll wager that's how most of these smaller depressions were created. Over the years, water rose to fill them and this is the result. Ponds and lakes in abundance. Broadland has a strange beauty.'

'Not to my eye.'

'I could enjoy living here, my lord.'

'Even in winter?'

'Especially then.'

Ralph shivered at the thought. Brother Daniel was a jovial ascetic. Much as he liked living within the enclave at Winchester, he found the Norfolk broads full of appeal. He was unworried by the fact that the area would be exposed to the extremes of climate. That was part of its attraction. To suffer in the service of the Almighty was a form of joy.

'There it is!' he said, pointing excitedly.

'At last!' sighed Ralph.

'It can't be more than a mile or two now, my lord.'

'Even less if you could arrange for us to walk on water.'

Daniel laughed. He had recovered from the shock of finding the dead body near the castle and was ready to lend his assistance in the murder inquiry. A visit to the abbey of St Benet at Holme was an incidental bonus to him. When he took the cowl, he never expected to leave the cloistered world of Winchester, still less to see a distant monastic house about which he had heard so much. His curiosity would now be satisfied. More to the point, crucial information might be gleaned about the theft of the gold elephants.

The abbey was constructed in the shape decreed by tradition. Occupying pride of place, the church looked down on all the other buildings that had grown up around it. Chapter house, cloisters, kitchen, refectory, cellarium, reredorter, infirmary and warming room were arranged to best advantage. Bakehouse and brewhouse were kept in regular use. The large gardens were tended with care by monks who subsisted on what they could grow. Holy brothers whose life in the Benedictine Order had run its full course now rested in the cemetery. When the visitors arrived, the hospitaller came shuffling out of the main gate to welcome them and to learn their business.

While the men-at-arms were given refreshment, Ralph and Brother Daniel were conducted to the abbot's lodgings, which were above the cellar and next to the chapel. The monk who escorted them went into the private chamber alone to announce their arrival. Reappearing almost at once, he beckoned them inside before taking his leave. The visitors found themselves in a large room with few concessions to comfort or decoration. Seated behind the table and below the crucifix on the wail was Abbot Alfwold, a frail old man with a silver tonsure around his gleaming skull. His face was emaciated. Bared in a smile of welcome, his teeth were chiselled and discoloured by time. Alfwold set aside the Bible he had been studying to rise to his feet.

Introductions were made in French but the old man then spoke to Brother Daniel in Latin. Ralph refused to be excluded from the conversation and used the tongue that he had learnt from his wife. Alfwold was pleasantly surprised.

'Few Normans have mastered the intricacies of our language,' he said, lapsing into it himself. 'You're to be congratulated, my lord.'

'My wife is a Saxon. She taught me well.'

'Then your union is clearly blessed.'

Ralph held back the ribald rejoinder that immediately came to mind. He and Daniel were waved to a bench and their host lowered himself carefully back into his chair. Before he could disclose the purpose of their visit, Ralph heard a tap on the door and looked up to see a tray of food being brought in by a young monk who placed it respectfully on the table. Wine was served to Ralph but Daniel preferred a cup of ale. Both men were grateful to chew the cakes that were offered. When the young monk withdrew, Alfwold sat back and appraised his visitors.

'What do you think of the abbey of St Benet?' he asked.

'Inspiring, Father Abbot,' said Daniel. Truly inspiring.'

'It lacks the grandeur of Winchester but it has other virtues.'

'I've just eaten one of them,' said Ralph, before washing down the cake with a sip of wine. This is self-denial indeed. Living in a stone citadel, miles from anywhere.'

'Isolation is vital, my lord.'

'It wouldn't suit me, Father Abbot. If I'm isolated from my dear wife for one night, I feel lonely and deprived. And I could never live so close to water.'

'It supplies fish and attracts all manner of birds. When you come to know it, you realise that Holme is a species of paradise.'

'Save your breath, Father Abbot,' said Ralph, genially. 'You'll not persuade me to take the cowl, whatever attractions your abbey may offer. I'm too besmirched by sin to move in the direction of sainthood.'

Daniel's grin was immediately vanquished by a reproachful glance from Alfwold. 'This is not a chance visit, I take it?' said the abbot.

'Certainly not,' said Ralph, candidly. 'Only a very good

reason would make me ride through that endless broadland.'

'What is that reason, my lord?'

'The theft of two miniature gold elephants.'

A look of anguish flitted across Alfwold's face. 'Ah, yes,' he said, rubbing his temple with a skeletal finger. 'That unfortunate business.'

'You can confirm that they were stolen, then?'

'There's no other way that they would have left this abbey.'

'When did they go astray?'

'Ten days or so ago. The sacristan will be able to tell you the exact date.'

'Do you know who took them, Father Abbot?'

'We have our suspicions,' said the other, sadly, 'But we can't be sure. Those two elephants were very precious to us. Not simply because they were made of gold. Their value lay in their origin.'

'Oh?' said Ralph, ears pricking up.

'They were brought from Rome, blessed by the Pope himself.'

'Who made them in the first place?'

'A Venetian goldsmith, my lord. A master of his craft.'

'So I understand.'

'They were presented to the abbey as a gift and we've cherished them.' A weak smile touched his lips. 'We like to believe that we are the only abbey in England that houses elephants beneath its roof.'

'Who gave them to you?' asked Ralph.

'A good, kind, God-fearing man called Jocelyn Vavasour. A soldier like you, my lord, but one who was deeply troubled in his mind by all the blood he had spilt on English soil. He wanted to make amends in some way.'

'A penance?' said Daniel.

'Yes,' replied the abbot. 'But the lord Jocelyn didn't ride on his destrier to Rome. Like a true pilgrim, he walked every inch of the way. When he saw those elephants, he said that he felt impelled to buy them for the abbey.'

'Why here, Father Abbot?'

'The lord Jocelyn had estates nearby until he forfeited them.'

Ralph was taken aback. 'Voluntarily?'

'Yes, my lord. Some years ago.'

'Did he enter the Benedictine Order?'

'That was the strange thing,' said Alfwold, pursing his lips. 'He refused to do so.'

'Why?'

'He felt unworthy of us. He wouldn't have been the first soldier to exchange the sword for a cowl but it was never even considered. A moment ago, my lord,' he recalled, 'you jested about being besmirched by sin.'

'It wasn't entirely a jest,' admitted Ralph.

'The lord Jocelyn was in earnest. He came to see that the taking of life is a heinous sin even when sanctioned by a state of warfare. His past actions haunted him so much that he couldn't bear to enjoy their fruits. He surrendered his estates and this abbey, I'm pleased to say, was among the beneficiaries.'

'What happened to Jocelyn Vavasour?'

'He became an anchorite, my lord.'

'Where?'

'Nobody knows,' said the old man. 'He had no family to keep him so he just wandered off alone. All that I can tell is that he lives alone somewhere, enduring a life that's even more austere than the one we embrace here.'

'What would he do if he knew his gift had been stolen?'

'He'd be deeply upset, my lord. I hope that he never finds out.'

'He has a right to know.'

'True, my lord.'

'Have you taken any steps to retrieve your gold elephants?'

'We've prayed day and night,' explained the abbot, 'and we've made a few enquiries of our own but without success. When the crime was first reported, I wanted to go in search of the malefactor myself but my bones are too brittle. It's thirty years since I left this abbey and I'll not step outside its walls again.'

'Somebody ought to,' said Ralph. 'When property is stolen, it's your duty to alert the sheriff so that he can apprehend the thief.'

'But we've no idea who that thief is.'

'I thought you told us that you had your suspicions.'

'We do, my lord. Or, to be more exact, Brother Joseph does.'

'Brother Joseph?'

'The sacristan.'

'A sacristan looks after the contents of the abbey church,' said Daniel, helpfully. 'The vestments, linen, robes, banners, gold and silver plate, and the vessels of the altar.'

'Did he keep those elephants under lock and key?'

'Some of the time,' replied the abbot, wheezing slightly. 'On other occasions, all our treasures are on display so that the holy brothers can draw strength from them. Brother Joseph had arranged them in the church when the traveller came to stay.'

'Traveller?'

'He was exhausted from a long ride, he said, and begged a night's rest in the guest lodging. The hospitaller naturally took him. Next morning, the man left early. It was only after he'd gone that Brother Joseph discovered that the elephants were missing.'

'Why didn't you give chase at once?' said Ralph.

'We had no notion which road he'd taken, my lord. Besides, it might just have been a coincidence. The traveller may have been innocent. The thief could have been someone else altogether. Even – though I dread to think it – one of our own.'

'Did this mysterious traveller give a name, Father Abbot?'

'Oh, yes. One that we all grieve to remember.'

'What was he called?'

'Starculf,' said the old. 'Starculf the Falconer.'

Their friendly manner slowly helped to weaken her reserve. When he had recounted the details of the murder, Gervase was invited into Olova's hut with Eustace Coureton. It was a large, rectangular building, its thatched roof supported by wooden pillars sunk into the ground and its wadis made up of overlapping timbers, cut to size and trimmed to uniform smoothness. The interior was divided by vestigial screens into three bays, two of which contained beds. Some rough benches provided seating in the central bay. Cooking implements stood beside the slow fire over which a pot was suspended. Steam curled up lazily into the air. Competing smells of fish, smoke, animal skin and general mustiness filled their nostrils. Squatting on the one chair in the room, Olova indicated a bench. She watched her visitors shrewdly as they sat down. Her tears had been wiped away now and bitterness had returned.

'Hermer the Steward was a monster,' she said. 'We'll not mourn him.'

'Why do you despise him so much?' asked Gervase.

'He drove me off land that I inherited from my husband.'

'Only because he was ordered to do so by the lord Richard. Hermer was simply his agent. He obeyed orders.'

'No,' corrected Olova, vehemently. 'He enjoyed making us suffer, Master Bret. He did more than obey orders. He humiliated me. And it didn't end there.'

'What do you mean?'

She looked away. 'Nothing,' she said, quietly. 'It's a private matter.'

'He slighted you in person?'

'It was far worse than that.'

'Go on.'

'There's no point,' she said, shaking her head vigorously. 'Hermer is dead and there's an end to it. These are glad tidings and I'm grateful to you for bringing them.'

'Ask her about Starculf,' suggested Coureton.

Mention of the name made the old woman withdraw into herself. Folding her arms, she sat back in her chair with an expression of quiet defiance on her face. Gervase noted the change in her.

'Well?' he said. 'Do you know a man called Starculf?'

'I might have done,' she replied after a long pause.

'Did you ever meet him?'

'No.'

'Are you quite certain of that?'

'Yes,' she said, sourly.

'Yet you confess that you might have known him.'

'I heard his name, Master Bret. That's all. Hermer the Steward spoke of him.'

'Starculf was his assistant.'

'So I gathered.'

'What else did you gather?'

'Nothing.'

'Come, now,' he reasoned. 'You're an intelligent woman.'

'Don't try to flatter me. I'm too old for that nonsense.'

'It's not nonsense. I spoke to one of the commissioners who visited his county earlier on. He remembered how well you marshalled your case when you appeared before them in the shire hall.'

'I was only fighting to reclaim what was mine.'

'Fighting against the lord Richard. Except that he was absent from the fray so had to be represented by his steward. You and Hermer created sparks when you clashed.'

'So?'

'Legal battles are not only won by clever advocacy.' he said. 'A wise disputant finds out as much as he can about the person who'll challenge him before the judges. It's a case of knowing your enemy. I suspect that you knew everything that could be known about Hermer the Steward.'

'I did!' she said, scowling darkly. 'I knew him for the villain he was.'

'What of Starculf?'

'He's not important here.'

'But he is.' insisted Gervase, seeing that she was holding something back. 'If he was Hermer's assistant, Starculf would have travelled with him. You might not have met him in person but I dare say you picked up what information you could about him. It would've been in your interests to do so.'

Olova went off into a rueful silence. Gervase turned to Eustace Coureton.

'She won't help us.' he said, speaking in French. 'She claims

154

that she never met Starculf. I'm not sure that I believe her.'

'Press her a little harder, Gervase.'

'That's not the way to get her on our side.'

'No,' sighed Coureton. 'I suppose not. She's a fiery character, isn't she?'

'Fiery and determined.' He looked back at Olova and slipped back into her language. 'My colleague was just saying that he has great sympathy for you. '

'You're lying,' she said, crisply. 'I've picked up enough French to guess at what he told you. Know your enemy. As you suspected, it's advice that I took long ago. One way to know your enemy is to learn something of his language.'

'I didn't come here as an enemy.'

'You're a Norman.'

'My mother was a Saxon like you, my father was a Breton.'

'That makes no difference.'

'I'm not your enemy.'

'You're in the pay of King William. What else can you be?'

'Tell me about Starculf.'

'Why should I?'

'Because it might stand you in good stead when you come before us,' he said, appealing to her self-interest. 'Starculf was Hermer's assistant but the two of them had an argument and Starculf was dismissed. Do you know what that argument was over?'

'Ask the lord Richard.'

'I have a feeling that you might know.'

Olova pondered. 'All I can say is this.' she volunteered at length. 'Starculf was trained as a falconer but he had higher ambitions than that. He wanted to be the estate reeve like

Hermer. Starculf worked himself into the lord Richard's favour and was taken on as Hermer's assistant. He was good at his job until the two fell out.'

'Over what?'

'I don't know but I could hazard a guess.'

'Money?'

'No, Master Bret.'

'Then what?'

'Women. That was what interested Hermer most, as we discovered to our cost.'

'In what way?'

'That's not important,' she said, abruptly.

'Why should Starculf argue with him over women?'

'It's just a guess, Master Bret.'

'Based on your knowledge of Hermer. Do you know where Starculf is now?'

'If he had any sense, he'd have fled the county.'

'Why?'

'Because the lord Richard doesn't like people who let him down,' she said with rancour. 'He wouldn't merely have dismissed Starculf. He'd have hounded him. Beaten him, probably.' Her eyelids narrowed. 'What's your interest in the man?'

'We'd like to talk to him about Hermer's death.'

She went silent again and glowered at her two visitors. After collecting another meaningful look from Coureton, Gervase smiled at Olova and changed the subject. 'I'm sorry if I said anything to offend you,' he began. 'A few more questions then we'll be on our way again.'

'You won't be detained,' she muttered.

'Do you know the abbey of St Benet at Holme?'

'Everyone in Norfolk knows it, Master Bret.'

'Something was stolen from there recently. Something very valuable.'

She bridled instantly. 'Are you accusing me?'

'Of course not. I just wondered if you'd heard what was taken?'

'Abbot Alfwold would hardly tell me.'

'He might,' said Gervase, remembering some details he had seen when going through the returns for the county. 'Your late husband was a generous man. He endowed the abbey with land. You must have had dealings with the monks.'

'That was many years ago.'

'Isn't the gossip from the abbey carried this far? If you and your husband took such an interest in the abbey, I'm surprised that you don't at least keep in touch with it.'

Olova was trenchant. 'My husband gave them land,' she said, 'but what good did it do us? When the Normans came and we fell on hard times, where was Abbot Alfwold? He turned his back on us like everyone else. My husband was a thegn,' she said, her chin jutting out with pride. 'Our house was much bigger and finer than this. We had land in four different hundreds in Norfolk. The abbey was glad of our friendship then. Not now, Master Bret.'

'Shall I tell you what was stolen?'

'I haven't the slightest interest,' she said, rising angrily to her feet. 'To be honest, I don't care if they lost all the valuables they possessed. Don't ask me about the abbey. I don't care if it got burnt to the ground.'

Olova was so upset that further conversation with her was clearly pointless. After bidding her farewell, the visitors left the house and mounted their horses. Olova stood in the doorway and watched the little troop ride off. None of the men looked back. When they were out of sight of the old woman, Coureton reflected on their visit.

'We learnt something, anyway.'

'Did we?'

'Given the chance, Olova would've strangled Hermer with her bare hands.'

'She was delighted when she heard about his murder, that was obvious. We brought some cheer to her house with that news. I just wish that she'd told us more about Starculf,' said Gervase, thoughtfully. 'I had a distinct feeling that she was hiding something from us.'

'Is it worth talking to her again?'

'No, my lord. We'd only be wasting our time.'

'You're probably right.'

'The person I'd really like to question is that grandson of hers.'

'Skalp. A surly fellow, if ever there was one.'

'I didn't see him when we left. Did you?'

'How could I when he was hiding behind the hut.'

Gervase looked across at him. 'Olova's house?'

'Didn't you realise that?' said Coureton. 'He heard every word that was spoken.'

Brother Joseph was a tall, slender, lugubrious man in his fifties who seemed to be carrying all the cares of the world on his stooping shoulders. As the sacristan of the abbey, he was responsible for the safety of its valuables and he looked upon the theft of the miniature elephants as the grossest failure on his part. No sooner had he met Ralph Delchard than he was apologising to the commissioner for the loss of the treasures. The three men were in the abbey church. Hands fluttering like a pair of renegade doves, the sacristan was showing the visitors the table on which the elephants had been displayed along with the abbey's extensive stock of gold plate.

'I'll never forgive myself,' he wailed. 'Abbot Alfwold assures me that it was not my fault but I believe that it was. I should have taken more care.'

'Where are your valuables normally kept?' asked Ralph.

'In a locked chest.'

'Is that where they spent the night in question?'

'No, my lord,' said Joseph. 'To my eternal shame, I left them on this table.'

'Had you ever done so before?'

'Many times. The one place you do not expect theft is inside an abbey, especially one as remote as this. Don't you agree, Brother Daniel?'

'Yes,' said the monk. 'It's the same at Winchester. Gold plate, sacred vessels and holy relics are frequently set out yet are never under the slightest threat.'

'When did you become aware of the theft?' said Ralph.

'Not until after Prime.'

'Wasn't that rather late, Brother Joseph?'

'Horrendously late,' confessed the other, wincing at the memory. 'Had I noticed it at Matins or at Lauds, we could have taken swifter action.'

'Only if the thief had already struck,' argued Ralph. 'The elephants might have been here during the first two services of the day then been taken before Prime.'

'Not while we were all still in church, my lord. There's no gap between Lauds and Prime. We don't move from here.'

'Perhaps not,' ventured Daniel, 'but you'd all be engrossed in prayer.'

Joseph was shocked. 'Not even the vilest thief would steal from us at a time like that, surely? It would be sacrilege.'

'I don't think this man is hoping to claim his reward in heaven,' observed Ralph, tartly. 'Though the abbot did hint at the possibility that he might already wear a cowl.'

'That's inconceivable.'

'Is it?'

'I simply can't bring myself to accept that.'

'Nor can I,' said Daniel, loyally.

Ralph was characteristically blunt. 'I side with Abbot Alfwold. When a crime like this is committed, *everyone* must be under suspicion, regardless of whether or not he belongs to the Benedictine Order. After all,' he said, indicating the table, 'the monks go right past herein single file. Even with candles, it must be gloomy in here during Matins and Lauds. What would be easier than for one of your number to sweep up the elephants in his hand and put them into his scrip?'

'No, my lord!' protested Joseph.

'What could he hope to gain?' challenged Daniel. 'Monks take a vow of poverty. Gold is no use to them here. There's no motive, my lord.'

Ralph shrugged. 'Perhaps someone liked elephants.'

'They were taken *out* of the abbey. That much we do know.'

'Granted, but that doesn't let the holy brothers off the hook.

Who was better placed to know when and where the treasures would be on display? It's not beyond the bounds of possibility that one of the monks stole the elephants then passed them to a confederate outside the abbey.'

'Such a thought appals me,' said Joseph with a shudder.

'Then let's set it aside while we consider your theory.'

'It's more than a theory, my lord. It's the only explanation.' The sacristan gave an apologetic smile before relating his narrative. 'On the night in question, three travellers were staying at the abbey. Two were pilgrims, on their way to Yarmouth to take ship. The other was a man named Starculf. He told us that he was a falconer, riding north to Lincoln to collect a peregrine for his master. Starculf hailed from an estate on the Suffolk coast. He'd been in the saddle for a whole day when he arrived at our gate.'

'Who admitted him?'

'The hospitaller. He had no call to turn him away.'

'Did you meet this Starculf yourself?'

'Yes, my lord. I'm not such a poor steward as you might think. Since the abbey's valuables are under my protection, I make a point of talking to all our guests in case I sense that they are here for nefarious purposes.'

'What did you think of Starculf?'

'He seemed honest and open. I had no qualms.'

'Until the following morning.'

'He left before any of us really knew that he was gone.'

'But not on the road to Lincoln,' said Ralph. 'He had a shorter journey ahead of him than that. Can you describe this man to us, Brother Joseph?'

'I'll never forget him,' said the sacristan. 'He was a short man of some thirty years or more. Stout and well built. He carried himself with confidence and was grateful for our hospitality.' He gave another shudder. 'Now I know why!'

'You mentioned that two pilgrims also spent the night here.'

'They joined us here in church for Prime.'

'Were they still in the abbey when the theft was discovered?'

'Yes, my lord. They were so upset that we might think them responsible that they offered to let us search their belongings. But there was no need,' said Joseph. 'All I had to do was to search their faces. They were no thieves.'

'That brings us back to Starculf.'

'We feel that it must have been him.'

Ralph was puzzled. Starculf had been dismissed from the service of Richard de Fontenel and had every reason to hate his former master. If he had stolen the gold elephants, he would hardly have surrendered them to a man he loathed. There had to be some other explanation of how they came into the possession of de Fontenel. Was it possible that Starculf himself had been robbed of them? Or had he sold the treasures to a third person who made a handsome profit by passing them on to the man who wanted them as a wedding gift? It was evident that de Fontenel knew he was receiving stolen property. He had gone to some lengths to give the impression that the gold elephants had come from abroad. Ralph thought about the lady Adelaide. Pleased at the notion that her suitor had scoured the Continent on her behalf, she would be horrified to learn that he was giving her plunder from the abbey of St Benet.

'How did you know that the elephants had been stolen, my lord?' asked Joseph.

'I picked up a rumour.'

'From whom?'

'I can't remember,' said Ralph, careful not to give too much information away. 'It may have been from Richard de Fontenel. Do you know the man, Brother Joseph?'

The monk grimaced. 'Only by repute.'

'Has the lord Richard ever visited the abbey?'

'No,' said the other firmly. 'From what I hear, he has no interest in monastic houses. The lord Richard is not among our benefactors.' He slipped his hands inside his sleeves. 'How did *he* come to hear of our robbery?'

'I'm not sure that he did,' said Ralph, dismissively. 'I may have caught wind of it from someone else. That's why I came here today. I wanted to establish the facts. I don't hold with theft, Brother Joseph,' he added, hand on his sword hilt. 'I'll do everything in my power to see the elephants returned to the abbey.'

'Thank you, my lord.'

The sacristan followed him out of the church, showering him with gratitude. Ralph summoned his men and they mounted up to depart. Brother Joseph followed his visitors outside and waited until Ralph was in the saddle.

'Will you be able to recover our little elephants, my lord?' he asked.

'If at all possible. To tell you the truth, I'd rather like to see them.'

'Where will your search begin?'

'With the man who gave them to the abbey in the first place.'

'Jocelyn Vavasour?'

'Yes,' said Ralph. 'He sounds as if he might be a holy treasure himself.'

It took well over an hour to gather his men from the surrounding estates but Richard de Fontenel's temper did not cool in the meantime. When fifteen armed men had answered his call, he mounted his horse and led them off at a canter. Impelled by the desire to strike at Mauger Livarot, he had no precise idea what form his action would take. At the very least, he intended to wreak havoc on his rival's land, destroying crops, pulling down fences, even setting fire to barns or dwellings. Confrontation with Livarot himself was what he craved most, however, hoping to provoke him into a duel that he was confident of winning. Surprise was the crucial factor. As they thundered along the bone-hard track, de Fontenel prided himself on the suddenness of his attack. His enemy would be taken completely unawares. Livarot would not merely be humiliated – even killed in single combat – he would be lessened in the eyes of the lady Adelaide. It was de Fontenel who would assuredly rise in her esteem. His assault on his rival was also a road to marriage.

But the road was unaccountably blocked. Cresting a hill, de Fontenel expected to lead his men down the incline to Mauger Livarot's undefended manor house. The sight that confronted him and his troop made them bring their horses to a sharp halt. Waiting for them in front of the house were twice their number of men, armed and poised for a charge. Richard de Fontenel's strategy paled in the face of resistance. Mauger Livarot was ready for him, inviting attack and sure of success. He gave a signal with a raised arm, then led his men forward at a trot until they were only twenty yards from the newcomers. Ordering them to halt, Livarot grinned at his visitors.

'Did you want something, my lord?' he taunted.

'I'd like your head on a plate,' said de Fontenel, glaring at him.

'You're welcome to come and take it.'

'Don't tempt me, Mauger.'

'We outnumber you. Why not use what little brain you have and go home?'

'You *knew* that we were coming. How?'

'That's my business.'

'Who warned you?' Richard de Fontenel drew his sword and was about to nudge his horse forward when he heard the sound of approaching hoofbeats. Looking to his left, he saw the sheriff riding round the angle of a copse with several of his men at his back. Roger Bigot took in the situation at a glance. He rode into the gap between the two rivals and reined in his horse, his men pulling up in a line behind him. Richard de Fontenel was startled by the appearance of the sheriff but Mauger Livarot was delighted.

'Welcome, my lord sheriff!' he said, smirking happily. 'I'm glad that you got my message in time.'

'What's going on here?' demanded Bigot.

'We're giving our knights a little exercise.'

Bigot turned to de Fontenel. 'You're trespassing, my lord. Do you realise that?'

'Stay out of this,' was the surly reply. 'It's none of your business.'

'Keeping the peace in this county is my business.'

'That's why I sent for you, my lord sheriff,' said Livarot with false piety. 'At least one of us has a healthy respect for law and order.'

'Disperse your men, Mauger.'

'Gladly – when these interlopers have been driven off my land.'

'Well?' said Bigot, addressing de Fontenel. 'What are you waiting for?'

De Fontenel scowled. 'I'll be back!'

'Not if you have any sense.'

'Mauger killed my steward!'

Bigot was calm. 'Bring me the proof and I'll arrest him for the crime. Cause any more trouble on his land, however, and I'll be forced to arrest you instead. Is that clear, Richard?' he said, his voice ringing with authority. 'Nobody takes the law into his own hands while I hold the office of sheriff. Now, away with you!'

Richard de Fontenel glowered at his rival, then looked back at the sheriff. Roger Bigot was a man of his word. Further provocation would be foolish. With a snort of disgust, de Fontenel swung his horse round and dug his spurs into its flanks. He went galloping all over the crest of the hill with his men, enraged, frustrated and outmanoeuvred by the rival he had come to punish. It was a long and cheerless ride back to his home.

Chapter Eight

It was mid-evening by the time Gervase Bret and Eustace Coureton rode back into the bailey of Norwich Castle. Their return journey had been spent in a long discussion about the value of their visit to the combative Olova. The men disagreed. Gervase, who had spoken to her in her own language, felt a natural sympathy for the woman and was inclined to accept her word. Coureton, however, relying on her manner and gestures to form an opinion of her, was a little more sceptical.

'I think it was deliberate, Gervase,' he said.

'What was?'

'Inviting us into her house like that so that her grandson could eavesdrop outside.'

'There was nothing sinister about that,' said Gervase. 'Skalp was simply making sure that no harm came to Olova. Besides, what did he hear? We were hardly giving away any great secrets inside that hut.'

'I distrusted him.'

'Not as much as Skalp distrusted us, my lord.'

'He was a truculent character. Just like his grandmother.'

'I dare say that Olova wasn't quite so truculent when she was the wife of a thegn with appreciable holdings in the county. She was a dignified lady then.' he said, recalling the proud way she bore herself. 'The Conquest changed her life completely.'

'Yes.' said Coureton. 'It brought Richard de Fontenel into her life.'

'And Hermer the Steward. She had nothing but scorn for him.'

'I couldn't understand why, Gervase.'

'Nor me,' confessed the other, 'but it seemed to have something to do with Hermer's fondness for women. I didn't see any there apart from Olova. Did you?'

'No, but they probably went into hiding when they saw us coming.'

'Why should they do that?' wondered Gervase.

When their horses had been stabled, they made their way to the keep and went off to their separate apartments. Alys was dozing on the bed when her husband entered but awoke at once, sweeping aside his apologies for disturbing her and insisting that she was just taking a short nap. As she talked about how she and Golde had spent the afternoon, she was bright-eyed and animated. It was Gervase who had to suppress an occasional yawn, feeling a slow fatigue settling in. He gave her only the briefest outline of his visit to Olova.

'She wasn't exactly pleased to see us,' he admitted.

'It was like that in the market this morning. Pure resentment.'

'I didn't blame her, Alys. In her position, I'd have harboured a grudge.'

'No, you wouldn't. It's simply not in your nature.'

'Oh, I bear a grudge from time to time.'

She was hurt. 'Not about me, I hope?'

'Of course not. You'd never give me the slightest cause.'

'Is that the truth?'

'You know it is,' he assured her. 'Why do you think I agreed that you should come with me to Norfolk? I wanted you there at the end of the day, Alys. And first thing in the morning as well.'

'What about the time in between?' she asked with a smile.

'Any time spent with you is pure joy.'

She gave him a kiss on the lips. 'Thank you.'

Though he embraced her warmly, his mind was not entirely on his wife. Gervase was still remembering his talk with Olova, wondering if he might have got more out of the awkward old woman if he had taken Brother Daniel with him instead of Eustace Coureton. It was the sight of Norman soldiers in helm and hauberk that rankled with her. Gervase had the feeling that Hermer the Steward might have visited her in the past with an armed escort. Intimidation was patently a weapon he had often used. Cowed by his master, it was he who became the bully when dealing with others.

'We're bidden to the hall whenever we're ready,' said Alys, giving him a playful push when he failed to reply. 'You're not listening to me, Gervase!'

'Yes, I am.'

'What did I say?'

'Something about the hall.'

'You didn't hear me, did you?'

'Yes, I did.'

'You were miles away.' Pretending to be upset, she stalked across to the window and stared out. Gervase went up to put his arms around her waist, nestling his head into her wimple.

'I'm sorry, Alys.'

'Are you?' she asked, pouting.

'I'm back with my wife now, I promise.'

'You're not the only one.'

'What?'

'Look down there,' she said, pointing to the bailey. 'Ralph has just ridden in through the gate with Brother Daniel. Golde is there to welcome them.'

Gervase gazed over her shoulder to watch the reunion down below. Ralph dismounted to collect a kiss from his wife then walked towards the keep with an arm around her. There was a decided jauntiness in his step.

Alys smiled approvingly. 'He's pleased to see Golde again.'

'That's not the only reason he's in such good spirits.' said Gervase, reading his colleague's manner and movement. 'His visit was more profitable than ours. He found out something important at the abbey of St Benet. I wonder what it was.'

Mauger Livarot, dining alone at his manor house, sat back in his chair and drank the remains of the wine. When he set the cup down on the table, he was still grinning broadly. The steward stood a few yards away, smiling obsequiously and rubbing his palms together. Livarot went off into a sudden peal of laughter.

'The look on his face was a joy to behold, Drogo,' he recalled.

'I'm sure it was, my lord.'

'Richard de Fontenel thought that he'd take me by surprise and instead he found us ready and waiting. We'd even alerted the lord sheriff to the prospect of trouble.'

'Forewarned is forearmed,' said his steward.

'Yes, your man did well.'

'That's what I told him.'

'Give him a just reward.'

'I already have, my lord. He earned it.'

'It's just as well the lord Richard is too stupid to realise that we have a spy in his house. You picked exactly the right man for the job, Drogo.'

'He misses nothing.'

'The fellow has been worth his weight in gold.'

'Just like those two elephants.'

They shared a throaty laugh, then Livarot became serious. He beckoned his companion closer. After biting hungrily at a leg of chicken, he tossed it aside, chewed noisily and spoke through a full mouth. 'I want those miniature elephants.'

'Why, my lord?'

'Never you mind. Just get them for me.'

'But how?' said Drogo, alarmed. 'I've no idea where they are.'

'Then you'll have to conduct a search, won't you? It's crucial that I get my hands on them before the lord Richard does. Then I can put them to the purpose for which he acquired them,' said Livarot, swallowing the last of the chicken. 'That will give me the utmost satisfaction. To use his own bait in the trap.'

'Trap, my lord?'

'A personal matter between the lord Richard and me.' He poured more wine from the jug and sipped it. 'Find out where those gold elephants are, Drogo.'

'That won't be easy.'

'I didn't say that it would be.'

'The lord sheriff has failed to track them down so far.'

'That's all to the good,' said Livarot. 'If he recovers them, he'll only give them back to the one man who must never set eyes on them again. They must belong to me.'

Drogo was anxious. 'Have you ever seen them, my lord?'

'No, but I've seen the effect they have.'

'How big are they?'

'Who knows?'

'Could you give me a detailed description?' asked the steward.

'No, I can't.'

'That complicates matters. It will be even more difficult searching for something when I have no idea what it looks like.'

'They're elephants, man. Two small, smooth, shiny gold elephants.'

'That doesn't help me. I've never seen such an animal.'

'Well, you'd better make sure that you see one now,' said Livarot, shooting him a warning glance. 'Two of them, to be exact. This is not an idle request, Drogo. It's an order. And it takes precedence over everything else.'

'Yes, my lord.'

'Use the man you have at the castle. That's the best place to start.'

'I'll get word to him this evening.'

'Roger Bigot may not be able to track down the missing elephants but Ralph Delchard and Gervase Bret might. They've sharper noses to sniff a trail,' he said with grudging admiration. 'Follow them, Drogo. They'll lead you to the elephants.'

'Will they?'

'If anyone can find those beasts, they can.'

'I hope so, my lord.'

'All you have to do is to make sure that you grab them first.'

The steward looked doubtful. Livarot took another swig of his wine. 'Take care,' he said, raising a finger. 'This means a lot to me. Get me those two gold elephants and you'll be richly rewarded. Fail me,' he added, menacingly, 'and I may be looking for a new steward. Now, off with you!'

The feast was not as lavish as the banquet on the previous evening but it was still much larger and more appetising than any meal the commissioners would normally have enjoyed. The cooks who toiled in the castle kitchen had mastered all the arts of choosing and preparing food. Venison was the main dish, garnished with a delicious sauce and served with a selection of vegetables. Wine and ale flowed freely. Roger Bigot and his wife entertained their guests in the hall, controlling the arrival of each course with a series of unobtrusive signals. Minstrels played at the far end of the room. Dozens of candles burned brightly. Famished after his long ride, Brother Daniel accepted the invitation to join his colleagues and he ate as heartily as any of them. Eustace Coureton was delighted to be seated next to the monk, enabling him to talk in Latin and to quote his favourite Roman authors. Daniel was responding with whole paragraphs from St Augustine's *De Civitate Dei*.

Disappointed that the lady Adelaide was not present, Ralph Delchard enjoyed the occasion immensely, moving easily from inconsequential chatter to a discussion of more serious topics. He was fascinated to hear of the sheriff's intervention in the threatened outbreak of violence between Richard de Fontenel and Mauger Livarot, but the real value of the evening lay in the fact that he was seated beside Gervase Bret and thus able to exchange information about the irrespective visits that day. At the mention of a certain name, Gervase sat up with interest.

'Jocelyn Vavasour?' he repeated.

'He was the man who presented the gold elephants to the abbey in the first place and started all this trouble. Apparently, he's become an anchorite.'

'I wondered what happened to him.'

'You know the man?'

'Only through my study of the returns from this county,' said Gervase, making an effort to recall the salient details. 'His name appeared time and time again. At one point, Jocelyn Vavasour had a number of holdings in the county, then seemed to lose them all.'

'He gave them away, Gervase.'

'Why?'

'Madness.'

'That's your way of saying that he wanted to live a more spiritual life.'

'What's to prevent a man from owning property and having religious impulses?'

'Try reading the Bible,' advised his friend.

'The lord Jocelyn gave everything away.'

'Not quite everything,' said Gervase, brow furrowed with thought. 'If memory serves me, he retained one of his outliers. A small acreage in the hundred of Holt, to the north of here.'

'Then that's where we might find him.'

'Possibly. I can't think why else he should keep that patch of land.'

'I'll search for him tomorrow.'

'Take a boat with you, Ralph.'

'Why?'

'It's a coastal property,' explained Gervase. 'My guess is that it's more water than land. In short, an ideal place for a hermit to live and to commune with God.'

Ralph frowned. 'I saw enough water on the way to the abbey.'

'Would you rather I went in search of the lord Jocelyn?'

'No, Gervase. He's mine. We have the same background. I want to know why a man who fought hard for everything he has tosses it foolishly away instead of settling down on his estate with a beautiful wife.' He looked fondly at Golde. 'As I've done.'

'There's a simple answer to that.'

'Is there?'

'You were lucky enough to meet Golde before he did,' Gervase pointed out, mischievously. Ralph laughed appreciatively. 'By the way,' Gervase went on, 'did you tell Abbot Alfwold that the missing elephants turned up in the lord Richard's hands?'

'No, I thought it better to say nothing.'

'Why?'

'Because I had no proof that the lord Richard was behind the theft. If I'd mentioned him as a potential suspect, the abbot would probably have sent word to the bishop, inciting him to take action. That would have confused matters even more.'

'Yes,' sighed Gervase. 'The last thing we want is for Bishop William de Bello Fargo to come charging up here from Thetford to join in the hunt. He'd only get in our way and put the lord Richard on the defensive.'

'That was my reasoning,' said Ralph. 'We also kept Brother Joseph, the sacristan, ignorant of what we knew though I floated the name of the lord Richard past his anxious eyes. It's curious, Gervase. I never thought I'd feel sorry for anyone inside an abbey but I was overwhelmed with sympathy for poor Brother Joseph. He's positively writhing with guilt.'

'The kindest thing we can do is to return the elephants to him.'

'As soon as possible.'

'But you want to speak to Jocelyn Vavasour first.'

'I'll go in search of him at first light.'

Ralph turned to look up the table at his host. Roger Bigot was just breaking off a conversation with Alys in order to wave to the minstrels. They struck up a more lively tune and the sheriff nodded his approval. Ralph caught his eye.

'Perhaps you could help us, my lord sheriff,' he said.

'Gladly.'

'You must have heard of one Jocelyn Vavasour?'

'Heard of him and known him, my lord,' said Bigot with admiration. 'I fought alongside him more than once. He was a doughty soldier, brave and loyal. But if you wish to know about Jocelyn Vavasour, the man to ask is the lord Ivo.'

'Ivo Tallboys?'

'The same. It was he who commanded the siege of Hereward the Wake in the fen county. Jocelyn Vavasour was one of his ablest lieutenants. I remember the lord Ivo telling me how valuable an asset he was. Jocelyn Vavasour knew the fens almost as well as Hereward. He was completely at home there.'

'That settles it!'

'Settles what?'

'The location of his refuge. He's probably hiding in the marshes.'

'That's very likely,' agreed Bigot. 'A second Hereward.'

'I hope I don't have to lay siege to the lord Jocelyn.'

'He's known by another name now.'

'Vavasour the Madman?'

'No,' said Bigot, solemnly. 'Jocelyn the Anchorite.'

Made out of rough timber and roofed with thatch, the hut amid the marshes was small, bare and primitive. From a distance, it looked less like a human dwelling than a random collection of logs washed up by the sea. Birds perched familiarly on it. Wind plucked at the thatch and carried salt spray in its wake. It was remote and unwelcoming terrain. The man who emerged from the hut had chosen its location with care, yearning for a solitary existence where he could atone for what he saw as the sins of his past life. No comforts were needed, no company sought. Jocelyn Vavasour was a true anchorite, spending his days in prayer and meditation before sleeping at night on the cold ground. When he came out of his simple abode, the birds on his roof were not disturbed. They were used to him by now, accepting him as one of their own, a creature of the marshland.

Vavasour was a big, powerful man in his forties, muscles hardened by long years as a soldier, face craggy and weather-beaten. A hot summer had darkened his complexion and his bare arms. Dressed like a Saxon peasant in ragged tunic and gartered trousers, he had almost nothing of a Norman lord about him now. His earlier swagger had been replaced by a gentle gait, his boldness by complete self-abnegation. He had shed the personality of Jocelyn Vavasour like an outer skin that had died and become useless. The world of the anchorite brought him deep satisfaction. Only one book shared the hut with him and he read from his Bible at regular intervals throughout each day, educating himself and searching for guidance in its wonderful Latin cadences. Psalms had been learnt by heart, favourite passages studied again and again. Nobody ever disturbed him. A life once committed to violence was now dedicated wholly to God.

The sky was almost dark now and a breeze had grown up to ruffle his hair and his long, curly beard. It was the time of day that he liked most. Alone with the elements and unable to see anything apart from the crescent moon and a scattering of stars, he felt closer to his Creator and more keenly aware of his own purpose on earth than at any other hour. Inhaling deeply, he smiled up at the heavens. Then he fell to his knees to begin his prayers.

The first lash of the whip produced a howl of anguish. A plea for mercy soon followed. Richard de Fontenel ignored it and wielded the whip even harder the second time, slicing open the man's naked back and sending a rivulet of blood curling its way down his body. Clamahoc jerked and struggled but there was no escape. His wrists and ankles were tied to a wooden hurdle. By the light of a flaming torch, his master administered some more punishment, turning the white flesh into a raw expanse of agony. The tall figure of Clamahoc sagged under the onslaught, his cries of pain dwindling to mere whimpers.

Grabbing him by his bushy hair, de Fontenel glared into his face. '*Now* will you tell me?' he demanded.

'Yes, my lord,' gasped the other.

'No lies, mark you.'

'I'll tell you everything, my lord.'

'Or I'll flay you.'

Richard de Fontenel had been in an irate mood when he returned to his house. Not even a surprise visit from the lady Adelaide that afternoon could assuage his fury. Indeed, her presence only served to remind him of the ignominy he had faced at the hands of his rival. Not only had he been outflanked by Mauger Livarot, but the sheriff had been alerted to his strategy and caught him in the act. There was nothing he could do but slink away with his tail between his legs. One thought occupied his mind. If his adversary knew of his imminent arrival, he must have been forewarned by a member of de Fontenel's own household. Stern questioning of each and every man had eventually delivered the culprit. Clamahoc was the last person he suspected: a young man who courted the shadows and gave least offence yet one who was well placed to listen at doors and to spy on his master. He deserved no compassion.

Taking the torch from his servant, de Fontenel held it close to Clamahoc's face. 'I want the truth.' he insisted.

'You'll have it, my lord.' groaned the other.

'Who paid you to spy on me?'

'Drogo.'

'The lord Mauger's steward?'

'Yes, my lord.'

'Did you warn him that I was riding against his master?'

'I had to,' said Clamahoc, still wincing at the pain. 'If I'd failed him, he'd have taken his revenge on me.'

'That's nothing to the revenge I'll take on you, if I don't get the answers I want. Do you hear me?' he said, thrusting the torch closer so that its heat made Clamahoc yell. 'I'll send your head back to Drogo with your eyes burnt out.'

'No, no, my lord! Please!'

'Then tell me all you know.'

'I will!' exclaimed the other. Take the flame away and I will.'

The torch was drawn back. 'How long have you been spying on me?'

'For months.'

'What were the lord Mauger's orders?'

'To report anything that happened under this roof,' said Clamahoc, breathlessly. 'I was to take a particular interest in what happened between you and the lady Adelaide.'

'You eavesdropped on those conversations?' roared de Fontenel.

'I had to, my lord. Drogo forced me to do it.'

'And paid you, no doubt,' sneered the other. 'Let's have no more talk about being forced. I'm your master, Clamahoc, not that weasel of a steward. Your first loyalty was to me yet you betrayed me.'

Clamahoc hung his head in shame. His back was on fire, his temples pounding. Ropes were biting into his wrists and ankles. His only hope of clemency lay in complete honesty. He had neither strength nor duplicity enough to hide anything.

'What did you tell them about those gold elephants?' asked de Fontenel.

'That they were a wedding gift for the lady Adelaide.'

'Did you say where they came from?'

'That you brought them back from Normandy.'

'Are you sure?' said the other, squeezing the man's throat.

'Yes, my lord,' spluttered Clamahoc. 'It's what I heard you say to the lady Adelaide. I was outside the door at the time.'

'Those elephants were stolen from my house not long afterwards.'

'It was none of my doing, I swear it!'

'What about Hermer? Was he in the lord Mauger's pay as well?'

'No, my lord. He couldn't be bought.'

'So Hermer didn't steal the elephants on his behalf?'

'How could he?' said Clamahoc, relieved that the grip on his throat had been relaxed. 'The lord Mauger didn't know of the existence of the gold elephants until I told him and that was after they'd disappeared.'

His master was at once annoyed and reassured. He was angry that his assumptions about his rival wrere false. Mauger Livarot had not instigated the theft nor, it now seemed, the murder of the steward. At the same time, Hermer was exonerated. Instead of being another traitor in the household, he was a faithful servant who became a hapless victim. It was one consolation; there was another. Mauger Livarot, it now transpired, did not know the true origin of the gold elephants. Fortunately, that had been kept from him. Richard de Fontenel was baffled by the revelations. If his rival was not responsible for Hermer's death, the killer had to be someone else. He looked back at Clamahoc.

'Who killed Hermer?' he said, still holding the torch.

'I don't know, my lord.'

'But you were listening outside my door.'

'Only until you called for Hermer to bring the wedding gift,' said Clamahoc. 'I hid in the kitchen until he went out again. I heard him open the door of the strong room to put the gold elephants away again.'

'What else did you hear?'

'What you said to the lady Adelaide.'

'Didn't you hear a cry from Hermer?'

'No, my lord.'

'Not even the sound of a scuffle?'

'Nothing. I had my ear pressed to your door.'

'But while you were doing that, someone was overpowering Hermer and stealing my priceless wedding gift. They must've made some sort of noise.'

'I didn't hear them, my lord,' whispered Clamahoc. 'Truly, I didn't.'

'Who else was in the house at that time?'

'Nobody, as far as I know.'

'Then how did Hermer and those gold elephants disappear?'

'It's a mystery.'

'Don't you dare lie to me, Clamahoc,' said the other, waving the flame close to his victim's face again. 'Tell me everything you know about Hermer's death.'

'There's nothing to tell, I swear.'

'You were the one who brought his hands back in that box.'

'I found it lying outside your door, my lord.'

'Did you put it there in the first place?'

'No!' protested the other as the torch made his eyes smart. 'If I'd known what was in that box, I'd never have looked into it. The sight of those hands turned my stomach.'

'Be glad that I don't cut off your own hands and hang them up in front of you.'

'Please don't!' begged Clamahoc. 'I'll do anything for you.'

'It's too late.'

'But it isn't, my lord. It's true that I spied on you but I can work against the lord Mauger instead. I can find out things that will be of use to you,' the man gabbled, desperate to avoid further punishment. 'I can mislead them, if you wish, I can give false information to Drogo. I'll do anything, if only you'll spare me.'

Richard de Fontenel handed the torch back to the servant and toyed with his whip. He looked at the sweating face and blood-covered torso in front of him. Clamahoc had suffered enough for the time being. He might yet come in useful. His master turned to the two brawny men in attendance on the beating.

'Lock him up without food,' he ordered. 'Just give him water.'

After one final swipe with his whip at Clamahoc's back, he walked quickly away.

To travellers who had come all the way from Winchester, it was a relatively short ride. The lady Adelaide lived in the hundred of Humbleyard, slightly to the east of Heigham. It was attractive countryside, making the journey from Norwich a source of pleasure and curiosity. Alys and Golde were accompanied by four of Ralph's men, for whom it was an easy assignment and a welcome change from the long ride to the abbey of St Benet.

'What did *you* think of him, Golde?' asked Alys.

'Of whom?'

'Richard de Fontenel.'

'I thought him a veritable ogre.'

'Could the lady Adelaide ever love such a man?'

'The question I'd ask is whether or not he could ever love her,' said Golde with scepticism. 'All that interests a man like him is power. That's what he loves. Power over his servants, power over his rivals and power over his wife.'

'She must see that.'

'The lady Adelaide is an astute woman. She sees everything.'

'Then why does she let such a man near her?'

'He's one of two suitors, remember. We haven't seen the other yet, though Ralph tells me that the lord Mauger is every bit as abominable.'

Alys gave a wan smile. 'It makes me feel grateful for Gervase.'

'Yes.' said Golde. 'Ralph may not have wooed me with a pair of gold elephants but he's a paragon compared with that oaf who interrupted our banquet the other night.'

'Which one of them will the lady Adelaide choose?'

'I don't know, Alys. Let's hope that she tells us.'

They rode on until the manor house rose up before them in the middle distance. Constructed of local flint, it was a long, low building with large windows and a thatched roof whose eaves undulated gently like golden waves. At the front was an avenue of trees and shrubs, at the rear a well-tended garden. It was an impressive house, larger than the one that Golde shared with Ralph on his Hampshire estate and much bigger than the modest abode in Winchester where Gervase and Alys lived. The visitors were duly struck with the size and solidity of the exterior. Once inside the house, however, they had even more cause for approbation.

'What a beautiful house, my lady!' exclaimed Golde admiringly.

'Thank you.'

'There's so much colour and ornament.'

The lady Adelaide nodded. 'I could never live in drab surroundings.'

'It's more comfortable than the castle,' said Alys in wonderment.

'Give the lord Roger more time and that will be improved out of all recognition. It was only built of timber in the interests of speed. When a stone fortress is erected, I'm sure it will be more daunting on the outside and more opulent within. That, at least,' she said with a confiding smile, 'was what the lady Matilda told me. Norwich is still growing. It's only a matter of time before Bishop William moves his seat here.'

'Why, my lady?' Golde wanted to know.

'Thetford is too small a town from which to administer a diocese.'

'Is it?'

'Can you imagine anyone wanting to build a cathedral there? Norwich is the only fitting place for such a structure. Come back in five or ten years and we'll have a stone castle and the foundations of a magnificent cathedral.'

They were seated in the parlour of the house. Golde and Alys had both worn their finest attire but it seemed dowdy beside the pale blue silk chemise and gown of the lady Adelaide. A gold necklace and a large brooch sparkled in the sunlight that flooded in through the open shutters, and her fingers were adorned with rings. The lady Adelaide looked supremely at home in a room that featured oak furniture, splendid wood carvings, a series of tapestries on the walls and some gleaming gold plate, worthy of display in any cathedral. Sitting in the middle of it all, she exuded wealth and sophistication. As she talked about the future of Norwich, her visitors were astonished at how well-informed she was.

'You seem to know everything about the city, my lady,' said Alys, curiously.

'I like to keep abreast of affairs. I know that women are not supposed to take an interest in such things but I don't see why men should make all the decisions.'

'I agree with that,' said Golde, firmly.

'Do you influence the lord Ralph's decisions?'

'As often as I can.'

'What about you, Alys? Your husband seems to me a most considerate man.'

'He is, my lady. Gervase is an angel. He does everything I could wish.'

'Does he discuss his work with you?'

'No,' admitted Alys. 'He fears it would bore me.'

'Is that the only reason?'

'What do you mean?'

'Well,' said the lady Adelaide, casually, 'When I spoke to the lord Ralph at the banquet, he told me that this was the first time Gervase had brought you with him on one of his outings as a royal commissioner. Whereas you, I believe,' she went on, looking at Golde, 'Have been at your husband's side a number of times.'

'That's true,' said Golde.

'So your husband is much more open with you.'

'Gervase is very open with me, my lady,' said Alys, loyally.

'He is,' confirmed Golde. 'I'm sure that he wasn't deliberately trying to keep Alys ignorant of his work. What concerned him was the tedium of travel and the dangers involved. Gervase didn't want to expose Alys to either.'

'Well, I'm glad that he changed his mind,' said the lady Adelaide, sweetly. 'Or I shouldn't have had the pleasure of meeting her. I'm so glad you were both able to visit me here. It was impossible to talk properly at the banquet.'

'Yes,' said Golde. 'Especially when the lord Richard barged in.'

'That's his way,' said the other, tolerantly. 'The lord Richard will never be renowned for his good manners but he has other things to commend him.'

'Does he, my lady?'

The arrival of a servant with refreshments saved his mistress from having to answer the question. Wine and honey cakes were served to the visitors, while the lady Adelaide looked fondly around.

'I love this room,' she said softly. 'My husband and I designed it together. Geoffrey was so amenable. He kept nothing from me and always took my advice before he made an important decision.'

'Ralph is just the same,' said Golde, proudly.

'And Gervase,' said Alys, determined not to be left out of any display of marital credentials. 'He's so kind and patient with me.'

'Yet he never confides in you about his work.' noted the lady Adelaide. 'And I dare say the lord Ralph is equally secretive about affairs of state. Like most men, he believes that a mere woman could never begin to understand them.'

'You're quite wrong.' replied Golde, stung by the implication but remaining cool. 'My husband frequently talks about his work as a royal commissioner.'

'Oh?'

'There've been times when he's deliberately sought my counsel.'

'When was that?'

'In York, for instance. Or when we visited Exeter.'

'You were excluded from those visits, I gather,' said the lady Adelaide, glancing at Alys. 'Didn't you mind being left behind?'

'It was only proper, my lady. Gervase and I were not married at the time.'

'No,' said Golde, 'and if they hadn't managed to speed up their deliberations in Exeter, Alys might not have been married at all. As it was, Gervase had to race back to Winchester to get there in time. He was a rather breathless bridegroom.'

Alys beamed. 'But all the more welcome.'

'When will the commissioners start work in the shire hall?' asked their hostess.

'Not until the murder of Hermer the Steward has been solved, my lady.'

'There's the other crime as well,' added Golde. 'The theft of two gold elephants. You've actually seen them, I believe, my lady. Are they as exquisite as report has it?'

'They were.' said the other with feeling. 'I have a passion for gold that amounts to an obsession but even I have never seen anything like those two miniatures. They were works of art. Simply to hold them in my grasp was a privilege. To possess them would be a form of ecstasy.'

'And will you possess them?'

'How can I when they've been stolen?'

'If they're recovered, I mean,' said Golde, fishing gently.

'We shall have to wait and see.'

'Would you be ready to accept them as a wedding gift?'

A noncommittal smile. 'I'd be prepared to accept them, most certainly.' The lady Adelaide deftly shifted the conversation to another topic, and her visitors gradually relaxed. They could see why suitors were drawn by her beauty but they were now able to appreciate her other qualities as well. She would be no timid wife. After one happy marriage, she would clearly impose stringent conditions before she entered into a second. Alys marvelled at her self-possession. Golde liked her candour.

'Have they any idea who the killer is yet?' said Adelaide, after a brief pause.

'No.' confessed Golde, 'but my husband says that they are getting closer all the time. He's gone to search for a man called Jocelyn Vavasour today.'

The other woman sat up. 'Why on earth should he do that? He surely can't suspect the lord Jocelyn of being the murderer. The man has become an anchorite.'

'So I understand.'

'What possible help can he be to your husband?'

'I'm not sure,' said Golde, sensing that she should not divulge any more details. 'It was late when they got back last night and I had no time to talk to Ralph. Shortly, after dawn, he and the lord Eustace set off.'

'Didn't your husband go with them, Alys?'

'No, my lady. He's continuing the search nearer home.'

'Where?'

When she felt Golde's gentle nudge, Alys bit back her reply. 'I don't know,' she said with a shrug. 'I'm not sure that I want to know. It was such a foul murder. I just want them to arrest the culprit. We'll all sleep safer in our beds then.'

'The lord sheriff thinks that the steward was killed by the man who stole the elephants,' observed Golde, watching the lady Adelaide. 'Would you still want to possess them, knowing that they'd provoked a murder?'

'Of course.'

'I wouldn't,' put in Alvs.

'Nor me,' said Golde.

'That's only because neither of you actually saw them. Or held them in your hands, as I did.' The lady Adelaide's eyes ignited. 'They were like nothing I've ever seen before. As for provoking a murder, the elephants can hardly be blamed for that. Men kill for lust or gain. Would you condemn a woman because her beauty led a man to kill for her sake? That would be absurd. Why be so coy about those gold elephants?' She looked from one to the other. 'If they'd provoked a dozen murders, I'd still want to own them. In some ways, it would give them even more value.'

Alys was shocked but Golde was simply intrigued, wondering if there were aspects to the woman's character that had been carefully concealed until now. In that one fleeting moment, the lady Adelaide had not looked quite so incongruous a partner for Richard de Fontenel. The conversation returned to the visitors' impressions of Norfolk. Both of them spoke at length about the journey they had endured and the cordial welcome they had received. Alys talked movingly about their visit to the market. The open hostility she had met still worried her at a deep level. It was only when they were leaving that she and Golde realised that they had failed in their mission.

Each of them had been asked by their respective husbands to sound out the lady Adelaide about her two suitors. Golde was to ask questions and Alys was to listen to the answers, but neither of them had fulfilled their duty. Riding back to the castle at a leisurely pace, they reflected on their visit and reached the same conclusion. Instead of finding out more about the lady Adelaide, they had been manipulated into volunteering information about themselves and their husbands. The invitation was not as innocent as it had at first seemed. Golde and Alys had not gone to the house simply as honoured guests.

They were there to be interrogated.

Chapter Nine

Ralph Delchard was soon regretting his decision to embark on a hunt for Jocelyn the Anchorite. Forced to leave the castle when he was only half awake, he missed the comfort of a soft bed and the presence of his wife beside him. He also began to have doubts about the wisdom of searching for a man who, whatever else he might be, was obviously neither a thief nor a murderer. The confidence of the night before had vanished and he was sceptical about his chances of finding the anchorite at the exact spot suggested by Gervase Bret. Because he had retained a tiny pocket of land, it did not mean that Jocelyn Vavasour still inhabited it. All sorts of motives might have prompted him to hang on to the last vestige of his estates. The instinct that prompted Ralph to go there now seemed like recklessness. The further they went, the less certain he became, chiding himself for setting out on what might well be a long, wasted journey.

The one saving grace was that Eustace Coureton had volunteered to accompany him, intrigued, like Ralph, by the notion of a soldier's becoming a hermit. Defying his years, Coureton was up early and without complaint. Four of his men rode with two from Ralph's escort to give the search party some flexibility and to safeguard the two royal commissioners who rode at the head of the little cavalcade. They went north-west from the city, making the most of the early start before the sun was fully up to dazzle their eyes and set the sweat running beneath their hauberks. Flat terrain made for swift progress. They met no obstacles on the way.

Sensing his friend's mood, Coureton tried to cheer him up. 'I'm sure that this visit will be profitable,' he said.

'Will it?' moaned Ralph. 'What if we don't find the man in the Holt hundred?'

'Then we look elsewhere.'

'Why, my lord?'

'Because it's important.'

'What can he tell us?'

'When and for what reason he gave those gold elephants to the abbey.'

'It was when he took leave of his senses and became an anchorite.' Coureton smiled. 'I can see that such a life has no appeal for you.'

'What's the point of needless suffering?'

'It isn't needless. You should talk to Brother Daniel.'

'No, thank you,' said Ralph, rolling his eyes. 'I like the man as much as I could bring myself to like any Benedictine but I heard all that Brother Daniel had to say on our ride to the abbey. On the way back, I heard it all for the second time,' He gave a quiet chuckle. 'At least, he didn't try to quote Horace at me.'

'Is that a complaint?'

'No, it was a gasp of relief.'

'I take the hint,' said Coureton, affably. 'Even though my beloved poet wrote a line that describes your state of mind perfectly.'

'Me?' said Ralph.

'Yes. *Post equitem sedet atra Cura.*'

'Does it come with a translation?'

'It comes with my translation, though Gervase and Brother Daniel might give you slight variations of their own. My version is this. "At the rider's back sits dark Anxiety." Am I right?'

'Not quite. It's more a case of sheer irritation.'

'At whom?'

'Myself,' said Ralph, disconsolately. 'My convictions don't seem so trustworthy in the light of day. I have a horrible feeling that we'll never find this elusive anchorite, and that even if we do he'll be of no practical use to us.'

'I disagree,' said Coureton. 'When I woke up, I felt that fortune would smile on us this morning. We'll track the fellow down, I'm convinced of it. He is, after all, entitled to know the fate of those gold elephants. They have great significance for him. Don't forget that we're talking about someone who went all the way to Rome on foot in order to acquire those treasures. They were blessed by the Pope.'

'I don't care if they were made by St Peter and polished by the Archangel Gabriel. Popes are not held in high esteem by me. Nor,' added Ralph, grimacing, 'are bishops, monks, nuns and anchorites.'

'I'll wager that Jocelyn Vavasour might be the exception.'

'Will you back that wager with your purse?'

Coureton laughed. 'I'm not that headstrong. I'm just more optimistic than you. What I can say is that well most definitely find him.'

'And what do we gain from that?'

'An interesting story, to start with. Come, Ralph,' said the other, 'you're as eager as I am to know why he traded in his hauberk for the holy cross. He was one of us, born and brought up in Normandy, moulded into a warrior just as we were. Why did we end up as royal commissioners while he prefers the company of birds and a Bible?'

'I'm very keen to learn that,' conceded Ralph, 'but that's a personal matter. I'm just having second thoughts about his usefulness to our enquiry. How can a hermit possibly help us to solve a murder?'

'By giving us the history of the treasures whose theft started the whole business off.'

'And?'

'By telling us what he knows about some of the characters we've so far met.'

'Such as?'

'Olova,' said Coureton. 'That potent lady whom Gervase and I visited yesterday. I may speak Latin and Greek but I've never felt my deficiency in the Saxon tongue more painfully than in her hut. I was longing to speak to Olova.'

'Why didn't you try a line or two from Horace on her?'

'I don't think she'd have much sympathy for noble Romans, somehow. But she and her husband did have sympathy for the abbey of St Benet, it seems. According to Gervase, they endowed the place generously.'

'Was that a case of generosity or spite?'

'What do you mean?'

'We've seen it so often, Eustace,' said the other. 'Wealthy Saxons who gave property to a monastic foundation to save it from falling into the hands of people like us.'

'That wasn't what happened here, I'm sure. Olova may have been aggressive but I detected a piety about her as well. She and her husband donated that land to the abbey out of Christian impulse. That gives her an immediate connection with Jocelyn Vavasour.'

'Except that he took his Christian impulse to extremes.'

'He must have known Olova. Some of his holdings were in the same hundred as hers. He also had land in the Taverham hundred atone time so he must have been acquainted with Richard de Fontenel and Mauger Livarot. And if he knew them, he'd be familiar with the irrespective stewards. You see?' Coureton, reached across to pat his companion on the shoulder. 'He knows almost everyone of importance. This anchorite will tell us things that we could never get from anyone else.'

'That's true,' admitted Ralph, revived by the thought.

'You can even discuss Abbot Alfwold with him.'

'And poor Brother Joseph.'

'I told you that an anchorite would be able to help us.'

'In more ways than one,' said Ralph, buoyed up. 'I'd like to hear what he has to say about the movement of property in this county. A man who's willingly forfeited his lands has no vested interest. Jocelyn Vavasour will be honest and dispassionate. He'll know who stole what from whom and be prepared to name them. It may well be,' he went on, grinning as the idea took a firm hold, 'that he can provide weaponry for us to use in the shire hall against the likes of the lord Richard and his ilk. Imagine that. It'll save us endless time.'

'Doesn't that make you glad you got up early today?'

'No,' replied Ralph, still grinning.

'It must have some benevolent effect.'

'It does, Eustace. It makes the pain easier to bear.'

Riding in pairs, the travellers clattered over a rickety bridge and continued on their way. Their eyes were trained on the twisting road ahead. None of them thought to look over their shoulders and therefore remained completely unaware of the fact that they were being trailed by a man at a cautious distance.

The decision to make the visit had been reached after a long debate with his fellow commissioners and Roger Bigot on the previous night. Since it called for tact and diplomacy, Gervase was felt to be the best person to send on the embassy. While Ralph and Coureton were riding in the direction of the Holt hundred, therefore, he was making his way to the estate of Richard de Fontenel, accompanied by Brother Daniel and two of Eustace Coureton's men-at-arms. The monk was as talkative as ever.

'The lord Eustace speaks Latin better than I do,' he confessed.

'But for a different purpose,' said Gervase. 'His interest is in ancient Rome.'

'Mine is in eternal life.'

'You have something in common, then. His passion is for the Eternal City.'

'St Augustine wrote unforgettably about it.'

'I know, but he didn't have Rome in mind.'

Gervase was pleased to be riding beside the monk, even though the latter's shortcomings as a horseman were all too apparent. It gave the young commissioner an opportunity to ask about the discoveries of the previous day. Having already heard Ralph's version of events, he wanted to see if it tallied with that of Brother Daniel.

'Did you enjoy the visit to the abbey?' he asked.

'Very much.'

'Why?'

The monk needed no more invitation. He gave a detailed account of the journey, the architecture of the abbey and the people they met within it. Nothing he said contradicted Ralph's version but it was considerably embellished. The monk may have said little but he had looked and listened with care.

'What did you make of the sacristan?' asked Gervase.

'He was far too trusting. He should never have been taken in by a guest.'

'We're not absolutely certain that's what happened, Brother Daniel.'

'What other explanation is there?' said the monk. 'Someone stole those gold elephants from the abbey. They didn't stampede out of there of their own accord. They were taken by Starculf and given to the lord Richard.'

'Even though Starculf swore revenge against his former master?'

'An intermediary must have been involved. Hermer, perhaps.'

'Starculf hated the man.'

'Those elephants came into the lord Richard's possession somehow.'

'Yes,' said Gervase. 'That's why we're going to see him. But we must be sure not to accuse him of anything, Brother Daniel. That will get us nowhere. We must try to draw information out of him by more subtle means.'

'I'll leave the talking to you.'

'Watch his reactions.'

'From what I've heard about the lord Richard,' said Daniel, worriedly, 'you'd be well advised to watch how close his hand gets to his sword. He's inclined to violence.'

'Only if he's provoked. Ours will be a softer approach.'

'I'm glad to hear it.'

Men were working in the fields as they drove past. They looked up briefly at the passing visitors before returning to their work. Sheep were the only animals on view, scuttling out of their way with noisy protests. When the travellers got to the manor house, a servant met them at the door. They were soon conducted into the empty parlour. While Gervase took a swift inventory, Daniel clicked his tongue at the ostentatious display of wealth in the room.

Richard de Fontenel swept into the parlour, more puzzled than irked by their unannounced visit. Gervase performed the introductions but that only deepened the lines in their host's forehead.

'Why have a royal commissioner and a monk come to see me?' he wondered.

'We come in other guises, my lord,' explained Gervase. 'I'm

helping the lord sheriff to solve the crimes that have occurred here and Brother Daniel is the person who actually stumbled on the dead body of your steward.'

'I shudder whenever I recall it,' said Daniel.

'What exactly happened?' pressed de Fontenel, interested to hear. 'Why did you look into that derelict house in the first place and what state was Hermer in when you saw him?'

Brother Daniel took a deep breath before he told his story once again. Gervase was grateful to him. He could see the effort that it was costing the monk but the grim details were lapped up by their host. When they were offered seats, the visitors began to feel more welcome. Richard de Fontenel wanted to know everything that the monk could tell him, making him repeat some parts of his narrative. Beneath the man's simmering anger, Gervase could sense a real affection for the dead steward.

'Thank you,' said de Fontenel at length. 'I'm glad to hear it all from your own lips, Brother Daniel. It was good of you to come here.'

'That wasn't the only reason for our visit, my lord,' said Gervase, taking over. 'I'm here on the lord sheriff's behalf to talk about the theft that took place.'

'Well?'

'I understand that the objects stolen were extremely valuable.'

'They were solid gold, Master Bret, and fashioned in Italy.'

'Is that where you bought them?' asked Gervase, softly.

'Not exactly.'

'Then how did they come into your hands?'

'Does that matter?'

'I'm afraid it does, my lord.'

'A merchant sold them to me.' said de Fontenel briskly. 'When I was in Normandy, I heard that this man had something very special to sell and it was exactly what I needed at that particular time. So I bought the elephants from him.'

'In Normandy?'

'Further south than that, Master Bret.'

'When was this, my lord?'

'Quite recently.'

'Could you be more specific, please?'

'It must have been – what? – ten or twelve days ago. I only returned to England earlier this week. The two elephants were a gift. Before I could present them to the person for whom they were intended, they were stolen and my steward was murdered.'

'Let's just concentrate on the elephants,' suggested Gervase. 'Would you describe the merchant from whom you bought them as an honest man?'

'Of course.'

'You had no reason to doubt him?'

'Why should I?'

'Because what he sold you, my lord, was stolen property.'

'Never!'

'It was,' maintained Gervase, 'and I think that your memory may be at fault with regard to the precise time of the purchase. Ten or twelve days ago, you said.'

'That's when it was, Master Bret.'

'Somewhere in France.'

'Do you have any proof to the contrary?'

'I don't, my lord, but Brother Daniel has.'

'Yes,' said the monk, taking up his cue. 'I had the pleasure of visiting the abbey of St Benet at Holme yesterday. According to Brother Joseph, the sacristan, those gold elephants belonged to them and were regarded as holy objects. Unfortunately, they were stolen from the abbey church at the very time you claim to have bought them in France.'

Richard de Fontenel's face was ashen. There was a long pause before he spoke. 'I think there's been a mistake,' he said at last. 'The elephants that I bought didn't come from Holme. They may have been similar to the ones stolen from the abbey but they couldn't possibly have been the same ones.'

'We believe that they might be, my lord,' said Gervase.

'But that's impossible!'

'On the face of it, yes. The objects could hardly have been taken from the abbey and sold in France on the same day. As far as I'm aware, elephants don't fly.'

'Don't jest with me, Master Bret.'

'I'm in earnest, my lord.'

Brother Daniel nodded vigorously. 'Theft of holy treasures is an abomination.'

'I didn't steal them!' shouted de Fontenel.

'Nobody is suggesting that you did, my lord,' said Gervase. 'Our fear is that you were the victim of an unscrupulous merchant. In which case, the transaction between the two of you must have taken place more recently than you have told us.'

'Well, yes, that's true,' mumbled the other. 'I can't be precise about the date.'

'It would have taken days for them to reach you in France.'

'I'm aware of that, Master Bret,' said de Fontenel through

gritted teeth. 'But. I'm still not convinced that the gift I bought in good faith came from the abbey of St Benet. Who gave you the idea that it did?'

'Judicael the Goldsmith.'

'He's never seen my elephants.'

'He hasn't seen the ones at the abbey either,' said Gervase, patiently, 'but he had a very clear description of them from a goldsmith who had. That description matched in every detail the one you gave to the lord sheriff. The objects are quite unique. There's no room for error here.'

'There must be!'

'Two holy treasures are stolen from an abbey and you buy identical objects shortly afterwards? No, my lord. That would be far too great a coincidence. In any case,' said Gervase, blithely, 'the matter will soon be resolved.'

'How?'

'When the elephants are recovered, the abbot and sacristan will be able to identify them as belonging to the abbey. You'll be allowed to examine them yourself, of course, but there'll be an even more important witness.'

'Witness?' echoed de Fontenel.

'Yes, my lord.'

'Who are you talking about?'

'The man who presented the gift to the abbey – Jocelyn Vavasour.'

'But he's disappeared. The lord Jocelyn has become an anchorite.'

'My colleagues are on their way to find him at this very moment.'

Richard de Fontenel was checked. His jaw tightened and his eyes darted. He was mortified by the notion that, even if they were located, the missing elephants would not be returned to him. His wedding gift would be confiscated and his plans thrown into confusion. He was caught unawares by the next question from Gervase.

'Does the name Olova mean anything to you, my lord?'

'Who?' said the other, blinking in surprise.

'Olova. She lives in the Henstead hundred. Your steward had dealings with her.'

'That may well be, Master Bret. I didn't keep track of every person that Hermer saw in the course of his duties. I've never heard of this Olova.'

'Even though you acquired land that once belonged to her?'

'It was done legally, I assure you.'

'Not in her opinion. The lady is ready to challenge you in the shire hall.'

'Let her.'

'She didn't speak too highly of your steward.'

'You've talked to her?'

'The lord Eustace and I rode out to see Olova yesterday.'

'Do you give preference to a Saxon?' said de Fontenel, flaring up. 'The place to settle a dispute is in the shire hall, not behind my back. I'll register the strongest complaint about this, Master Bret. Judges should be quite impartial.'

'Olova made no attempt to influence me, my lord,' Gervase assured him.

'Then why visit the woman?'

'To seek her views on another subject.'

'You went all that way to listen to an embittered old Saxon crone?'

'Olova is half Danish, my lord. Her late husband was a thegn with estates large enough to match your own. I found Olova a woman of intelligence and determination.'

'Neither will do her any good when she takes me on in the shire hall.'

'Are you trying to influence a commissioner, my lord?' said Brother Daniel, waspishly.

'Not at all,' blustered the other. 'I didn't introduce Olova into the conversation.'

'The only reason that I do so,' said Gervase, 'was that she talked about Hermer. She was less than grief-stricken when I told her of his fate.'

'I'm not interested in her, Master Bret.'

'Then let's forget her for the moment, my lord. What I wanted to ask you about was your steward's hands. Why do you think they were cut off?'

'Sheer savagery!'

'I was appalled when I saw the mutilation,' recalled Daniel.

'The hands were returned to you,' resumed Gervase. 'Why was that, my lord?'

'I wish I knew.'

'Was it a symbolic gesture, perhaps?'

'Symbolic of a brutal mind. It would be typical of the lord Mauger.'

'The lord sheriff has absolved him of the crime.'

'I know,' grunted the other, 'and I've learnt for certain that it was not his doing.'

'How?'

'That doesn't concern you, Master Bret,' said the other, eager to move them on their way. 'You come at an awkward time. I'm a busy man and have much to do. If you've told me all you came to say, I'll bid you farewell.'

The visitors rose to their feet and walked across to the door, where Gervase halted. 'I believe that you once employed a man called Starculf,' he said.

'Not for long. He was dismissed.'

'What did he look like, my lord?'

'A tall, handsome, upstanding young fellow. A strong one, too, who used to be a falconer. To look in his face, you'd have thought him the soul of honesty. But he let me down, Master Bret. Nobody does that with impunity.'

'So I understand.'

There was an exchange of farewells, then Gervase led the way out. It was only when they were riding away from the house at a trot that he spoke to his companion.

'What did you learn from that, Brother Daniel?'

'That the lord Richard is a poor liar. He didn't buy those elephants in France.'

'No,' said Gervase. 'He knew exactly where they came from. He may not have stolen them in person but I'm certain that he instigated the theft. Without knowing it, he may even have told us who the thief was.'

'It wasn't Starculf,' said the monk. The description he gave of the man was nothing like the one we had from the sacristan at the abbey. Brother Joseph told us that the thief was short, stocky and thirty years or more. He was no handsome young man.'

'The sacristan was not describing Starculf at all, Brother Daniel.'

'Then who was he talking about?'

'Hermer.'

Drogo had important news to report. Expecting approval, he strutted into the house with more confidence than he had shown when he left it. Mauger Livarot was in the parlour, fastening the gold brooch that held his mantle on. He swung round on his steward. 'Well?'

'I've spoken to my man at the castle, my lord.'

'What did he say?'

'There's much activity there. Ralph Delchard and Eustace Coureton rode off at dawn in search of Jocelyn Vavasour.'

'Why?'

'He didn't know, my lord. He simply overheard them talking about going to the Holt hundred. That's where they believe they'll find him.'

'I thought that the lord Jocelyn became an anchorite.'

'He did. Nobody quite knows where he is.'

'They must be very anxious to track him down,' said Livarot, stroking his chin, 'though what use a holy man is to them, I fail to see.' He gave a cackle. 'Unless they want the mad fool to bless their enterprise.'

Drogo preened himself. 'I'll know more detail in due course,' he said. 'As soon as I heard where they'd gone, I sent a man off in pursuit. He'll shadow them all the way.'

'Well done, Drogo.'

'The lord sheriff is also being followed.'

'How is Roger Bigot spending the day?'

'Searching for one of the men they suspect – Starculf.'

'That'll keep him busy. Is Olivier Romain with him?'

'Yes, my lord. They're making every effort to hunt the man down.'

'Then we must get to him first,' said Livarot. 'I remember Starculf well. He was driven off the lord Richard's estates. Rough treatment breeds revenge. Find him, Drogo. Organise a search of your own.'

'I've already done so,' said the other, complacently.

'Good.'

'We'll recover those gold elephants somehow, my lord, I promise you that. We might even catch a murderer into the bargain.'

'All that I'm interested in is a pair of elephants. As for the man who killed Hermer, I'm more likely to congratulate him than hand him over to face justice. Hermer was as loathsome as his master,' Livarot sneered. 'I've been saved the trouble of killing him myself.'

'Yes, my lord.'

'Two commissioners have ridden off, you say. What of the other?'

'Gervase Bret is paying a call on the lord Richard.'

'Oh?'

'Brother Daniel, their scribe, was in attendance.'

'You have eyes everywhere, Drogo.'

'I spend money wisely, my lord. But we'll soon know what passed between the lord Richard and his visitors. I have eyes and ears inside that manor house. I've arranged to meet Clamahoc later,' the steward said airily. 'He'll tell me every word that was spoken.'

'This is cheering news, Drogo. I sense that we're moving forward.'

'We are, my lord.'

'Is there anything else to report?'

'Not unless you wish to hear about the commissioners' wives?'

'Have they gone in search of Starculf as well?'

'No, my lord,' said Drogo, washing his hands in the air. 'They accepted an invitation to visit the lady Adelaide. I dare say they're on their way back to the castle by now. Unfortunately, I have no spy in that particular household.'

'We don't need one,' boasted the other. 'I'm on my way to see the lady Adelaide myself. With careful questioning, I'm sure that I can find out exactly what happened when the two ladies called on her. The lady Adelaide confides in me.'

'With good reason.' Drogo followed his master out and waited while Livarot mounted the horse that was saddled in readiness for him. Reins in his hand, the latter looked down at his steward with a puzzled expression.

'Where does he fit into all this?' he asked.

'Who, my lord?'

'I can understand why men are out in search of Starculf and I can think of many reasons why one of the commissioners should want to question the lord Richard. But it simply doesn't make sense to go haring off in pursuit of a crazed anchorite.'

'That surprised me as well,' admitted the other.

Mauger Livarot shook his head in bafflement. 'What possible use can Jocelyn Vavasour be to them?'

Sitting cross-legged on the ground, he ignored the sharp pinch of the wind as it came in off the sea with mischievous intent. He was too engrossed in his work to feel the periodic hot embrace of the sun as well. Vavasour was using a knife to carve a small piece of driftwood. It was slow, careful, demanding work that allowed for no lapse of concentration. He did not even lift his head when eight riders approached him from behind. It was only when the wading birds suddenly took to the air in fright that he realised he had company. The anchorite turned to look up at his visitors.

Ralph Delchard was the first to dismount and stride across to him. 'We're looking for Jocelyn Vavasour,' he announced.

'Then your journey has been in vain, my lord,' said the other, getting up. 'He doesn't exist any more.'

'In that case, I'll talk to Jocelyn the Anchorite. Do you answer to that name?'

'Not by choice.'

'You're ashamed of your calling?'

'I'm embarrassed by company, my lord. I chose a hermetic life in order to shun it. I've never had to answer to any name since I came to this place. Why have you sought me out?'

Ralph signalled to the escort and the men dismounted, glad to be out of the saddle and able to water their horses. Then he introduced himself and Coureton, explaining that they had suspended their work as royal commissioner while they helped the sheriff with a murder investigation.

'I know nothing about any murder.'

'There's a related crime,' said Ralph. 'The theft of two gold elephants.'

'From the abbey?' said Vavasour, anxiously.

'Initially.'

'Who took them?'

'We're not entirely sure. Let me tell you the sequence of events.'

The anchorite grew increasingly tense as he listened to Ralph's account. An anger he had not felt for years began to surge up inside him. He banked it down as best he could.

'Those elephants were holy treasures,' he declared. 'They belong to the abbey.'

'When we find them, they'll be returned there.'

'But you have no idea where they are.'

'We will do in time,' said Coureton.

'Yes,' said Ralph, confidently. 'They obviously came into the lord Richard's hands by some nefarious means. In one sense, justice has been served. The original thief is now the victim of a theft himself.'

'I care nothing for that,' said Vavasour. 'Those elephants are highly important to me, my lord. They symbolise a solemn vow I made. I went to Rome as a soldier and came back as a new man.'

'What took you there in the first place?' asked Coureton.

'Shame and disgust.'

'At what?'

'Myself, my life, my dreadful sins.'

'You were a soldier like us. You did as you were told.'

'No, my lord,' admitted the other, gloomily. 'I did more than that. Some killed because they had to but I did it to satisfy a lust that raged inside me. Do you recall the penances imposed on us by Bishop Ermenfrid of Sitten?'

'What do bishops know of warfare?' said Ralph.

'They can see the results strewn all over the battlefield. Like you, I suspect, I paid little heed to the penitentiary when it was issued. But its decrees slowly took hold on me. Bishop Ermenfrid was the papal legate. He spoke with the authority of the head of the Roman Catholic Church. Would you defy the Pope himself?'

'It depends on the circumstances.'

'Did both of you fight at Hastings?'

'We did,' confirmed Coureton.

'Then you will know what the first decree was,' said Vavasour. '"Any man who knows that he killed a man in the great battle must do penance for one year for each man that he killed." The next decree was just as unequivocal. "Anyone who wounded a man and does not know whether he killed him or not must do penance for forty days foreach man he struck (if he can remember the number), either continuously or at intervals." That is what was ordered.'

'We know, my friend. And rightly so.'

'That's a matter of opinion,' said Ralph.

'You both know mine,' continued Vavasour, holding his arms out wide so that they could see his ragged attire. 'I killed or wounded seven men at Hastings. And that was only the start of it. Don't tell me that I was young and impulsive. I revelled in the slaughter. I fought on the Welsh border, in the north and in several other battles. I helped to smoke out Hereward the Wake from the Fens. A year of penance for every man I killed or mutilated? I'd not live long enough to manage that.'

'Is that what led your footsteps to Rome?' asked Coureton.

'I went in search of forgiveness.'

'Did you find it?'

'In some small measure, my lord. Everything I possessed was harvested by the sword. I gave it all away. Since the abbey of St Benetlay close to land I once owned, I wanted to bestow something special on it.'

'Two gold elephants.'

'Beasts of burden transformed into holy treasures. They were magnificent,' said Vavasour, wistfully. He turned to Ralph. 'We must find them. I won't rest until they're back where they belong. I'll do anything to achieve that.'

'Good,' said Ralph. 'The first thing you can do is to tell us what they looked like. The simple truth is that we've never seen a real elephant. To be honest, I thought they were creatures of fable. I had grave doubts that they actually existed.'

'Oh, they exist, my lord.' affirmed Vavasour. 'When I was in Rome, I had the good fortune to see a live elephant with my own eyes. The animal had been brought back from Africa and was kept in a huge cage.'

'Describe it to us.' urged Ralph.

'The sheer size is what first strikes you. The creature was enormous. Stand on its back and you could probably look over the walls of Norwich Castle. Then there was this curious nose.' said Vavasour. 'It's a long trunk that reaches right down to the ground and is used by the elephant to feed itself. I watched it in Rome using its trunk to load hay into its mouth. That's the other strange thing.' he added. 'Though it's by far the largest of all animals, it doesn't prey on any of the others. Elephants eat no meat. They feed entirely off leaves, shoots and grass.'

'They sound like gentle giants,' observed Coureton.

'There was a lumbering gentleness about the one I saw,' recalled Vavasour, 'but there was also a tremendous strength. To defend itself, it has two vast tusks of ivory that stick out either side of its trunk. Even a lion would think twice about attacking a beast as large and powerful as an elephant.'

'I still can't picture it in my mind.' admitted Ralph. 'As high as Norwich castle, you say, and with a trunk and ivory tusks.'

'And two great ears that flap like wings.'

'I'm more confused than ever now.'

'Then let me help you, my lord.' said Vavasour with a smile. 'If you really want to know what an elephant looks like, I can show you because I've been trying to fashion one myself.'

He held up the piece of wood that he had been carving so painstakingly. It was a miniature elephant, reproducing all the features he had just described to them. Ralph and Coureton stared in astonishment at the object.

'So *that's* what all this is about, is it?' said Ralph. 'Now, I understand.'

Gervase Bret was pleased with what he had learnt from his visit to Richard de Fontenel but disappointed that Ralph Delchard was not at the castle to hear about it. He repaired to his apartment in the keep and was delighted to find both Alys and Golde there, deep in conversation about their own visit that morning. He settled down on a bench.

'How were you received by the lady Adelaide?' he asked.

'Very warmly,' said Alys. 'She was glad to see us.'

'But not for the reason we thought,' added Golde.

'Why not?' he said.

'I thought that we'd be questioning her, Gervase, but we were the ones providing all the answers. The lady Adelaide showed a very keen interest in your work.'

'Did she?'

'Yes. She was very subtle about it, but it was almost as if she were trying to wheedle something out of us for her own advantage.'

'Will she be appearing before you in any dispute?' said Alys.

'No, my love,' he replied. 'But two friends of hers will.'

'Lady Adelaide's two suitors?'

'I wonder which one of them put her up to it?'

'Neither, in my view,' decided Golde. 'The lady Adelaide is a person who knows how to look out for herself. And she likes to flaunt her wealth, doesn't she, Alys?'

'Oh, yes! Her house was a small palace.'

'No wonder she has two men after her,' observed Gervase.

Golde raised an eyebrow. 'They're not only interested in her house.'

Helped by Alys, she gave him a detailed account of their visit, admitting that she could not entirely make up her mind about the lady Adelaide. Of the latter's essential kindness and intelligence there could be no doubt, but Golde suspected that there might be a darker side to the woman.

'She was *using* us, Gervase.'

'To what end?'

'That's what I couldn't quite understand. But we felt manipulated.'

'I felt overwhelmed,' said Alys. 'I've never been in a house like that before.'

'You're staying in a castle,' teased Gervase. 'What could be grander than this?'

'It wasn't just a question of size, it was the way that the lady Adelaide lived. Wherever we looked, we saw the woman's touch. She has that house exactly the way that she wants it, doesn't she, Golde?'

'Yes. I can't see her giving it up to marry either the lord Richard

215

or the lord Mauger. She belongs there. It fits her so snugly.'

'The lady Adelaide would hardly invite a husband to join her there,' said Gervase. 'If any house were surrendered, it would naturally have to be hers.' He became pensive. 'Did she say anything about the theft of the elephants?'

'No more than we've already told you.'

'Yet she was in the lord Richard's house when they were stolen.'

'She's very conscious of that.'

'What she did say was that she had an obsession about gold,' recalled Alys. 'If I had the opportunity, I dare say that I'd be the same.' She beamed at her husband. 'Would you buy a pair of gold elephants for me?'

'Not this particular pair, my love,' he said. 'They're too troublesome.'

'But if you had the money, you'd spoil me, wouldn't you?'

'He already has,' said Golde, fondly. 'Gervase married you.'

'Yes. That's better than any amount of gold.'

He grinned shyly. 'I'm very flattered, Alys, but it doesn't get us anywhere nearer to solving either of these crimes. I'm still thinking about the fact that the lady Adelaide was with the lord Richard at the exact moment they and Hermer disappeared.'

'So?'

'Could it be that she was deliberately keeping him occupied?'

'You mean that she was party to the crime, Gervase? Oh, no!'

'I'm not so sure,' said Golde, ruminating. 'The lady Adelaide would certainly not be involved in murder but I fancy that she'd go to any lengths to acquire something whose sparkle attracted her enough. She's very single-minded.'

'She must be,' said Gervase, 'to be able to keep men like the lord Richard and the lord Mauger at bay. There's more than single-mindedness in action there. The lady Adelaide is not easily dismayed, either. Brother Daniel was shocked to the core when he chanced on that dead body but the murder didn't put the lady Adelaide off her food. She was also the one person who remained calm when Richard de Fontenel burst in.'

Alys shivered. 'That was terrifying,' she said. 'Is it always like this when you visit a city as a royal commissioner, Gervase? Theft, murder, violence and heaven knows what else? Is this what usually happens?'

'Our work is never entirely without incident, my love.'

'That's putting it mildly,' said Golde. 'What will you do next?'

'Nothing at all until I've spoken to Ralph. And I'll want a word with the sheriff to see if he has any news about Starculf's whereabouts. Beyond that, I'm not sure, to be honest.' He got to his feet. 'I know what I'd like to do.'

'What's that?'

'Pay a second visit to Olova.'

'Is she the lady in the Henstead hundred?' said Alys.

'Yes, my love,' he said, touching her shoulder. 'It was wrong of me to ride there with the lord Eustace and an armed escort. Olova was a Saxon lady who's suffered much at the hands of Norman soldiers. I just couldn't get through to her properly.'

'Do you think it was important to do so?'

'Very important, Alys. I'm certain that Olova knew more than she told me.'

Golde smiled. 'Would you like *me* to speak to her?' she offered.

*　*　*

Drogo the Steward was annoyed when he reached the appointed place and saw no sign of either the man or his horse. It was so untypical of Clamahoc. He was always very punctual. Drogo made sure of that. The servant had been corrupted by a judicious mixture of threat and money. He was too involved to turn back, too frightened of the consequences. Drogo resolved to instil his own brand of fear when the man finally arrived. His spy would be roundly chastised for his lateness. Dismounting from his horse, the steward tethered it to one of the bushes. He and Clamahoc always met near that copse, taking advantage of its cover and its convenient position midway between the two estates. In the shade of the trees, much invaluable information had been passed between them.

No more would be forthcoming. Drogo had the odd sensation that he was not alone. When a muted groan came from the heart of the copse, he reached for his dagger. A second groan gave him some idea of where to go and he pushed his way cautiously through the undergrowth, it did not take him long to find him. Clamahoc had been punctual, after all. Lying face down on the ground, he squirmed and twitched in agony, his bare back crisscrossed with lacerations and smeared with dried blood. A savage punishment had taken him close to death.

Drogo let out a cry of alarm then used a tentative foot to turn the man over. 'Who did this to you?' he demanded.

But his spy imparted no useful information this time. His tongue had been cut out.

Chapter Ten

Ralph Delchard studied the animal with intense interest. Holding the wooden elephant in his hand, he turned it slowly around to examine it from all angles. Eustace Coureton was equally fascinated. The carving was crude and unfinished but the main features of the elephant's physiognomy were all there. Jocelyn Vavasour had vanished into his hut. When he reappeared, he brandished an earlier attempt at woodcarving.

'This is the first one that I did,' he said, passing it to Ralph. 'It will give you a clearer idea of what an elephant looks like.'

Ralph was intrigued. 'Look at the size of that trunk!'

'And those ears!' said Coureton, reaching out to touch them. 'So large and yet so smooth. You've got a rare talent, Jocelyn.'

'No,' said the other modestly. 'They're poor copies of the originals.'

'At least, they give us an idea of what we're looking for.'

'But for one thing, my lord. I wasn't able to carve the cross that stood on the animal's head. That was beyond me. I tried very hard,' he said, sadly, 'but my hand slipped and the knife cut the cross off at the base. I wasn't patient enough. I'll be much more careful with the second one.'

Ralph held them up side by side to compare them. He sighed with admiration. 'Remarkable work!'

'Wait until you see the originals, my lord,' said Vavasour. 'They capture the essence of the creature. The Venetian goldsmith who made them had actually seen elephants. His miniatures had a life to them.'

'So do these, my friend.'

'But they're made of driftwood and not solid gold.'

'It's not the material,' said Ralph, 'it's the way it's shaped. Besides, these two carvings of yours have a glow all of their own.'

'The wood dries that colour in the sun.'

'So you have two gold elephants of your own,' said Coureton with a chuckle. 'When the second is finished, you'll be able to present them to the abbey as well.'

'No, my lord,' said Vavasour, taking the two carvings from Ralph. 'These are carved from memory rather than inspiration. The abbey deserves only the best. I carried them all the way from Rome with a papal blessing on them and I want them restored to their rightful place.'

'They will be.'

'What if the thief has already had them melted down?'

'We've taken steps to prevent that,' said Ralph. 'I visited the three goldsmiths in Norwich myself and the lord sheriff has sent out word to every other one in the county. The moment they're offered those miniatures for sale, they're to report it to him or they'll suffer the consequences.'

'But the elephants may already have left Norfolk.'

'True, but I think it unlikely.'

'Why?'

'Whoever stole them knew where to find them,' Ralph explained. 'Nothing else was stolen from the lord Richard's strong room even though it was full of other treasures. Hermer the Steward was overpowered by someone who thus had possession of his keys. Had the thief simply wanted booty, he could have opened every chest in the strong room, but he didn't. Do you follow my thinking here?'

'Yes, my lord. You believe it to be someone who knew his way around the lord Richard's manor house. Someone from the locality.'

'And someone with a particular reason for wanting those gold elephants.'

'That's why the name of the lord Mauger had to be considered,' said Coureton. 'When they were taken from the abbey, they were destined to be a wedding gift to the lady whose hand he's been seeking in marriage himself.'

Ralph explained the situation in detail. The anchorite listened intently throughout, interrupting only to clarify a point or to challenge an assumption. He was impressed by the way that the commissioners had thrown themselves wholeheartedly into the pursuit of a thief who was, in all probability, also a killer. After spending so long alone on the marshes, it took him some time to adjust to the workings of the world he had renounced so completely, but memories gradually surged back. He was able to furnish them with new information about the long feud that existed between Richard de Fontenel and Mauger Livarot, but it was his comment on the lady over whom the two men fought that was most illuminating.

'How closely have you questioned the lady Adelaide?' he asked.

'We haven't spoken to her at all,' said Ralph.

'You should, my lord.'

'Why?'

'There's an odd coincidence here that you couldn't be expected to see. But I'm more familiar with the people involved.'

'Go on.'

'I've no wish to malign the lady Adelaide,' said Vavasour with emphasis. 'She's a good Christian with a charitable disposition and was a loyal wife to her late husband. But there's an aspect of her character that's a little less admirable. The lady Adelaide is fond of manipulating people for her own advantage.'

'Yes,' said Ralph, nodding in agreement. 'We've observed the way in which she's keeping both suitors at arm's length and playing them off against each other.'

'It began with Geoffrey Molyneux, my lord. The lady Adelaide loved him dearly, I've no doubt, but that didn't stop her from exploiting him. He doted on her. Since you've met her, I'm sure that you can understand why.'

'Oh, yes!' said Coureton. 'Any husband would dote on her.'

'The lord Geoffrey showered her with gifts. Her passion was for jewellery and he would travel hundreds of miles just to buy a particular necklace or brooch for her. Gold is the lady

Adelaide's weakness,' continued Vavasour, looking down at the two carvings in his hand. 'The lord Richard understood that only too well. He acquired those gold elephants because he knew they might be the one gift that would ensnare her.'

'Not if she realised that they were stolen property, surely?'

The anchorite hesitated. 'I can't answer for that.'

'You think that she would accept them in those circumstances?' pressed Ralph.

'All I can say is that she loves gold more than anything else in the world. And that, alas, even includes her children. Did you know that they're being brought up in her parents' household?'

'No. She never mentioned the children to me.'

'The lady Adelaide likes to see them if and when she wishes.'

'Would you call her an uncaring mother, then?'

'No, my lord. She seemed affectionate towards them on the few occasions I saw them all together. But she chooses not to have them living under her own roof. I find that a peculiar decision, especially now that she's a widow. It comes back to what I said earlier.' Vavasour added. 'The lady Adelaide likes to exert control over people.'

'Over men,' said Ralph, bluntly.

'It's more difficult to do that with children plucking at the hem of your gown.'

'All this is very interesting. I spoke to the lady at length myself and saw none of these defects. But as it happens, my wife went to visit her this morning. I dare say she'll have discerned things about the lady Adelaide that are less flattering.'

'There's one last thing, my lord.'

'Yes?'

'You mentioned a man called Starculf.'

'The lord sheriff is searching for him high and low.'

'What did he tell you about the fellow?'

'That he once served the lord Richard and was expelled from his estates.'

'Do you know how Starculf came into his service in the first place?'

'As a falconer.'

'But who recommended him?'

'I've no idea.'

'The lady Adelaide,' said the anchorite, softly. 'That was the odd coincidence I referred to earlier. Starculf learnt his skills on her estates. When her husband died, she offered the man to the lord Richard. It may just be that she had no need of a young falconer although, of course, he was soon promoted to a higher position.'

'On the other hand,' concluded Ralph, 'she might have recommended the fellow to Richard de Fontenel for a purpose. To act as her intelligencer.'

'Perhaps that's why Starculf and Hermer fell out,' suggested Coureton. 'The steward realised that his assistant's loyalties lay elsewhere.'

'I don't know about that, Eustace. What is obvious is that the lady Adelaide will bear closer examination. I'm keen to hear what Golde found out about her.'

'Not as much as we've just done.'

'No,' said Ralph, turning to Vavasour. 'Thank you, my friend. Our journey has been more than worthwhile. You've taught us what an elephant looks like and given us valuable insights about some of the people with whom we're dealing.' He gazed across the marshes to the rolling waves of the sea. 'I never thought we'd harvest so much in this wilderness of yours.'

The anchorite smiled. 'It's no wilderness, my lord.'

'But you're completely alone.'

'I have the birds, I have my Bible and I have God. That's company enough for any man.' He held up his carvings. 'I have these as well.'

'We won't disturb you any longer,' said Coureton.

'I'm very grateful that you came.'

'We felt that you deserved to know what happened to your generous gift to the abbey. Having met you, we can see why you venerate those gold elephants.'

'And now,' said Ralph, 'we'll get on with the task of finding them.'

'Wait, my lord,' said the anchorite, holding up a hand.

Jocelyn Vavasour was torn between the past and the present, reflecting on the person he once was and the strength he drew from the new life he had chosen to lead. He wrestled with his conscience for some time, searching the heavens for counsel. They could see the anguish in his face and the tension in his body. With great reluctance, he eventually came to a decision. He straightened his shoulders. After taking a nostalgic look around the marshes, he walked swiftly back to his hut.

'Give me a few moments,' he said. 'I'm coming with you.'

Drogo the Steward was not entirely without compassion. When he recovered from the shock of finding Clamahoc in the middle of the copse, he carried the man back to his horse and led it slowly homeward, wondering what he might say to his master and speculating on how it would be received. The message was as vivid as the blood on the servant's back. Clamahoc had been unmasked as a spy. Retribution had been severe. Richard de Fontenel had ensured that he would never tell tales of any kind again. When they reached the manor house, Drogo took his passenger around to the stable sand propped him against some sheaves of hay. After reviving the wounded man with a cup of water, he washed away the blood from around his mouth. When he tried to clean the raw wounds on his back, however, he sent Clamahoc into convulsions. The howls of pain were heard by Mauger Livarot as he returned on horsebackfrom his visit.

Leaping down from the saddle, he came to the stables to investigate. 'Who's this?' he demanded, looking down at the tortured figure.

'Clamahoc, my lord,' said his steward.

'Your man in the lord Richard's household?'

'I fear that he's been discovered.'

'How?'

'I'm not quite sure, my lord.'

'Well, ask him!' ordered Livarot.

'He can't tell us,' said the steward. 'His tongue was cut out.'

'What?'

'This is how I found him at the place where we arranged to meet. The truth was beaten out of him before he was silenced for ever. Look at the marks on his back, my lord. It's a wonder that the poor fellow's still alive.'

'Why did you bring him here?'

'He was our man, my lord.'

'Your man, Drogo,' corrected the other harshly. 'He was never mine. And in that state, he's no use to either of us.'

'That's not his fault.'

'Of course it is. He was found out.'

'Only after he'd given us good service.'

'Horses and dogs give me good service,' said Livarot with callous indifference, 'but when they grow old or lame, I nevertheless have them put down at the earliest opportunity. I don't carry burdens.'

'Clamahoc is not exactly a burden.'

'What else is he?'

'Proof of the lord Richard's brutality.'

Livarot snorted. 'As if we needed another example of that!'

'We should report this to the lord sheriff and have the lord Richard arraigned.'

'On what charge?'

'Attempted murder. '

'Talk sense, man,' said the other, grabbing his steward to shake him. 'No murder was attempted here or you'd have found a dead body awaiting you. If everyone who had a servant whipped was reported to Roger Bigot, half the landowners in the county would be held to account. The lord Richard did no more than I'd have done in his place.'

'But he cut out the main's tongue!'

'Can you prove that?' Livarot pointed at the servant. 'Can he?'

'It's self-evident, my lord.'

'All that's evident to me is that this idiot let himself be caught and got his just deserts. Knowing his master, I'd say that Clamahoc got off lightly.'

The servant groaned in agony on the ground. Drogo took pity on him. 'He needs a doctor, my lord.'

'Not at my expense!'

'Those wounds need to be dressed.'

'Don't look to me for sympathy, Drogo. You may feel sorry for the wretch but he's little short of a traitor to me. He betrayed us. Not only have we lost the advantage we had over the lord Richard, he'll want his revenge. And there'll be nobody to warn us when he's coming next time.' He kicked the servant hard and produced another cry of distress. 'Get rid of him.'

'Can't he stay here until he recovers?'

'No!'

'But he's in no fit state to travel.'

'That's not my problem,' said Livarot coldly. 'Get rid of him.' After kicking the wounded man again, he marched out of the stable.

Anxious to hear their news, Gervase Bret was waiting for them in the bailey when they returned late that afternoon. Ralph Delchard and Eustace Coureton dismounted from their horses and removed their iron helms. Both were perspiring freely and their tunics were covered in dust. Their horses were led away by ostlers.

'Well?' asked Gervase. 'Did you find Jocelyn Vavasour?'

'Unfortunately, no,' said Ralph.

'Oh.'

'What we found instead was Jocelyn the Anchorite. He's turned his back on everything he stood for and vowed to pass a contemplative life among the birds. He lives in the remotest part of the marshes.'

'I admire the man,' said Coureton. 'What he's done shows rare courage.'

'Courage or stupidity?'

'A little of both, perhaps, but there's a fine line to be drawn between the two. Be honest, Ralph. Both of us have done impulsive things in battle that were afterwards viewed as acts of bravery. Had they failed, we'd have been condemned for our stupidity.'

'The lord Jocelyn's case is surely different,' said Gervase. 'What he's done is no sudden or impulsive move. He must have brooded on it for a long time.'

'Months, by the sound of it, Gervase.'

'Then he's shown the courage of his convictions. There's no folly involved. Did he seem unhappy or rueful?'

'Quite the opposite. He was at ease with himself.'

Ralph scratched an itch on his neck. 'That's more than I am,' he complained. 'This is no weather for a hauberk. I was almost roasted alive. Come with us, Gervase. I need to change. We'll talk on the way.'

The three of them walked in the direction of the keep, Gervase between his two colleagues. Holding back his own news, he poured out a steady stream of questions.

'Was the journey worthwhile?' he said.

'Yes,' said Ralph. 'It opened our eyes.'

'In what way?'

'Jocelyn the Anchorite told us all sorts of interesting things.'

'About whom?'

'Almost everyone involved in this enquiry,' said Coureton. 'But principally about the lady Adelaide. She's an intriguing woman.'

'Alys and Golde discovered a few things about her themselves.'

'I was hoping they would,' said Ralph. 'We must compare our findings.'

'Was the lord Jocelyn upset to hear about the theft from the abbey?' said Gervase.

'Horrified, but glad to be made aware of the crime.'

'I had a feeling that he might be.'

'It was the one thing that could have got him out of there, Gervase.'

'Out of where?'

'His lonely hut in the marshes,' explained Ralph, as they ascended the rough timber steps to the keep. 'He wants to join in the hunt. He came with us.'

'Then where is he?'

'We dropped him off on the way back at the house of some friends.'

'Yes,' added Coureton. 'We offered to wait for him but he insisted on travelling alone. He was hoping to borrow a horse from his friends.'

'Only a horse?'

'What do you mean, Gervase?'

'Well, I know that he's an anchorite who yearns for solitude, but it's dangerous to ride alone through open country. Might he not also want to borrow some weapons?'

Jocelyn Vavasour made good speed. Unencumbered by armour and riding a fresh horse, he rode south by a different route taken by the two commissioners who had visited him, eager to act on his own without help or supervision. The theft of the holy elephants had stung him badly and spurred him to leave the hut on the marshes where he led his life of self-denial. Since he had brought the gift from Rome in the first place, he felt it his duty to reclaim it on behalf of the abbey and, though he had given Ralph Delchard and Eustace Coureton some guidance, he had not told them everything that might help them. There were lines of enquiry that he wanted to reserve for himself. Riding at a canter throughout the afternoon, he reflected on the details of the theft again, mortified that the treasure he had bestowed on the abbey of St Benet had led to a cruel murder.

His mind had been eased by his penitent existence but the instincts of a soldier had not entirely deserted him. When he saw a stand of oak trees ahead of him, he knew that it would be an inviting place for an ambush and remained vigilant. His alertness saved him. Three men awaited the traveller, lurking in the shadows and seeing a lone rider as easy prey. Though the unkempt stranger did not look as if he would be carrying much money, he sat astride a fine horse that would fetch a good price. They took up their positions. As the anchorite plunged in under the overhanging branches, he found his way blocked by a fallen tree that had been dragged across the track. He slowed his horse to a trot. The robbers pounced at once. One man grabbed the reins of the horse, the second threatened the rider with a dagger and the third tried to haul him from the saddle.

Vavasour reacted violently. Kicking away the man who tried to pull him off, he swung his horse sharply round so that its rump knocked the man with the dagger hard and sent him rolling into the undergrowth. When he saw his confederates lying dazed on the ground, the man holding the reins let go and took flight. Vavasour went after him, overhauling him quickly and delivering a kick to the back of his neck that sent him somersaulting over the grass. He brought his horse to a halt and leapt down from the saddle to run back to the man. Shaken by his fall, the latter hauled himself up and pulled out his dagger to thrust at Vavasour, but the weapon was instantly twisted from his grasp and tossed harmlessly into a ditch. When the man tried to escape, he was held by the shoulders. The anchorite pulled him close and spoke with controlled anger.

'You've committed a sin, my friend,' he said. 'Ask for forgiveness.'

'Who are you?'

'Someone who bears his own burden of sin.'

The other was aghast. 'But you've no weapon to defend yourself.'

Vavasour took him by the scruff of his neck and pitched him back down the track. 'I don't need one when I have God to do that for me,' he said.

A combination of cold water on his face and a warm welcome from his wife helped to revive Ralph Delchard after his long ride. When he joined Gervase Bret in the hall for some refreshment, he was wearing a clean tunic and a bright smile. The two men settled down opposite each other at the table and picked at the food set out for them.

'Golde has just told me about her visit this morning,' said Ralph. 'She felt that the lady Adelaide only wanted them there as a means of checking up on us.'

'Alys was of the same mind.'

'Perhaps it's time that one of us went calling, Gervase.'

'I think that you're the more suited to that task,' said the other with light irony. 'You and the lady Adelaide are already acquainted to some degree. Besides,' he went on, reaching for his mug of ale, 'I want to pay my respects elsewhere.'

'To whom?'

'Olova.'

'But you've already spoken to her.'

'I know, Ralph, but the circumstances were wrong. A second visit will yield much more, I'm certain. Did Golde mention it to you?'

'No. Why should she?'

'Because I'd like to take her with me.'

When he explained his reasons for wanting to do so, Ralph gave his approval at once. Ordinarily, he tried not to involve his wife in work that befell him in the course of an assignment, but he felt that this was a special case.

'Golde's father was a Saxon thegn,' he said. 'She'll be able to talk to this woman on her own terms. In fact, she may get more out of her than you could, Gervase.'

'No question of that.'

'Then it's settled. As long as you take a sizeable escort.'

'I will, Ralph, though I won't ride up to Olova's house with them this time. But tell me more about your encounter with the anchorite. What sort of man is he?'

'A holy fool.'

'Did he explain why he had renounced all his possessions?'

'Yes,' said Ralph, munching a piece of bread. 'Eustace pressed him on that point. I think that the solitary life has a

233

sneaking attraction for our colleague. He could quote Horace at the birds all day long. Though I doubt that he'd have the same skill as a woodcarver.'

'Woodcarver?'

Ralph explained that they had seen wooden replicas of the two elephants that had been stolen from the abbey. He also gave a fuller account of his conversation with the anchorite and speculated on where the man would begin his own search for the stolen property. Gervase waited until he had heard every detail.

'Now I can tell you what I found out,' he said with quiet excitement.'

'How was the lord Richard?'

'Less than welcoming until I introduced Brother Daniel. When he realised that I'd brought the man who actually discovered the corpse of his steward, he showed much more interest. He even managed to display a muted affection for Hermer.'

'That's more than anyone else seems to do, Gervase.'

'I know.'

'Did you challenge the lord Richard about the theft from the abbey?'

'I was more tactful than that. He denied that his gold elephants were the same ones that had been taken but he obviously knew that they were. He was even obliging enough to tell us who stole them for him.'

'Starculf.'

'That was a false name, given to mislead them at the abbey. When he gave us a description of Starculf, I knew that it couldn't possibly have been him.'

'Then who was it?'

'Who else?' said the other. 'Hermer.'

Ralph was astonished. 'Are you sure?'

'More or less. The description you got from the sacristan certainly fits him. And what better guise for Hermer to take on than that of a man he disliked enough to have dismissed? When the theft was uncovered, suspicion naturally fell on Starculf.'

'A clever ruse, Gervase.'

'But an expensive one. It cost Hermer his life.'

'You think *that* was the motive for his murder?'

'I believe that the theft of those elephants was instrumental in bringing it about,' said Gervase, piecing it together in his mind. 'Someone wanted them enough to kill for them. Who knew that they'd gone astray?'

'Only the monks in the abbey. The crime wasn't reported.'

'I can't believe that a Benedictine would commit a murder. In any case, the only reason that a monk would reclaim those elephants would be in order to restore them to the abbey. What we're looking for is someone who's outraged enough by the theft to take revenge on the thief, even to the extent of cutting off the hands that actually stole those holy objects. And yet,' he continued, drinking some ale, 'greedy enough to hold on to the booty himself. In short, we're looking for a human contradiction, Ralph.'

'A monk with a streak of wickedness in him?'

'A killer with a keen moral sense.'

'Where's the morality in murder?'

'He may have seen it as an act of divine retribution.'

'Are you saying that God instructed him to kill and mutilate Hermer?'

'No, Ralph. I'm just wondering if the man we're after confuses good and evil so much that he's unable to tell the difference between them. In meting out punishment for one crime, he doesn't accept that he's committing an even more heinous one. By all accounts,' added Gervase, 'Hermer wasn't a weak man. In order to overpower him, his attacker would have had to be strong and trained to fight.'

'A soldier?'

'With a warped sense of right and wrong.'

Ralph sighed. 'There are plenty of those to choose from, Gervase. God knows, I've met enough of them in my time and so have you. Where do we begin?'

'Let's consult with the lord sheriff first. This is, after all, his investigation.'

'But it has such a direct bearing on the work that brought us here.'

'We still need his permission before we take independent action,' said Gervase. 'I can't see any reason why he'll object to my speaking with Olova once more and he can hardly stop you from paying a visit to the lord Richard.'

'I'm looking forward to that encounter. I've a complaint to make.'

'About what?'

'The way he barged into the hall the other night when I was in the middle of eating. It gave me indigestion, Gervase. And it upset the ladies. Yes,' he said with feeling. 'A meeting between Ralph Delchard and Richard de Fontenel is long overdue.'

Judicael the Goldsmith was scrutinising a gold ring when the customer came into his shop. As soon as he saw who his visitor was, he jumped to his feet and gave an obedient smile, flapping his hands about and emitting a mirthless laugh.

'Good day, my lord.'

'Good day to you,' grunted the other.

'What can I do for you?'

'First of all, you can tell me exactly what you told him.'

'Who, my lord?'

'The man who came asking after a pair of gold elephants.'

Judicael took a step backwards and ran his tongue slowly over dry lips. Richard de Fontenel was glowering at him with cold hostility and he needed to appease him at once. The man was pulsing with impatience.

'His name is Ralph Delchard, my lord,' he said, 'and he's a royal commissioner, lately arrived in Norwich in connection with the Great Survey that's been set in motion.'

'I know all about that,' said the other irritably. 'Just tell me what happened, man. And don't you dare leave anything out, or you'll soon regret it.'

Judicael cringed in fear. 'Yes, my lord.'

In a quavering voice, he recounted all that had passed between himself and Ralph Delchard, hoping to mollify his companion but only succeeding in deepening the man's frown. Richard de Fontenel did not like what he heard. When the goldsmith finished, his visitor leaned in close to him.

'Nobody else must know what I'm about to say to you, Judicael.'

'I understand, my lord.'

'As far as you're concerned, I never even came into your shop.'

'No, my lord.'

'If one word of this conversation ever gets out,' said the other, darkly, 'I'll come looking for you in person. Do you hear? Ralph Delchard and the other commissioners are only in Norwich for a short while. When they leave, I'll still be here.'

Mouth agape, Judicael nodded obligingly. 'Yes, my lord.'

'Who was the man who first told you of those elephants?'

'His name is Heinfrid. He's a goldsmith from Thetford.'

'And he actually visited the abbey of St Benet?'

'Yes, my lord. Heinfrid was invited to take on a commission by the abbot. He has a good reputation. Bishop William has employed him before now.'

'So this Heinfrid was able to give you a good description of those elephants?'

'As exact as only a craftsman could give.'

'What was your reaction?'

'Curiosity, my lord. Followed by a natural envy.'

'Did you wish that you'd created such beautiful objects?'

'Yes, I did. Very much so.'

'Then you may have your opportunity,' said de Fontenel. 'How long would it take you to make something very similar to the elephants described by your friend?'

'It's not a question of time but of ability, my lord. I'd be unequal to the task.'

'Nonsense!'

'I would. I have great skills but they're no match for a Venetian goldsmith. The only man who could even begin to design what you want is Heinfrid. After all, he's seen and held the objects. Why not approach Heinfrid, my lord?'

'Because I want you to have the commission.'

'Heinfrid is the better man.'

'He's also worked for Bishop William and been employed by the abbey. I want nobody with those connections,' said the other, firmly. 'I need someone I can trust, Judicael. Someone who'll work in secret and do exactly what I want.' He gave him a conciliatory smile. 'Set your price. It'll be paid in advance.'

The goldsmith was tempted. Rubbing his hands together, he took a moment to examine the implications. Refusal of the commission would be dangerous, yet acceptance also brought hazards. He feared his customer's reaction if the work were not exactly to his taste and specification. Greed, however, slowly got the better of apprehension. 'I'd have to speak to Heinfrid first, my lord,' he said.

'As long as you don't tell him what you've been asked to do.'

'Oh, no. But he can help me. Perhaps even provide a drawing.'

'Excellent!'

'Only when I see that,' the goldsmith explained, 'can I tell you how long it will take and how much it will cost. When do you want the pieces, my lord?'

'As soon as possible!'

'And I'm to work on them in secret?'

'Discretion is absolutely vital.'

Judicael gave a nervous laugh. 'I think I know why,' he said, grinning. 'It's the reason you don't want Heinfrid of Thetford to have the commission, isn't it? He might spoil the surprise.'

'What are you burbling about, man?'

'Those gold elephants, my lord. You want to present them to the abbey, don't you?'

Richard de Fontenel's expression made him back away.

Anxious to make up lost ground, Drogo went off to find his master as soon as he had something to report. Mauger Livarot was at the rear of the house, testing a new shield he had had made, engaging in mock combat with one of his men and fending off his adversary's sword with deft use of the shield. The steward waited until the clang of iron ceased and the two men stepped apart. He wished that he had not come upon his master when the latter had a weapon in his hand. After dismissing his man-at-arms with a rod, Livarot putdown the shield and turned to his steward.

'I hope you've brought no more bad tidings,' he said.

'No, my lord.'

'Next time one of your spies is caught, leave him to rot where he lies.'

'Yes, my lord. I'm sorry that I brought Clamahoc back here.'

'What have you done with the man?'

'Sent him on his way with food and a little money.'

'More fool you!' sneered the other. 'You're too soft-hearted, Drogo.'

'That's not a complaint you'll be called on to make again,' promised the steward. 'But I've other news. I spoke to the man who trailed the two commissioners. They tracked down Jocelyn Vavasour somewhere near the coast.'

'Why?'

'That I can't say, my lord. It was impossible to get close enough to overhear them. But the visit had an unexpected result, it seems.'

'Unexpected?'

'Yes, my lord,' said Drogo. 'The lord Jocelyn left with them.'

'But he vowed to live as an anchorite.'

'Something they told him made him abandon his hermetic life for a while.'

'We must find out what it was, Drogo.'

'They'll be dining at the castle this evening. I've a man there who might overhear what we need to know. He's among those who'll be serving the guests.'

'Is the lord Jocelyn at the castle as well?'

'Apparently not,' said the other. 'The commissioners returned without him. They parted company with the anchorite on the way.'

'Where did he go?'

'We don't know as yet.'

'What of the lord sheriff?' asked Livarot, sheathing his sword.

'He and his men haven't ridden into the city yet. As soon as they do, I'll have a report on where they went and what they found. Meanwhile,' said Drogo, allowing himself a smirk of self-congratulation, 'I've search parties of our own in action. They, too, should be bringing back news before long.'

'What I want brought back to me is two gold elephants.'

'You'll have them, my lord.'

'I hope so,' said Livarot. 'I need them to honour a promise I gave once again this afternoon. I don't care to disappoint a lady, Drogo. That means we must recover the missing animals before anyone else does. There are too many hounds in this chase – the lord sheriff, his deputy, royal commissioners, Richard de Fontenel – and my fear is that one of them may run the elephants to ground before us. That mustn't happen!'

'We're doing all we can.'

'At all events, they must never he returned to the lord Richard. Take note of that. My plans will be ruined if they are. They're the key to everything.'

'I understand that, my lord.'

'Good.' He cleared his throat and spat on the ground. 'It's such a pity that Clamahoc was caught. We need an eye on the lord Richard.'

'We still have one,' said Drogo, ready to part with what he thought would be the most intriguing piece of information. 'There's a lorimer in the main street below the castle whom I pay to watch who comes and goes. He can be useful at times. While he makes spurs for his customers, he keeps the whole street under surveillance. This afternoon, he saw someone call at a shop not far from his own.'

'Who was it?'

'Richard de Fontenel.'

'What was he doing in Norwich?'

'Visiting a goldsmith.'

Mauger Livarot raised his eyebrows in surprise. The steward gave a snigger.

'I thought you'd be interested to hear that, my lord,' he said.

Ralph Delchard and Gervase Bret were still in the hall when Eustace Coureton joined them. Having taken off his armour, he now wore a fresh tunic and mantle. Though he had a contented smile, he moved rather stiffly and was grateful to lower himself on to a bench near his colleagues.

'My old bones are starting to creak,' he said with a chuckle.

'I had difficulty climbing the stairs to my chamber.'

'Have you been asleep?' asked Ralph.

'No, I refreshed myself by reading for a little while.'

'Horace, no doubt.'

'Cicero, actually. A more cunning politician.'

'Too cunning for his own good in the end,' noted Gervase. 'He was executed.'

'Not before he wrote some sublime speeches and essays.'

'Spare us any quotations from them,' said Ralph, holding up his hands. 'Gervase and I have been comparing what each of us found out today. It's mystifying to me.'

'What is?' asked Coureton.

'The more information we gather, the further away we seem from the man we're after. As for those tiny elephants, we might as well search for an ant in a cornfield. They're so easy to conceal. They could be anywhere.'

'I was musing on them as well, Ralph. We came to Norwich to settle a dispute between two human elephants. At least, that's how Richard de Fontenel and Mauger Livarot seem to me. Big, strong, ungainly creatures who trample everyone in their way and who bellow aloud while they're doing so. Instead of which,' he said, resignedly, 'We're spending our time in pursuit of two small four-footed elephants and I'm coming to the view that, it might be safest for everyone if they're never found.'

'Why do you say that?' asked Gervase.

'I'll tell you later. I don't wish to upset Ralph.'

'With what?'

'Another Latin quotation.'

'Oh, go on,' sighed Ralph. 'I'll steel myself to bear it.'

'*Aurum irrepertum et sic melius situm.*'

'Cicero?'

'Horace.'

'I feared that it might be. Will someone tell me what it means?'

'I'll try,' said Gervase. 'My translation would be, "Gold undiscovered, and all the better for being so." Is that close enough, my lord?'

'I can't fault it,' said Coureton. 'I know that those elephants were blessed by the Pope and brought all the way from Rome but they're leaving havoc in their wake. Our friend, the anchorite, must be regretting he ever bought them.'

'They're holy treasures.'

'That hasn't stopped them being stolen.'

'Twice, my lord. First from the abbey and then from the lord Richard.'

'Did you tell him they'd have to be returned to Abbot Alfwold?'

'Yes,' said Gervase. 'A look of panic came into his eyes. There's no way that he can use them as a wedding gift now. Indeed, if we can prove that he ordered them to be stolen, he won't be in a position to marry anyone.'

Gervase went on to tell Coureton about his earlier visit, abbreviating detail that Ralph had already heard. The old soldier heard it all with philosophical calm. The three men were discussing the implications of what they had learnt when the door opened and Roger Bigot came in. Hot, dusty and tired from several hours in the saddle, he gave them a weary greeting and stood with his hands on his hips.

'I hope that your day has been more fruitful than ours,' he said.

'Very fruitful, my lord sheriff,' said Ralph, cheerily. 'We not only found Jocelyn the Anchorite, we spurred him into joining the search for those elephants.'

'It was Gervase who made the most crucial discovery,' said Coureton. 'When he called on the lord Richard, he found out who stole the objects from the abbey.'

Bigot was startled. 'The lord Richard confessed?'

'On the contrary,' explained Gervase. 'He swore that he bought the wedding gift from a merchant in France. But he unwittingly gave me the name I wanted. It wasn't Starculf who spent the night at the abbey and made off with their treasures.'

'Then who was it?'

'Hermer.'

'He used a false name?'

'Yes, my lord sheriff. So that no trail would lead to his master. I don't think that Starculf went anywhere near the abbey of St Benet.'

'He did, Master Bret. That's the one thing we did learn.'

'Oh?'

'Several sightings have been made of him in the county. Starculf is here without any doubt. I feel it,' he said, ruefully. 'Someone is hiding him.'

Chapter Eleven

Gervase Bret was slightly concerned about his wife. When the visitors dined with their hosts that evening in the hall, Alys was unusually subdued and had little appetite for the rich fare that was served. Though she assured her husband that she was well, he sensed that she was putting on a brave face in order to conceal some malady. Once back in their chamber, however, Alys seemed to recover her spirits at once. She was bright, talkative and almost exuberant. Seeing the anxiety in his eyes, she gave him a kiss and squeezed his arms byway of reassurance.

'Stop worrying about me, Gervase,' she said. 'I feel fine.'

'You didn't appear so in the hall.'

'That was only because I was so shy. You must remember that this is in the nature of an adventure to me. I've never stayed in a castle before as the guest of a sheriff and his wife. I know they've both been very hospitable but I feel a little overwhelmed.'

'You've no need to be, Alys.'

'I'm taking time to get used to the honour.'

'It's no more than you deserve, my love,' he said, fondly. 'Make the most of it in the same way that Golde does. She's always completely at her ease.'

'I do admire her for that, but I'm more reserved than Golde. It was the same when we visited the lady Adelaide. Golde was quite relaxed while I found it an effort to join in the conversation.'

'Why?'

'The lady Adelaide has that effect on me, Gervase. She's so beautiful.'

'Beside you, she's practically invisible,' he said, loyally.

Alys laughed. 'That's not what Ralph thinks – or any of those men who were at the banquet on our first night here. The lady Adelaide enchanted them all in a way that I could never match. It's very sweet of you to flatter me,' she said, beaming gratefully, 'but I won't pretend that I can compete with her. And it wasn't just the lady herself. It's the house where she lives. It's sumptuous, Gervase.'

'Golde found that ostentation rather tasteless.'

'It overpowered me. I felt so small and insignificant.'

'Well, you're neither of those things to me,' he said, enfolding her in his arms. 'I'll admit I had grave doubts about asking you to join me on this visit but they've all faded away now. I'm so glad that you came.'

'Are you?'

'Very glad, my love.'

'Does that mean I can ride out with you tomorrow?'

'Tomorrow?'

'Yes,' she said, smiling. 'Golde has offered to go with you to the Henstead hundred and I want to come as well.'

Gervase hesitated. 'That might not be such a good idea, Alys.'

'Why not?'

'To begin with, it's a taxing ride.'

'No more taxing than the ride from Winchester to Norwich.'

'I don't think you've fully recovered from that yet.'

'Of course I have.'

'I'd rather you stayed here and rested.'

'But I don't want to rest,' she said, breaking away from his embrace. 'I've seen little enough of you during the day since we got here. All that I want to do is to ride beside you, Gervase. If you can take Golde, why reject your own wife?'

'It's not a case of rejection.'

'Then what is it?'

'Diplomacy, my love.'

'I don't understand.'

'But you were there when I explained it,' he reminded her. 'I have to speak to the Saxon woman Olova again.'

'You don't think she was responsible for the crime, surely?'

'No, but I'm convinced she's holding back information that may be valuable to us. She wouldn't divulge it in the presence of lord Eustace but she may do so to another Saxon woman like Golde.'

Alys grew petulant. 'What you're saying is that I'd be in the way.'

'Not at all.'

'Your own wife would be an embarrassment to you.'

'That's not the case at all,' he insisted. 'It's just that you're likely to make Olova feel uncomfortable and that wouldn't serve our purpose at all.'

'Then I'll make sure that she doesn't even see me. It's easily done. When we get there, I'll stay completely out of sight.'

'No, Alys.'

'You just don't want me to go, do you?' she challenged.

'It wouldn't be appropriate, that's all.'

'Is it more appropriate for me to stay here on my own?'

'I'm afraid it is.'

'So you're forbidding me.'

'Of course not.'

'Then why do I feel so hurt and neglected?'

Gervase fell silent as he struggled with the dilemma. To leave his wife behind on the morrow would make her upset and resentful. Taking her with him, however, involved a number of risks, not least of which was that she would distract him from the work in hand.

Gervase knew that he would not be able to concentrate properly if he was worrying about his wife's safety and comfort. He thought about the sad, pale, uncommunicative woman who had sat beside him in the hall earlier on. Alys might be in a more buoyant mood now but along ride that began at dawn would be an ordeal for someone who never enjoyed the most robust health. His wife was putting him to the test. He had to be firm.

'I'm sorry, Alys,' he said calmly, but you'll have to remain here.'

'Why?'

'Because that's what I've decided. You promised that you wouldn't interfere with my work if I let you come to Norfolk with us and you've been scrupulous in keeping that promise until now. There's a conflict here between duty and pleasure. You know which one I must choose.'

'Yes,' she said, gloomily. 'You're always so dutiful.'

'I have to be, Alys. This is no enjoyable ride into the country that we make tomorrow. It's part of a search for the truth about a serious theft and a brutal murder.'

'I know that.'

'And since Olova is also implicated in one of the disputes that we have to settle in the shire hall, it impinges on my work as a royal commissioner. We were appointed by the King himself. He expects diligence and commitment from us.'

Alys was deflated. 'It might have been better if I hadn't come at all.'

'That's not true.'

'But I'll be so lonely tomorrow.'

'Visit the market again. Or take the opportunity to rest.'

'If you say so,' she agreed with a disconsolate nod.

'And you won't be wholly alone. Brother Daniel will be here.'

'What about Ralph? Is he going with you?'

'No,' said Gervase with a smile. 'He'll be confronting another redoubtable woman. Ralph will be calling on the lady Adelaide tomorrow. He thinks it's high time that she knew the truth about the wedding gift she was offered.'

'The two gold elephants?'

'The lord Richard didn't buy them in France at all. They

were deliberately stolen from the abbey of St Benet, much to the chagrin of the man who brought them back from Rome – Jocelyn Vavasour, soldier turned anchorite.'

'He's the man that Ralph and the lord Eustace tracked down today.'

'Yes. He's engaged in a hunt of his own now.'

When he first saw the visitor, Brother Joseph did not even recognise him. Hirsute and ragged, the man knelt in prayer in the empty church and looked more like a beggar than anything else. Compline had long since ended another day at the abbey and most of the monks had retired to their dormitory, but the sacristan had stayed behind to put away all the vestments and holy vessels before sitting in contemplation beside the chest in which the valuables were kept. A scuffling noise had alerted him to the presence of someone in the abbey church. Taking the candle with him, Joseph went quietly into the church and walked silently down the nave. The circle of light suddenly included an unknown man, kneeling in submission before the altar and reciting a prayer to himself in Latin. It was only when the visitor rose to leave and turned to face him that the sacristan had an idea of who he might be.

'Bless my soul!' he said, holding up the candle. 'Is that you, my lord?'

'I answer to no title, Brother Joseph,' said Vavasour. 'I'm plain Jocelyn now.'

'You've changed so since we last met.'

'Outwardly, perhaps. Inwardly, I'm still the same miserable penitent.'

'When did you arrive?'

'Shortly after Compline.'

'I should have been told,' said the sacristan, flapping his arms like a black swan struggling to take flight. 'I could have given you a proper welcome. Come. Let us talk.'

He led the guest into the vestry and offered him a seat. Vavasour preferred to stand, making it clear that it was not a social visit. An outbreak of guilt sent Brother Joseph into a paroxysm of apologies.

'I don't blame you,' said Vavasour, silencing him with a soft touch on his shoulder. 'You couldn't stand guard over those elephants twenty-four hours a day, Brother Joseph. What I wish to hear, from your own lips, is what actually happened.'

The sacristan composed himself before relating details that caused him the utmost distress. Interweaving his account with more apology, he explained how they had no choice but to conclude that the traveller who stayed the night there had been the thief. Vavasour pressed him for a description of the man then shook his head.

'Your guest was lying to you, Brother Joseph. I've met this Starculf and he's not the man you just described to me. Someone was using his name as a convenient disguise.'

'Who would do that?'

'I don't know, but I intend to find out.'

'We were so dismayed that your precious gift went astray, Jocelyn. It grieves me more than I can say. My only consolation is that the lord sheriff is now aware of our loss. He sent a man called Ralph Delchard to the abbey.'

'I've met the lord Ralph. He seems honest and capable.'

'He assured me that the treasures would be found and returned.'

Vavasour was emphatic. 'I'll make sure that they are, Brother Joseph. Nothing else would have torn me away from my little hut in the marshes.' A distant smile showed through the beard. 'I'm very happy there. It's home and church to me.'

'Abbot Alfwold will be delighted to see you.'

'I'll not be able to stay long. My search will begin early.'

'Where will you go?'

'Everywhere.'

'But the lord sheriff and his men have searched in vain so far.'

'I know people and places that they may have overlooked.'

'Those elephants of yours have brought us such joy,' said the sacristan, eyes moist with sadness. 'It's remarkable that something so small can occupy so large a place in our hearts. It's not their value as gold pieces. It's what they represent.'

'The penance of a sinful man.'

'Your pilgrimage to Rome purified you, Jocelyn.'

'Not completely,' sighed the other, 'But I have a second chance of redemption now. If I can recover those little elephants and return them to the abbey, I hope that God will forgive my past misdeeds and offer me His succour. This isn't simply a search for missing property, Brother Joseph,' he declared. 'It's a mission.'

It was a dry morning but dark clouds obscured the sun and held the threat of rain. As he rode through the outer edges of the estate, Ralph Delchard looked up at the sky.

'I hope that we're not in for bad weather,' he sighed. 'Gervase and Golde have a long ride ahead of them this morning. They'll be soaked to the skin.'

'It may hold off,' said Eustace Coureton. 'If it doesn't, we'll get wet as well. It would be a great pity if two royal commissioners turn up at the lady Adelaide's door looking like a pair of drowned rats. She'd refuse to admit us.'

'She's far too gracious to turn us away, Eustace.'

'How gracious will she be when she has heard what we have to say?' Ralph grinned. 'It'll be interesting to find out.'

With four men by way of an escort, they rode at a brisk trot so that they could take stock of the land through which they were passing. Dispensing with their hauberks for such a relatively short journey, they wore bright tunics under their mantles. Verdant pasture stretched out to their left, dotted with hundreds of sheep who were in skittish mood. Harvesting was taking place in the fields to their right, the men so busy with their scythes and sickles that they did not even raise their heads to look at the passing riders.

The two commissioners continued on their way until the house finally came into view. Ralph emitted a whistle of admiration. 'Now I can see what Golde meant when she said that it was magnificent.'

'Yes,' said Coureton. 'Rather more so than the anchorite's hut.'

'That had a certain charm,' observed Ralph with light sarcasm. 'Not that it worked on me, I hasten to say.'

'Doesn't self-denial have any attraction for you?'

'Only when it's practised by someone else.'

'I don't think you'll find the lady Adelaide is an example of it.'

'I agree. At heart, I fancy that she's something of a sybarite.'

When they got closer, servants come out to take charge of their horses while they went inside. Concealing her surprise at their sudden arrival, the lady Adelaide welcomed them into the parlour as if they were expected guests. They were offered seats and refreshment soon arrived. The conversation had a neutral tone to it at first.

The lady Adelaide occupied a chair that was built like a small throne. 'I was so pleased that your wife could visit me yesterday, my lord,' she said.

'Yes,' replied Ralph. 'Golde had a very enjoyable time.'

'I'm glad to hear that.'

'She was impressed with your lovely house but even more impressed with you.'

'Indeed?' said the other with a self-deprecating laugh. 'There was no reason.'

'It was kind of you to invite her and Alys to call on you.'

'I wanted to be able to speak to them both at leisure. It was a pleasure to get to know them a little better and, indirectly, to learn more about you and your colleague, my lord. You're honoured guests in Norwich.'

'Even though we came at an awkward time?' asked Coureton.

'A grisly murder is hardly a cordial welcome,' she agreed, quietly.

'That's what brought us here today,' said Ralph, becoming serious. 'The murder and the crime that preceded it. I understand that you were present in the lord Richard's house when those gold elephants disappeared?'

'Yes, my lord. It was a great shock to both of us.'

'Did you know where the gift actually came from?'

'Somewhere abroad,' she said. 'The lord Richard brought them back when he returned from Normandy. They were exquisite.'

'So we're given to understand.'

'I'm surprised that anyone was ready to part with them.'

'They weren't, my lady,' said Ralph, choosing his words. 'The lord Richard was correct to say that they came from abroad. The objects were made in Venice and sold in Rome before being presented to the abbey of St Benet at Holme.'

She was astonished. 'That can't be true.'

'I had the story from the abbot himself, my lady. Yesterday, we met the man who actually offered the elephants to the abbey as a gift. His name is Jocelyn Vavasour.'

'The lord Jocelyn?'

'He's forfeited his lands and become an anchorite.'

'I know. It caused us great amazement.'

'Why was that?'

'Jocelyn Vavasour was hardly the most devout Christian, my lord. He was only happy when he was fighting a battle or laying a siege. My husband and I entertained him here more than once. He was a strange, restless, uneasy guest. I heard tales about his going to Rome but I had no idea that he brought back a gift for the abbey.' A thought made her sit up. 'Is the lord Richard aware of this?'

'He is now, my lady.'

'I understood that he bought those elephants abroad.'

'He may very well have done so,' said Ralph, careful not

to tell her too much. 'He obviously didn't realise that what he acquired in good faith was, in fact, stolen property.'

'I see.'

She retained her composure but her mind was racing. Profound disappointment surged inside her. The gold elephants she coveted might never be hers now. If they were taken from the abbey, they would have to be returned there. Anger soon followed. The wedding gift that was dangled in front of her was no more than the booty from a monastic house and she sensed that her suitor must have known that. What remaining appeal the lord Richard still had now withered swiftly away. Curiosity soon took over. Mauger Livarot had given a pledge to recover the objects for her. Was he trying to buy her affection with stolen goods or was he unaware of their true origin? If ignorant, would he still continue his search when he knew the facts of the case? In the space of a few seconds, her attitude to both of her wooers underwent a transformation.

'How well did you know the lord Richard's steward?' asked Ralph.

'His steward?' She came out of her reverie. 'Quite well, my lord. It was Hermer who brought the wedding gift in on a platter.' She pursed her lips and shook her head. 'It was the last time that I saw him alive.'

'How would you describe him?'

'He was a conscientious man who did his job well. The lord Richard wouldn't have employed him in the office otherwise. He had complete faith in Hermer.'

'Until the man's corpse turned up, that is,' said Coureton. 'He lost all faith in his steward then, my lady, and accused him of stealing the elephants from him. I think he's learnt that Hermer was innocent of that crime.'

'If not, perhaps, of others,' resumed Ralph. 'What about his assistant, my lady?'

'Starculf?'

'I believe that you recommended him to the lord Richard.'

'That's true,' she said, airily. 'I'd no use for the man's skills after my husband died. I don't hunt myself and I knew that Richard de Fontenel was looking for a new falconer so I put in a word for Starculf.'

'Was he a good man?'

'My husband always found him so. Strong, reliable and intelligent.'

'He must have given sterling service if he was promoted by the lord Richard.'

'Yes, my lord.'

'And yet he was dismissed soon after.'

'I was sorry to hear that.'

'Do you know what caused the rift with Hermer?'

'No, my lord. It was none of my business. Why should it be?'

'Because it was you who recommended Starculf in the first place,' said Ralph, noting the way her hands had tightened slightly in her lap. 'I would have thought you'd show some interest in his fate. Indeed, I'd expect the man to turn to you for help.'

'I can assure you that he didn't,' she said briskly.

'Even though you were probably the one person who might assist him?'

'Starculf was my husband's falconer, my lord. I hardly knew him.'

'You knew him well enough to suggest his name to the lord Richard and he's the sort of man who expects the highest standards from anyone in his service. I can't believe that you'd recommend someone you hadn't met and liked.'

'I had met him,' she admitted. 'And I knew his pedigree.'

'What of his character?' said Coureton. 'Was he a violent man?'

'Not to my knowledge.'

'Did you see any change in him when he worked with Hermer?'

'Why are we talking about Starculf?' she said with irritation. 'He left the area some time ago, my lord, for reasons that are quite unconnected with me. I've no opinion to offer on the man beyond the fact that he served my husband well.'

'Let's go back to the two gold elephants,' suggested Ralph. 'Until we met Jocelyn the Anchorite, we couldn't understand their appeal. Then he showed us some replicas he was carving out of driftwood. They were adorable creatures.'

'Prime examples of a goldsmith's art.'

'And blessed by the Pope,' said Ralph, piously. 'Did we mention that?'

'No, my lord.'

'That's why they were presented to the abbey. As holy objects.'

She inhaled deeply before speaking. 'I was quite unaware of that.'

'I'm sure you were,' he continued. 'If you had not been,

you'd have been horrified when the lord Richard offered them to you as a wedding gift. You'd have demanded that they be returned to the abbey immediately.'

'Of course.'

'I can't imagine that you'd accept anything that bore the slightest taint.'

'That's quite right, my lord,' she said, levelly. 'I, too, have high standards.'

Her manner had become condescending. Ralph resorted to bluntness. 'High standards, my lady?'

'Extremely high.'

'Then why did you consider marriage to Richard de Fontenel?'

The travellers were fortunate. Though the sky remained dark, only one shower actually broke out and they were able to shelter from it beneath the overhanging branches of a tree. When the rain eased off, they emerged to continue their journey with more urgency.

Gervase Bret did not make the same mistake twice. The six men who escorted them were left a short distance away from the destination. Gervase and Golde proceeded on alone until they came to the circle of thatched huts. More inhabitants were visible this time. Skalp was trying to repair one of the derelict dwellings with the help of a much older man. A third man was hacking at a length of timber with his axe. Two small children were playing in the long grass. A young woman was weaving a basket. An older one was waddling off to feed the chickens. Everyone looked up as the strangers rode into the little encampment but there was less hostility this time. Ambling forward towards them, Skalp showed more curiosity than antagonism.

'Why've you come back?' he asked.

'To see Olova again.' said Gervase.

'We can't help you.'

'You can if you try, Skalp.'

The young Saxon indicated Golde. 'Who's this?'

'A friend of mine.'

'Why have you brought her?'

'Come with us and you'll find out.' said Gervase, easily. 'You can sit in Olova's hut with us this time. There's no need to lurk outside to listen.'

Skalp's eyes flashed but he bit back a comment. He followed them across to the largest of the huts. Gervase dismounted and helped Golde down from the saddle. On his advice, she was not wearing the fine apparel that befitted the wife of a Norman lord but had chosen more homespun garments, comfortable for the journey and reminiscent of the clothing she had worn when she lived in Hereford. Olova stepped outside to give them a wary greeting and to be introduced to Golde. The visitors were invited into her hut. When Skalp tried to follow, a nod from his grandmother sent him back to his work. Inside the musty hut, the guests were waved to seats.

Olova settled into her own chair and gave them a stern warning. 'I hope that you've not come to insult me as well, Master Bret.'

'Insult you?'

'That's what my other visitor did.'

261

'When?'

'Not long ago. If you'd come earlier, you'd have caught him here.'

'Did he give a name?'

'Jocelyn the Anchorite,' she said, chewing on bare gums. 'I think that's what it was. He didn't speak our language as well as you.'

'It's my language as well.'

'And mine.' added Golde. 'How did this man insult you?'

'He told us about a theft from the abbey,' said Olova.

'I tried to do that myself.' Gervase reminded her, 'but you wouldn't listen to me.'

'I wouldn't listen to this man and it made him very angry. I thought that an anchorite was a man of peace but this one had more of a warrior about him. When I wouldn't tell him what he wanted, he more or less accused me of having taken those holy objects myself. That was an insult. I may loathe the abbey for the way it treated me but I'd never steal property from consecrated ground.'

'I'm sure that you wouldn't.'

'We're God-fearing people, Master Bret. We're not thieves like the Normans.'

'Not all Normans steal,' said Golde.

'Some of them stole our land, that's all I know. I told that to the anchorite.'

'What was his reply?'

'That he was ashamed of his own part in the pillaging. He'd been a Norman lord himself and grabbed his share of property along with all the other vultures. At least, he had the grace to say that it was unjust. I admired him for that.' Her voice darkened. 'But I won't forgive him for insulting me like that.'

'Why did he come to you in the first place?' said Gervase.

'He was looking for the man that you mentioned.'

'Starculf?'

'The anchorite had heard rumours that he'd been seen in this area.'

'And has he?'

'Not that I know, Master Bret. It's more likely that someone was up to mischief when they sent the Norman here. We have enemies. This is the kind of thing they do. I don't believe that Starculf is within a hundred miles of here.'

'Jocelyn is after the wrong man.'

'How do you know?'

'Starculf didn't steal those treasures from, the abbey.'

'Then who did?'

'Hermer the Steward.'

A look of sheer contempt came into her eye but she said nothing. Gervase nudged Golde. On the journey from Norwich, they had already discussed how to approach the old woman. Golde gave a sympathetic smile and leant forward.

'I can understand how you feel,' she said with quiet sincerity. 'My father was a thegn in Herefordshire with five manors to his name. We lost them all. I was married off to a brewer. It wasn't what my father had hoped for me. He died a bitter and disappointed man.'

'My husband didn't live to see the worst of it. I thank God for that.'

'We can't change the past, I'm afraid. We just have to accept it.'

'You might do that but I won't. I'll fight to get some of my land back.'

'You're perfectly entitled to do that,' Gervase put in.

'But that's not what brought us here,' resumed Golde. 'You know that Hermer was killed and I can see why you shed no tears at his passing, but even the murder of a bad man must be paid for, Olova. The taking of life is a crime.'

'I know that.'

'Then help us to find his killer.'

'What can I do?'

'Tell us why you hate the man so much.'

'I hate anyone who steals land from me.' said the old woman, bitterly.

'Hermer was only a servant of someone else. He didn't have the land for himself. I think there's another reason why you despise him so much.' Olova turned away. 'We have to know what it is.' Coaxed Golde. 'Did Hermer threaten you or beat any of the family? We know he was cruel. We met an old man called Alstan who'd been whipped by Hermer and chased off the lord Richard's land. What did Hermer do to you?'

Olova looked first at Golde, then at Gervase. She forced herself to speak. 'If I tell you, will you leave me alone for good?'

'We swear it!' vowed Gervase.

Golde nodded gently. 'You have our word, Olova.'

The old woman was still unconvinced. She regarded them both with a mixture of suspicion and interest, unwilling to trust them yet sensing a distant bond with them. It was minutes before she spoke, hands clutched tight and voice almost a whisper.

'You called Hermer a bad man,' she began, biting her lip.

'You never met him. He wasn't bad – he was evil. Whoever killed him rid the world of an affliction. I'm not just speaking about his work for the lord Richard, though that gave him the power that he wanted. Power to bully, cheat and rob at wall. But there was something else.'

'What was it?' asked Golde.

'Something that will take him straight to hell.'

'Cruelty?'

'Lust!' said the other woman. 'A lust that burnt inside him like a fire. We'd all heard the stories about him. Hermer took what he wanted wherever he could find it. If a young widow could not pay her rent, Hermer would exact payment of another kind. If someone caught his eye, he'd stalk her carefully for months until he had his way.' She winced as if feeling a sudden pain. 'Then Aelfeva came to live with us.'

'Aelfeva?'

'Her parents died and she had no kinfolk apart from us. We took her in. A sweet, innocent girl of no more than sixteen summers. But she wanted no favours.' said Olova. 'She worked hard and did more than her share of chores. Aelfeva was a joy to have around. She became part of the family. Until he laid eyes on her.'

'Hermer?'

'Whenever he was in this hundred, he made an excuse to call here to see Aelfeva. He stalked her until the poor girl was in a state of terror. Whenever he came, she'd run away and hide.' Olova let out another sigh and her body sagged. 'That was her undoing.'

'Hermer found her hiding-place?' said Gervase.

'He did more than that, Master Bret. He violated the girl. We heard the screams from half a mile away. By the time we got there, of course, he'd ridden off. Aelfeva was in a terrible state. She cried for days.'

'Didn't you report the crime?' said Golde, smarting with indignation.

'To whom?'

'The lord sheriff.'

'What was the point?' retorted the old woman. 'If we'd accused Hermer, his master would have lied on his behalf. Who'd believe the word of a young girl over that of a Norman lord? There was nothing that we could do – except remember it,' she added with a glint in her eye. 'Besides, Aelfeva wasn't able to bring a charge against him. The shame of it was too much for her. A few days later, she drowned herself. Skalp found her body floating downstream. He was heartbroken – it was a tragedy.' She looked at Gervase. 'Can you see now why I thanked God when I heard that that devil had been killed?'

'Yes,' he said, 'and I'm very grateful that you explained it to us. I can see how difficult it was for you, Olova. But it's not the end of the story, is it?'

'What do you mean?'

'I think there's more.'

'No, there isn't.'

'Let's hear it all, please.'

'You already have.'

'Tell us,' he persisted. 'It's to do with Starculf, isn't it?'

She went off into a flurry of denials but Gervase was not deflected. 'It could be important, Olova. We must know the

266

full truth. It's the only way we can solve this crime.' She glared at him but her anger was tempered by wistfulness. 'Once you've told us, we'll leave at once,' he said quietly. 'That's a promise.'

There was a long pause. Her breathing became heavier. She weighed her words. 'I did know Starculf,' she said at length. 'He came here to apologise.'

'Apologise?'

'For what Hermer had done to Aelfeva. Some time after he got back, Hermer boasted about it to his assistant. Starculf was a hard man but he was an honest one as well. He taxed Hermer with what he'd done to the girl and ordered him to make amends.' She gave a snort of anger. 'How can anyone atone for what he did to her?'

'Is that how the two men fell out?' said Gervase.

'Yes. Starculf was dismissed and driven out. He came straight here, hoping to offer his sympathy to Aelfeva, but we'd already buried her by then. Suicides don't lie in consecrated ground, Master Bret. It was one more indignity for the girl to suffer.'

'What did Starculf do?'

'Apologised to us and swore to take revenge on our behalf.'

'Was that the last time you saw him?'

'Yes,' she said. 'And the last time I wanted to see him. He'd only remind me of what happened to Aelfeva and I can't bear to think about that.' She stood up abruptly. 'I want you to go, Master Bret. I want you both to leave now.'

'Of course,' he agreed, getting up and helping Golde to her feet. 'I'm sorry that you had to confront some painful memories but you've been a great help to us. Thank you, Olova. What you've told us explains a lot.'

'Just go,' said the old woman, almost pushing them out.

They bade her farewell and left the hut, hearing the sound of her sobbing as they walked away. The other inhabitants were still engaged in their work or play. Skalp was using a heavy stone to hammer a timber support into position. He spared only a glance as Gervase went past, escorting Golde on his arm. A minute later, their horses were heard setting off in the direction from which they had come. Skalp waited until the sound of hoofbeats died away before ambling slowly across to a clump of bushes near the stream.

'You can come out now, Starculf,' he said. 'They've gone.'

Roger Bigot arrived back at the castle with his men as the two commissioners were dismounting from their horses in the bailey. The sheriff joined them and dropped down from the saddle.

'Did you enjoy your visit to the lady Adelaide?' he asked.

'Yes,' said Ralph. 'I think we enjoyed it far more than she did.'

'That was your fault,' said Coureton with a chuckle.

'She was patronising us. I wasn't going to stand for that. When she boasted that she had extremely high standards, I asked her why she was considering Richard de Fontenel as a husband.'

The sheriff laughed. 'I can see why that upset her.'

'It was a fair question, my lord sheriff.'

'I dare say that it earned you a warm reply.'

'It did,' said Ralph with amusement. 'But I just wanted to know why the lady Adelaide would even look at someone as disreputable as the lord Richard. Or, for that matter, at someone as devious as Mauger Livarot.'

'They're the only choices available to her.'

'You mean she's so desperate to be married that she'd rather take on a confirmed reprobate than remain a widow?'

'No,' said Bigot, 'I mean that the lady Adelaide enjoys the idea of being wooed even if her suitors are not perhaps the most ideal of men. She's kept the two of them at bay for several months now. I'm not sure that she'll commit herself to either.'

'I'd not put money on the lord Richard's chances,' said Coureton.

'Why not?'

'She was shocked to hear that the gold elephants came from the abbey.'

'Did you tell her that we know who stole them?'

'No, my lord sheriff,' said Ralph. 'The lady Adelaide doesn't know that Hermer took them on behalf of his master. I thought it better to let her reach her own conclusions.'

Coureton grinned. 'And she did. I could see it in her face.'

'So could I, Eustace. The lord Richard's hopes have foundered. I'd love to be there when she confronts him. The lady Adelaide has a sharp tongue when she's roused, as we found out ourselves.'

'What else did you learn?' asked the sheriff.

Ralph gave full details of their visit, drawing particular attention to the discomfort she had shown when questioned about Starculf. Bigot listened with interest. When Ralph had finished, the sheriff passed on his own news.

'There've been more sightings of Starculf,' he announced. 'I still have search parties out looking for him. We know that he's in the area and has been for some time.'

'How did you find that out, my lord sheriff?' asked Coureton.

'From a locksmith in Wymondham.'

'Locksmith?'

'Yes, my lord. What puzzled me was how the man who stole the elephants and abducted Hermer actually got into the house. He must have had a key. The first thing I did, naturally, was to check on the locksmiths in Norwich itself to see if any had done work recently that might possibly be connected with the lord Richard's house. None of them had. So we widened our search to Wymondham.'

'I remember seeing that name in our returns,' said Coureton. 'Its fortunes seem to have taken a turn for the worse. Sixty plough teams are recorded in 1066 but little more than a third of that number now survive.'

'The town was much reduced in size in the wake of the Earl Ralph's rebellion,' explained Bigot. 'Wymondham suffered more than most from that unfortunate business. But it still supports a few locksmiths and we spoke to all of them.'

'Profitably, it seems.'

'One was given a commission a fortnight ago to make two keys for a young man who wanted them in a hurry. The locksmith remembers how intense he was. The customer didn't live in the town. He gave his name as Alstan.'

'Alstan?'

'But that was the name of the old man we met on our way here,' remembered Ralph. 'A slave from the lord Richard's estate. Whipped and driven out.'

'That's perhaps where he got the name from,' said Bigot. 'The locksmith had the feeling that there was something odd about the man. But he did the work nevertheless and handed the two keys over to him. Alstan paid him and left.'

'Did the locksmith give you a description of him?'

'A good description, my lord. I think that the customer was Starculf.'

'What was he doing in Wymondham?'

'Having duplicates made of keys to the lord Richard's estate. At least, that's what I believe. The time is critical,' reasoned Bigot. 'Two weeks ago, the lord Richard was still in Normandy. That would have been the perfect time for someone to break into his house to borrow his keys. Starculf knew the premises well. He wanted the duplicates made in a hurry so that he could return the originals before the lord Richard came back.'

'That makes sense.' opined Coureton.

'Not necessarily.' said Ralph, slowly. 'Consider his purpose. Starculf needed those duplicates so that he could have access to the house in order to kill Hermer. Why wait so long until he did so? Why not attack the steward when he returned the stolen keys to the house?'

'Because Hermer wasn't there, my lord.'

'Where was he?'

'Spending the night at the abbey in order to make off with the elephants. Before that, he was absent for some days, visiting his master's estates in the hundreds of East Flegg and Walsham. Don't you see?' Bigot went on. 'Starculf deliberately chose a time when neither the lord Richard nor his steward was at home.'

'But how could he possibly know they'd both be absent?'

'By waiting and watching. Starculf is a cunning man.'

'I can appreciate that.' said Ralph. 'He must have guessed that you'd talk to all the locksmiths in Norwich so he had the work done some distance away. And now I come to think of it there's another reason why he didn't kill Hermer earlier.'

'What is it, my lord?'

'He wanted the lord Richard to be there. To be shocked by the discovery. To suffer. Look at the way he sent the steward's hands back in a box. That, too, was meant as a taunt to his former master. The only thing I don't understand,' Ralph admitted, rubbing his chin, 'is why he stole the elephants, Starculf couldn't possibly have known they'd be in the house.'

'There are lots of questions still to be answered,' said Bigot, solemnly, 'but I feel that the villain is now identified beyond any doubt. Starculf is the killer and he's still somewhere in the county.'

'Are all the main roads being watched?'

'Yes, my lord. The net is closing in on him.'

The storm caught them in open country. Alerted by the first rumble of thunder, the posse increased its speed to a gallop as it tried to outrun the threatened downpour. No cover offered itself. A second rumble of thunder was followed by a flash of lightning that made the horses neigh and roll their eyes. Rain soon followed, a heavy, relentless, blinding downpour that soaked them within seconds and formed puddles on the track. The sheriffs officers had an important task to do but they could not perform it in the middle of a thunderstorm. When a hamlet finally appeared ahead of them, they drew extra speed from their horses with a jab of their spurs. Bent low in their saddles, they rode on through the swirling rain and cursed aloud as another flash of lightning illumined their plight.

The man hiding in the ditch curled himself into a ball until all the horsemen had charged past. It was the third posse he had encountered in the past few hours. Travelling on foot slowed him down but it made it easier for him to move unseen in the ditches or behind hedgerows. He waited until the drumming of hooves was drowned out by another roll of thunder before he hauled himself out of the little stream that was forming around his ankles. Nobody would search for him in that deluge. It was a welcome friend. Lashed by the rain, Starculf broke into a loping run and headed due east.

Chapter Twelve

On the last stage of their journey back to Norwich, their luck finally ran out and they were soaked bv torrential rain. Gervase Bret was not dismayed, feeling that his second visit to Olova was well worth being caught in a violent storm, but he was sorry that Golde had to suffer alongside him. It was some time before they could find shelter and it was far too late by then. They were well and truly sodden. Capricious clouds eventually cleared to allow the sun to peer inquisitively through but the damage had already been done. It was a wet and dispirited troop that Gervase led back into Norwich castle.

After conducting Golde to her apartment, he went off to change out of his damp clothing. Alys was waiting for him in their chamber.

'Gervase!' she exclaimed as he entered. 'You're dripping wet!'

'I don't need you to tell me that, Alys.'

'You look as if you've been swimming.'

'It felt rather like that.'

'What happened?'

'We were caught in the rain three or four miles south of here. The skies opened. It could have been worse, I suppose,' he said, starting to take off his things. 'We might have been drenched on the way there.'

'Did you see Olova?'

'We did.'

'Were you able to get the information you wanted?'

'I got even more than I dared to expect, Alys. I'm so glad I went back.'

'And I'm so glad that I stayed here,' she confessed, looking at his bedraggled condition. 'It was a long day here but at least I was dry. We heard thunder in the distance earlier on. I was afraid that you'd get struck by lightning.'

'I was,' he said, fondly. 'The day I met you.'

She moved in to give him a kiss then recoiled at the soggy touch of his apparel. Gervase laughed. While he continued to undress, she told him about the pleasant time she had spent with Brother Daniel during his absence and apologised for being so difficult when he insisted on travelling without her.

'I can see now that it wasn't my place to go with you, Gervase,' she said. 'Am I forgiven?'

'There's nothing to forgive, my love.'

'The truth is that I felt so very tired today.'

'Did you manage to get any sleep?'

'Yes, this afternoon.'

'You couldn't have done that on horseback.'

'I know,' she said, cheerfully. 'All things considered, I was better off here.'

Gervase was pleased at the way in which she had come to accept the situation. A sincere apology made for a warmer welcome than would a sharp rebuke for leaving his wife behind. When he had put on dry attire, he gave her a hug of gratitude. Knowing that he would not divulge them, Alys had sensibly not pressed him for details of what he had learnt on his visit. That, too, earned his thanks. By the time they adjourned to the hall to join the others, they had put their disagreement completely behind them.

The visitors were dining with the sheriff and his wife, attentive hosts who made sure that their guests lacked for nothing. Brother Daniel ate with them again, appetite heartier than ever, mind alert to engage in any friendly debate that arose. Golde seemed to have recovered from the exhausting ride, having shed her wet garments and looking resplendent in a blue chemise and gown. While Eustace Coureton amused the ladies with a succession of anecdotes about his own wife, Gervase took the opportunity to pass on his news to Ralph Delchard and Roger Bigot, hearing in turn what progress each of them had made with their enquiries. The sheriff was interested to hear that Olova had actually met Starculf.

'What sort of man risks his place by castigating the steward under whom he works?' he said, thoughtfully. 'A brave one, surely.'

'And an honourable one,' added Gervase. 'The argument between them arose because Hermer boasted about violating Aelfeva, a defenceless girl whom he'd stalked. Starculf was outraged on her behalf.'

'Yes,' added Ralph. 'Even to the extent of finding the victim's kinfolk in order to apologise to them. Starculf is a considerate man.'

'He's a murderer,' said Bigot, sternly. 'He showed little consideration to Hermer.'

'How much consideration did Hermer show to that girl?'

'That's not the point at issue, my lord.'

'Starculf was provoked by what the steward did.'

'It doesn't excuse his own actions.'

'No, my lord sheriff,' agreed Gervase, 'But it does suggest that Starculf is a man with a strong moral sense. It may have driven him to extremes but it can't be entirely ignored. I'd like to meet him.'

'You will, Master Bret. When my men arrest him.'

'Where are they searching?'

'All over the county. The main roads are being watched to cut off his escape.'

'What about the ports?'

'Word has been sent to all of them. A reward has been offered for information leading to the capture of Starculf. It's only a matter of time before we take him.'

'I wonder how the lady Adelaide will react.' said Ralph.

'She'll rejoice at the arrest of a killer.' replied Gervase.

'Oh, I think she'll be pleased that the crime is solved but I suspect she'll wish that the perpetrator were anybody but Starculf. She liked the fellow, I could tell, and knew him far better than she was prepared to admit. Though she'll deplore what he did, I fancy that the lady Adelaide will show him a little sympathy as well.'

The sheriff was brusque. 'That's more than I'll do!'

'Or me,' said Ralph evenly. 'But the lord Eustace and I were both struck by the way she talked about Starculf. Her denials were far too hot to be taken seriously.'

'The lady Adelaide won't have all that much sympathy for him.' said Gervase. 'Had it not been for Starculf, she might now be the owner of the gold elephants she covets so much. If the murder had not occurred, the earlier theft of the treasures might never have come to light and she would have regarded herself as their rightful owner. Instead of which, she now knows that they're beyond her reach.'

'Yes, Gervase. They'll be returned to the abbey.'

'As a wedding present, they're null and void.'

Ralph chuckled. 'That puts paid to the lord Richard's hopes.'

'But it raises an interesting question.' noted Gervase. 'Now that Richard de Fontenel is no longer a possible suitor, will the lady Adelaide turn to his rival? Are we to hear the announcement of a marriage between her and the lord Mauger?'

'That depends on what he has to offer.'

The blow was so hard that it sent him reeling backwards until his body slammed against the wall. All the breath was knocked out of Judicael the Goldsmith.

'Tell me!' demanded Mauger Livarot.

'My lord,' gasped the other, shaking with fear. 'Don't strike me again.'

'I won't use a fist next time,' warned Livarot, drawing his dagger.'

'Now, speak!'

Judicael shook his head. 'I can't, my lord.'

'Yes, you can.'

'I gave my word.'

'Who cares about that?'

'I do.' whimpered the other. 'I have to. I'm a craftsman. My customers trust me. If I abuse that trust, I lose their faith.'

'You'll lose more than that if you continue to defy me!'

Livarot brandished the dagger and the goldsmith cowered against the wall. It had been the worst possible start to a new day for Judicael. No sooner had he opened his shop than Mauger Livarot burst into it, demanding private information and threatening violence if it were not forthcoming. Impatient and irascible, he had already demonstrated his readiness to resort to physical assault. Judicael was neither brave nor resourceful. He lacked the courage to stand up to his visitor or the guile with which to talk himself out of his predicament. The blow across his face had not only shocked him and left the first tentative signs of a bruise, it made him fear for the safety of his hands, the essential tools of his trade. If his truculent customer were to inflict serious damage on them, Judicael's occupation would be gone.

Standing up straight, he made a doomed effort to assert himself. 'If you come any closer.' he said, 'I'll report this to the lord sheriff.'

'Go on, then.' taunted Livarot, blocking his way.

'I must ask you to leave the premises, my lord.'

'What if I refuse?'

'*Please!*' he begged.

'Not until you tell me what I came here to find out.'

'That's impossible, my lord.'

'I won't wait much longer, Judicael.'

The goldsmith tried to sound firm. 'I'll be forced to summon the lord sheriff.'

'Will you?'

'Yes, my lord.'

'And what will you tell him?'

'That you assaulted me for no reason at all.'

'But I've a very good reason.'

'My lord—'

'And you're giving me an even better one,' continued Livarot, jabbing the point of his dagger at the man's throat to pin him against the wall. 'You won't be able to say much to Roger Bigot if I slice that ugly head of yours from its fat body.'

'No, no!' pleaded Judicael.

'Then answer my question.'

'It's more than my life is worth.'

'You won't have a life if you don't tell me the truth.'

'You've no right to treat me this way.'

'Try stopping me.'

'I implore you, my lord. Leave me be.'

'Only when you have the sense to tell me.' His dagger pricked the goldsmith's neck hard enough to draw blood and to instil terror. Eyes bulging and mouth agape, Judicael was now running with sweat. There was no way out. Mauger Livarot would not be denied. The goldsmith gently touched the scratch on his throat and saw the blood on his finger. He shuddered.

'You're asking me to break a confidence.' he said, weakly.

'No, Judicael. I'm ordering you to do it.' A second jab with the dagger produced a yelp of pain. 'You had a visit from the lord Richard yesterday. I have a witness who saw him come into your shop. He'd not take the trouble to ride all the way here unless it was on important business. What was that business?'

'It's a confidential matter.'

'The lord Richard brought you a commission, didn't he?'

The dagger drew more blood from his throat and Judicael capitulated. 'Yes, my lord,' he said, trying to stem the flow with a hand.

'Well?'

'He asked me to make something for him.'

'Some jewellery, perhaps?'

'Two gold elephants.'

'Elephants!' repeated Livarot. 'Are you sure?'

'The commission was very specific, my lord,' said Judicael, relieved that the dagger had now been lowered from his neck. 'The lord Richard had two miniature elephants stolen from his house recently. They were crafted out of solid gold by a Venetian master. The lord Richard wanted exact copies to be made.'

'How could you possibly do that?'

'By taking details from another goldsmith who actually saw the objects.'

'At the lord Richard's house?'

'No, my lord,' said Judicael. 'At the abbey of St Benet at Holme.'

Mauger Livarot needed a moment to absorb the shock of the announcement. 'Did I hear you aright?' he said, dagger lifting again. 'Are you telling me that these gold elephants belonged to the abbey?'

'They were holy objects, brought back from Rome.'

'Then how did they come into the lord Richard's greedy hands?'

'I don't know, my lord.'

'Did he buy them from the abbey?'

'Hardly,' said the other. 'Abbot Alfwold would never part with holy treasures. How they went astray, I've no idea. But when they're found, the lord sheriff will no doubt restore them to their rightful owner.'

Livarot was not sure whether to be pleased or annoyed at the tidings. 'Did the lord Richard say why he wanted two gold elephants made?'

'I understood that he wished to give them to someone, my lord. I thought at first that he meant to present them to the abbey but now I'm not so sure.'

'Well, whoever it is won't receive them from the lord Richard.'

'But I have a commission.'

'It's just been cancelled.'

'You can't speak for the lord Richard.'

'I'm not,' said Livarot, grinning to himself. 'I'm speaking for the lady to whom they were due to be presented. When she was offered the original pair she was very taken with them, but there was a significant omission. The lord Richard somehow forgot to mention that they were stolen property.' He sheathed his dagger and gave a laugh of triumph. 'When she learns the truth, she'll be livid.'

'They were stolen from the abbey,' said the lady Adelaide, pulsing with quiet fury.

'I didn't know that,' he replied.

'You must have done.'

'No, Adelaide. I bought those elephants in France.'

'Then how did they get there from the abbey of St Benet?'

'Who can say?'

'You can, Richard. Stop lying to me.'

'I'm not lying,' he said, trying to conceal his embarrassment beneath an affectionate smile. 'I'd never lie to you, Adelaide. I bought those gold elephants because I wanted the best for you. I knew that you'd appreciate them.'

'I did – until I heard that they were stolen property.'

'Who told you?'

'Ralph Delchard, one of the royal commissioners.'

'Why is he poking his nose into this?'

'That's irrelevant. The point is that I now know the truth about this so-called wedding gift. You had those elephants seized from the abbey so that you could wave them in front of my eyes to entice me into marriage.'

'But I didn't. I swear it.'

'That was despicable!'

Richard de Fontenel had been delighted when he saw the lady Adelaide riding towards his manor house, but that delight turned swiftly to misery when he learnt the purpose of her visit. Having brooded overnight on what she saw as a reprehensible act, she had decided to confront her erstwhile suitor. He had never seen her in such an angry mood. She moved around his parlour with her eyes smouldering.

'And to think that I was tempted,' she said, her voice full of self-reproach. 'I let myself be dazzled by two pieces of gold.'

'Purchased especially for you, Adelaide.'

'Stolen especially for me.'

'Not by me.'

'No, you'd use one of your underlings for that. Hermer, probably,' she speculated. 'From what I hear, he was corrupt enough for anything.'

'What do you mean?' he said, stung by the remark.

'Your steward had a reputation.'

'He gave me excellent service.'

'So I begin to see.'

'Hermer was killed because of his loyalty to me,' he reminded her. 'Murdered and mutilated.' He went quickly on to the attack. 'And do you know? who was responsible for that? The man you recommended to me, my lady, Starculf.'

'There's no proof of that.'

'There's ample proof.'

'Starculf is no longer in the county.'

'Then why is the lord sheriff sending out men in search of him? He's the prime suspect. Roger Bigot assures me that he has evidence enough to convict the villain.'

'Starculf is no villain.'

'Yes, he is.' retorted the other. 'That's why I dismissed him.'

'Wrongfully.'

'Are you telling me how to manage my estate?'

'No, my lord.' she said, backing off slightly. 'But I know Starculf better than you. He was a mere youth when my husband took him on. I saw him grow to manhood. He was honest and straightforward. Starculf had integrity.'

'Killing my steward?' he shouted. 'Is that an example of his integrity? And why did he have to cut off Hermer's hands? Tell me that. Starculf is a vicious animal who deserves no mercy. I'll be searching for him myself.'

The lady Adelaide was dismayed. She had lost her momentum and been thrown on the defensive. The one person she did not wish to talk about was Starculf. It was important to regain the initiative in the conversation.

'So you no longer accuse the lord Mauger?' she mocked. 'When the crimes were first committed, you immediately pointed to him.'

'With cause. Mauger is more than capable of theft and murder.'

'But not in this instance.'

'He's no picture of innocence.' sneered the other. 'Mauger had a spy working for him under my roof. A wretch called Clamahoc. What sort of a man contrives that?'

'A cunning one.' she said, calmly.

'Are you saying that you approve?'

'It's not for me to make any comment.'

'When I showed you those gold elephants, Clamahoc overheard every word that we exchanged.' He saw her wince. 'Yes, my lady. A marriage proposal is something that should concern only the two people involved. How do you feel, knowing that the private remarks you made to me were then passed on to Mauger?'

'I'm not exactly pleased,' she admitted.

'That's the man you might have taken for a husband.'

'At least he didn't order someone to steal holy treasures from an abbey.'

'Neither did I!'

'Then how did they come into your possession?'

'I bought them from a merchant.'

'What was his name – Hermer?'

Richard de Fontenel's expression gave him away. Turning from her, he circled the room and worked himself up into a rage to deflect her from further accusation.

'Hermer is dead,' he said, punching a fist into the palm of the other hand. 'Cut down and foully abused by Starculf. He was slaughtered, Adelaide, and all you can think about is a pair of gold elephants. Don't you have any concern for human life? Hermer was never popular – he never tried to be – but he didn't deserve to be murdered. I spoke to Brother Daniel, the monk who discovered the corpse, and he was still in a state of shock over what he saw. That was all Starculf's doing.' He rounded on her. 'The man you were so keen to recommend to me. Don't you think you should accept some of the blame for what happened? Starculf was your man, after all.'

The lady Adelaide was too embarrassed to answer. After meeting his accusatory glare for a few seconds, she turned on her heel and hurried quickly out of the house.

There was a flurry of activity in the bailey as Roger Bigot marshalled his men before riding out of the castle to continue the hunt. Eager to help in the search, Eustace Coureton volunteered himself and his escort. They were assigned to the group led by the sheriffs deputy, Olivier Romain. It was a beautiful day. With the morning sun on their backs, the respective parties felt a surge of confidence. They were convinced that they would at last catch their elusive quarry.

Ralph Delchard and Gervase Bret had already left the castle. Accompanied by Ralph's men, they rode at a comfortable pace in a south-easterly direction. Though he responded willingly to his friend's leadership, Gervase was puzzled that they had not put themselves at the disposal of the sheriff.

'Why are we riding on our own, Ralph?' he asked.

'We make more speed this way.'

'Is that why we left before them?'

'It's part of the reason, Gervase,' said Ralph, cheerily. 'I didn't want us to get too entangled in the search for Starculf.'

'But he's the man we're after, surely?'

'Indirectly.'

'I don't follow.'

'You will,' promised the other, grinning. 'We'll both follow, Gervase. The lord sheriff and his men know this county well, yet they've so far failed to capture Starculf. We'll hunt more wisely. While they charge along the main roads, we'll follow someone who knows the smaller paths.'

'And who's that?'

'Jocelyn Vavasour.'

Gervase was surprised. 'The anchorite?'

'He's turned huntsman now and my guess is that he has a keener nose than Roger Bigot and his officers. Find Jocelyn and – very soon – I think we'll find Starculf.'

'But we have no notion where Jocelyn might be.'

'Yes, we have. Thanks to you.'

'Me?'

'Didn't you say that he'd been to see Olova as well?' said Ralph. 'Before that, I feel sure, he would have repaired to the abbey itself toget full details of the theft.'

'So?'

'We put ourselves in his position, Gervase. We try to get inside his head.'

'That's a troubled place to be. His mind is beset by demons.'

'They're driving him on to recover the elephants at the moment. Jocelyn Vavasour was no ordinary soldier, remember. He helped the lord Ivo to flush out Hereward the Wake from the fens. That means he knows how to stalk his prey. My guess is that he'll have looked under every bush and behind every tree. He'll certainly have talked to anybody and everybody he met along the way. If we make enquiries, it's only a matter of time before we pick up news of him.'

'Norfolk is a large county. It could take us all day.'

'I don't think so. We'll be crossing land where we know he's already been.'

'Is that why we're heading south?'

'South-east, Gervase. Towards the coast.'

'The coast?'

'That's the way Starculf will be going.'

'How do you know that?'

'I don't,' confessed the other. 'But it's what I'd do if all the roads were being watched. Even if Starculf slips past a posse and crosses the boundary, the lord sheriff's writ runs in Suffolk and he has influence in the other neighbouring counties. If he stays on land, Starculf will never be safe.'

'But the ports have been alerted as well.'

'That's why he won't make for a port, Gervase. A boat could put out from almost anywhere along the coast. Starculf may already have one in readiness. All I can say is what my instinct tells me. Starculf will travel towards the coast and the anchorite will be on his tail every inch of the way.'

Ralph's predictions were soon borne out. When they stopped at a hamlet, they heard that Jocelyn Vavasour had called there the previous evening, asking after a lone man on the run. Having picked up the anchorite's trail, they followed him due east and soon gathered more evidence of his route from the priest in a village church. They quickened their pace and pressed on. Ralph remembered something.

'I've forgotten to give you an apology, Gervase,' he said.

'For what?'

'Hauling you out of bed so early this morning, I was so anxious to get off that I knocked far too hard on your door. I'm sorry if I disturbed Alys as well.'

'She was already awake.'

'There's nothing worse than being interrupted at a time like that,' said Ralph with a smile. 'No wonder you were so quiet at the start of our journey. I deprived you of the delights of the marital couch.'

'But you didn't,' explained Gervase. 'I was sad to leave because I wanted to comfort Alys. She slept badly last night and felt sick in the early hours. Alys hasn't been enjoying her food since we got here.'

Ralph was concerned. 'Then there's even more reason to apologise,' he said. 'Why didn't you tell me, Gervase? I could have ridden out with my men and you could have stayed to look after your dear wife.'

'It was Alys who urged me to go.'

'I hate the thought that she's unwell.'

'She was considerably better when I left, Ralph. But I still worry about her.'

'I hope you have no qualms about bringing her with us. it's been wonderful for Golde to have such a companion. She and Alys have become almost like sisters.'

'I'm glad that I brought her.' said Gervase. 'I just wish that she could start to enjoy the visit to Norwich rather more than she is doing. It isn't only her ill health that's upset her; she was horrified by the murder. She's had nightmares about it.'

'Then let's do what we can to solve the crime once and for all,' said Ralph. 'Then we can get on with our work and your wife can sleep more soundly at night.'

A mile down the track, they stopped to question an old shepherd who was tending his flock in the bright sunshine. The man was largely inarticulate but he did manage to give them some heartening news. Earlier that morning, someone who sounded very much like Jocelyn Vavasour had passed that way and interrogated him. They were getting closer. It encouraged Ralph to set an even faster pace, collecting evidence of further sightings of the anchorite whenever they paused in a hamlet or met someone on the road. It was afternoon when they finally caught up with him. Ralph raised an arm to bring the troop to a halt. He pointed to a derelict house. 'That's where we'll find him.'

'Can you see him?' asked Gervase.

'No, but I glimpsed a horse grazing nearby. Its rider must be Jocelyn.'

'Let's find out.'

They approached at a trot until they closed in on the dwelling. It was a Saxon hut, long abandoned and almost falling to pieces. Two of the walls had collapsed and very little of the thatch remained. Jocelyn the Anchorite was not pleased to see them. He stepped out of the ruined dwelling and stood with his hands on his lips. 'What are you doing here?'

'Looking for you, Jocelyn.' said Ralph. 'You're the hound that we knew would pick up the scent.'

'I'm hunting on my own account, my lord.'

'Nobody is stopping you, my friend. We'll just plod along behind you.'

Ralph gave the signal to dismount, then got down from the saddle himself. The anchorite saw the determination in their faces and knew that he could not easily shake them off. He elected to confide in them. 'Starculf is travelling on foot,' he said.

'How do you know?' asked Gervase.

'Because he's been seen by more than one person. Also, he'd have got much further than this if he'd been on horseback. He spent the night here.'

They followed him into the ramshackle house and looked down at the ashes in one corner. When Jocelyn raked them with his foot, a faint glow could be seen.

'He's a resourceful man.' he said, 'to light a fire in those conditions. It rained hard for most of the night. I should know. I was out in the storm for hours.'

'Wouldn't it have been dangerous to light a fire?' said Gervase. 'In country as flat as this, it could be seen from miles away.'

'Not if it was banked down properly.' suggested Ralph. 'He would have lit it to dry himself out, and my guess is that then he cooked something on it.'

Jocelyn nodded. 'He did, my lord. I found some small bones.'

'Which way is he going?'

'Towards the coast.'

'I guessed as much. He'll be travelling very slowly, if he's on foot. We should overhaul him.'

'That's easier said than done, my lord. Starculf will be more difficult to spot than he would be on horseback. There are ditches all over this land and lots of other hiding-places to choose from.'

'Then let's join forces and search them,' said Ralph. 'Shall we?'

Jocelyn the Anchorite hesitated. Irritated that his own pursuit of the quarry had been interrupted, he understood the advantage of additional pairs of eyes. He also had some admiration for Ralph Delchard, who had somehow found him in his refuge. That argued skill and patience on his part. He could be useful.

'Very well, my lord.' he said at length. 'But there's a strict condition.'

'What is it?'

'You can have Starculf – but I get the elephants.'

Ralph needed no time at all to consider the proposition.

'Agreed.' he said.

Olova was so angry that she waved her fists in the air. Skalp calmly stood his ground.

'He was here?' she said in disbelief. 'Starculf was here?'

'Only briefly.'

'Why didn't you tell me?'

'There was no need for you to know.' he said.

'There was every need, Skalp. Think of the danger he put us all in. Everyone is out searching for him. If he'd been caught here, we'd all have been arrested for hiding him from justice.'

'He wasn't caught.'

'He might have been.'

'He wasn't, grandmother.' he asserted, sourly. 'I hid him too well.'

'From me as well as from everyone else.' Olova scolded. 'How could you do such a thing, Skalp?'

'He was our friend.'

'What sort of friend puts us at risk like that?'

'There was no risk. I saw to that.'

'Well, I should have been told about it. Only yesterday, I gave my word to Master Bret that Starculf hadn't been near us for ages. You turned me into a liar.'

'You told the truth as you saw it.'

'Yet all the time, Starculf was lurking nearby.'

'Somebody had to help him.'

'Why did it have to be you?'

Her grandson fell silent. He respected Olova and would do her bidding without the slightest complaint most of the time. But he had an independent streak and it had shown itself clearly now. Because she rarely stirred from her hut, he had dared to conceal a fugitive from the law on her land. It shocked her. Olova would have been happier if she had never heard the name of Starculf again. It brought back sad memories for her.

'Why did it have to be you?' she repeated.

'I felt that I owed it to him.'

'You owe him nothing.'

'Yes, I do,' he said, vehemently. 'And so do you, grandmother. You were delighted when you heard that Hermer had been killed. I saw the joy in your face. It was Starculf who put that joy there. Don't forget that. But for him, Hermer would still be alive, doing to other girls what he did to Aelfeva. Is that what you'd have wanted?'

'No!' she cried in distress.

'You saw what happened to Aelfeva.'

'Don't remind me.'

'I was the one who found her body, floating in the water,' he reminded her. 'That's what Hermer drove her to, Grandmother. He had Aelfeva's blood on his hands.'

'I know that.'

'Then you should be grateful to Starculf.'

'I am – in some ways.'

'Hermer deserved to perish,' he said, harshly. 'His master took our land from us and he himself took Aelfeva. Was it Hermer who came here to apologise?'

'No, it was Starculf.'

'And because he spoke out, he lost his place.'

'That still doesn't mean you should have harboured him, Skalp,' she said, sternly. 'And you certainly shouldn't have done so without my knowledge. My property may have shrunk in size but I still own a little land and you get your living from it. That means you're accountable to me. Do you understand?'

'Yes, Grandmother.'

'Nothing takes place here behind my back.'

He gave a nod. 'I'm sorry.'

'I'd never have known if one of the children hadn't spotted a stranger coming out of the bushes. But I do know now, and I realise that you betrayed me.'

'I had to help Starculf. He was only here for a night or two.'

'I don't care if he was here for no more than an hour. He put us all in danger.'

'Starculf put himself in danger for our sake.'

'That was his choice.'

'I couldn't turn him away.'

'Why not? Is he more important to you than I am?'

'No, Grandmother.'

'Be honest,' she pressed, glaring at him. 'Do you put Starculf above me?'

Head on his chest, he shifted his feet and gave a noncommittal shrug. When he looked up at her again, his face was expressionless and his voice dull. 'I've got to get back to work.'

'Where is Starculf now?'

'I don't know.'

'Is that the truth?'

'Yes, Grandmother.'

'What am I to say if they come looking for him again?'

'Nothing,' he advised, sullenly. 'Nothing at all.'

Starculf moved more slowly by day, keeping to the ditches or hugging the occasional outcrops of hedgerow. The warm weather was a mixed blessing. Against the pleasure of being dry again he set the danger of being more visible in the bright landscape. Though the fields seemed to be devoid of almost any moving creature apart from sheep, he knew that a sharp pair of eyes could pick him out from a considerable distance. While a posse might not spot him so far off the beaten track, a shepherd or a cottar or someone else working on the land might pick him out and report his whereabouts. He travelled in short bursts, keeping low and running towards the next available cover. He was tired but he pushed himself on, ignoring the water that squelched under his feet in ditches that were still soggy from the previous day's rain. Birds watched his furtive progress across the countryside and put their comments into plaintive song. A fox was disturbed out of its den. Smaller animals also fled from a man who was himself in flight.

They were a mile away when he first caught sight of them over his shoulder. Starculf counted nine of them, moving steadily forward in a line that stretched out across a hundred yards or more. The sun glinted off the helms that most of them were wearing. They were methodical. He sank down behind a tree stump to watch them. Under the guidance of the rider at the end of the line, they rode at a brisk trot as they searched for signs of the fugitive's route. Eventually, one of them stopped near a ditch and called out. The others quickly converged on him. Starculf crawled away on his stomach until sloping ground took him out of their sight. Getting to his feet, he sprinted in the direction of a field of wheat that stood unharvested. They were on to him. He needed a refuge.

Ralph Delchard dismounted to see what Jocelyn the Anchorite had found. Crouched on the ground, the latter pointed to footprints in a patch of muddy ground near the ditch.

'I think he came this way, my lord.' he said.

'Someone did.' agreed Ralph. 'We've no guarantee that it was Starculf.'

'Who else would be in such a remote place?'

'Another anchorite, perhaps?'

Jocelyn acknowledged the jest with a rare smile, then dropped down into the ditch. He went back along it for some way before clambering back up the bank. When he reached the others, his feet were wet but his face was glowing.

'He's definitely been here,' he announced. 'There are footprints all the way along the ditch. It must be Starculf, trying to keep out of sight.'

'He's close,' decided Ralph, scanning the horizon. 'I feel it.'

'So do I.'

'How far can a man get on foot in a day?'

'It depends how much guilt is weighing him down.'

'I have the feeling that Starculf is not a man troubled by his conscience,' said Ralph, mounting his horse again. 'If he were, the crimes wouldn't have been committed in the first place.'

'Only a godless heathen would steal holy treasures,' said Jocelyn, pulling himself up into the saddle. 'I'll read him a sermon when I catch up with him.'

'You'll be wasting your breath, my friend.'

'He must be made aware of the gravity of his offence.'

'Murder takes precedence over all else,' insisted Ralph. 'That's the charge on which I'll arrest him. Save your sermons for ears that might wish to listen.' He waved an arm and yelled to his men. 'Fan out and stay in line with me. He's very close. Keep your eyes open!'

The men obeyed the order, stretching the line even further than before. At a signal from Ralph, they set off again, looking carefully for any clue that might help them. They moved on until they came to the tree stump behind which Starculf had earlier hidden. It was Gervase who called them to a halt this time. He was at the very centre of the line. Ralph and Jocelyn rode swiftly across to him.

'Look,' said Gervase, pointing to the grass that had been flattened. 'Somebody was here without a doubt. It's almost as if he crawled on his belly through the grass.'

'He's nearer than we thought.' said Ralph.

'He must have gone down that hill.'

'Then let's follow him!'

Taking out his sword, Ralph held it up in the air as if about to lead a charge. 'Forward!' he shouted. 'Starculf is here! I can smell him. I want the rogue taken alive. After him!'

When she returned to her house, she found Mauger Livarot waiting for her. The lady Adelaide needed a moment to regain her composure before she went into her parlour. Her confrontation with Richard de Fontenel had left her feeling jangled and she was not pleased to see that she had a visitor. It was an effort to manufacture a token smile. No effort was needed by Mauger Livarot. Smirking complacently, he got up from his seat to welcome her. After an exchange of greetings, he waited until she sat down before he spoke again, eyeing her possessively and standing close enough to inhale her fragrance.

'Your servant tells me that you paid a visit to the lord Richard,' he began.

'That's right.' she conceded.

'I think I can guess what sent you there, Adelaide. You learnt the truth about those gold elephants, didn't you? They were holy treasures, stolen from an abbey.'

'So I hear.'

'Richard de Fontenel was trying to trick you into marriage.'

'You're not above using a trick or two yourself, my lord.' she observed, tartly. 'You had a spy in his household until the man was discovered. I should imagine that he paid dearly for his betrayal.'

Livarot's face darkened. 'His back was whipped to shreds.'

'You must take some of the blame for that.'

'The man was a fool to get himself caught.'

'What will you do now that you no longer have someone to report on the lord Richard? It won't be so easy to stay one step ahead of him in future.'

'Yes, it will,' he assured her. 'But tell me what you said to him.'

'That was a private conversation. Unheard by any spy of yours.'

'Were hot words traded?'

'I spoke my mind,' she said, briskly. 'He knows my feelings now.'

He clicked his tongue. 'Only Richard de Fontenel would try to palm off stolen property on the woman he was hoping to marry.'

'Those hopes have been dashed.'

'That's why I came here this afternoon. To plead my own case.'

'I'm not in the mood for courtship, my lord.'

'I just thought you'd like to know the full truth about my rival,' he said, easily. 'He still planned to ensnare you with a pair of gold elephants.'

'How? If they're recovered, they'll go back to the abbey of St Benet.'

'Not in this case.'

'What do you mean?'

'The lord Richard didn't wish to disappoint you, Adelaide. He commissioned Judicael the Goldsmith to make two replicas, exact in every detail. Fortunately, I was advised of his scheme in time to stop it.'

'Stop it?' she said with interest.

'You'd hardly wish to receive anything from the hands of a man who deceived you so cruelly. The lord Richard betrayed you. He's nothing more than a common thief.'

'Tell me about these replicas.'

'They can never be quite as good as the originals,' he pointed out, 'But Judicael is confident that he can make them, given the help of another goldsmith who saw the treasures at the abbey before they were taken.' His voice was artless. 'Does the idea of replicas hold any attraction for you?'

There was a long pause as she examined the implications of the question. 'It might,' she said at length. 'It would, of course, depend entirely on the quality of the craftsmanship.'

He moved in close. 'You'll not find a better craftsman than me, Adelaide.'

'You intend to make the pieces yourself?' she teased.

'No, but I'll commission them on your behalf. Judicael can do for me what he would have done for the lord Richard. 'Unless, that is,' he said, searching her eyes, 'you prefer to own the originals.'

'I do. Without question.'

"How would you react if they were offered to you now?'

'That's impossible.'

'Not necessarily.'

'They belong to the abbey and must be returned.'

'They could belong to you,' he suggested. 'Ample recompense can be paid to the abbey. They'd not lose by it. They could purchase some other treasures.'

Her curiosity was aroused. A flame seemed to be lighted inside her. 'What are you saying, my lord?'

'That it's a matter of choice. Before I knew where they came from, I vowed to recover those gold elephants for you and I'm ready to keep that vow. If, on the other hand, you'll settle for replicas made by Judicael, then I'll commission them this very afternoon. Which is it to be, Adelaide?'

'Are you suggesting that I accept stolen property?'

'I'm suggesting that you have exactly what you want and nobody will be any the wiser. You saw those elephants, touched them, felt their quality. Could you be happy with something of lesser excellence?'

'No,' she said, thoughtfully. 'I don't believe that I could.'

Chapter Thirteen

Starculf had not been idle. While his pursuers were inspecting his footprints in the ditch and noting the flattened grass behind the tree stump, he was burrowing deeper into the heart of the wheat field, staying very low and doing his best to create as little visible disturbance as possible. As he strained his ears for the noise of hoofbeats, another sound could be heard faintly in the distance. It was the roll of the waves on the shore and it took on a seductive rhythm. Surrounded by stalks of wheat, he was only a mile or more from the coast to which he had been heading. Once there, he proposed to make his way south in search of a boat that would take him to safety. Starculf had money enough to buy his passage and reason enough to quit England for ever. All that stood between him and salvation were the nine men who were tracking him. Unable to outrun them, he had to stay where he was until they had gone past him. Patience was his watchword.

Ralph Delchard and Gervase Bret also had the gift of patience. When they reached the point where the land sloped sharply away from them, they tried to work out how far a man might get on foot, and came to the same conclusion. Ralph waved his men to a halt, then nudged his horse towards Gervase so that he could have a brief conference with him. Jocelyn Vavasour came over to join them. The anchorite's suspicion coincided exactly with their own.

'I think that he may be in that field of wheat,' he said, pointing a finger.

'So do I,' said Ralph, 'but I don't want to ruin the harvest by charging in there with my men. There's an easier way to draw him out.'

'Is there, my lord?'

'We ride on past the field and make for that stand of trees in the distance. Our hoofbeats will have faded by then. He'll think that we've gone.'

'All we have to do is wait,' said Gervase, surveying the field. 'If Starculf is in there, he'll soon come out when he thinks he's safe. If he isn't hiding amid the wheat, we'll not have lost much time and we won't have trampled over someone's harvest.'

'True,' said Jocelyn.

'You agree, then?' asked Ralph.

'Yes, my lord.'

The plan was put into action immediately. Signalling to his men, Ralph brought them all together then led them in formation at a brisk trot. They went down the hill and on past the wheat field, skirting its perimeter without even looking at it and continuing on for over a quarter of a mile until they reached a stand of willows and sycamores. Once they went round the angle of the copse, they were out of sight of any fugitive who might be lurking in the field. They reined in their horses and dismounted. Ralph, Gervase and Jocelyn crept through the trees in search of a vantage point from which they could observe the field. It was a hot afternoon. Cooled by a breeze that came off the sea, they could hear the waves rolling behind them quite clearly. If the fugitive headed for the coast, they had comprehensively cut off his escape route.

But there was no sign of Starculf. In the field, the wheat danced in the wind and shone in the sunshine. Nobody rose out of it to continue his bid for freedom. As time oozed slowly past, they began to lose faith in their instincts.

'He's not there,' Ralph decided.

'Give him more time,' advised Gervase.

'But he may already have reached the coast. We should be riding along the shore.'

'Only when we're sure he's not hiding in that field.'

'I prefer the lord Ralph's counsel,' said Jocelyn, worried. 'Starculf is ahead of us and not behind us. We should mount up and give pursuit.'

'Hold here a little longer,' said Gervase, restraining him gently.

'It's a needless delay,' Ralph complained.

'Yes,' said Jocelyn. 'Starculf could be getting away.'

'Not unless he has a horse hidden in that wheat field as well,' said Gervase, using a hand to shield his eyes from the sun. 'I can see movement.'

'Where?' said Ralph, tensing at the promise of action. 'Where is he?'

'Over to the left. Do you see him?'

Ralph let his gaze drift across to the left of the field and realised that Gervase had seen something that had eluded both him and the anchorite. No head had been lifted above the top of the stalks but a thin dark line was gradually snaking through the wheat. They were too far away to be certain of what they were witnessing. The parting of the wheat might have been caused by a dog or another animal making its way along but Ralph felt otherwise. He sensed that Starculf was about to make an appearance at last.

The fugitive was circumspect. When he had crawled all the way to the edge of the field, he did not break cover at once. Instead, he waited and watched until he was satisfied that there was nobody insight. With a suddenness that took them all by surprise, he then rose up and loped off.

'We've got him!' said Ralph.

'He's mine!' declared Vavasour.

'There's no hurry.' said Gervase. 'He can't possibly get away.'

But his companions were not listening. Engaged in a private race, they mounted their horses and kicked them into a gallop. Ralph's men were not far behind, spreading out in a semicircle to eliminate any hope of escape for the fugitive. When he saw them coming, Starculf changed the angle of his run, increasing his speed and aiming for the marshland off to his right, but it was a futile exercise. He was trapped. All that remained to be decided was who got to him first. Determined that he would have the pleasure of arresting the man, Ralph spurred his destrier on, but the weight of his hauberk slowed the animal slightly, it was the lighter figure of Jocelyn Vavasour, wearing no mailcoat and carrying no weapon, who surged ahead on his borrowed horse.

Reaching the edge of the marshes, Starculf zigzagged between the pools until he heard the splash of hooves in water. His flight was soon over. As he turned to see how far behind him they were, he was caught by a well-aimed foot that sent him tumbling to the ground. Vavasour was on him in a flash. Bringing his horse to an abrupt halt, he leapt down from the saddle and ran across to the man who was now struggling to get up, grabbed him by the shoulders and shook him vigorously.

'Where are the elephants?'

'First things first,' said Ralph, dismounting to hurry over. 'My name is Ralph Delchard,' he announced, taking hold of the prisoner, 'and it's my duty to arrest you on behalf of Roger Bigot, sheriff of Norfolk and Suffolk.'

Starculf was still too dazed to reply. Ralph misunderstood his silence. 'Would you rather I used your language?' he said in English.

'No, my lord,' answered the other, slowly recovering. 'Given the circumstances, I think I'd prefer to be arrested in French.'

'Then that's how it'll be,' agreed Ralph, reverting to his own tongue.

'Ask him about the elephants, my lord,' urged Vavasour, impatiently.'

'All in good time, Jocelyn.'

'But I want them now. That's the whole purpose of my mission.'

'There's the small matter of a homicide to discuss first.'

'I caught him, my lord. I want those holy treasures.'

'You'll get them,' said Ralph, firmly, 'when I'm ready and not before.'

'Search him!'

'I'll not be rushed.' warned the other. 'Starculf is my prisoner.'

Vavasour glared mutinously. 'If you say so.'

'I do say so.'

Gervase had now arrived and dismounted to join them on the ground. He took a close look at Starculf and matched him to the description they had been given of Richard de Fontenel's former servant. There could be no question of the prisoner's identity. He was a tall, handsome, well-built young man. Even in his dishevelled state, Starculf was a striking figure, his features smooth, his beard well trimmed and his eyes glistening with a quiet pride. Gervase discerned another cause for the enmity between him and the steward with whom he worked. The short, stocky Hermer, who had to secure his pleasures by force, was bound to resent a man to whom sexual favours would be freely offered.

Ralph returned to his interrogation. 'I'm arresting you on a charge of murder.' he said, solemnly, 'in that you did wilfully and maliciously kill one Hermer, steward to the lord Richard.'

'No, my lord!' protested the other.

'Don't lie to me!'

'On my oath, I didn't kill Hermer.'

'Then why are you running away?'

'Because I don't wish to pay for a crime I didn't commit.'

'Tell the truth, man!' ordered Ralph.

'That is the truth, my lord,' said Starculf, earnestly. 'I'll swear on the Holy Bible that I didn't lay hands on Hermer. The first that I heard about his death was when the lord sheriff's men started hunting for me.'

'Innocent men don't need to flee.'

'They do if they have little chance of proving their innocence.'

'What about the elephants?' demanded Vavasour.

'Let them wait!' said Ralph, irritably. 'Pinion him!'

Two of his men moved in swiftly to tie Starculf's hands behind his back and to remove his dagger from its sheath. The fugitive had noo ther weapon on him. Gervase was impressed with the man's bearing. Starculf was no cringing felon, begging for mercy or hissing defiance. Nor was there anything of a trapped animal about him. Upright and unafraid, he exuded a strange honesty.

'You claim that you're innocent?' said Gervase.

'I didn't murder the lord Richard's steward,' Starculf replied.

'Yet you vowed to get revenge on him and his master.'

'I confess it readily.'

'Now we're getting somewhere,' said Ralph.

'Let him finish.' suggested Gervase, touching his friend's arm. 'Go on, Starculf.'

'Hermer was a brutal man,' said Starculf, bitterly, 'and a lustful one at that. I tried to shut my eyes to his behaviour at first but it became too gross to ignore. So I spoke out against him. After what he did, Hermer didn't deserve to live.'

'So you *wanted* to kill him?'

'Yes.'

'And you planned to do so?'

Starculf hesitated. 'It was always at the back of my mind.' he said.

'I think it was at the forefront,' argued Ralph. 'If you didn't have designs on the man's life, why go to the trouble of getting duplicate keys to the lord Richard's house?' The prisoner was startled. 'Yes, my friend. A locksmith in Wymondham gave the lord sheriff a good description of you. On that occasion, you didn't use your own name. You called yourself Alstan.'

'That was the name of a slave on the estate, wasn't it?' said Gervase.

'You know more than I feared,' admitted the other. 'Yes, I did have duplicate keys made and I did use Alstan's name because I knew the man when I worked on the lord Richard's estate. Alstan was shamefully treated by Hermer.'

'Yet he didn't return in order to murder him.'

'Neither did I.'

'Then why did you have those keys made?'

'We're going round in circles here,' complained Vavasour, stepping forward. 'Ask him all you wish but first let me have the elephants so that I can return them to the abbey at once. You owe me that, my lord,' he said, looking at Ralph. 'I led you here.'

'That's so,' conceded Ralph. 'Take your treasures, Jocelyn. You've earned them.'

'Well?' said Vavasour to the prisoner. 'Where are they?'

'What?'

'The gold elephants you took from the lord Richard's house.'

'I took nothing.'

'Blessed by the Pope himself,' added Vavasour, 'and presented by me to the abbey of St Benet at Holme. Now, don't prevaricate, man. Where are they?'

'I have no idea,' said Starculf.

'They're hidden about you somewhere.'

'Search me, if you wish, but you'll find no gold elephants about my person. I've never laid eyes on such objects and I certainly didn't take them from the lord Richard's house. This is the first I've ever heard of them.'

Jocelyn Vavasour refused to believe him. Pulling him close, he subjected the prisoner to a thorough search, even to the extent of tearing off some of his clothing. Starculf bore it all with dignity. Nothing was found on him apart from some money. Ralph and Gervase were the first to accept that the prisoner was telling the truth.

'Leave him alone,' said Ralph. 'He didn't take them.'

'I never went into the lord Richard's house,' Starculf insisted.

'You must have!' shouted Vavasour.

'But I didn't. I give you my word.'

Pushed almost to despair, the anchorite grabbed him and shook him violently. 'I want those elephants!' he cried. 'Where are they?'

Long after Adelaide's departure, Richard de Fontenel was still fuming with anger. The woman he had planned to marry had just walked decisively out of his life. When he looked around for solace, he found none at all. In the space of a few short days, he had suffered a series of disasters. His steward had been murdered, two valuable gold objects stolen from his strong room, one of his trusted servants unmasked as a spy in the pay of his rival and the lady Adelaide had rejected him outright. What pained him most was that the advantage had now been decisively handed to Mauger Livarot. Not only would the latter be able to rejoice in de Fontenel's misfortune, he would probably wed the very person over whom the two of them had fought so long. It was intolerable.

After brooding on the malignancy of Fate, he was jerked into action. Since their origin had been revealed to the lady Adelaide, the recovery of the gold elephants no longer dominated his thinking. He would never get them back. Instead, he turned his attention to the capture of Hermer's killer. There was more than theft and murder to lay at his door. In exposing the earlier theft from the abbey, the culprit had rendered de Fontenel liable to investigation himself and deprived him of the woman he had been tempted to take as his wife. He had caused acute embarrassment to someone who was accustomed to unquestioning respect. Certain that Starculf was responsible for his downfall, de Fontenel now wanted retribution. He called for his horse to be saddled and summoned his men. They were soon riding towards Norwich castle.

A mile down the road, they were met by the unlikely sight of an adipose man, panting and perspiring as he struggled to control a small, wayward horse. Richard de Fontenel brought his troop to a halt and stared in amazement at Judicael the Goldsmith.

'What are you doing here?' he asked.

'I was on my way to see you, my lord.' said the other, anxiously.

'If it's about that commission of mine, you've made a pointless journey. The items will no longer be needed, Judicael.'

'I know. The order was cancelled earlier today.'

'By whom?'

'The lord Mauger.'

'But it's nothing to do with him!'

'That's what I told him.'

'When?'

'This morning, my lord,' said the goldsmith, feeling his throat ruefully. 'He came to my shop and demanded to know what you had commissioned from me. It seems that you were spotted visiting me yesterday.'

'Mauger has intelligencers everywhere!' growled the other.

'I refused to divulge any information but he drew his dagger on me. I had to tell him the truth, my lord,' he bleated, apologetically, 'or he'd have used the weapon on me.'

'You told him about my commission?'

'Only under duress.'

'You idiot!' De Fontenel swung an arm and knocked Judicael from the saddle. After rolling in the dust, the man got up on his knees to implore mercy. His horse seized the opportunity to bolt.

'What did you say to him?'

'As little as possible, my lord. I swear it.'

'I warned you to keep your mouth shut.'

'The lord Mauger used violence against me.'

'That's nothing to what I'll use,' snarled de Fontenel. 'And what's this about the commission to make those replicas being cancelled?'

'It was only your commission that was void,' said Judicael, scrambling to his feet and clutching at de Fontenel's leg. 'The lord Mauger told me that you'd no longer have use for the objects, but there was a chance that he himself might need the replicas. If it proved necessary, he was going to employ me himself.'

'What!'

Richard de Fontenel's bellow made the goldsmith jump back in alarm. Spurring his horse into life, he led his men off at speed, leaving a cloud of dust in their wake. Priorities had now altered. Instead of going to Norwich castle to berate the sheriff for his delay in bringing the killer to justice, de Fontenel concentrated his anger on his rival. He and his companions rode hell-for-leather towards the estate of Mauger Livarot.

Bruised and shaken, the hapless goldsmith started to search for his horse.

Mauger Livarot was also in the saddle. Accompanied by Drogo and with a dozen of his men at his back, he cantered over the gentle undulations of the Norfolk countryside in the direction of the coast. His steward was eager to claim his share of praise.

'I told you that I spent money wisely on your behalf, my lord,' he said.

'You did, Drogo.'

'I knew that it was worth having the lord Ralph followed.'

'He's a keener huntsman than Roger Bigot,' said Livarot, eyes on the landscape ahead, 'but will he lead us to the man we want? More to the point, will we be able to take those gold elephants for our own use?'

'I hope so, my lord.'

'I need more than hope.'

An expression of grim determination was on his face.

Mauger Livarot did not give his promises lightly. Since the lady Adelaide had made a request, it had to be met. She could not be satisfied with mere replicas. The joy of possession weighed more heavily with her than the knowledge that she would be guilty of sacrilege. Provided that secrecy was maintained, she wanted the gold elephants that were taken from the abbey so that she could gloat over them in private. Both she and Livarot had endowed the monastic institution in the past. Perhaps the lady Adelaide felt that her generosity absolved her from the charge of receiving stolen property. It would be the second time that the treasures would be offered to her and Livarot vowed that it would be the last. He was thrilled that she had chosen the original objects over the possibility of replicas made by Judicael. It was not simply an indication of her superior taste, it revealed an unscrupulous vein in her that boded well for their marriage.

She and Livarot understood each other. They were two of a kind.

The man was waiting near the derelict house where Starculf had spent the night. When the newcomers drew to a halt, he hastened over to report his news to his master. 'The lord Ralph went this way, my lord.'

'Who was travelling with him?' asked Livarot.

'His fellow commissioner and six men-at-arms.'

'Nobody else?'

'There was another rider whom I hardly recognised at first. He was dressed in rags and wearing a beard. I couldn't believe that it was the lord Jocelyn.'

'Jocelyn Vavasour?' said the other with alarm. 'What was he doing here?'

'The same as us, probably,' said Drogo. 'Hunting for those treasures.'

'We must get to them before he does!'

'Yes, my lord.'

Livarot was peremptory. 'Ride with us,' he ordered the other man. 'We may need every sword we can muster. There's no time to lose. Away!'

Urging on his horse, he set a fierce pace for them.

Hands still tied behind his back, Starculf rode between Ralph Delchard and Gervase Bret on a horse they had borrowed in a village through which they had passed. Two of the men-at-arms led the little column, four more brought up the rear, Detached from the others by a dozen yards or more, Jocelyn Vavasour followed dejectedly, still fretting over the loss of his beloved elephants and chiding himself for lapsing so easily into violence when he captured the fugitive.

They were moving at an easy trot. It enabled the commissioners to continue their interrogation.

'Why did you get those duplicate keys made?' asked Ralph.

'To gain access to the lord Richard's house,' confessed Starculf.

'Yet you claim that you never made use of them.'

'When I learnt of Hermer's death, it became unnecessary.'

'But you did plan to kill him?'

'I wanted revenge, my lord.'

'Why wait so long?' wondered Gervase. 'It was ages since you'd been dismissed by him. And why go to all the trouble of getting into the house when it would have been far easier to ambush him when he was out on the estate or visiting one of the outliers?'

'It wouldn't have been that easy,' said Starculf. 'Hermer never travelled alone. I'd have been one man against three or four. Besides, I wanted to deliver a personal message to the lord Richard. The best place to do that was under his own roof.'

'Yet the body wasn't found at the house.'

'If I'd killed Hermer, it would have been.'

'Why do you think it was left close to the castle?'

Starculf shook his head. 'I can't tell you that.'

'You must have some idea,' said Ralph.

'I didn't kill him, my lord. That's all I can say. I'd have done it very differently.'

'So you plotted murder but didn't have the stomach to carry it out.'

'No,' said the other with vehemence. 'I wasn't lacking in courage. I risked my life to get inside that house at night to borrow the lord Richard's keys. That took a lot of courage. The reason I didn't kill him was that someone got to Hermer before I did. I can't reproach myself enough for that.'

'For what?'

'Delaying my move for so long. I lost my prize.'

'Is that what you call it?' said Ralph, disapprovingly.

'Yes, my lord.'

Tired of riding adrift of the others, Vavasour caught them up and brought his horse alongside Ralph's mount. The anchorite still believed that the prisoner was deceiving them in some way. He listened carefully to Starculf s account of his movements since leaving Richard de Fontenel's estate.

'I was an outcast. The lord Richard didn't merely hound me off his land, he threatened to have me whipped if I was ever caught in the county of Norfolk again. I went down into Suffolk to lie low for a while, working as a falconer for a new master, but I never forgot the old one. I knew Hermer feared that I might return and that kept him on his guard. I let time pass so that he and the lord Richard would think they'd seen the end of me.' He gave a secret smile. 'Then I went back for the keys.'

'When both of them were absent from the house,' said Gervase.

'Yes.'

'That was very convenient for you, wasn't it?'

'I knew where the lord Richard kept his keys,' said Starculf. 'Nobody else was allowed to use them so they'd not be missed for a few days. I chose a locksmith in Wymondham because I thought I'd never be looked for there.'

'But you were.'

'Unfortunately.'

'Let's go back to the theft of those keys,' said Gervase, studying his profile. 'I don't think you would ride all the way up from Suffolk in the hope that the house you wanted to break into would be largely unoccupied. You knew, didn't you? You had an accomplice who told you the exact moment to strike.'

'Someone did give me a little help,' conceded Starculf.

'Who was it?'

'That's not important.'

'Of course it is,' asserted Ralph. 'The fellow is as guilty as you are.'

'No, my lord.'

'Tell me his name!'

'I'll never do that,' Starculf said, proudly. 'The person who gave me the information had no idea what use I meant to put it to. When I broke into that house – and when I returned the keys I borrowed from there – I had no accomplice.'

'What about the gold elephants?' asked Vavasour, bitterly. 'Did you have a confederate when you stole them?'

'I've told you before that I didn't steal them.'

'I say that you're lying.'

'Not about the elephants,' decided Gervase. 'I don't think he even knew that they existed until you mentioned them. And he's not lying about the murder either. He's doing something more subtle than that, aren't you, Starculf?'

'What's that?'

'Deliberately holding back the full truth.'

Further questioning was interrupted by the arrival of a body of riders on the horizon. Moving swiftly in pairs, twenty or more men were galloping towards them with the sheriff at their head. Ralph moved his party forward at a canter until the groups met.

Roger Bigot was delighted to see that they had a prisoner with them. 'Is Starculf taken?'

'He is, my lord sheriff,' said Ralph. We deliver him over to you.'

Slapping the rump of Starculf's horse, he sent it forward. One of the sheriff's officers took the reins, and two other men took up their positions either side of the fugitive. Roger Bigot eyed the prisoner with a mixture of relief and curiosity. 'So this is the man who murdered Hermer, is it?' he said.

'He denies the charge,' said Gervase, 'and we believe him.'

'I don't,' said Vavasour.

The sheriff noticed the hirsute rider for the first time. He peered at him. 'Saints preserve us!' he exclaimed. 'Is it really the lord Jocelyn?'

'That's not a name I answer to any more.'

'You've changed so much.'

'For the better, my lord sheriff. I've drawn back from the abyss. I lead a contemplative life now instead of one dedicated to greed and warfare.'

'Don't let him give us a homily,' implored Ralph. 'It's far too hot a day for that.'

'This man is guilty,' said Vavasour, indicating the prisoner.

Starculf was adamant. 'I didn't kill Hermer.'

'I agree,' attested Gervase. 'I think he's innocent of the murder.'

'So do I,' said Ralph. 'Guilty of much else but innocent of murder.'

The sheriff was dismayed. Hoping that the case had finally been solved, he was faced with an unexpected setback. Starculf's denial did not impress him but the firmness of the responses from the commissioners made Roger Bigot take the plea seriously. After staring at the prisoner, he divided a baleful glance between Ralph and Gervase.

'If Starculf didn't kill him,' he said with exasperation, 'then who did?'

The sunlit afternoon encouraged them to take a leisurely walk around the perimeter of the bailey. Having been thoroughly soaked on the previous day, Golde was pleased to be enjoying less trying conditions. Alys, too, blossomed in the bright sun.

'Isn't it beautiful out here?' she said. 'We might almost be in a garden.'

'Apart from the high walls and the guards on the ramparts,' replied Golde with mild cynicism. 'But it's good to be able to stretch our legs. There's a limit to how long I want to watch the lady Matilda work on that tapestry of hers.'

'It's such an intricate piece of work.'

'I'd never dare to undertake it.'

'Why not?'

'My hands lack the requisite skill.'

'Nonsense!' said Alys. 'They had skill enough to brew ale.'

Golde laughed. 'Brewing calls for rather different talents. In any case, I've put that life behind me now – thanks to Ralph.'

'He changed your life, didn't he?'

'Completely.'

'Are you ever afraid for him when he rides out with his men?'

'Never, Alys. He's a born soldier.'

'Gervase isn't,' sighed the other. 'I fear for his safety all the time.'

'There's no need. Gervase is well able to take care of himself. In fact . . .' Golde broke off as she saw a familiar figure ride in through the main gate. 'Is that the lady Adelaide?' she said in surprise.

'I think so,' said Alys. 'I wonder what she's doing at the castle?'

'Let's find out.'

They hurried across to the newcomer. The lady Adelaide was escorted by two men-at-arms, one of whom dismounted to help her down from the saddle. When she saw the two women approaching, she beamed regally and offered warm greetings.

'I was hoping to call on the lady Matilda,' she explained. 'Is she here?'

'Yes, my lady,' said Golde.

'Precious few of us still are,' Alys piped up, admiring the visitor's immaculate appearance yet again. 'The castle is almost deserted.'

Adelaide looked around. 'Where is everybody?'

'Joining in the search for the killer,' said Golde. 'The lord sheriff has set his heart on catching the culprit today. He's leading the search himself.'

'Is the lord Ralph involved in the hunt?'

'Yes, my lady. My husband left shortly after dawn.'

'So did mine,' said Alys. 'Ralph knocked on our door very early.'

'Do they hold out much hope of finding the man?' asked the visitor.

'I think so,' said Golde. 'My husband wanted the pleasure of arresting the killer himself. He has delayed the commissioners' work long enough. Ralph wants him put under lock and key so that they can begin their deliberations.'

'All of us want the fellow arrested as soon as possible.'

'I certainly do,' said Alys, widening her eyes. 'He not only committed murder. He stole some holy treasures that rightly belong to an abbey.'

'So I understand.'

'What sort of man would do that?'

'An ungodly one,' murmured Adelaide.

'Brother Daniel was shocked. He's the scribe to the commissioners. Stealing from an abbey is a most heinous crime in his eyes. I agree with him, don't you?'

'Of course, Alys.'

'But you know the man responsible, I hear.'

'Vaguely.'

'Ralph said that this Starculf once worked as your falconer.'

'My husband's falconer,' corrected the other with undue sharpness. 'I had no dealings with him myself. After he went to the lord Richard's estate, I never saw him. Starculf belongs very much to my past.'

'What drove him to kill and steal, my lady?' asked Alys.

'I haven't the slightest idea.'

'It sounds to me as if you're well rid of the fellow.'

'I am indeed,' said the other, moving gracefully away. 'But you'll have to excuse me. I need to speak to the lady Matilda. Goodbye.'

They waved her politely off then traded a puzzled frown. 'She was doing it again,' said Golde, turning to watch the departing visitor.

'Doing what?'

'Using us to get information about our husbands. The lady Adelaide wants to know what progress has been made. Now that she knows where Ralph and Gervase are, she'll see what she can find out from the lady Matilda about the sheriff's movements.'

Alys puckered her face. 'Why is she so keen to hear about the search?'

'It could just be natural curiosity. On the other hand . . .'

'Yes?'

'Well, the lady Adelaide is directly involved here,' said Golde, recalling what she had overheard. 'Those gold elephants were first offered to her as a wedding gift. Unbeknown to her, of course, they were stolen property but they must have impressed her greatly. They're reputedly works of art. We saw how fond she was of gold when we visited her.'

'The jewellery that she wears is always so striking.'

'Yes,' agreed Golde as the visitor ascended the steps to the keep, 'the lady Adelaide likes to glitter. It's important for her to be the centre of attention.'

Alys sighed. 'I'm too shy to want that. I prefer the shadows.'

'There's no shadow dark enough to hide the lady Adelaide.'

'Why did she stalk off like that, Golde?'

'Because we caught her on a raw spot.'

'I didn't think that she had any.'

'Neither did I until I mentioned the name of Starculf. Did you notice how quickly her manner changed? And she went out of her way to deny any real acquaintance with him, yet according to Ralph she recommended him to the lord Richard.'

'I found that rather odd as well.'

'There was something even more curious. Not in anything she said, but I saw it clearly in her eyes. The lady Adelaide gave me the impression that she didn't actually want Starculf to be caught.'

Alys was silent. She blinked rapidly as if feeling a spasm of pain.

'What's the trouble?' said Golde. 'Are you unwell?'

'No, no. I feel fine.'

It was Ralph Delchard's turn to be slightly baffled. When the long cavalcade reached a fork in the road, Gervase Bret suggested that they break away from the main body in order to continue their enquiries elsewhere. It was no casual suggestion. Ralph knew his friend was not given to wild impulse. If Gervase advised a course of action, a great deal of thought had gone into it. For that reason, Ralph detached himself and his men. While the sheriff took the prisoner back to Norwich castle, the commissioners plunged on into the Henstead hundred. Jocelyn the Anchorite went with them, sensing that Gervase might possibly lead him to the missing treasures.

'Are we to be told where we're going, Gervase?' asked Ralph.

'To search for the killer.'

'We've been doing that all day.'

'No, Ralph. We were looking for Starculf and he didn't commit the murder. In thought, perhaps – but not in deed.'

'I still have my doubts about him,' said Vavasour. 'He's no innocent man.'

'Oh, he's guilty of abetting the murder, that much is clear. But it obviously didn't go as planned. Starculf was saving Hermer for himself when his accomplice stepped in ahead of him.'

'What accomplice?'

'The man for whom he had those duplicate keys made. My guess is that they agreed to work together. Starculf needed someone to watch his back so he found a man who was only too glad to assist him.'

'And who was that?' pressed Ralph.

'Cast your mind back to that visit Golde and I made.'

'The one to Olova? I'll never forget it,' said the other with a ripe chuckle. 'Golde was drenched by that rain. When I first saw her, I thought that she'd fallen into a stream.'

'It was Aelfeva who ended up in the stream, Ralph. He found her.'

'Who?'

'The man we're going to see. Olova told me how heartbroken he was when he saw her dead body floating on the water. That kind of experience would embitter anyone. I can see why Skalp was fired up to attack the steward.'

'Skalp?' said Vavasour.

'Olova's grandson. You must have noticed him when you called there yourself. A big, strong, surly young man who was very protective towards the old woman.'

'I saw no sign of him.'

'Then he must have been hiding somewhere.'

'With cause, by the sound of it,' said Ralph, trusting in his friend's judgement. 'Are you saying that Skalp was guilty of both crimes, Gervase? Theft *and* murder?'

'I believe so.'

'On his own?'

'Probably. One man would attract less attention.'

'But he didn't know his way around the lord Richard's estate.'

'Starculf did,' said Gervase, 'and he would have told his accomplice all that he needed to know. He even gave him the duplicate keys to look after until the appointed time. Skalp couldn't wait. He wanted Hermer too badly.'

'How can you be so sure?' asked Vavasour.

Gervase raised a finger. 'Remember what Starculf told us. He wanted to kill Hermer in the lord Richard's manor house and leave the body there to shock his old master. The last thing he would've done is to drag it across country at night and deposit the corpse so close to the castle. Skalp wasn't content with upsetting the lord Richard,' he went on. 'He wanted to outrage the entire city. That's why he left the stench of death right there in the middle of it.'

'What about the severed hands?' said Ralph.

'Did Starculf look like the sort of person to do that?'

'I suppose not.'

'He had no reason. Skalp did. Those were the hands that had defiled Aelfeva.'

Ralph grimaced. 'I'm surprised he didn't cut off the man's pizzle as well.'

'Skalp made his point strongly enough.'

'Why did he return the hands to the lord Richard?'

'To give him a jolt, Ralph.'

'Just hearing about it jolted me,' confessed the other.

'Thank heaven I turned away, from that world!' said Vavasour with an upsurge of remorse. 'I hacked off limbs in my time. I blinded and maimed. In the name of duty, I fought and killed my way right round this country.'

'So did I, my friend. We had no choice.'

'But we did, my lord. We could've refused to go on with the slaughter. We could've renounced the violence as I've now done and tried to atone for it by leading a more spiritual life. We could've walked away.'

'Speak for yourself,' said Ralph. 'I have a wife to look after and I don't think she'd appreciate living in a pile of brushwood out on the marshes.'

'Can't you hear what I'm saying?' Vavasour reached out to

grab his arm. 'We revile this man Skalp for committing a foul murder yet you and I are just as bad in some ways. We've shed blood as well. We've sinned.'

Ralph removed his hand. 'I'll make amends for my sins in my own way.'

'And what way is that, my lord?'

'Dispensing justice and rooting out crime.'

Gervase had gone off into a meditative silence. He came out of it with a smile. 'Starculf had another accomplice,' he declared.

'There were three of them?' said Ralph.

'Only two were party to the murder. The third was an unwitting confederate.'

'Who was he?'

'The person who told Starculf when the lord Richard and his steward would be away from the house. That's what made possible the theft of the keys and everything turned on that. I can see why Starculf refused to tell us who it was! He wanted to protect her at all costs.'

'Her?'

'Of course,' said Gervase. 'It was the lady Adelaide.'

Mauger Livarot was mortified when he saw the sheriff and his officers approaching with a prisoner. It looked as if his hopes had run aground. If the killer had been caught, the elephants would have been recovered and there was no way that he could wrest them from Roger Bigot and his substantial escort. Livarot and his men waited until the other column reached them.

'Good day, my lord!' Bigot hailed him. 'What are you doing here?'

'Helping in the search,' said Livarot, looking at Starculf. 'But it seems that we came too late. You've caught him without us.'

'It was the lord Ralph who arrested him. We've taken charge of him now.'

'Has the villain confessed?'

'No,' said Bigot, irritably. 'Starculf claims that he's innocent of the murder. And the wonder of it is that the lord Ralph and Gervase Bret accept his word. The man is involved somehow and I mean to find out exactly how, but he may not actually have struck down Hermer.'

'What of the other crime?' said Livarot. 'The theft of the gold elephants?'

'I stole nothing,' asserted Starculf.

Bigot was astringent. 'Apart from the keys to the lord Richard's manor house.'

'I've never set eyes on these gold elephants.'

'Then where are they?' prodded Livarot.

'The lord Ralph has gone in search of them,' said Bigot.

'He knows their whereabouts?'

'Gervase Bret does. He was acting as guide.'

'Which way did they go?'

'They took the road to the Henstead hundred,' said Bigot, swivelling round to point a finger. 'A mile or so back.'

Livarot's hopes revived. 'We'll catch them up and offer our assistance.'

'I think they can manage well enough without you, my lord.'

'We've come this far,' said the other, eager to be off. 'We might as well ride on a little further. Who knows? We might arrive in time to be of real use.'

Giving the sheriff no time to reply, he led his men swiftly off down the track.

Skalp saw them coming. They were half a mile away when he first heard the noise of their harness and the sound of their voices carried on the light wind. One glimpse of them was all that he needed. When he recognised Gervase and saw the men-at-arms with him, he was off at once. Dropping the axe with which he had been splitting a log, he ran to his hut and disappeared inside. The old man who had been helping him to rebuild the other dwelling looked on in dismay as Skalp grabbed his dagger, thrust it into his belt, then reached up into the thatch for something that was wrapped in a piece of animal skin. He darted out of the hut and ran across to his grandmother who had come out to see what was happening.

'Don't tell them where I am!' he said.

'Who?' asked Olova.

'Say that I've gone far away.'

'Why?'

'Goodbye, Grandmother.'

'Skalp!'

'I must go.'

It was an unceremonious departure. Sprinting down the slight incline, he made for the bushes near the stream and dived behind them. Olova lost sight of him, wondering why he had gone so abruptly and in such a state of fear. Minutes later, Gervase Bret came into view with his companions. Olova folded her arms defiantly.

'You promised that you'd leave me alone!' she said.

'We've not come to see you, Olova,' he explained, courteously.

'Then why have you brought soldiers with you?'

'We need to speak to Skalp.'

'He's not here.'

'Then where is he?'

'I don't know.'

Her eyes betrayed her. Before she could stop herself, she glanced in the direction that Skalp had taken. It was enough of a clue for Ralph Delchard to seize on. 'He's making a run for it!' he cried, kicking his horse into action.

Jocelyn Vavasour was the first to respond. He gave pursuit with Ralph's men close behind him. Gervase shot a look of apology at Olova, then joined in the hectic chase.

Ralph was not going to surrender the pleasure of overhauling a fugitive this time. As soon as he reached the stream, he caught sight of Skalp's head, bobbing up and down in the distance. Swinging his horse round, Ralph galloped along the bank and ducked beneath the overhanging branches of a tree. Skalp vanished into some bushes and reappeared again, running at full pelt. It was all the admission of guilt that Ralph needed. He remembered the mutilated corpse that was brought into the castle. A man responsible for that crime deserved no mercy. As his destrier began to gain on his quarry, Ralph drew his sword.

Skalp was fast and guileful, dodging round bushes and threading his way through trees, seeking new cover all the time to make pursuit more difficult. Ralph was impervious to pain. As a branch lashed his face or a shrub beat his leg, he simply carried resolutely on. When he drew level with Skalp, he struck him across the back of his neck with the flat of his sword and sent him spinning on the ground. Tumbling uncontrollably, Skalp let go of his cargo and the animal skin rolled down the bank of the stream. Ralph was standing over the man within seconds, breathing heavily and holding the point of his weapon at Skalp's throat. The prisoner was undaunted.

'Go on!' he invited, spreading his arms. 'Kill me!'

'I'll leave that job to the sheriff,' said Ralph, sternly. 'I'm arresting you for the murder of Hermer, steward of the lord Richard.'

'He was an animal. He raped a girl of sixteen.'

'We know all about that, Skalp,' said Gervase, still astride his horse. 'But it doesn't excuse what you did.'

'This is where I found her,' howled the youth, indicating the stream. 'Aelfeva drowned herself here. She couldn't bear to live after what Hermer did to her.'

Vavasour's yell made them all look in his direction. Having jumped from his horse, he had retrieved the object that had rolled down the bank. The animal skin was unrolled to reveal two small, shiny gold elephants.

'They're here!' he said in triumph. 'I've found them!'

Skalp was quick to take advantage of the diversion. Rolling away from the sword, he took out his dagger, rose quickly into a kneeling position and plunged the weapon into his own heart. His face contorted with agony and his body twitched for a few seconds until, without a sound, he dropped lifelessly to the grass.

Cursing himself for his inattention, Ralph sheathed his sword and bent over to examine the corpse. Skalp had found a way to elude justice. He was for ever beyond their reach now.

Gervase dismounted and heaved a sigh of regret at what had happened. 'It's a pity that the lord Eustace isn't here,' he said.

'Why?'

'Falling on one's sword. He would have appreciated that gesture.'

'Would he?'

'That's the way that noble Romans took their own lives.'

Ralph was contemptuous. 'There's nothing noble about this man, Gervase. He was a ruthless killer. Skalp has cheated us. He got away.'

'I don't think that his grandmother will see it quite like that.'

'He's been caught,' said Vavasour. 'That's the main thing. The hunt is finally over. And I fulfilled my pledge to the abbey,' he continued, holding up the miniature elephants. 'I've recovered their holy treasures. They must be returned immediately.'

'We'll ride with you,' said Gervase.

'No,' replied the other firmly.

'But it's too dangerous to go alone.'

'No harm will befall me. I'm on my own now. That's the way I wish it to be. I'm grateful for your help but we must part here. I'm going back to my life as an anchorite.' He pointed at the corpse. 'Far away from this kind of thing.'

Concealing the gold elephants inside his tunic, he mounted his horse and rode off.

Ralph stood up and watched him go. He had mixed feelings about Jocelyn the Anchorite, but he did not begrudge the man the right to return the treasure he had once brought all the way from Rome. Then he remembered what Gervase had just said.

'We're going to the abbey as well?' he asked.

'We have to, Ralph.'

'Why?'

'For proof that it was Hermer who stole the elephants in the first place.'

'Does that matter any more?'

'Of course,' said Gervase. 'Otherwise, we let the lord Richard off the hook. He sees himself as a victim of crime but I'm certain that he instigated the theft from the abbey. We need evidence of that. Before we go there, however,' he continued, looking sadly down at the dead man, 'We'll have to take Skalp back to his grandmother. I don't relish the thought of having to explain everything to her.'

'Even Olova can't condone what this villain did, Gervase.'

'Maybe not, but he was still her grandson. It's the second suicide in the family. Olova will have to bury someone else in unconsecrated ground.'

Ralph motioned to two of his men. 'Pull out his dagger and put the body across the back of my horse.'

Drogo was tingling with excitement. Having pushed their horses hard, Mauger Livarot and his men had caught a glimpse of the column ahead of them as it reached the circle of huts. Livarot took cover behind some trees with his soldiers and sent his steward to reconnoitre. Drogo was nervous, fearing that the gold elephants would be out of their reach and knowing how vindictive his master would be as result. Making his way along the bank of the stream, he had to dive out of sight when someone came running towards him with a group of riders in pursuit. Drogo saw and heard it all. He could not wait to pass on the good tidings to Livarot. When the dead body was taken away across the back of Ralph's horse, the steward scurried back to his master, arriving out of breath but smirking happily.

'Well?' said Livarot.

'I saw them.' replied Drogo, gulping down air. 'I saw the gold elephants.'

'Who has them?'

'The lord Jocelyn – though he no longer looks like the man we once knew by that name. And he no longer talks like him either.'

'What did you see?'

Still panting, Drogo gave a rapid account of the scene he had witnessed.

Livarot grinned. 'Jocelyn Vavasour is on his own?'

'Yes, my lord. Riding to the abbey with the gold.'

'One man against all of us?' said the other. 'He doesn't stand a chance.'

'He put the elephants inside his tunic.'

'Then we'll take them out of there. Mount up, Drogo.'

'Yes, my lord.'

'We're going to get what we came for,' said Livarot.

Olova was overwhelmed with sadness when the body of her grandson was returned to her. Gently and tactfully, Gervase explained what had happened, but even his soft words could not ease a grandmother's pain. She asked them to lay Skalp inside the hut that he had been rebuilding. Though there was bitterness in her voice, there was also a note of resignation. She looked from Gervase to Ralph with tears welling in her eyes. There was no point in concealment. The truth came out of her between bursts of sobbing.

'I knew that something was wrong,' she said. 'Skalp went away for a couple of days. He wouldn't tell me where he'd been. Now I know.'

'He went to kill Hermer,' said Gervase.

'He was very quiet when he got back. He threw himself into his work. But something had changed in him. I could sense it.' She brushed away a tear with, the back of her hand. 'How did you realise that it was him?'

'We didn't at first,' admitted Ralph. 'We were after a man called Starculf. When we caught him, he protested his innocence so strongly that we were inclined to believe him. That meant we had to look elsewhere. Gervase brought us here.'

'It had to be Skalp,' said Gervase, simply. 'He never forgave Hermer for what he did to that young girl. You told me that it was Skalp who found her body. He took his own life close to the same place. In fact, I think he ran there deliberately.'

Ralph was rueful. 'I blame myself for letting him stab himself.'

'It wasn't your fault.'

'It was, Gervase. I caught him. I should have taken his dagger away.'

'You were distracted. We all were.'

There was an awkward silence. Olova glanced towards the hut where Skalp lay. 'He was here, Master Bret,' she mumbled.

'Who was?'

'Starculf. When you came for the second time. Starculf was close by. I didn't know it at the time, so I wasn't lying to you. Skalp was hiding him. I only discovered that afterwards.'

'They were accomplices, Olova.'

'In a sense, we all were,' she said, harshly. 'We all wanted Hermer dead. But not at this cost. I've lost everyone now. My husband, my children and now my grandson. They've all gone. What's to become of me?'

She went off into another fit of sobbing. Gervase put a consoling arm around her. 'I'm sorry that it had to end this way,' he said.

'But it hasn't ended yet,' Ralph reminded him. 'There's unfinished business.'

'I know.'

'Leave us,' said Olova, making an effort to compose herself. 'Leave us alone to grieve in peace. You've done what you had to do. There's nothing left for you to take from me now. Please go.'

After muttered farewells, Ralph and Gervase walked slowly back to their horses.

Jocelyn Vavasour did not become aware of them until he was well on his way. He was far too preoccupied, his mind grappling with the horror of Skalp's suicide. He could not understand how the precious gifts he had given to the abbey had ended up in the hands of the young Saxon. Still, they had been rescued now. Vavasour could give them back to Abbot Alfwold and return to his solitary existence on the coast. Riding at a steady canter, he covered some distance before he decided to give his tired horse a rest. When they reached an expanse of marshland, he slowed the animal to a gentle trot. It was then that he heard the pummelling of hooves behind him. He swung his horse round, expecting to see Ralph and Gervase coming towards him, but it was a larger troop of men that was approaching. They were a hundred yards away when he recognised Mauger Livarot. The instinct that had saved him from one ambush now warned him of another.

He looked over his shoulder. The abbey was still a long way off. His horse could never outrun the fresher animals on his tail. Vavasour had no cover to use and no weapon beyond that of prayer. Sitting bolt upright in the saddle, he faced the newcomers without fear. Livarot barked an order and his men drew up in a wide circle around the anchorite.

Social niceties were brushed crudely aside. 'Give them to me, Jocelyn,' demanded Livarot, holding out his hand.

'What?'

'The gold elephants.'

'They're holy treasures, my lord,' said the other with righteous indignation.

'I want them nevertheless.'

'They belong to the abbey of St Benet.'

'Not any more.'

'Would you dare to steal them?'

'I'd dare to do much more than that,' boasted Livarot, drawing his sword. 'Hand them over now or I'll cut them out of that ragged tunic of yours.'

Vavasour thought quickly. His fate was sealed. He was certain that, when he surrendered the two elephants, he would be killed on the spot. If Livarot wanted to keep the stolen property, he could not possibly leave the anchorite alive to accuse him of theft. The marshes offered countless places where a dead body could be hidden, but they also gave him an idea. As his appointed executioner moved closer, Vavasour reached inside his tunic to take out two small objects that he held up in the air. Burnished by the sun, they glowed proudly in his hands.

'Is this what you're after, my lord?' he asked.

'Those are the elephants!' exclaimed Drogo. 'Those are the ones I saw!'

'Give them to me!' yelled Livarot.

'How much do you want them?'

'Enough to kill.'

'You still won't get them,' taunted Vavasour.

Putting both animals into the palm of one hand, he flung them as far into the marshes as he could. Mauger Livarot went berserk. What he saw disappearing into the water was his one chance of marrying the lady Adelaide. Emitting a howl of rage, he dropped from the saddle and went lumbering after the elephants, splashing through water and kicking his way through beds of reeds. Single-mindedness was his downfall. He lurched towards the spot where he had seen the objects fall, oblivious of the dangers, and water suddenly gave way to quicksand. Instead of moving forward at speed, he was sucked inexorably downwards, the weight of his hauberk working against him. His men looked on in horror as their master was suddenly waist deep and sinking.

'Help!' shouted Livarot, threshing impotently. 'Get me out!'

Jocelyn Vavasour was the first to go to his rescue. Spurning his own safety, he ran to the edge of the pool and stretched out a hand. But the stricken man was tantalisingly out of reach. When one of the soldiers tried to grab Livarot's hand, he fell into the quicksand himself and had to be dragged out by the others.

'Do something!' begged Livarot. 'Quickly!'

There was no salvation. The more he struggled, the firmer hold the quicksand took on him, pulling him slowly and relentlessly down until only his head and hands were visible. After one last deafening cry, Livarot vanished from sight for ever beneath the loose, wet, treacherous pool of sand. His men were stunned. They stood there in grim silence until Drogo looked for revenge. Swinging round, he pointed accusingly at Vavasour.

'There's the man responsible!' he said. 'Throw him in there as well.'

Before the order could be obeyed, however, eight riders could be seen coming towards them. Livarot's men hesitated. They did not want witnesses to an act of cold-blooded murder. Vavasour was relieved and grateful to see Ralph Delchard and Gervase Bret coming to his rescue. Detaching himself from the others, he waved an arm in welcome. The newcomers brought their horses to a halt. Ralph sensed the tense atmosphere. He recognised Drogo.

'Where's the lord Mauger?' he asked.

The steward looked despondently across at the quicksand.

'He's still searching for two gold elephants,' said Vavasour.

Brother Joseph was in the abbey church when he was summoned. Fearing a reprimand and still writhing with self-reproach, the sacristan hurried off across the cloister garth. When he was admitted to Abbot Alfwold's lodging, he was surprised to find three visitors there. Ralph Delchard and Gervase Bret had escorted Jocelyn Vavasour to make sure that he arrived without further mishap. The anchorite exchanged warm greetings with

Joseph then raised his eyebrows hopefully.

'I've just heard the most remarkable story,' said the abbot, soulfully. 'It seems that our holy treasures were taken by a man called Hermer, steward to Richard de Fontenel. When he stayed at the abbey, Hermer gave us the false name of Starculf. This same Hermer was murdered and the treasures stolen by someone else. Earlier today, they were reclaimed from the thief by our courageous visitors.'

The sacristan gurgled with joy. 'We have them back, Father Abbot?'

'Not exactly, Brother Joseph.'

'But you said that they'd been recovered.'

'Recovered then lost again, I fear.'

'Employed to save a life,' explained Ralph. 'When someone tried to take them from Jocelyn by force, he flung them into the marshes. Two gold elephants are at the bottom of some quicksand with Mauger Livarot.'

Joseph paled. 'The lord Mauger?'

'You'll hear a full account later,' promised the abbot. 'Suffice it to say that the Lord has saved a good man and punished an evil one.'

'Yet we've lost our treasures, Father Abbot.'

'Not exactly,' said Vavasour, stepping forward. 'There's something that I haven't mentioned so far because I wanted you to be here when I did, Brother Joseph. You know what significance those gold elephants held for me and I was touched by the way in which you and the holy brothers revered them.'

'We did, Jocelyn. We mourn their disappearance.'

'Mourn them no more,' said the other, reaching inside his tunic.

To the astonishment of them all, he brought out the two miniature gold elephants and handed them to the sacristan. Joseph danced on his toes with pleasure. Abbot Alfwold had to hold back tears. Ralph shook his head in wonderment.

'You told us that you threw them into the marshes?'

'It's true,' admitted Vavasour with a smile. 'Two elephants did get hurled there but they weren't made of gold, as these are. They were carved out of wood. I brought them with me when we left my little home. That's the irony of it,' he added with a sigh. 'The lord Mauger didn't die in pursuit of holy treasures blessed by the Pope. He went into that quicksand after two pieces of driftwood that had dried yellow in the sun.'

Ralph grinned. 'I wonder what he'll say when he finds them.'

Epilogue

Richard de Fontenel was in a state of elation. Word had reached him that Mauger Livarot, his loathsome rival, had been sucked down into quicksand on the previous day, a fate that de Fontenel found singularly appropriate. It was the best news he had heard all week and it made him shake with laughter. At a stroke, he had lost an enemy and gained an unexpected opportunity to renew his pursuit of the lady Adelaide. With one suitor dead, she might come to see the other in a more favourable light. He decided to give her time to reflect and a chance to mellow. When he next tried to engage her affections, he promised himself that he would have two miniature gold elephants to offer, as irresistible as the pair that had first excited her. Judicael the Goldsmith would have a commission from him after all. Hopes rising swiftly, de Fontenel began to speculate on the pleasures of marriage to a beautiful new wife.

It was a dull morning and the sky was hung with grey clouds. When he came out of his manor house, however, he felt as if the sun were blazing down on him. That illusion was soon shattered. There was a drumming of many hooves before Roger Bigot appeared with a dozen men at his back. Ralph Delchard was among them, riding beside a Benedictine monk of middle years on a spindly donkey. When the visitors drew up in front of him, de Fontenel gave them a guarded welcome. The sheriff was brusque.

'We need to inspect your stables, my lord,' he announced.

'My stables?' said the other.

'Yes,' explained Ralph, indicating his companion. 'This is Brother Osbern from the abbey of St Benet at Holme. He's the hospitaller there and welcomes every visitor. One particular visitor turned out to be a thief. Osbern has come in search of his horse.'

'Why?'

'Because it's the only way to prove that Hermer, your late steward, was the man who stole some holy objects from the abbey.'

'But that's absurd!' blustered de Fontenel.

'Is it? How else could the little elephants have come into your hands?'

'I told your colleague, my lord. I bought them in France.'

'Then the merchant who sold them to you must also have been a magician who conjured them out of the air, because the stolen property from the abbey could never have made the journey to France in the time you allege.'

'Take us to the stables,' ordered Bigot.

'There's no point, my lord sheriff.' replied de Fontenel, evasively. 'Hermer's horse is no longer here. The animal had to be sold.'

'I think that very unlikely.' said Brother Osbern, speaking for the first time. 'The traveller, who we believe stole our treasures, was riding a fine bay mare in her prime. He gave his name as Starculf the Falconer and I remember wondering how a mere falconer could own such a magnificent animal. I'd recognise that horse anywhere.'

'Once we match the horse to its rider,' said Ralph with a grin, 'we'll have our thief. All we have to do then is to match the thief to the master who ordered him to steal.'

'I did nothing of the kind!' protested de Fontenel.

'Conspiracy to steal from consecrated ground is both a crime and sacrilege.'

'You can't prove anything.'

'We'll start with that bay mare. Let's see if Brother Osbern can pick her out.'

'Oh, I will, my lord. I'd spot her among a thousand.'

'Step over to the stables, Brother Osbern.' said the sheriff.

'No!' countered de Fontenel. 'The horse is not there.'

'Then you won't mind if we look, my lord, will you?'

Bigot gave a signal and two of his men conducted the monk around the side of the house to the stables at the rear. Richard de Fontenel was concerned. He knew only too well that his steward's horse was still there and that it would provide incontrovertible evidence against him. Unable to lie, bully or fight his way out of the situation, he flew into a panic and acted on impulse. He swung round, darted back into the house and slammed the door shut before bolting it from inside. Roger Bigot ordered his men to surround the building in order to cut off any possibility of escape, but Ralph acted of his own volition. Seeing the open shutters, he rode across to the window, dismounted on to the sill and jumped into the parlour. With his sword in his hand, he went in pursuit of de Fontenel and found him at the back of the house, fumbling with a key as he tried to open the strong room. Ralph was merciless. As his adversary pulled out a dagger and turned to confront him, he struck at the man's wrist, opening up a deep gash and making him drop his weapon to the floor.

Richard de Fontenel cursed and roared. Holding his wounded wrist, he tried to kick out at Ralph but the latter tripped him up with a deft movement of his foot and stood over him, his sword an inch above the man's face. Thunderous banging was heard behind them, then the front door burst open under the concerted weight of two burly officers. Sword out, Roger Bigot followed his men into the house. Ralph stood aside to hand the squirming prisoner over to them.

'He saved you the trouble of wringing a confession out of him,' said Ralph.

'Yes,' said Bigot, grimly. 'By his own actions shall he be judged.

'You have no evidence!' howled de Fontenel, wincing with pain as he tried to stem the flow of blood from his wrist. 'I was away in Normandy. I have no idea what my steward did while I was away.'

'Hermer did nothing without your command.'

'That's not true.'

'Starculf has told us how you treated those who served you.'

'I'd never send anyone to steal from an abbey.'

A loud whinny made them all turn round. Framed in the open door was Brother Osbem, leading a bay mare by a rope. The animal gave another whicker and flicked her tail playfully. The monk was beaming in triumph.

'This is the horse,' he said, confidently. 'I'd swear to it.'

* * *

After the delays and distractions of the past few days, the commissioners finally began their work that afternoon. Their first session in the shire hall was long but productive. A number of minor disputes were settled with brisk efficiency. Eustace Coureton proved to be a sagacious judge and Brother Daniel an able scribe. All four men worked so well together that they seemed to have been in harness for years rather than for one afternoon. Seated inline behind a table, they proved a formidable quartet. When the session finally ended, Coureton wanted more elucidation about recent events.

'What I can't understand is how Skalp actually did it,' he said.

'Neither can I,' groaned Ralph. 'Before we could get the details out of him, he thrust that dagger into his heart.'

'I think that we can work it out,' said Gervase, thoughtfully. 'With the lord sheriff's permission, I talked to Starculf this morning. A night in chains has loosened his tongue a little. He told me what his original plan had been.'

'To kill Hermer and leave him under the lord Richard's nose.'

'Yes, Ralph, but it was rather more complicated than that. Using Skalp as his lookout, Starculf planned to get into the house under cover of darkness with one of the duplicate keys. The second key would have got him into the strong room where he could spend the night without fear of discovery. Hermer, it seems, was the only person who would go into the strong room and did so at the start of each day. Starculf was going to be lying in wait for him.'

'Is that what Skalp did?' asked Coureton.

'He certainly spent the night in there, my lord, because he admitted as much to his accomplice. He chose his moment to pounce. My guess is that it was when Hermer paid his second

346

visit to the strong room to return the gold elephants to their box after they'd been shown to the lady Adelaide.'

'He couldn't have killed the steward then,' argued Ralph. 'There'd have been too much blood. According to the lord sheriff, there were no signs of a struggle in that strong room.'

'That's because the murder didn't take place there,' said Gervase, piecing it together in his mind. 'Skalp must have knocked him unconscious at first. We saw how strong he was. It wouldn't have been difficult to take Hermer unawares. The strong room was at the back of the house. Skalp could have carried the body out into the garden. He used the trees as cover to get far enough away to kill the steward and conceal the body.'

'Then he came back at night to retrieve it.'

'Exactly.'

'Tying a rope around Hermer's ankles and dragging him off the estate.'

'We all know what happened next, Ralph.'

'I'd rather you didn't mention any details,' said Brother Daniel, putting a hand to his stomach. 'I feel sick at the very thought.'

'It was only the hands that were cut off,' said Ralph breezily.

'My lord!' Clapping a hand over his mouth, the monk rose up from the table and hurried out with his satchel over his shoulder. Coureton shot a look of reproof at his colleague.

'That was unkind.'

'It was not meant to be, Eustace.'

'Brother Daniel is a sensitive soul.'

'I'll apologise to him this evening,' said Ralph, penitently. 'But let's go back to Gervase's theory of what happened. There's one thing he missed out.'

'Yes,' admitted Gervase. 'The two gold elephants.'

'Skalp couldn't possibly have known that they even existed, still less that they'd be in the house on the very day that he chose to get his revenge on Hermer.'

'The murder was premeditated, Ralph. The theft arose out of opportunity.'

'You mean that he just saw them and took them?'

'He must have done. The steward went into that room to put those elephants back into their strong box. Skalp saw them, two pieces of solid gold worth more than he would earn in a lifetime. The temptation was too much.' Gervase paused. 'It was also one more way to inflict pain on Richard de Fontenel. Stealing something of great value from him. When he knocked Hermer senseless, I believe that Skalp grabbed the elephants and took them with him.'

'Starting off a search that's taken us all over the county.'

'With compensations,' said Coureton.

Ralph was dubious. 'Compensations?'

'How else would we have got to meet Jocelyn the Anchorite?'

'That was a pleasure I'd happily have foregone.'

'But he was such an interesting man, Ralph. I can't help admiring what he's doing. And it was he, after all, who helped us to track down Starculf.'

'He also duped the lord Mauger,' observed Gervase. 'That showed bravery and guile. He sacrificed his own wooden elephants to save the real ones.'

'He'll have plenty of time to carve himself another pair now,' said Ralph.

They got up from the table and gathered up their documents. Coureton sighed. 'I suppose the person we should feel sorry for is the lady Adelaide,' he said.

'Never!' exclaimed Ralph.

'But one of her suitors died and the other is now in the castle dungeon.'

'Both got their just deserts. The lord Mauger was going to kill Jocelyn and the lord Richard is as brazen a rogue as any in the whole county. As for the lady Adelaide,' Ralph said, tartly, 'spare no tears for her. She was the person who told Starculf when the lord Richard would be in France and when his steward would also be absent from the house.'

'Be fair to her, Ralph,' counselled Gervase. 'The lady Adelaide didn't know that Starculf intended to steal those keys as part of his plan. She knew and liked Starculf. That's why he turned to her for help. All that she gave him was information. She'd never have countenanced murder.'

'I'll wager she'd have provoked theft.'

'Surely not.'

'She wanted those gold elephants so much, Gervase.'

'She's lost them for good now,' said Coureton. 'Along with her two suitors. It's been a very chastening experience for the lady Adelaide.'

'She'll be even more chastened when Roger Bigot has spoken to her,' commented Ralph with a smile. 'He knows that her hands are not entirely clean in this business and means to roast her ears a little with some hot words.'

Ralph led them out of the shire hall and into the street where four of his men had been acting as sentries. The commissioners were in a contented mood. The murder investigation into which they had been drawm was satisfactorily terminated and their load had been lightened in consequence.

'In some ways,' said Coureton, 'it's a pity. The major dispute we came to settle has vanished into thin air now. I was rather looking forward to watching Richard de Fontenel and Mauger Livarot battle it out in front of us.' A thought made him turn to Gervase. 'Where will this leave Olova?'

'In a strong position, my lord.'

'She'll regain some of her land?'

'Most probably.'

'I have reservations about that,' said Ralph. 'Her grandson was a killer.'

'Olova isn't,' said Gervase, 'and she's the person on whom we must pass judgement, not Skalp. Olova had no part whatsoever in what went on.'

Ralph was about to reply when he saw his wife riding towards him, accompanied by one of the guards from the castle. Thinking that she had come to greet him after his work in the shire hall he gave her a welcoming wave, but it was Gervase to whom she spoke.

'Alys is unwell.' she told him, 'A doctor has been summoned.'

'What's wrong with her?' he asked in alarm.

'I don't know. But you'd better come.'

'We all will,' said Ralph.

Gervase did not wait for the others. Mounting his horse, he set off at a gallop that scattered people in the narrow street. By the time the rest reached the castle, he was running up the stairs to the keep. Ralph and Golde dismounted to hurry after him. When they reached the apartment that he and Alys shared there was no sign of Gervase, but they could hear voices from inside the chamber, and waited anxiously for news.

The doctor eventually emerged, a small, fussy man who

waved away their questions. 'It's for Master Bret to tell you,' he said. 'Wait until he is ready.' He went off down the steps and left them even more worried.

'What can it be, Golde?' Ralph asked.

'I don't, know,' she replied. 'Alys has not been well since we arrived here. In the bailey yesterday, she seemed to have a spasm of pain.'

'Why wasn't the doctor called then?'

'Alys denied that there was anything wrong with her.'

After a further delay, the door finally opened and Gervase came out. His face was so pale that they feared the worst. Golde reached out a comforting hand. But then a ghost of a smile touched his lips. There was an air of disbelief about his announcement.

'Alys is with child,' he said.

'That's wonderful!' exclaimed Golde, embracing him. 'May I go to her?'

'Please do.'

'Congratulations!' said Ralph as his wife slipped into the room. 'This is the best news possible, Gervase.'

'It's so unexpected, Ralph,' said the other, still dazed. 'I'm not sure that I'm ready to be a father just yet.'

'Of course you are. And think how proud the child will be.'

'Proud?'

'Yes,' said Ralph, slapping him on the back. 'You've been a royal commissioner and you've had glorious adventures in the service of the King. Look at what happened here in Norfolk, for instance. You'll be able to boast that you saw a pair of elephants.' Ralph cocked an eyebrow. 'How many people can say that?'

Gervase thought about all the problems that the two gold elephants had created. 'Far too many,' he said.

EDWARD MARSTON has written well over a hundred books, including some non-fiction. He is best known for his hugely successful Railway Detective series and he also writes the Bow Street Rivals series featuring twin detectives set during the Regency, as well as the Home Front Detective series.

edwardmarston.com